a&b

The Sweet Smell of Decay

The Chronicles of Harry Lytle

PAUL LAWRENCE

Allison & Busby Limited
12 Fitzroy Mews
London W1T 6DW
www.allisonandbusby.com

First published in Great Britain in 2009.
This paperback edition published by Allison & Busby in 2014

The author would like to acknowledge his use, at the beginning of
chapters, of brief quotes from *Flora of Cambridgeshire*, Ray, John, translated
and edited by A.H. Ewen & C.T. Prime, Wheldon & Wesley Ltd, Hitchin,
1975. All efforts were made in seeking permission to use these quotes. Any
omissions will be rectified in future editions.

A CIP catalogue record for this book is available from
the British Library.

10 9 8 7 6 5 4 3 2 1

ISBN 978-0-7490-1542-8

Typeset in 10/15 pt Sabon by
Allison & Busby Ltd.

The paper used for this Allison & Busby publication
has been produced from trees that have been legally sourced
from well-managed and credibly certified forests.

Printed and bound by
CPI Group (UK) Ltd, Croydon, CR0 4YY

For Ruth, Charlotte, Callum, Cameron and Ashleigh

Chapter One

Muscus ex cranio humano
The mosse on a dead man's skull.

As I gazed upon her face a small black beetle emerged from the ruins of her right eye. It stood uncertainly upon the crest of her cheekbone as if suddenly reluctant to step out further. Though I looked upon the beetle as if it was something unutterably revolting, still I felt like we two had something in common. The butcher reached over, picked it up gently between his thumb and stubby forefinger then crushed it. I could hardly protest. He wiped its remains upon his shirt.

He smiled at me like we were two brothers engaged in holy conspiracy then poured fluid into the two ravaged sockets out of a small wooden cup before setting to clean out the holes with a piece of soiled linen, humming quietly as he worked. The smell was sweet and rich, like an ancient suet pudding. Great lumps of congealed sticky flesh he extracted with the cloth, which he wiped upon his trouser leg. Swallowing gently,

I stood back, giddy for a moment, and breathed in some of the icy, wet air that hung about us like a damp mist. All I could think of was that when we were done here we would not be leaving all of the body behind. Some of it would be walking out with us, stuck upon the butcher's arse. The cold in the room was a mercy. Walking about the table I positioned myself beside the butcher's left shoulder so that I could see all, yet not too close.

Her face was white, so white that it must have been her complexion before death also. Pale orange freckles were still visible upon her nose and cheeks, though the rest of her face was now covered with a thin layer of green mould, which hid all subtleties of skin tone. What looked like moss had started to grow about the edges of the thin rope that was still tied across her mouth, biting into its corners so that she seemed to smile. It was not a happy smile, more like the smile of one that has swallowed a fly thinking it was a currant, yet would feign that it was a currant to those watching suspiciously.

Despite the awful empty eyes and her frantic grin, still I could tell that she had been beautiful – this cousin of mine. The butcher looked round at me as if checking my whereabouts, seemingly concerned with my welfare. Then he took a short-bladed knife from inside his coat and carefully cut the cord at the middle of her lips. He had to peel the rope away from the skin where it had become embedded by the bloating flesh. It came away with a sound that reminded me of walking through thick mud. Behind it her teeth were crooked, some still standing as they had before, others wrenched from their roots pointing backwards towards her throat. Tiny wriggling worms played about exposed roots.

'He pulled it tight with all his strength,' the butcher

murmured. His face was ripe and weathered, thick-pored skin unblemished by pox. A big, friendly face. The way he spoke was strange – it sounded like Scots. Tall and broad, he had thick arms and he wore thick canvas trousers and a rough, stained linen shirt. His nails were cut very short, the ends of his fingers a dull red. Flakes of old dried blood sat in his cuticles and in the lines of his knuckles. Silver hair grew straight and strong upwards out of his head as if determined to escape the bloody grime that coated his scalp. He was a walking graveyard.

Staring into the girl's mouth, he cautiously prised her jaws open wide with two giant forefingers. He was having to squint in the poor grey light that seeped into the vestry from inside the church, so I took a candle from the single shelf and held it that he might see better. Grunting, he stuck his knife into her mouth at which point I looked away. The room was bare save for a wooden crucifix on the wall, a cupboard, an array of wooden candlestick holders on the shelf and the table upon which lay the body of Anne Giles. *What* was I doing here in this cursed place?

The butcher stood up gradually and rubbed his back with his palms. Then he exhaled slowly and returned to his work. Lifting up her head with one hand, he carefully unwound the cord from her mouth, then dropped it into a cloth bag that he pulled from within his jacket.

'We will burn it,' he explained.

And your clothes with it, I thought to myself, but said nothing.

He took another length of cloth, moistened it, and cleaned up the rest of her face. The edges of the skin where the rope had bitten marked the edges of a jagged, deep ravine now sculpted across her face permanently, at least until the beetles came back and ate the rest of it later.

'There she lies,' said the butcher, wiping his hands on a new piece of cloth in a poor effort to clean them. There she lay indeed, her small, thin body shrouded in a thick cloth dress the colour of which I couldn't tell in the small, dark room in which we three were grouped together. Her long red hair lay in waves across her shoulders and over her breasts but her face was mutilated almost beyond recognition.

'You are sure that she be your cousin?'

'No,' I replied. 'I have never met my cousin, indeed never knew she was my cousin.'

'Oh.' The butcher looked at me strangely.

I shrugged. Though she was supposed to be my cousin, I had never met her before and so felt no kinship. It was a grim experience to behold her in her current state, but in truth she looked no worse than the severed heads that blew in the breeze over Nonsuch House. The sooner we could get out of this room the better. The air was foul and I was worried that it would seep into my lungs and infect my humour.

Though he had a kindly face and a generous disposition, the way that the butcher looked at me was vexing. Something of his manner made me feel like I was being judged in all that I said. It wasn't a feeling I much liked. He stared at me now as if I should tell him what to do next.

'What do you conclude from your inspections?' I asked him.

'That some wicked villain cut both her eyes out with a short, wide blade and then tied a cord tight round her mouth so hard that her teeth broke.'

That much was obvious. Standing above me with his hands on his hips, it seemed that he was waiting for me to ask him another question. We stood in uncomfortable silence.

'The body has been lying there for three days,' he said at last.

'Three days? They left the body in here three days?'

'Aye, news got about quickly as to the nature of her death. The congregation will not return until they understand the meaning of it.'

'And so what has happened in three days?'

The butcher watched me like he was suspicious. 'Little. The King had to be consulted and agents appointed.'

And then they appointed the butcher? This was too strange. And who was it that went all the way to Cocksmouth to tell my father? Odd fish, indeed.

I peered about the small, unventilated room. Thick stone walls were damp to the touch and condensation fell from the ceiling in small drops. Little wonder that the body had started to go green so quick. 'Has no one told the relatives that she lies here?'

He looked at me as if I were a simple buffoon. 'You are the relative.'

'Of course.' I kept forgetting.

Fixing me with his big brown eyes he seemed determined to extract from me some explanation as to what was going on. You are looking at the wrong man, I thought, but felt no inclination to enlighten him just yet. My brow had started to prickle and my stomach was doing those things that it does just before you vomit. I grasped for the handle of the door that led outside, but the door was locked, so I turned and fled down the aisle of the church, out into the weak winter sunshine. Taking another breath, relieved that I had managed to get this far without unloading, I headed out as far as I could get into the more remote corners of the churchyard before I had to stop and discharge. The relief, when it came, was blessed.

The ground where I squatted was soft. Birds flitted from bush to grave looking for worms. They seemed interested in the pile that I had deposited. Wild teasel grew close to the hedge. Rainwater that gathers at the base of the plant's leaves acquires the power to remove warts from a man's hands. I stroked its wet leaves with my fingertips. 'Seek peace, and pursue it,' I said to myself, in an attempt to quell all that was disassembled in my mind and body.

'An *abundance* of peace, so long as the moon endureth.' I jumped up and around and found myself staring once more into the face of the butcher. How did such a big lump manage to stay so quiet? Standing with his arms folded, a calm smile upon his lips and eyebrows raised, he eyed the vomit on the ground.

'Feel free to examine it.' I stood up and brushed my jacket with my hands, checking that it stayed clean.

He grunted. 'What do you suggest we do now?' he asked.

Go to the nearest inn and have a breakfast of cleansing ale and a piece of beef pie is what I felt like doing, but I kept the thought to myself.

'I suggest we take a look around the church,' he answered himself.

'Good idea. I'll wait here.' The cold, clean air was good for me.

'No, sir. This is your game. If you have no appetite for it, then I will go back to my butcher's shop and cut up cows.' He stuck his thumbs into a broad, black leather belt and then stuck out his big lump of a chin. Godamercy – the temperament of a small child!

So we went for a walk through the cowquake and got very wet. We revealed nothing out in the graveyard – he poked about in the leaves a lot with his toe and we wasted an hour of our lives. Then he led us back into the dark, foul church where we walked slowly down the centre aisle, me casting a lazy eye down each pew as we went, he walking down each and every one. Though I walked as slow as I could I still reached the ancient pulpit first. Its surface was scratched, worn and unpolished and the base of it was stained black. Someone had been scrubbing at it. Although I gazed at it a while I couldn't see anything much to note and my head began to cloud over with boredom and weariness. I sighed and sat myself down in the front pew. It was very quiet. All to be heard was a slow drip coming from some dark, green corner and the sound of the butcher poking around. At last he reached the pulpit, which seemed to fascinate him. He kept rubbing his forefinger up and down the grain of the wood.

'What have you found?' I asked when I could stand the tedium no longer.

'Into Hell, where the worm dieth not, and the fire is not quenched.'

'What is that supposed to mean?'

'The air in here is wicked and foul.' On that we could agree.

He dropped his heavy frame onto the pew next to me then laid his legs out before him straight. Musing with his thumb and forefinger on either side of his nose, he at last answered the question properly. 'I would venture that the man that did this planned it well. He killed her where you are sitting. There is a bloodstain just behind your left shoulder. New it is, you can tell by the colour and the texture of the wood.'

I looked slowly over my shoulder, with dreadful visions of blood dripping from the wood like the tears of an angel, praying silently that the red stain did not curse my jacket. I need not have worried, for all that was to be seen was a small circle that seemed a little darker than the rest. Who was to say it wasn't a pattern of the grain? But then I wasn't a butcher. 'You'd know about blood,' I muttered.

'Aye,' he growled. 'I would say that she was hauled from here to the pulpit and tied to it. It was while she was bound to the pulpit that the man took her eyes out. You'll have seen the big bloodstain on the floor where the wound dripped. No sign of it anywhere else. The rest of the church is clean.'

'How did she die, then?' I asked with foreboding.

'She bled to death.' He looked again to the pulpit. 'Someone has been hard at work with a brush and pail.'

I felt ill again.

'That's the way it appears to me.' Standing up, he turned to face me, looking down. 'See, there are no marks on the door of the church.'

I stood up too, uncomfortable with him looming over me. You never knew what might fall off his head. 'Why should there be?'

'It means the murderer had a key to the door, else the door frame would have to be broken.'

'How so?'

Waggling a finger, he explained. 'No one leaves their doors unlocked these days, certainly not in these parts, and this killing was carefully planned. So the murderer had a key.'

'Maybe they were just passing, in a carriage, and the man saw the door open.'

'Call me cut if you would.' Bending down he picked something up off the floor. A dead mouse.

I stepped away and folded my hands behind my back. 'To take a person's eyes out is surely madness. Why should madness not strike a man suddenly?'

'The madness you are talking of is born of fury. The madness that happened here was cold and planned. Beside, it is too much to credit that the door was left unlocked, here near to Alsatia, off the road from Fleet Ditch. Too unlikely. The rector would never have left it so. The man had a key, which signifies that he was scheming ahead.' He headed out back into the wintry graveyard. Out on the porch he stretched back his arm and threw the dead rodent into the bushes, then he wiped his hand on his backside. I made a mental note never to buy meat at his shop. Then he placed the same grisly hand upon my shoulder! My body went rigid.

'Now, sir. Would you be so kind as to tell me what brings *you* here?'

A fair question. My father's letter sat snug next to my chest, my ears still burnt from the shrill lecture I had received from Prynne and my courage was still recovering from the threats made to me by Shrewsbury and his henchmen. These were things I knew I would need to share with someone were I to make sense of them, but I didn't at that time think that I wished to share them with him.

'All I can tell ye is that Anne Giles is supposed to be my cousin, yet I only discovered it this morning. Before that I had never heard of her. Now I am asked by my father to find out who killed her.'

He looked down at me like he was my uncle, knowing that I didn't lie; yet knowing also that there was more truth to be told. Given that my uncle had been a foolish man (that had been kicked to death by a cow) this did not endear me to him any the more.

'And your name is really Harry Lytle?'

Also I did not want to talk about my name. I had spent

most of my life listening to witty comments that compared my name to my lack of stature. 'Aye.'

He mused, like he was weighing me up like an order of meat. Then he smiled a cheery grin and proffered the same dreaded hand. 'David Dowling.'

I took his hand briefly. It was cold and clammy. I quickly let it drop, wondering whose blood I now carried upon me. I didn't know what to say to him next – I think I was hoping that he would just tell me who had done it.

'You speak well for yourself,' for a butcher. 'How do you come to know the Mayor?'

'I served as constable, elected five years in a row. Not here, that wasn't. That was when we lived out in the village. Stealing, vagrancy and drunkenness mostly. I helped out our local alderman a few times since coming to London. That's how the Mayor knows of me.'

'Most men would avoid such appointments.' Men like me.

He puckered his lips like a woman, he showed no inclination to say more. 'Aye, sir. That they would.'

'I am supposed to find out who killed Anne Giles. A job best done swiftly, I think. Are you accomplished at such tasks?'

Dowling smiled again, though this time I thought I saw something prickly in his eye. 'I don't know, sir. I have never tried it.'

I grunted. So much for having the thing finished by Friday. 'You must be able, else the Mayor would not have spoken for you.'

'If not pleased, then put your hand in your pocket and please yourself.'

I sighed. 'What did you do for this alderman that he thinks so highly of you?'

'Some thievery and nonsuch. He had a friend he was fain

16

to see left alone.' When he stretched and yawned I saw that most of his back teeth were missing. He offered no more and I wasn't interested enough to press him.

'We should go talk to the rector,' I suggested.

'Yes, sir. Your cousin's husband, besides. He lives in Bishopsgate. First thing tomorrow, if you don't mind; I've still got work to do before the day ends.' He turned on his heel, left the churchyard and headed back towards Fleet Street. Seemed I had offended him, which was no great shame. I couldn't stand folks that exuded their anxieties like they felt it was your duty to share them. Serenity was my objective in life.

A gust of wind blew through the grass and played with my ankles. I looked down at my sodden boots and then around the deserted cemetery. Some stinking horehound was growing up a flint wall. Though my heart bid me follow the butcher back into the City and head for the nearest alehouse, my feet started to walk back towards the church. It was a strange sensation being carried by my body to a place I never wished to visit again, but my feet kept walking all the way back down the aisle, past the battered pulpit and through into the vestry. I pushed the door open with a fearful heart, half expecting the body to have hidden itself somewhere, else be sitting up waiting to converse. But no; it lay as it had, wretched and torn. I looked once more into its face, trying to divine some family resemblance, but seeing none. Perplexing. I fished into my pocket and brought out the letter that I had received that morn to read aloud. I decided to share its contents with the corpse.

Son,
Still here. In this lairy place. Your mother seems
happy tho. Must be the pigs that they breed here coz

she likes pigs. Nothing here to gladden a man's heart
in Cocksmouth. Nothing for me to do save help her
brother in the shed. Can't make shoes here. You caring
for the shop? Some hope. I note you haven't been to
visit. Your mother notes it too. You have a cuz, name
of Anne. Married to a man called John Giles. Don't
think you knew your cuz Anne. Not likely to now
coz she dead. Someone killed her. I took the liberty of
telling William Prynne esq. that you have to leave his
employ. We'll be back when your grandmother is died.
About time, I say.
Your father.

It still made no sense. It was improbable that there were
two men working for Prynne that had fathers in Cocksmouth,
so the author *was* presumably my beloved parent (male). In
which case it was one of God's most wondrous miracles since
he had never written to me before in his whole life nor indeed
had hardly spoken to me since I had learnt the art of speech
myself. I didn't even know he *could* write.

'So who are you, Anne Giles? And how is it that I never knew
you before?' I asked the body. It made no reply. I thought I knew
all my cousins intimately. Thieves and cutpurses most of 'em – on
my mother's side anyway – thou and thee-ers on my father's side
– drier than old biscuits. None of them was called Anne.

Chapter Two

Mushromes of severall sorts
*Any kind of fungus is always evil and when eaten, although
its effect may not be felt immediately, after some time it has a
bad effect on the inner working of the bowels.*

The holy house was thin and tall. It leant crooked over the
street like a very old man about to fall over, held up only by
the efforts of its sturdier neighbours. Evil looking heads stared
down from corbels on every corner of the grim facade onto the
busy street life below.

Dowling waited for me with a sour face. He muttered at
me and I mumbled back. We stepped through the buzzing
throng without meaningful conversation and stood upon the
threshold. A note was pinned to the door that said: 'we walk
by faith, not by sight'.

'Corinthians.' Dowling winked at me like it was a great
secret. Why was he winking at me? I knew it was Corinthians.
One of those sayings that rectors and other holy folk pronounce
with great solemnity, yet is empty of all practical meaning. Try

walking down Cheapside with your eyes closed – faith or no faith you'll end up betwixt the hooves of a horse with every bone of your body broken.

A servant showed us into the hall. He was more hideous than the corbels. The floor was laid with yellow and green Flemish tiles, suggesting a mercantile interest, and the walls were covered with wooden flower motifs and thick carved rings. Expensive. The servant bowed and led us up a polished staircase to a lovely old wooden door. It had its own knocker in the shape of a lamb's head. Running my fingers over its rough bronze surface, I suddenly noticed that the servant was waiting to use it. Embarrassed, I stepped to one side and he opened it. Beyond it was dark.

'Enter please,' the servant leered, showing no signs of crossing the threshold himself. I obeyed, if only to escape the sensation that he sought to devour my kidneys. The door closed behind us.

Darkness was relieved only by feeble tendrils of weak winter light that wriggled through small holes in the drawn curtains, and the glow of a small fire burning in the grate. Walking slowly towards the window I was careful not to bump into anything. The curtains were made of thick red velvet, luscious and gorgeous to touch. Worn thin in places, the pattern of light betrayed their age. Squinting into the warm gloom at the paintings and tapestries that hung from the wall opposite I could see that they were old and black, years of dirt hiding all but the brightest shades. Stern faces peered down at me with disapproving yellow eyes. Contorted figures stared at the ceiling – mostly representations of Christ. The air was thick with heavy scent, musty and clinging. The other walls were covered with books, leather-bound and thick. Not many people could afford to buy books, but the rector had hundreds. Slowly my eyes got used to the absence of light. So it was that I finally noticed a figure behind a great desk at the far end of the room sat in the shadows by himself.

'Good morning,' the man greeted us softly in a rich plummy voice. After standing up slowly, he adopted an elegant pose. 'I was engaged in serious contemplation.'

Dark, curly hair sat above black, bushy eyebrows like a mop. Stubble covered his lip and ran down his olive cheeks. He looked quite young, surprisingly, not much older than me. He wore a stiff black coat despite the warmth of the room and a collar that forced him to hold up his chin. The desk was made of thick carved oak and was covered with reams of paper, scattered goose-quills and stacks of books, carefully placed I reckoned.

Sighing as if he was in great pain, he put the back of one hand against his forehead. 'How gratifying that you should take such an interest in the desecration of my church. The people of this parish talk of little else. I fear that they will not cease their prating until the whole wicked affair is resolved. Until that time, law or no law, they will not venture past its doors. They will stay at home or else go to other parishes to do their worshipping.'

Stifling a yawn I neglected to tell him that I held no interest whatsoever in his predicament. 'Aye, it was my cousin that was killed.'

He looked at me sharply with one beady, calculating black eye, then, lowering the hand, he proceeded to walk over to a shelf where he pulled down one of his books, the spine of which he stared at blankly. 'There are dozens in London, some in this parish I know, waiting for a church appointment. They would see me in the gutter and not give a damn. They would call it providence, the will of God.'

If that was truly the case then I should feel much better disposed towards God, for I didn't like this fellow much, walking his study like it was a theatre stage.

'Aye, the will of God,' Dowling repeated solemnly. I looked at him in surprise. His face was blank and wore no expression that I could read.

'Providence.' The rector turned, suddenly animated. 'There exist three possible reasons why the foul deed took place at Bride's. You should know this; it may help you in your investigation. The three reasons are providence, popery and maleficium. We will deal with each in turn. Providence we shall dismiss first.'

This man reminded me of the odious intellectuals I escaped from at Cambridge. Never consider the obvious, for it means you can't quote the Holy Book.

'Why does it have to be any of the three? Why not chance?'

The rector looked at me as if I was a fool. It was a feeling I was used to in my life so it had no influence on me. 'There is no such thing as chance, sir. The woman was not bound to the pulpit of my church and struck down by satanic agents by *chance*. She was killed for a reason, and she was killed at Bride's.'

I resisted the urge to growl. 'Whoever killed her had to kill her somewhere. Bride's is as good a place as any.'

Laughing like Betty Howlett, he made a noise that was loud and shrill. I exchanged glances with Dowling – it was not a sound you expected to come from the rector's big lips. '*Sir.*' He spread his palms and shook his head sorrowfully. 'A church is not as good a place as any to commit a murder.

Were a man to kill in so abominable a fashion with no clear intention as to where he would do the deed, then providence or maleficium should intervene, else he would do it somewhere more appropriate. He would commit the foul deed in a place quiet and desolate, where the deed was unlikely to be discovered. Would you not say so?' To my annoyance he turned to Dowling.

'Aye.' Dowling nodded slowly, lower lip protruding in serious contemplation. I considered poking him in the ribs. Why was he encouraging this bumble-turd?

'So. Then we must consider why the deed was done at Bride's. As I said, there are three possible causes. First, providence. Providence is God's will.' He nodded at me as if I did not know the meaning of the word 'providence'. 'You will accept that I do not favour the theory of providence, for it implies that God has no regard for the good fortune of one of his own.'

'You, you mean?' If I was God, then this was precisely the kind of fellow I would like to strike down with a thunderbolt or two.

'Yes, sir. I mean me. If it was God's will, then it was God's will that it happen at one of his own houses, in this case the house that I look after on his behalf. Were it providence, then it is difficult to consider why he should want to desecrate one of his own houses were it not to comment upon the keeper of that house.'

'Or the people in it?' I looked sideways to see what Dowling was thinking. His face was bright and innocent and he wouldn't look me in the eye.

'Yes sir, or the people in it. And it is indeed true that we have some of the worst vagabonds and ne'er-do-wells of London in this parish. There are those who come to my church every prayer time, always late, and proceed to chat and gossip with their neighbours, or even fall asleep. I have had to have serious words with some young men of this parish, who I know for certain come here to meet young ladies and proposition them. Those are the ones that come. The ones that don't come go bowling or drinking. We have most of the City's whores living in Fleet Alley and most of its criminals in Alsatia. This is clear, but it does not make the theory of providence any easier. For if the death of the woman is providence, then it suggests that the parish is beyond redemption and the efforts of its minister hopeless.' The rector leant forwards with his hands upon the desk.

Indeed I imagined that his efforts probably were hopeless. About as hopeless as a dog with no balls.

'This is, however, a credible theory, and one which the people of this parish will be considering even now. England is God's chosen land and yet the efforts of its children are lewd, wicked even, in honouring God for that privilege. My flock are amongst the lewdest, and look forward to the day when they may return to the wine and the dancing and the bawdy houses. They seek the easy route to salvation, and would have me provide it for them.'

'So we may dismiss the theory that Anne Giles was killed at Bride's because it was God's will,' Dowling summarised before I could argue with the man's conceited logic. The summary was for my benefit, I realised, that I waste no further time upon an argument that we both knew to be ludicrous in any case.

'Granted,' the rector nodded, as if the logic was ours. 'So now we will dismiss popery, the work of the Catholics.' He placed his forefingers at the top of his nose. 'This is not so clear, for I have heard of such things before. In this case, though, I cannot see any reason why Catholics should have chosen my church.' The rector looked to Dowling again, eyebrows arched and palms spread wide. Clearly he did not want to debate it with me, which was just as well, for I had little tolerance for those that blamed the Catholics for everything that went wrong in their lives.

'I don't see why Catholics should select your church, good sir, unless you have particular argument with them. Even if you did, then I would not credit even the Catholics with the devilry that took Anne Giles.'

Well spoken, butcher – I commended him silently.

'The Catholic Church is led by the Antichrist, and I am not so certain that the nature of the deed excludes popery, but as you say – why choose Bride's? Which leaves maleficium. Maleficium, as you know, is that power to do harm by use of supernatural powers.' He was looking at me again.

Enough of this nonsense. 'How many keys are there to Bride's?' I demanded. The rector didn't answer, just looked at me with his mouth slightly open.

'Good sir, the man that killed Anne Giles entered your church with a key – betimes you left the door unlocked,' Dowling explained gently.

The rector shook his head vigorously. 'Impossible.'

'Unless you left the door open, how else may we explain the fact that there is no damage to the door?'

'Well, I don't know, I hadn't thought about it. As you say, it is very strange. This is an interesting piece of information that would further support a theory of maleficium. That someone managed to enter the church even though the door was locked points to witchery and sorcery.'

Godamercy – the man was ingenious. 'How many keys are there?' I asked again, unable to suppress from my tone the impatience that gnawed at my guts. Looking down, the rector slowly pulled open a drawer of the heavy chiselled desk. He poked about it with a long elegant forefinger before slowly closing it. 'There are two keys,' he said at last, 'and one is missing from my desk. I don't know who took it.' He didn't even have the grace to look sheepish.

'The man who took that key was likely the man that killed Anne Giles, else gave it to the man that killed Anne Giles,' Dowling rightly identified the need to spell out the obvious.

'Yes, sir. That is a credible *theory*, but do not rule out maleficium. It should be easy for a witch to take the key and spirit it away without even having to enter the house. Or perhaps persuade one of my servants to take it against their will and outside their waking memory.' The rector looked into space, apparently deep in thought.

'It seems to me, sir, that the theory of maleficium is most attractive to you only because it permits you to be done with the notion that it was providence,' Dowling remarked. I regarded the butcher with a new admiration. Now we were getting closer to the point.

'Not so,' the rector blinked. 'You forget that the murder was bloody and very wicked. The woman was not by any account a wicked person, yet the deed itself was wicked. The curse of the Lord is in the house of the wicked, not the house of the Lord himself. And all of this reminds me of something that happened not so long ago.'

'What was that, good sir?'

'There is an old woman that until lately came to prayer without fail. She didn't sing the psalms, nor even did she appear to pray. Always she would sit at the back and watch, never said anything, never spoke. In the two years I have been here I have not heard her proclaim any word. Then recently she applied for the pensions list. Well, she was widowed many years ago and nothing had changed of her circumstances. She continued to earn money from the selling of meats, I certainly saw her doing so on several occasions. It seemed to me that she merely desired to stop working, and sought a pension to support her idleness. On that basis I turned her down.' He looked away with pink cheeks.

'And what was her response, sir?'

'She made no response. She stopped coming to church,' he answered severely. 'I've seen her since, selling meat on the street. Why, then, did she stop coming to church? Only on the basis that she was refused a pension? After so many years? That indicates to me that although she said nothing upon being refused her pension, still she was maddened. Perhaps she cursed me. Maybe she has been cursed herself and can no longer stand to be in God's house.'

'Maybe she doesn't like your sermons,' said I before I could stop myself.

'Exactly!' exclaimed the rector, thankfully missing the point. 'It is well known that she has a teat on her upper body from which she may give sustenance to whatever wicked spirits there are that may dwell in these parts, which God knows are likely very many. Never was she able to recite the Lord's Prayer nor the Creed, not word for word.'

Witch-hunting was an old sport. An accusation would be followed by torture until a confession was obtained. Then the rector would be free to stage a public exorcism, a cleansing of his church and parish with him as blessed cleanser, and the poor wretch hung by the neck, burnt alive or drowned. I looked to Dowling for help. He sat expressionless and impassive.

'Sir, I know you by your noble reputation,' Dowling said cautiously. 'I know you as a learned man and a wise man. I am much surprised to hear you talk of witchery. It is my understanding that the learned give little to notions of witchery and maleficium. These are the superstitions of the poor and uneducated, and the Presbyterian Scots.'

'I think you are telling me your *own* views, sir,' replied the rector firmly, 'but they are not the views of the secular courts, one of whose tasks it is to ensure the prosecution of black magic and maleficium. God himself spake through Moses; "Thou shalt not suffer a witch to live." Until two years ago this church was ministered by an Independent, I know not what he preached to these people, for none will relate it to me, so I must presume that it was heresy. Where there is the stink of heresy one cannot rule out that witchery has grown from the seed so planted. Give up witches, give up the Bible.'

'I am a humble man,' I said untruthfully, 'but in my turn I also divine that you disfavour providence because of its consequences. How can you be sure that the slayer did not take the key from your desk?'

'I cannot. That is my sadness, sir. Now that you bring it to my attention the theory of providence becomes strong again. I simply cast my net wide so that I might catch the right fish.' The fisher of men ran his talons through the tight black curls upon his head.

'The Devil needs no witches to do his deeds. He is able to do his own deeds.' Dowling looked cross.

The rector nodded thoughtfully. 'You may not dismiss

maleficium so easily. The Devil uses witches because he uses witches. The issue of need is not at issue here. If you are investigating this murder, then you must consider witchery. Indeed, even if the key *were* stolen, it is just as likely to be maleficium as providence. You must agree!'

'Very well,' Dowling replied, before I could debate the point further, 'but what of the key?'

The rector looked at us both with a slightly guilty expression. 'You should know that I lost a servant three days ago, a poor, mean, dishonest young man who I would be rid of anyway. He departed without a word. Strange that he should leave about the same time the key is taken from my desk.'

God save my pickled soul! This was too much to bear! 'It isn't strange at all,' I said slowly through gritted teeth. 'Perhaps now we can dispense with all this talk of popery and witches. What's his name and where does he live?'

The rector observed me thoughtfully before picking up his quill and writing. 'His name is Simpson and he lives in a tenement near to St Martin's. If any one of my servants took that key – it was he.' He wrote some more. 'And here is the name and abode of the woman that I suspect of witchery. If you do not pursue her then I will find others that will.'

'Sir,' I spoke carefully, 'we visited your church yesterday, and examined it indoors and outdoors. We saw no evidence of witchery, no markings, no herbs or smells or concoctions. You should pay heed afore you accuse an old woman of witchery. Should you send one of your parish to the secular court only because you did not aid them when they demanded it, and they in turn went wanting, then we should take a personal interest and make full use of the Mayor's influences. In this age, as you said yourself, there are many folks not to be intimidated by the word of the Church.'

The rector's big eyes glistened. 'Yea,' he muttered, 'but then you know little of witchery. Perhaps I should not raise the issue with you at all, but seek an audience with the Lord Chief Justice.'

Dowling coughed. 'There is no need for that, good sir. We will find the woman. You in turn, sir, I think should be less hasty. You may be a great man. Certainly it would be a pity to be a small man with such a great head.' Dowling gestured to all of the books. Indeed it was true – he did have an extremely large head.

The rector's cheeks turned bright red and he clasped his fingers together just below his nose. 'I read you and take you, Mr Dowling. Maybe I was not so much in need of your wise words as you would think. Meantime I hope you will indeed proceed hastily, for the sake of my parish, and I will do what I need to do, and I will thank you not to tell me how to go about my job.'

'Aye sir, thank you, sir. We should take our leave now,' Dowling exclaimed abruptly before seizing me by the arm and pulling me roughly. Though I was much offended I let myself be led. The rector waved a hand, dismissively. We hurried out the house and back onto Fleet Street.

'You would remove one of my arms?' I demanded, straightening my coat sleeve and checking that he had neither stretched the cloth nor left a print on it.

'I know that man by reputation. Clergy can be dangerous, and the time was right to leave.' He patted me on the shoulder like a puppy and looked up at the sky. 'We must find this witch!' he called, striding out ahead.

*　*　*

If you have the sense that you were born with, then you will have understood by now that neither Dowling nor I believed for a moment that a witch killed Anne Giles. I am intelligent and educated and the butcher can read and write. But it says in Exodus, 'Thou shalt not suffer a witch to live'. So if there are no such things as witches, then why does the Bible say so? The answer of course is that the Bible is both extremely long and very badly written; such that you can find in its pages whatever message you seek. This is not an argument worth pursuing in public, however, unless you are inclined to lose your liberty, selected pieces of your body or even your life. So we went to find the woman, whose name was Mary Bedford, on Fleet Street, to save her the role of rector's scapegoat. This was a gallant deed that made me feel unusually worthy.

We walked the streets towards the west, for the City had choked up already, such that walking was the quickest mode of transport available. Dowling strode down the middle of the road by himself, oblivious to the evil broth that splashed about his legs, body and ears, while I trod the higher ground with those that knew the difference between man and dog. So it was that he crossed the bridge at Fleet Ditch before me, the filthy stream that served the slums of Alsatia and Bridewell.

Tiny, dark, airless alleys branched off Fleet Street like dead twigs, every one of them a choking rotten tributary of streaming slops that crept slowly down to the river. Most of the ramshackle buildings were built of wooden planks nailed to posts, covered with pitch and roofed with rough tiles. The only warmth in those hovels was generated from the bodies of those that lived there, nested together many to a room, like rats in a nest. The stink was the foulest stink in the whole of England, a poisonous cloud fed by the soap makers, dye houses, slaughterhouses and tanneries. The curing pits of the tanneries nestled alongside the outside of the city walls and were full of dog shit, a key ingredient in the tanning process.

The house that Mary Bedford lived in was tiny and unsteady, tucked in at the top of one of the foul alleyways just behind the much grander half-timbered houses of Fleet Street. It was closed up and the door was shut.

Dowling looked at me and shrugged, his mind back at his shop I reckoned, but given the rector's ramblings about witchery we were committed to make greater efforts to find her, fearful of what might become of her were others to discover her whereabouts first.

The first house we tried was a large family house on Fleet Street. We didn't hold out much hope of getting sense from the master of the house, for what man of standing would admit to noticing a poor wretch of a woman that sold meats on the street? But we hoped to find out something from the servants. The one that opened the door stared at us uncomprehending and unspeaking, even after we had explained our objective three times, ever slower and clearer. Finally he shook his head in bewilderment and wandered off into the house to find someone else. An imbecile. London was full of them – they came in from the villages, like Dowling. A short time later he returned, accompanied by a middle-aged woman wearing a coarse brown dress and white apron, with a white hood tied around her head. Her face was ruddy and rough, her expression impatient and puzzled. Another imbecile. She listened to Dowling's questions, mouth agape and hands on her hips. Then she closed the doors in our faces. Washing day, as Dowling pointed out brightly.

We moved on to the next house and another street full after that.

'Good morning to you.' A grizzled face looked out through a ground floor window, a man maybe forty years old with a thick welt on his nose and one eye missing. Dowling recited his introduction for perhaps the twentieth time while I stood with my hands in my pockets. It was past lunchtime and my stomach wailed pitifully. The man leant on the sill with his arms crossed, chewing the inside of his cheek, apparently in the mood for a conversation.

'Aye, I know Mary Bedford, Old Mary. Known her since she was a child.'

'Have you seen her today?' I demanded, astounded.

'Not today. But she'll be around.'

'Around where?'

'Somewhere.'

'You know why she doesn't go to church any more?' Dowling probed.

The man nodded. 'Same reason I don't go no more. She asked to be put on the pensions list after she couldn't stand her giddiness no more, but the new man told her she was lazy. She was ashamed. I had to tell her not to pay no heed, but she's afeared to go back. Meantime she has to sell meats or else starve. If she's not been home, then likely she's lying on her face in a gutter somewhere. She's too ill to be out working.'

'Where does she sell?'

'She won't be far away, doesn't like to wander. Shy of strangers too.' His eyes were suspicious 'Why do you want to know?'

'We want to make sure she's safe,' I replied. The man shook his head and emitted a sorrowful cackle before closing the window. Dowling tutted sorrowfully, sighed and walked off.

'What's wrong with you?' I asked the back of his head.

He turned to regard me solemnly. 'The notion that a man wearing your fine clothes is likely to have an interest in the fate of one such as Mary Bedford is not to be believed.' One of his big dirty hands landed on one of my finely clothed shoulders. He was right, of course. I tried not to look too disappointed, hopeful that he would relieve me of his filthy great paw.

The next house to yield an answer was dark and unlit. All the windows were closed and there was a smell like liniment, sharp and acidic, with perhaps a hint of alcohol and fruit. The man that lived there was no less unattractive than the one we had just left, though he did have two eyes. His pupils were locked up tight like pinholes and the whites were covered with scabrous yellow patches. His nose was red and his eyes flowed. He twisted a piece of cloth between his fingers, which was clearly what he used to clean his nose. Poisonous green gases seeped from twixt his lips. He also knew 'Old Mary', but less intimately.

'There's some say she's a witch,' he told us through weeping eyes, in between sneezes. 'She suckles the Devil, so it is said.'

'Who says so?' Dowling asked gently.

'Folks,' was the only reply we got, and nothing else of any use.

By seven o'clock that night we were practically in Whitefriars. Some people spoke to us but we learnt nothing new. Confirmation of her poor circumstances, more loose speculation as to whether or not she might be a witch. This was nothing very interesting, since all old women living by themselves elicited images of witchery in many folk's minds. As darkness fell we made our final house call. A woman pushed open the top half of a door and stood there simpering. Her face, body and limbs were shrunken and wrinkled like an old, dry apricot. She smiled sweetly and broadly and her eyes shone bright. We'd spoken to a few like this, this endless afternoon.

'Ye-es?' The old lady smiled so broadly that her eyes threatened to pop right out. It was a frightening sight. A tiny spittle of saliva trickled down her chin that she did not seem to notice. Dowling started to describe Mary Bedford using information that we had gleaned from others that day.

'Ye-es. Mary.' Smiling and staring into Dowling's eyes she nodded slowly. He didn't seem to mind. Probably used to it, being a Scot.

'Tell me about her.'

'Mary is my frie-nd.' She continued to smile and waved her head from side to side like a snake, paying us scant attention. She seemed more interested in the darkening sky above our heads. Then she suddenly announced, 'She is a witch!' She said it quietly, melodically, as if she was talking about the weather, as if she did not understand the import of her words, which I suppose she didn't. At that Dowling relaxed, as if he had seen it coming all along. When I quizzed him afterwards he told me that in his unfortunate experience living in the country, witches were always accused in pairs, never alone. Whilst I had never heard it said before, it explained Dowling's persistence that afternoon, and his excitement in finding this woman, for she was, he told me, 'the sort'.

What followed then was deeply disturbing. She told us tales of the two of them suckling children with their old dry breasts. How they would change their forms at night and visit children that mocked them during the day in the form of great toads. They had the power to cause children to die if they were too wicked in their ways, she claimed. We shouldn't worry too much about Mary Bedford, she assured us, since being denied her pension she had subjected herself to spells that enabled her to walk freely again. She talked of how they were able to play with men's senses, remove and bestow at will hearing, sight and the use of limbs. And the more that she spoke, the more miserable I became. Not because of the words themselves, for I had no doubt that the woman was speaking nonsense. No, this was not my source of dread. What disturbed me was that I had heard these tales before, that they were in fact very well known. Two years before, two old women, Rose Cullender and Amy Denny, had been tried by the Lord Chief Justice himself, and were found guilty of witchery. The tales that this old woman was relating to us were clearly lifted from the account of their trial, which was printed and widely distributed and read. This old woman was clearly bucket-headed and weak minded, but her state of mind would be held as proof, not as grounds for dismissal. And so long as she was disposed to stand at her door and talk such nonsense to strangers such as us, both her life and the life of Mary Bedford were in very great danger should the rector take steps to pursue his theory. The Lord Chief Justice Keeling himself had tried the Lowestoft witches in his previous role as Lord Chief Baron of the Exchequer.

At the end of it Dowling pressed five coins into her hands and pleaded with her that she say no more of witchery. She nodded her head, and smiled happily, but neither of us believed that the money would change her behaviour. We left Fleet Street that evening, with troubled minds and troubled hearts, though not before Dowling asked me to reimburse him the five coins.

As the weak winter light slowly faded and a bloody red sheen slid forward over the cobbles and stones, we finally hurried to the address that we had for John Simpson. But all we gained was a vague description of an ordinary-looking man. Simpson himself had left the premises and taken what belongings he had with him. We would have to find him too, but not that night. I headed home exhausted and anxious.

Jane waited for me in the hall, simmering and full of tension. Waving her hands at me and making signs, she shepherded me towards the door of my front room. Then she put her lips to my ear and hissed, 'Get him out!'

I looked into her eyes, but saw no fear, so I pushed the door slowly open and entered the room. A strange little man stood looking about him at every article of furniture and detail. His manner matched his strange appearance, ponderous yet threatening, like a mangy dog that would soonest flee yet still sink its teeth into your throat should you block its passage. Even with his funny hat on, tall with a wide brim in the style that the Puritans used to wear some twenty years before, the man did not quite match even me in stature. Yet his legs were long like a rooster. Shiny black leather boots reached nearly up to his knees, and were so loose from his leg that I found myself wondering what would happen were I to pour water into them. The top of his head was covered with tightly curled hair; the bottom of it sprouted a pointy little beard. With one hand he carried a stick that was taller than he, a thick, twisted branch of wood, gnarled and black. Finally he looked me in the eye. Once he had it, he would not let it go, just stood there looking glum, staring.

'You have not found Mary Bedford.'

What business was it of his? 'Who are you?'

Blinking and frowning, he muttered something to himself, before looking at me with sad eyes and turned-down mouth.

37

A look of pity. I should have been angry, but instead felt intimidated. He cleared his throat and licked his lips. 'I am John Parsons. I was told that you are trying to find out who killed Anne Giles. Seems I was told false. I beg your pardon.' He made as if to leave.

'I *am* trying to find out who killed Anne Giles. What's your business?' As I spoke it suddenly occurred to me who the man might be. His old-fashioned Puritan dress, his mercenary aspect – all reminded me of the pictures I had seen and stories I had read of Matthew Hopkins and John Sterne. 'You are a witchfinder,' I exclaimed, horrified, making no attempt to disguise my contempt.

He had the temerity to smile modestly and bow his head. 'If I don't find her in one day, then you have my word that I will press no claim upon you for money. But I will find her.'

Matthew Hopkins died young, just twenty-five-years old. He came from Ipswich where he was a lawyer, a man of no reputation nor social standing. Yet before he died he managed to torture and kill more than two hundred poor folks, most of them women. He was a parasite that had fed upon the fears of the poor ignorants that lived in the countryside and the small towns. This man reminded me of him. He gave off a stinking malodour of the same horrible zealousness. A calm certainty exuded from his tiny body, my sharp words fell against him like leaves falling from a tree. My instinct was to be rid of him, but then what would he do? Men like him demanded money for their services, yet it wasn't money that drove them. They were conceited and proud, over sure of their own worth and righteousness. If I turned him away, I knew that he would market his services about the parish until he found one that would pay. So I tried to be clever. 'How much money do you want?'

His steady gaze made me feel like he could read my mind and was challenging me to rebuke him. 'We can agree the sum after I have apprehended the woman and tested her.'

'Tested her? You mean watching, searching or swimming?' I tried to hide the rising fear and loathing that this man was eliciting in my soul. Hopkins had forced his victims to sit on a stool in the middle of a room for days and nights on end. Witnesses would be told to watch for familiars sneaking out into the open to suck blood from the witch's hidden extra nipple. Every witch had familiars. He would keep them seated on the stool until they were exhausted, driven half mad by lack of sleep. Then he would extract his confession. Or he would search them, strip them naked and search every part of their body, looking for the hidden nipple and for witch marks. Or he would bind their hands and feet and throw them into a river or pond. Men would push them down to the pond to see whether or not they would rise to the surface. If they rose they were dragged out and hung. If they sank, then they were innocent, but dead.

'I will make that judgement based on what I see.'

I was angry enough now to return his black stare without trepidation. 'I will pay you well, Mr Parsons,' at which he nodded calmly and let his gaze drop, 'if you follow my instructions, and proceed as I instruct you.'

Looking up he seemed surprised, as if to ask what could I possibly know about his gory trade. He snorted.

'You will find her, and you may apprehend her, but you will do nothing else until talking to me. You will not test her, nor indeed do anything to her whatsoever, until I have visited and we have agreed what next to do, together. Is that acceptable to you, Mr Parsons?'

The witchfinder looked at me for a moment as if I was the weakest and least resolute man in the whole of England. Then he smirked, nodded, and confirmed that he was prepared to do my will. I should have felt satisfied, but as I watched him leave I felt my cold skin prickle. God help us.

'Who was that?' Jane glared at me from beneath the red tangle on top of her head.

I grunted. Not having a wife of my own, I had managed to acquire a bit of wealth. Indeed I was worth a hundred pounds, money that I kept in a small brown casket that was buried beneath the floor of the cellar. Those hundred pounds were the fruit of my efforts over five long years spent toiling every waking hour over at the Tower. Once I had saved a hundred pounds I had decided that it was enough. As long as I had money for food, wine and tobacco, that was funds sufficient. It was at that point I had employed Jane.

She had been a quiet girl when I first offered her employ. She'd worked for a lot of different households and came to me without any references whatsoever, but she did have this astounding wild red hair that I found instantly fascinating. For the first couple of days she did everything I told her to without comment, but on the third day, I think it was, she threw a cooking pot at my head for no reason at all and started shouting – all kinds of blasphemies – some of which I'd not heard before. After that we got on much better. She doesn't often do what I tell her to, but knows better than I what needs doing. Deep down I know that she wants to lie with me, but I think she's concerned that she may spoil our master and servant relationship. She keeps telling me that I ought find a wife, but not with any sincerity.

It was after she had been with me for three months that

she introduced me to her brother. He was a thin fellow that walked with permanently stooped back like he was in constant fear of being struck. He had six children, one of whom was always ill and had once been close to death. A month after that she introduced me to her sister whose husband had only one leg and so was unable to work. Then there was the uncle with the swollen head. The consequence of all these meetings was that I found myself having committed some small sums to all their livelihoods. It was not so much money, and still I could afford to do all that I wanted and keep untouched my hundred pounds. It was also enough to stop her prating, for each time she told me what a fool I was for not marrying, I reminded her that it would likely mean my no longer being able to afford to support her and hers. It stopped the nagging but did nothing for her temper, for she deeply resented her obligation, I think.

So all the money I earn I spend and all I spend is covered by what I earn, which is a balance that keeps my soul sweet and heart content. And if I ever do decide to marry then it will be to a wealthy woman anyhow, for liberty carries a high price.

She made me some dinner that I ate in silence. I prayed that I had been wise in my treatment of Parsons, but I didn't feel wise – I felt confused and lost. Were I to adopt the common view, then my new dead cousin was the victim of maleficium and Mary Bedford was the culprit. Whatever the truth of the matter – that wasn't it. This was a complex challenge for which I would need a good night's sleep. Later.

Chapter Three

Prunella
The flowers may be blue, flesh-coloured or white.

Hurrying through the wintry dusk, drawn forwards by a soft, warm light, I relished the safe haven of the Crowne. It is difficult for me to describe the sense of solace I find inside the walls of such great taverns. As I pass over the threshold it is as if all my troubles are taken away and hung on a peg. By the time I come to collect them again my soul is brighter and my heart sings a merry song. Also some of the warmest and softest women in London are to be found at the Crowne.

I had already arranged to meet William Hill there for no other motive than to drink and be merry. Yet this night I crossed the threshold with a fresh motive, for Hill possessed a sharp wit and I savoured the prospect of sharing my preoccupation with him, that he might hold forth his staff and put everything to right. He knew other people's secrets.

Hill had been a pensioner at Cambridge at the same time that I was a sizar – I had waited on the wealthier students to earn *my* passage. Now he was a merchant, like his father before him. He had left the year before me to travel Europe at his father's expense. I assume that the object of the trip was to build his own networks of colleagues and acquaintances, for that is how it seems to work in his line of business. He was still a good friend, of sorts, though the nature of his trade meant that there were always things that he did and people that he knew that he would tell me nothing of. Were I in a similar position then perhaps our relationship would have been more balanced. As it was there was nothing hidden in the yellowed parchments of the Tower that I would withhold from Hill other than from fear of boring him to death. So sometimes I wearied of his tales, the inevitable expression of regret that he could tell me no more. I think I was a little envious, but he was fun to be with, a bowl of sauce wrapped up in a thick layer of goose fat. While others walked wearily from pillar to post, Hill bounced.

Tonight, though, he sat in a corner by himself huddled over a mug of ale, a plate of bones at his elbow, miserable. He looked up at me and grunted as I approached, blinking with red eyes, his mouth curled in a surly snarl. Not the horny dog I knew so well. I asked what ailed him but he just muttered at me. I didn't know whether to stay or go for I had never seen him cloaked in such a foul black mood before, but he kicked a chair aside for me to sit in. Before obliging I called for another jug of ale and two pipes. Taking one of the pipes he leant back and acknowledged me with a forced grin. I thought better of asking him again what troubled him, assuming it must be some deal gone wrong. Perhaps he had lost a cargo, or had a shipment impounded at the docks, or some such disaster. He pulled at the pipe then watched the exhaled smoke drift away into the yellow fog.

'What's news at the Tower?'

'I no longer work at the Tower.' Putting down my mug and taking my time I recounted the events of the day. I told him how Prynne had gleefully informed me that my father had already been in touch with him to request that I be permitted to resign. Before I could recant the request he had berated me for being 'effeminate, whorish and abominable' then commended me for my noble resolution that he hoped would be my salvation. My interview with Shrewsbury had been little better. He had bid me attend him at Whitehall, then took me for a ride in his yellow coach, berating me my wasteful life. It was he that told me where my cousin's body lay, he that told me with great pompous majesty that he had deigned to support my efforts – again at my father's request – to the extent that he had arranged for someone from the Mayor's office to lend the butcher. Yet he also placed a sword at my throat and made me vow to tell no man of his involvement.

Hill listened with the face of a huge bull, big black eyes locked onto mine. As I spoke his brow slowly lowered and his jaw tightened, his china pipe waggling between his teeth. A little muscle twitched, just where his jaw met his neck. 'A vow that you have already broken at least once today, then?'

A fair point, I reflected, though spoken strangely. His tone was unusually guarded this evening. I had been half hoping that he would pull a face, flick the stem of his pipe in my direction and announce contemptuously that everyone in London knew who had killed Anne Giles. 'It's only you I've told.'

Hill shook his head slowly. 'Shrewsbury is a good patron to have, Lytle. You are fortunate to have a friend like him. If your loose lips land him in trouble with the Lord Chief Justice, then he will cut off your balls and sew them into your cheeks.'

'Aye,' I nodded. My mouth felt uncomfortably dry, so I wet it. He kept staring at me with his black beady eyes. 'What do you know of Shrewsbury?' I asked him.

'He's your patron, not mine.'

'It was my father that knew him. He used to come into the shop and smoke his tobacco during Cromwell's reign. He gave me my post at the Tower in exchange for my father's kindnesses, I suppose. Which was strange enough.' I shook my head. 'Why should he concern himself with my father's affairs now that he is rich and famous?'

Shrugging and looking away at last, Hill blew out his cheeks so his head looked like that of a pig. 'Shrewsbury sits on the Privy Council, Harry. He was loyal to Charles Stuart and diverted funds to his war on Scotland, and he helped Monck, indeed was a member of the Sealed Knot, those that planned the Restoration while Cromwell was still Lord Protector. Shrewsbury was one of those that went to Holland to bring Charles back.'

'Then I don't understand why he gives off such an air of things politick. I barely understand what he says half the time. If he's so close to the King, I would expect him to be sitting pretty at the Palace, wouldn't you?' I spoke quietly, despite the covering din.

Hill shifted his chair awkwardly so that his mouth was close to my ear. 'Aye, well you are artless of the workings of the Court. There is room for the whole of London in all the secret passages that worm their way between the Palace walls. Some of them are not so secret neither. I myself have been down the one between the King's quarters and Lord Arlington's rooms. The whole of London knows about the passage from the King's bedroom to the quarters of the maids

45

of honour, it is a sign of the way things are down at Whitehall. Once you find a secret passage then it is no longer a secret, it loses its worth, but when a spy is found he can be replaced, and Whitehall swarms with them. I would wager that Charles sets up his games just to keep the Court busy.'

'The King shows no gratitude to those that put him where he is?'

He turned away to drink from his mug. 'I didn't say that. The King is mindful of the fate that became his father. Parliament cut off his head because they said he was waging war upon his own people and soliciting support from France. Charles knows what happens when a king lifts his chin too high. Many complain that we wage war with the Dutch when Holland resists popery with such resolve, and say he is plotting with the Spanish, who are the natural harbingers of the papists. Others say that the war with Holland is a wall of smoke that causes the French and Spanish to be lax. None really know his intentions, for he confides in none, or rather confides in all, but confides particularly with each. He knows that the mood of the people may not be counted on to be steadfast, so he pleases them and their natural inclination to dance, play music and drink, whilst befuddling the Court with puffs of smoke and tastes of honey.'

I leant forward eagerly. 'And what of Shrewsbury in all of this?'

'Shrewsbury cannot be said to be anything other than a Royalist, for he has been steadfast and true. Yet he is plagued by tales that he forged some alliance with the Republic to safeguard his land and property. That he doesn't deny, but he forcefully denies that he made deals with those that slew the King. I am not so reckless to say that the King makes the most of his anxieties, and the multitude of others like him. I will leave others to say so if they will.'

'Lord Shrewsbury is not listened to, then?'

'I observe that the King listens and speaks to Shrewsbury as much as he does any man, but no man is secure. Shrewsbury seeks every opportunity to demonstrate his loyalty. I have even heard it said that he led discussions with the Dutch to stage a war that may later become a solid alliance against the French and Spanish. The French and Spanish fight each other lustily, so might come out of it with no navy and empty pockets.'

'Does he have enemies?'

'You may be sure of it, but I cannot list for you their names, and doubt that he can neither. Such is life at Court. It is well known that he and Lord Keeling cannot tolerate each other. This is an interesting thing that you ought know of, because this William Ormonde, the father of the dead girl, is a close friend of Keeling's. They were once neighbours at Epsom.'

'Then why does Shrewsbury help *me*? If Ormonde is Keeling's friend, then surely Keeling will make special efforts to see the killer brought to justice?'

Hill took a deep breath and had a drink. 'Your father asked him for help.'

My father. Asking Shrewsbury for help to catch the killer of someone I'd never heard of? I would have to talk to him, but he was away in Cocksmouth.

Watching me like he could read my thoughts, Hill licked his lips. 'Like I said, Harry, Shrewsbury's a good patron to have.' He called for more ale. 'Tell me more of the murder itself. A knife in the eye and teeth broken, you say? An eye for an eye, and a tooth for a tooth. It sounds like a strange and evil act of revenge.'

'Aye,' I replied, startled, for this had not occurred to me at all. 'Though what revenge could a man want on Anne Giles?'

'She may have been killed as revenge upon another,' answered Hill without enthusiasm, shifting his genitals into place with his left hand while smoking with his right. 'I'll tell you something for nothing.'

'What?'

'If I was in your place, then I would make speed to Epsom. Now that Ormonde has been informed of his daughter's death the funeral will be tomorrow or the day after. If you are her cousin then you should be able to gain access.'

'How do you know so much?'

Hill shrugged, his usual gesture that meant I should mind my own business. Switching his attention to the thin plume of smoke that drifted out of the bowl of his pipe he evaded my efforts to catch his eye, again behaving as if it was I that had sabotaged his affairs. We sat in gloomy silence for a while until he inadvertently poured ale down his nose and nearly choked himself. Then he drenched me in a giant sneeze. Laughing loud despite himself, his mood switched suddenly. He wiped an arm across his mouth and launched into a crazed partisan monologue about the Dutch war. It transpired that he had lost two shipments – of what he would not tell me – one from the Indies and one from Africa. He complained about the superior tactics of the Dutch, and how they beat our navy senseless every time they met. He derided Mings, Sandwich and Barkely in terms that he would not have used outside tavern walls, and generally vented his spleen. Then he downed a pot in one draught as if to draw a curtain upon the subject. It was loud now and the air was hot and full of ale fumes. At the end of the table a group of six men were singing a simple lewd song at the tops of their voices to the sound of a guitar and flagelette. Two of them sat playing their instruments, while the other four stood with their chests inflated, singing with their eyes screwed up in concentration.

'Come aloft, my little dwarf – have at thee!' Hill leant over, whisked off my wig and dragged his fingers across my cropped head. I fought him off with a well-aimed punch, then aimed another at his chin. He roared with laughter just before I caught him square, then sat back grinning ruefully, hand on jaw. None called me a dwarf, not even he. I may be short but I am well proportioned and very attractive to women. Lifting his full pot, he drank it down in one great swig before filling it again. More food arrived, and we ate heartily. Hill picked up on a melody that others were developing a short way down the table and began to join in the bawdy songs, singing at the top of his voice and sweating heavily. Leaving him to it I sought out some familiar company who let me touch her and play a little. By eleven the place was a melee of drunken oafs, singing, roaring and staggering stiff-leggedly like frothing horses. Coats got stained, stockings slipped down legs and wigs fell crooked. Hats were danced on and trampled, lace was torn and shoes were scuffed. Hill was in the middle of it singing the loudest as I stumbled out into the silent night.

I had drunk more than I intended, but was not senseless. The moon was brighter now and the streets emptier. I walked carefully past St Mary's, onto Poultry and stopped at the Great Conduit to douse my face in its cold water. The King's Head and the Mermaid were both still full. The night air was freezing, the filth was hard and frozen into lumps, the sewers were thick and ran slowly. This was night air, which would kill you by asphyxiation if you stayed out too long.

Drink took the edge off the prickly cold but I hurried anyway, knowing that frost's fingers would quickly find a way through my defences. Banging on my door with my fist I stomped my feet impatiently. Jane would be sitting up waiting for me in her own little bed, knees drawn up to her chin. As I stood waiting for her to come downstairs and open up, I looked back down the street. I fancied I saw a man hanging about under the eaves of a house fifty yards or so away, but the figure quickly turned and disappeared into the Mermaid. Lost or drunk, sucked into the warmth like iron filings to a magnet. I banged my fist on the door again, then looked at my knuckles. They were wet. There was paint on the door – I could just make it out – gleaming wet. I dabbed at the markings with my finger. It was paint all right, red paint. Why would someone paint my door? I stepped back to see if mine was the only door painted.

'What hour do you call this?'

I jumped, not having noticed the door open. Jane stood there in the doorway hissing at me, standing bent in a thick white nightgown with a shapeless white hat pulled down to the top of her eyes. Her feet were bare, her ankles too, long legs and fleshy hips. Then I heard something, or thought I did, and swung around, again catching a glimpse of movement at the end of the street. A light danced from side to side. It was a Charley and his dog walking slowly. The Charley rang his bell and called out in a thin, reedy voice, 'Past one o'clock, and a cold, frosty, winter's night.' There were shivers in the man's voice.

'I call it one,' I answered her. 'Some knave has painted a red cross on my door!' Looking up and down the street again, I checked. Sure enough mine was the only door painted. 'Was it you?'

Jane looked at the door and dabbed at the paint with her finger. 'Fie to you! What a foolish question.' She knelt down. 'There are words too.'

Crouching next to her I had a closer look. '*To the pest-house*,' I read. Very strange. It was what they used to write on the doors of those infected during the days of the plagues. 'You haven't got the plague have you?'

'No, of course I haven't got the plague.'

'Well it must be the wrong door, then. What about next door? Do they have the plague?'

'There hasn't been a plague in London for forty years, and there isn't a plague tonight. If there were, then I would know it, even if you didn't.' She seized me by the lapel of my poor fine jacket and manhandled me over the threshold. My hand brushed against her breast. It was warm and soft.

'Someone's idea of a jest, then.'

'All the children are in bed well before one o'clock at night and this paint is still wet. Strange foolery for a grown man to play.' She bundled me into the kitchen and sat me down at the table upon which stood a plate of cold meats and a cup of hypocras.

My stomach now declared itself to be very hungry. I smiled blearily.

'I have enquired of my colleagues about the town. They tell me that they allow themselves to be merry with their servants and their servants do not object. They may run their hands where their hands do please.' I had been thinking on it a while.

'These colleagues of yours are gentlemen, I suppose?' Jane snorted before turning on her heel and disappearing, only to reappear a minute later with a bucket and scrubbing brush, face taut and pale.

'Is your rhubarb up, old woman?' I felt myself stiffening.

'My rhubarb?' Jane exclaimed. 'You run your hands where you fancy, Lytle. You may place them where you please, but when you wake in the morning you will find them nailed to the bedpost.'

I thought about it for a moment. 'That sounds like a reasonable proposition.' She glared furiously. Time to put her in her place. 'God created Adam. Then later he created Eve, that man might be satisfied.'

'God created animals before he created Adam. Was that so that Adam might satisfy the animals?' I felt her slap me hard somewhere proximate to the top of my head. My eyelids fell down over my eyes and the muscle that could have lifted them fell asleep.

My eyes gave up and I let my head fall back. 'You are right. I will not run my hands where I please.'

'God save us both.' Picking up the bucket and brush, she headed back out towards the street.

I felt guilty. 'You don't need to do that now, do it tomorrow instead,' I called after her as she marched out.

'Oh aye, what wit!' She stopped, turned, and stamped back into the kitchen. 'Have the whole of London town saying that we have the plague in our house. Word would be all over the country by lunchtime.'

'Oh aye. Best do it now then,' I muttered. The door opened and that was that.

Chapter Four

Hairie River-weed
In stagnant waters.

Dowling danced like a dervish, all fingers and fairy steps, eyes blinking like a big green frog. Then he started stomping his left leg on the floor like a wormy horse. Jane lingered, fascinated, until she noticed what looked like a piece of gizzard stuck to his shirt, whereupon she left us to it. Mercifully, for else I think Dowling would have eaten his arm.

'We have a man locked up at Newgate,' he declared. 'They say he is the man that killed Anne Giles. A multitude of witnesses saw him running out of the church the night that she was killed with blood dripping from his hands.'

'Praise the Lord!' I exclaimed. The answer to all my prayers. 'So they will hang him, I suppose?' Would Shrewsbury be at Westminster today, or ought I visit his house to deliver the good news?

Dowling shook his head. 'He hasn't confessed it. The mob swears in God's name it's him, but we cannot take the word of the mob.' The mob usually meant apprentices, groups of inarticulate ne'er-do-wells that spoke with one voice and followed each other like newborn chickens. The mob would swear that the King was a horse if it meant a poke full of plums. Staring down at my feet, brown eyes unfocussed, Dowling's mind was clearly wandering. 'What perplexes me is that they brought him to my shop. Their usual inclination would be to beat him with sticks and hang him themselves at Cheapside.'

'They reckon he'll be hung anyway.' I pulled on my stockings and put on my shoes. 'Let's go and get that confession.'

Newgate gaol was another place I had not anticipated becoming acquainted with. It consisted of two square straight towers, sixty feet tall, on either side of the gateway in and out of the City. Three wenches without clothes stood over the gate draped with flimsy pieces of fabric, very yardy. All I could see that day, though, was the portcullis, with its sharp pointy teeth and eleven black windows, each one covered with a tight lattice of bars. I followed Dowling up five flat steps at the base of the left-hand tower into a gloomy little room. Two scabby-looking wastrels sat in the anteroom drinking and trying to play cards. They looked up as we entered, all lolly headed and winey. Their shoes were a disgrace; battered and uncared for, leather peeling off in torn patches. One of them nodded at Dowling as we entered, our permission to pass deeper into the prison, it seemed. We left behind a thick fug of cheap wine and walked into a mist of old sweat and stinking shit.

'This floor isn't too bad.' Dowling led us across large square flagstones. Not bad? The air was so thick you could feel it cling to the inside of your nostrils, greasy brown and sticky. It clogged your lungs and made your eyes water. Worse

than anything I had ever experienced, though it was true that –
unlike him – I did not spend my days in a merry slaughterhouse
soaking in the spirit of dismembered bodies.

I peered through a barred window into the room beyond.
It was large and very dark with just one small window set at
the top of the far wall. Once my eyes got used to the gloom I
saw movement, lots of movement, like a sea of maggots in an
open wound. The room was full of men, forty or fifty of them,
lying on pallets on the floor, all lined up next to each other.
A bucket stood by each pallet, used to piss in and shit in, no
doubt. Every man was chained. I had seen chickens boxed up
like this, but never men. Chickens pecked each other's eyes out
and started to eat each other. What would men do? It was a
foul disgrace. Dowling drew up beside me.

'They pay for fire, candles, clothes and food. They can be
rid of those chains if they want, but again they must pay for
the privilege. Given that most of them are in here for stealing
or for not paying their debts . . .'

Torture of the mind. 'Is our man in there?'

'Our man is downstairs in the stone hold, God have mercy
on his soul.'

Worse. The stone hold was notorious. Tiny underground
cells with no windows where they locked men up alone in the
dark. My head was so giddy with the stench of shit that I could
hardly stand. I tried to breathe shallow. Dowling took a deep
breath and pulled a face like he was tasting fine wine. 'This
way.'

I followed him to the end of the corridor towards a small
door. He pulled it open and we peered into the darkness below.
A cesspit.

He shuddered. 'I don't think they post a guard down there

any more, don't think any will stand for it. We'll need a flame.'
Taking a torch from the wall, he stepped forward tentatively.
Tasting the bile in my mouth I resigned myself to follow him.

The walls were damp and covered in a thin slime. All we
could hear was the sound of our own steps and the occasional
moaning above. Otherwise the silence was like a dirty wet
blanket, the sound of a man's heartbeat in his own ears. The
smell was no longer just a smell, but a foreign body that
displaced the air with something foul and evil. It was only
the knowledge that men were living down here, and the
impossibility of it, that stopped me from emptying my guts
and hurrying back into the daylight.

'Marry!' a voice shouted from behind us. 'You can't go
down there by yourself!' One of the drunken gaolers staggered
down the corridor carrying a torch of his own. 'You follow
me!' Pushing past us, he almost lost his balance as he missed
the first step. He led us the rest of the way down the twisted
narrow staircase, the ceiling so low that we had to walk with
bent backs. 'He has his own room, just like you said,' the
gaoler leered at Dowling with rotten discoloured teeth.

I watched Dowling's jaw clench. He wasn't smiling. 'I
didn't mean the hold.'

'I know you didn't,' laughed the gaoler with his mouth
wide open. The stair took us to a small square anteroom just
two foot wide by six feet long. At the end was a door and two
more on either side. Floors, walls and ceiling were all made of
cold, damp stone.

'The sorrows of hell got hold upon me,' Dowling whispered.
I knew what he meant for they had got a hold of me too. It
was silent.

The gaoler pointed to the cell on the left. Inside there wasn't enough room to move, let alone hide, but it still took me a while to make out the figure squatted on the floor of the cell, squeezed into a corner. Sitting with his heels dug into the stone floor, his body was pressed into the wall. Squinting, I tried to find form in the shadowed bundle of rags and pale skin. A red scabby head, translucent arms, white and rotten. He sat in a pool of his own piss and the smell was choking.

'Open the door,' I said aloud, staring up into the gaoler's bleary white face, red-lined and greasy. I could see fat lice walking about his hair in the light of the flame. His eyes wandered, drunk.

Out stretched a hand. 'Shilling.'

'If you let us take him upstairs.'

'Two shilling.'

I was about to argue, but then he belched in my face a cloud that stank of pig fat and vomit, foul beyond description. I gave him the money. Then he put a big iron key into the lock, and as the door opened I saw bright green eyes lit up by the light of the torch. The rest of his face twitched. He wriggled and squirmed away from the gaoler as far as his chains would allow. Eyes shone out brightly from above a large angular nose. The stubbly head stilled, motionless above quivering body. As he becalmed, his eyes stopped flitting and fixed on us. Watching us, wide-eyed and alert, his head craned slowly forward. Then the gaoler elbowed him in the head so hard you could hear the crack.

Dowling erupted, pushing the gaoler hard against the wall with both hands 'God have mercy, you drivelling rogue!'

The gaoler dropped the torch on the floor so that all I could see was the stone flags, but I could hear the sound of two men breathing heavily and the sound of a man being struck solidly in the guts. Then I heard the sound of a man losing his guts and smelt it too. The torch rose, held now by Dowling, who stood over the lumpen figure of the gaoler kneeling on the floor, his head touching the stones.

'Unlock that chain,' Dowling commanded. I wondered if the gaoler would plead incapacitation. Wisely he did not. Instead he staggered to his feet, reached clumsily for his key and did as he was told. Dowling took the prisoner by the arm, then wound his thick, burly right arm around the man's chest and sort of carried him back up the stairs and out of the hold. I followed as close as I could. The gaoler made a wheezing noise that might have been a plea for his torch but Dowling ignored him. So the butcher that could read and write had a short wick. I followed him to an empty cell, one with light and space and even a table and chair.

'This must be where they put the King when he doesn't pay his debts,' I remarked. It was supposed to be a joke, but none laughed. Dowling's face was set grim.

'That was a foolish thing for me to do,' he said in a whisper. 'They will take their revenge upon him when we are gone.'

True, I supposed, but if he was to be hung, probably drawn and quartered too, then all was pretty much lost anyway. I didn't share the thought with Dowling, who was busy propping up our man on a chair. Then he was gone, his footsteps ringing out down the corridor. Soon he was back with a bowl of thin mutton soup and a hunk of bread. The prisoner licked his lips and drew his shredded jacket about his narrow shoulders. His breathing steadied and the shaking diminished.

'What is his name, do we know?' I asked.

'Richard Joyce,' the man himself answered, his voice calm and melodious, the least likely voice you would have imagined from his appearance.

'Well, Mr Joyce. Is it true that you killed Anne Giles?' I asked. 'She was my cousin, you know.' Not that it mattered, but I hoped that he might be shamed into confessing. Murderers and thieves had a habit of denying their crimes and I didn't want to spend all day listening to fantastic stories or tales of incredible hardship.

'No,' he replied before picking up the bowl with two hands and sipping quietly.

We waited, Dowling patiently, me less so, but every time I cleared my throat to speak he put a hand on my shoulder. When Joyce had finished eating, Dowling sat himself on the second chair, leaving me to perch on a small three-legged stool.

'Tell us something about yourself, Joyce.' Dowling leant back as if he was planning to spend all morning there. Straw moved in a dark corner of the room and there were sounds of rustling. Rats.

Joyce sat back and met Dowling's gaze. 'I was a soldier. I fought for the Republic. Paid for it ever since.'

'Not *just* a Republican, though – is that not right, Joyce?' What was the butcher talking about now?

'No,' Joyce replied after a lengthy pause, 'I was a Leveller besides.' A Leveller?

'God has revealed the way of eternal salvation, only to the individual faith of each man, and demands that any man who wishes to be saved should work out his beliefs for himself,' Dowling recited. These words were written by Milton, and reflected a philosophy that had been outlawed after the Restoration. Milton was still in prison somewhere.

Joyce smiled, his head leaning back against the cradle of the chair. Still he held the bread in his lap. 'Abel's art made the earth more fruitful than Cain, thereupon Cain would take Abel's labour away from him by force.'

'Kingly government may well be called the government of highwaymen.' Dowling leant forward speaking the words carefully. I listened hard to see if any were close that might hear – this was treasonous talk and I rather wished Dowling would show more discretion. The Levellers were a raggedy bunch of fanatics that had been led by a man called John Lilburne, another extreme lunatic, a dangerous man whose views were rejected even by Cromwell. After many years in prison, he died in poverty seven years before. Pity. He would have got on well with Prynne.

'Aye, I was one of Lilburne's men. And I still believe that every man should be free and that he has no need of a King.' Joyce stuck out his chin defiantly. As if I cared what he believed. Then he grimaced and looked out the window at the cold grey sky. He shook his head and wiped at his eye. 'I was a fine man once. Had a house and land and a fine wife.'

Now he was levelled. 'Where is she now?'

He bowed his head. 'She fell when carrying a child. They say her blood went bad and poisoned the baby. She was ill for a while with wandering womb and died when it got to her head. That was twenty years ago.' We let him reflect in silence for a while. 'A long time ago.'

'You fought for Cromwell, sir,' said Dowling.

'I fought for England and for God,' Joyce corrected him, 'against the man of blood.' The man of blood was a name that some had bestowed upon Charles I before they chopped his head off to prove the point.

'I fought at Stamford, Gainsborough and Winceby. And Marston Moor. It was at Marston Moor I was wounded.' He leant forward and pointed to the back of his head. There was a bare patch of skin about the size of a man's hand with no hair growing on it. The skin was ridged and red like the surface of an angry sea at dusk. 'I should have died at Marston Moor.' He hawked and spat into the sawdust. 'It was summer, though ye wouldn't know it for all the rain that fell. The rye fields were like bogs, the water filled our shoes and sat next to our skin. We stood on the left of Marston Field with Manchester's footmen to the right of us, and the Scots on horses behind. We stood there shivering for hours, thinking of putting up camp, when the heavens opened up again, buckets of black water pouring on our heads. We were sure that all would stand down until the next day. Then late in the evening while there was still light, the Protector led us in a charge. Cavaliers met us halfway, but we went through them like blades. Then they had us from the flank but we beat them away besides, then went back and rescued Fairfax. It was a great victory for us. Near seven thousand of them were fallen, so it is said, less than three hundred of us. But numbers don't tell all.'

'What else, sir?'

'My horse was shot away with a bullet, and it fell onto me. They took me off the field and carried me back home. They made two holes in my head, but it didn't do no good.' He sighed. 'I was ill for a very long time, and good for nothing when I did recover.'

'You live here in London now?'

'My estate was delivered unto my cousin that vowed to care for me, so they say. But he died soon after and his wife sold it. The parish wouldn't keep me, so I came here.'

'What do you do?'

'There's a poor house where I shelter if I have to.' He spoke in a staccato. Despite his calm demeanour I think he

61

was trying not to weep. I found myself wondering how often he had the opportunity to talk to people nowadays, before it suddenly occurred to me that this had nothing at all to do with the murder.

'You were seen running from Bride's, Joyce. Yet you say you didn't kill my cousin?'

'Will you give me money if I tell you what happened?' he asked, chewing at the bread. I blinked and looked at Dowling. He looked to the heavens. It was hard to credit.

'Joyce.' I made sure I had his attention. 'They will hang you for her murder, cut you down, then slice open your belly and burn your guts in front of your face. You may wish you had died at Marston Moor, but there are far better ways to die than what lies in wait for you.'

Joyce nodded with blanched face. Pulling himself upright and leaning forward, he suddenly appeared anxious to speak. 'I was stood by myself, outside the Playhouse. A good enough place to beggar.' The last word he said sadly. 'It was very cold. I had some coins from those that went in. Now I was waiting for them all to come out. While I was waiting I saw this woman on her own walking towards the Playhouse. I made my way over the street towards her. She looked like the sort that would give me something. She wasn't a lady, but she wasn't a whore, nor a trader neither. Anyway, as I got closer to her she stopped. Not because of me, she hadn't noticed me, but I think she was looking for someone, like she had come to meet someone. I took care not to frighten her. Anyway – she gave me a coin. I went back over the street. Then I saw it was a sixpence she gave me, not a penny. She was kind. So I looked back to see if she was still there.'

'Was she?'

'Aye. Staring up Drury Lane. Anyway, then the crowds started coming out. Everyone dived in, the pedlars and hawkers. There was some pushing and likewise as folks fought for sedans and coaches. Soon enough they was all gone, but she was still there, still looking down Drury Lane. Then this man came out the theatre, a big man. He had about him a thick black cloak down to the ground. I couldn't see his face – it was hidden beneath the brim of his hat and he had some sort of scarf over his chin. He came up to her from behind, made her jump. She recovered, though, and put a hand on his sleeve like she knew him. He pulled down the scarf so he could talk to her, but I still couldn't see his face – the light was poor. They talked for a bit, and she seemed to get anxious, worried. He was holding her arm and she didn't seem to like it. So then they moved off, towards Drury Lane. She walked with her head bowed, fussing with the knot of her headscarf. They turned right at Drury Lane towards the City and I followed them to Bridget's. They went inside.'

'Did you follow?'

'In time. I stayed where I was for a while. When they didn't come out I thought I'd go and have a look, make sure she was alright. The door was open so I went in. Inside it was dark and cold. I crouched at the back. I could just see them sitting down at the front. They was talking it looked like, though all I could hear was her weeping. He was doing most of the talking, judging by the way his head went up and down. Then I sneezed, didn't I?'

'He heard you?'

'I didn't wait to see. I dropped down on my hands and knees and lay down on the floor. I was frightened, God's truth. I lay there for ages. I thought about going out, but there was distance between the pew where I was lying and the door and I thought he might be there waiting. I made myself look up eventually, but it had got even darker then and I couldn't see nothing. I could still hear the woman sobbing, but that was all. Couldn't see the back of the church neither, only a black hole behind the font. I thought about staying there all night, but it was too cold. I stood up straight and made a dash for the door. Ran right into him, didn't I? Should have heard me shout!' He paused with his hand on his heart and his mouth wide open as if he were reliving the moment.

'Then what happened?'

'Well, all I could see was the shape of him and that hat. I thought he'd make a grab for me, but he didn't. He just stood back and opened the door, held it open for me. Couldn't believe my luck – din't stop running 'til London Bridge!'

'Folks say you had blood dripping from your hands.'

Crossing his arms Joyce sat back again. 'Folks say all sorts of things. That's all I can tell you. Believe it or not. I don't hold out much hope for myself, so you can stop looking at me like I'm an idiot fool from Bedlam.'

It was a fanciful story, yet much to my dismay I recognised it as truth. Dowling too, judging by the look on his face. Joyce looked up at us both sadly. I regretted my harsh words, my selfish joy upon first hearing he was captured. I mumbled a useless farewell and wandered out. Dowling offered him some biblical platitude and was quickly at my side. We looked at each other – nothing to say.

On the way out we stopped to talk with the gaolers. The one that Dowling had punched sat sullen, staring out from beneath his single black eyebrow with beady little eyes. Dowling attempted to repair the damage by handing over the vast sum of ten shillings in exchange for fire, food, water and a new set of clothes. My ten shillings. Yet we didn't hold out much hope that he wouldn't be back down in the stone hold soon as we'd gone.

Once we were ten paces down the road I took off my coat and held it cautiously to my nose. It stank.

'It is little different to the alehouses you usually frequent.' Dowling watched me in grim amusement. 'Small damp rooms full of sinners, bathing in the foul odours of all that is sinful.'

I glared at him with teeth clamped hard upon my green tongue. Righteousness dripped from the corners of his curt smile. I kept my mouth shut and concentrated on forgiving him.

Heading back towards Cheapside in a foul temper, this affair was beginning to worm beneath my skin. If Joyce didn't do it – and my heart said he didn't – then who did? Looked like I'd have to go to Epsom after all. Then Cocksmouth. Dowling could stay behind and play with his chops.

Chapter Fiue

Dioscoridis his Milk-tare
*The short pod of this plant contains the seed which is similar
to the shape of a heart that is drawn in love letters!*

No one had invited me to Anne Giles's funeral, of course, but
since she was my cousin I supposed that none would overly object
to my appearance, and if she wasn't my cousin, an assertion
which still didn't feel snug with me, then I could pretend to be
simple in the head. I had met plenty of folks whose behaviours I
could mimic to that effect these last couple of days.

It was a long and unpleasant journey and cost two pounds
for the privilege. The coach lurched and rocked over frozen
ruts and I felt very ill – in need of some Epsom waters!
Some men would drive all the way from London to Epsom
Common, drink a pot or two from the well and then run off
into the bushes to pass a stool. I reckon you can achieve the
same effect by drinking two mugs of ale from any tavern on
the Southbank. Much quicker, twice as reliable and save you
the hell of the journey.

When at last we got to Epsom we stopped at the King's Head, a large inn sat in the middle of the high street. Little though I craved being welcomed to the Ormonde bosom, still I felt obliged to have a wash and sprinkle on some more of that lavender oil before showing my face. It was also an opportunity to ask a few questions of the locals about my newly unearthed relatives.

A large man with a big belly stepped across my path to the inn. He was bald, though a few last remnants of black hair grew wild about his ears. The apron upon which he wrung his hands was dirty and stained, reeking of old beer, wine and sweat. Standing squarely in front of me, he told me that the inn was full, for which I congratulated his good fortune. He wrinkled his nose at me in puzzlement, so I explained to him my purpose.

Looking me up and down he informed me that it was mostly gentry going – 'you knows'.

Straightening my wig I looked down at my clothes. Clean enough, I considered, crumpled maybe. I was wearing dull, black mourning cloth, though my shoes were russet. I didn't own any black shoes then, and certainly couldn't afford to buy any just for this one funeral. A decent pair of shoes cost thirty shillings. I asked him (again) with great politeness for access to a pump. Also for the loan of a fresh horse to get me to and from the Ormonde house.

'Aye, though I will have the money first. Touch pot, touch penny. Come in.' Beneath his apron he wore only a short-sleeved shirt, despite the perishing cold.

At one end of the large front room was a big roaring fire. Wooden pillars propped up a low ceiling. The floor was made of flagstones, worn and chipped. A long table filled the centre of the room, one end up against the fire where two men sat in silence. A tidy middle-aged woman stood dutiful and smiling next to a barrel of ale. I followed him to the kitchen where he waved a lazy hand at a half-full pail of cloudy water. Things hung suspended in it and its surface glistened with an oily sheen. He waited expectantly.

'Do you know Mr Ormonde?' I asked, eyeing the water.

'Aye, I know him. Lives on the road to Ashstead. Every man know him.'

I took off my hat and coat. 'What is he like?'

Looking at me suspiciously, he wrinkled his nose again. 'You going to his house for the funeral and you don't know him?'

The water was freezing cold. 'He is my cousin – my cousin's father, better said – but I've not met him.'

'Not met him?'

'No. What's he like?'

'He's tall, thin,' he stared at my coat, 'old.'

I turned, wiping my hands on my thighs. 'Do you see him often?'

'No. He don't come in here, squire. This is an inn.'

'Have you seen him walking about the town?'

'He don't walk about the town, does he? Want 'owt to eat or drink?'

I looked again at the pail of water. 'Just a horse.'

The innkeeper looked at me as if I was mad. 'We don't serve horse.'

He was not joking. What sort of cretins and morons lived out here in the country? Simpletons and whoballs, obviously. I learnt nothing of interest and left, bemused.

* * *

Ormonde's residence was out of town on top of a small hill in its own grounds, walled off from the general population. Today the tall, black, wrought iron gates stood wide open, inviting entry to the wide sweeping driveway, hidden from the fields by a row of poplars on either side. The house was painted white, three storeys high. My borrowed horse trotted up the driveway past seven coaches that stood there waiting. At the door a servant came running up to take the horse from me and to find out who I was and what I wanted. When I told him I was a cousin he hurried off into the house to consult. While I waited I watched the other guests arrive. They were all finely dressed. The men wore long black mourning gowns, black silk sashes across their tunics, black buckles on their shoes and black hats with thin black silk weepers falling down the back. I was the only one there with coloured shoes and the only one wearing a periwig. Though it *was* black.

After a time a very tall, thin old man emerged, walking stiffly down the low stone steps towards me using a thick cane to support himself on his right side. His face was long and worn, his eyes grey and watery. He regarded me sternly, mouth twitching with impatient irritation. From his lips came a low grumbling noise, though whether it was for my benefit or whether it was a noise he made all the time, I could not yet determine.

Towering over me with both hands on the top of his cane, legs akimbo with a terribly severe expression on his face, he looked like he was trying to pass an Epsom stool. 'You say you are a cousin?' he said in a low, thick slur. 'I think not.'

I smiled brightly. 'You may be right, sir. It was my father said that we were related, and the Lord Shrewsbury. I have no evidence of mine own to support it.'

At the mention of Shrewsbury's name his eyes widened and he began to breathe noisily through his nose. The mumbling stopped. His eyes fell and he began a long slow shuffle as he manoeuvred himself to face back towards the house. He hobbled back up the steps. I followed, not knowing whether I was to be admitted or not. A servant came up to me and stared at my brown shoes. After some consideration he offered me gloves and a hatband. I took them, though I didn't have a hat.

Inside it was quickly evident that the men were downstairs and the women were upstairs. The servant led me to the drawing room, from which all the furniture had been taken, except a line of red leather upholstered chairs standing around the edge. A big window, standing the full height of the room, allowed the winter light to bring a glow to the polished floor. A coffin stood in the middle of the room on a dark oak table. I went over to pay my respects, wondering if the casket was open, as was the custom – just in case the deceased should change its mind. I guessed not and indeed the box was nailed down. Nice box, though, unblemished elm, sanded, smoothed and lovingly polished. A dozen men sat around the border of the room, all wearing black broadcloth, all wearing the same design new gold ring with black enamelling, and all staring at me. I was the only one bereft of such a ring. Putting my gloves on quickly I walked over to the panelled fireplace. I pretended to admire the tapestries that hung on either side of it and accepted a cup of wine, although I didn't really want it. None spoke. Prynne would have had a ball.

At last a bell rang. The men stood up as one and headed for the hallway and the women descended from upstairs in small

70

groups of two or three. They all flocked like black sheep too, all dressed in the same black woollen gowns. I reckon a lot of people must die in Epsom, for everyone seems to know exactly what to do and wear. London is not so formal. As I walked out the door, a servant handed me a sprig of rosemary to throw into the grave.

Four special coaches stood waiting outside, all of them decked out in the family crest. For the chief mourners and family, I presumed. William Ormonde climbed into the front coach together with a very unhealthy-looking young man and two women, both veiled. One of the women had a very shapely behind beneath quite a tight black dress. The coaches pulled off towards the town with the rest of us following on foot.

Outside the very small church the mourners filed in slowly. It was a tiny church and at the last moment I decided that I had no stomach for sitting so intimately with such an ugly and bitter congregation, so I made up my mind to wait outside – the gathering afterwards would be had enough. I needed to gather my wits, so I sat on a wall and enjoyed the fresh, cold air and the hoarse cawing of crows from the treetops of Minnes' wood. When my behind got sore I went for a walk in the cemetery in search of the grave, a freshly dug hole. It was easy to find, in a small clearing beneath a giant oak tree surrounded by sanicle and periwinkle. Sanicle keeps away the surgeon, according to the French, whilst periwinkle stops nosebleeds when chewed. Neither of much practical use now for Anne Giles. The gravestone was small and arched, finely polished and chiselled.

Anne Ormonde

Born January 18th 1644
Died January 18th 1664

Thee didst hide thy face, and I was troubled.
Now shalt thou lift thy face unto God.

Composed by William Ormonde, no doubt; I was pretty
sure it wasn't from the Bible. Interesting that the husband's
name was ignored. Was the unhealthy-looking man with
Ormonde her husband? Anne Giles died on the same day that
she was born, her twentieth birthday.

Half an hour later the chief mourners emerged, and led
a small procession up the shallow hill. I positioned myself
that I might watch the woman with the shapely behind from
the rear. The mourners took their positions around the grave
and the local priest began to read from the Book of Common
Prayer.

'Man that is born of woman hath but a short time to
live, and is full of misery,' the priest read. This really is the
gloomiest nonsense and I cannot abide it. What is the purpose
in complaining how short a time we have to live on the one
hand, then moaning that even though it is short it is also
miserable? If it be so miserable then best that it is short –
for those that are miserable. I am not myself miserable but
will enjoy what life I do have and thank my blessings for it.
Not waste my time decrying how short it is, for if I did that
– then I would be truly miserable. Nonetheless some people
were moved enough to cry, others even wailed, apparently
in great distress. As the gratified minister read on, the coffin
was lowered into the ground. Ormonde stood straight and
still with his head slightly lowered. The woman whose behind

made me want to whimper wept quietly. The unhealthy man that I now decided looked like a stoat, stood by himself, eyes fixed upon the coffin.

The priest paused to give the mourners time to take a hand of earth. Most did, and made their own farewells quietly while the priest proceeded through the rest of the service. Out of the corner of my eye I saw the stoat take advantage of the movement of people to step swiftly away. Once he was apart then he broke into a trot and ran quickly into the woods. I caught his eye for a second before he vanished. Though I felt some sympathy with his desire to be elsewhere, still it was an odd way to behave.

'The love of God be with us all for evermore. Amen.'

Amen indeed.

'Mr Lytle!'

Turning, startled, I found myself face to face with the woman with the behind. My heart skipped merrily and tripped through the fields singing songs of love. She lifted her veil and brushed back a hair from her forehead. Her nose was small and upturned at its tip; the end of it faintly freckled. Her mouth was wide and curved with full lips. Her hair was long and brown with a red sheen. Her eyes were green and looked straight into my soul. It was the face of the dead woman. My yard collapsed like a softly boiled mushroom.

'My father told me about you and how you would help us.' She spoke so softly that I found myself leaning forwards, stretching my neck like a chicken. I straightened quickly.

When did I offer help to her father? 'You are Anne Giles's sister?'

She bowed her head. 'Mary.'

Though I expressed my sympathies, clumsily probably, for

etiquette is not a particular strength of mine, I saw in her face that whatever she sought, it wasn't kind words.

'Mr Lytle, I pray that you will enjoy of our hospitality?'

Bowing awkwardly I contemplated with anxiety the prospect of going back inside that house with this group of wailing ranters. It was easier to do with an invitation, though, and I don't suppose any would stop me leaving if I felt so disposed. I accepted her invitation.

'Then I will see you at the house.' She smiled at me with lovely white teeth then hurried away to her coach. Ormonde sat in it waiting, peering out through the little window like a malevolent rabbit.

At the house she squeezed my hand as I entered in the line and gave me a look with those green eyes that I found difficult to interpret – under the circumstances. If we hadn't been exchanging pleasantries at her sister's funeral then I would have been encouraged to tickle her chin. Her father nodded at me suspiciously and made the mumbling noise. It stopped once I had passed.

Once inside I did honestly try to make conversation with a couple of the more composed visitors, but my attempts fell flat. They looked me up and down as if I was a naked bearded woman. My mood brightened when I saw oysters, biscuits and mulled claret. I ate, then ate some more. There was nothing else for me to do in the absence of any that would talk to me.

'Mr Lytle, come with me, please.' Mary Ormonde appeared at my elbow like an angel of mercy. She steered me away up the staircase and into a library on the first floor. After shepherding me in she left me there while she went off to find a servant. They returned quickly, and the servant went straight to the fireplace and set about building a blazing fire.

'This is the warmest room in the house.' She sat next to me, close to the hearth, with her hands on her knees. Looking sideways, I found myself staring at her chest. 'My name is Mary. It was good of you to come all this way, Mr Lytle.'

'It's not so far.' I shrugged.

'You said you are our cousin?'

'That's what my father told me in a letter. It comes as a surprise to me, I own. There again he is quite old now and not very sensible. I thought I ought come anyway, just in case.'

She smiled at me like a hungry dog. 'My father says you are a wicked man without morals. Shrewsbury has devoted himself to your moral development because he owes a debt to your father.'

'Did he say that?'

'You have lain with many women.'

I didn't really know what to say. It was not so many women – but I didn't think that to be an appropriate response. Still she was looking at me. My lavender oil was mixing with whatever scent it was she was wearing and the brew was heady. I swallowed. I had come here to learn more about the Ormonde family and so far had found out little. Here I was in private audience with the sister – an ideal opportunity to find out all I wanted to know. All I had to do was stay calm and control my emotions. Then she reached over and put her hand on my plums. A strange thing to do to a man who might be your cousin, especially on the day of your sister's funeral, but the world is a strange place and you can't spend all your life shaking your head trying to make sense of it. That was about as far as my thoughts had progressed before she lifted her skirts and sat on my lap. Whilst I continued to contemplate, events developed their own momentum. Then, just as we were getting to the best bit there was a sudden crash. I jumped up, my heart pounding, Mary's arms still clinging about my neck. Looking around, I saw a cloud of grey ashes drifting slowly through the shadows.

'A dead bird,' said she calmly. 'It must have nested at the top of the chimney. Poor thing.' She climbed off me, rearranged her skirts and left the room without further ado.

On my way home I reflected that Hill had been wise to commend me to travel to Epsom, though what light it had shone upon the great mystery was not evident to me at the time.

Chapter Six

Holly
*Throughout its life this plant only bears spiny leaves
at the extremities of its branches.*

Three chickens strutted amongst the piles of rubbish that
layered the tide of thick mud that covered the tiny courtyard
in which we stood. A pig waded through the open sewer that
disappeared down the tiny alley through which we ourselves
had walked, snuffling and sniffing with its dirty wet nose. Big
blue flies coasted lazily about the seas of dead rotting vegetation
and old bones. I saw the swish of a scaly tail by a hole in the
far wall. This was not the part of Bishopsgate where the rich
merchants lived, this was the square where John Giles was said
to reside. On the near side of the square was the house we were
looking for. The front door was split, the top half already open.

I hadn't shared with Dowling all of my adventures in
Epsom, of course, but I did describe the man that looked like
a stoat and my theory that he might be John Giles. Rather
than bow before my keen observational skills, Dowling asked

me why I hadn't thought to introduce myself. Such a question did not merit a reply – his wife was being buried – hardly a time for new acquaintances. Today, though, I wanted this man to tell us who killed his wife. I was uneasy that all we had for suspects were a Roundhead with a hole in it and a decrepit old woman, both of whom were in danger unless we unearthed the real murderer. Also I was doing all of this for no payment and needed it finished with, that I might get a job. I was already more than three pounds out of pocket.

I stuck my head through the door and peered in. The room was bare save for two wooden chairs and what looked like another coffin lying on a rickety table. Rush mats covered the dirt floor. There was a doorway at the rear. Through it, as I watched, a short, thin man slid into view. Save for the expression on his face and the greasiness of his skin he was quite handsome, yet he resembled a petty villain with sly, dark eyes that slid about their sockets like beads of black soap. When he saw me he stopped in his tracks, fingers extended like short, sharp claws, before hurrying back to whence he'd come. It was indeed the man I had seen at Epsom, though he showed no sign of recognising me. I looked to Dowling, who shrugged.

'Good sir, my name is David Dowling and this here is Harry Lytle, appointed by our good Mayor to find the man that killed your wife. If we don't find him, then God Almighty will,' Dowling shouted before letting himself into the house.

A voice cried out from behind the thin board partition, 'Leave me alone.'

'Sir, painful though it be for you, we would ask some questions, so that we may be hasty.'

'Begone, and let me be hanged!'

'Sir, we would talk with you quietly. Your neighbours are

gathering.' Indeed, I observed, three women and a man had joined the chickens out front and stood watching curiously. The man was old and frail, his back was crooked and his eyes rheumy. His breathing was strained and noisy. Holding out a shaking palm he mouthed unintelligibly. The women were a bit younger, though well past their best. They stood next to each other in a line, one dominant to the fore, and the other two at her flanks. The middle one looked at me suspiciously, her mean eyes and sour mouth topping and tailing an ugly large misshapen nose. She wore a scarf and shawl, long dress and jacket, hat and apron, and lots of padding beneath it all.

Giles ventured out from his retreat, and upon seeing that we spoke truthfully he hurried to the door, slamming it closed. As we watched, the top door slowly opened again and the large-nosed woman's head poked through, eyes scanning the room beadily.

'Go away!' screamed Giles at the head, which slowly withdrew. I stepped over and closed the door softly.

Standing before us wringing his hands, Giles eyed us nervously. 'I don't want to talk to you,' he said in a low pleading whisper.

'Cursed is he that perverts the judgement of the widow, but the wicked flee even when no man pursueth. Time runneth where no man may follow.' Dowling removed his hat. Giles frowned, as confused as I. 'It is our task to find the man who killed your wife, sir.'

'And my cousin,' I added.

'My wife is dead,' Giles replied, face sullen and angry, 'and she is not your cousin.'

'How do you know?' I demanded, for he seemed very certain.

'She is not your cousin,' he repeated, shaking his head with his eyes screwed up like he had a great pain in the head.

'Who killed her?'

'I don't know who killed her or I wouldn't be here, would I?' Giles glared. He twisted away, twitching and rubbing his hands constantly.

I wasn't sure how the one determined the other. While I was thinking, Dowling butted in. 'Where were you the night she was murdered, Mr Giles?'

'I was out working.' Giles waved a hand then sat down. Crouched, ready to spring. 'I work for important people.'

A bumblebee in a cow turd thinks itself a king. 'Important, you say? They might be able to help you.'

'Aye, important people, people can help me if I need it, so I ain't afraid of you.' Giles smirked, but beads of sweat filled the cleft between his nose and upper lip.

'Who do you think killed her, sir?'

'I told you, I don't know! Go away and let me alone!' He spluttered loudly, punching the air with his fists.

'What be all the screeching?' I startled as the front door flew open, crashing against the board wall. The voice was strident, piercing and rough. Its owner was the woman with the large nose. 'You be letting me in, John boy. What's all the shouting for?'

Giles glared at her a moment before approaching the door more meekly than before. He closed it more gently, but so that she remained inside the room. Stout and in her forties, every pore on her face was blackened. Reaching out she took John Giles's chin roughly between her thumb and forefinger then pulled his face round and stared into it, eyes scrunched up and lips pursed. 'What are you shouting about, John boy?'

John Giles wailed in strangled misery before taking her hand in his and throwing it away. Then he put his own hand to his face, shielding it in embarrassment. 'Go away!'

'What's the news?' The woman turned away from him and came up to me with stooped gait and crooked back. Brown, black and yellow teeth lined up like coloured pegs in her mouth, rooted in shrivelled gums. Reaching to my dark-green jacket she started to finger the cloth. What was this fascination with my clothes that all people with dirty hands seemed to have?

'We labour at the Mayor's behest. We seek the killer of Anne Giles,' Dowling answered her.

She pulled lightly at a bright button on my jacket. With her other hand she fingered the simple lace. Her nails were cracked and broken. 'My John has fine clothes like yours,' she said, and indeed he did. It had not occurred to me before, but he was wearing a very fine cloth shirt and silk burgundy jacket even though they were stained and unwashed many weeks. His shoes were cobbled by a master craftsman. Very smart, quite fashionable, and extremely expensive for someone living in a weatherboard house in a slum like this. Where did the money come from?

She simpered at me. It was not pleasant. 'Lucky for you, John boy, that the Mayor himself has sent these men here to catch the devil that killed poor Anne.'

John Giles hissed quietly, sidling up to the woman that seemed to be his mother. 'I want to be on my own. I don't want to be answering questions.'

'Why was Anne at Bridewell?' I demanded.

The mother pushed him towards us with both hands. 'Go on, John boy. Answer them.'

His mouth turned down at the sides and his eyes dropped to the floor. 'She went out. I wasn't here.'

'Who did she meet there?'

Giles shrugged with drooping shoulders, eyes red and unfocussed, lower lip protruding like a naughty schoolboy's. Frowning, he flicked his eyes up momentarily to meet mine. They slipped away again just as quick. His nose ran, and he wiped his sleeve across it. 'I didn't know she was going out.'

'You're not telling us much are you, sir?'

'What does that mean?' Giles snapped, head jerking up. 'Do you call me a liar?'

'Be quiet!' his mother scolded. 'You tell them what they would know. Maybe the Mayor will give us some money to help, what do you think?'

'When hens make holy water is what I think, Mother! Will you stop prating! I just want to be left alone!' Giles was practically screaming now, his face was red and the veins on his forehead stood out. Strutting about the room with little steps, he put his palms to his eyes and a desperate shrill came out of his mouth. It was a horrible noise. Walking faster and faster, his eyes darted to the door over and over. He started talking to himself, muttering, asking himself questions and answering them, as if he were trying to give himself assurance. He was behaving like a mad fellow, yet his mother seemed oblivious to it. She edged closer to me, eyeing again the cut of my clothes.

'He says he works with important folk. What is his line of employ?' Dowling asked her quietly.

Giles stopped his pacing. He walked up to Dowling and looked into his face with rodent eyes. 'It's done now, isn't it? You can't raise her, can you?'

'No sir, we can't do that. All we can do is bring peace to thee, to thine and to all that thou hast.'

'I don't hast nothing. And nothing you do can bring peace to me.' Giles walked out, into the back room. Neither of us tried to stop him.

'I can tell ye something,' his mother chirped up. 'She had a golden necklace that she wore. Never took it off. It was cast in the shape of a cross, with a surface rough to the touch. A strange object; I never did see nothing like it anywhere else. When they laid her down it was missing, gone. John was very upset when he found out.'

'Valuable, was it?'

'I reckon.' She nodded. 'Her father gave it to her.'

'William Ormonde?'

'Aye, Ormonde – lives at Epsom. They have a family house there. I never seen it, never seen him neither. He didn't want his daughter to marry John, which is why they lived here and not in a big house of their own. Don't think Anne nor John saw him neither, not since they was married.'

'What is the casket for?' I asked.

'It's where we were going to lay Anne until a man came round, said that her father wanted to give her a good *proper* burial at his house in Epsom. Said that her father wanted to bring her back to the family plot. John didn't seem to mind, didn't say much, anyhows. Good for him, you ask me. John hasn't the gold to give her much of a fare-thee-well, nor me neither.'

The woman's lined face was unwashed and weather-beaten, rough and aged, an animal cunning in her eyes. Not a hint of self-pity, just a scavenger's sharp eye.

'John went to see her. Couldn't bear the sight of her face.'

She grimaced. 'She was a good girl. She would visit me in my house – I live just around the corner.'

'Where is he gone?' I poked my head into the back room. There was a bucket, a fire, two poor beds and three chairs. Giles was nowhere to be seen, a small window his only exit. The sly, greasy dog had fled us while his mother kept us talking. I turned back to the woman and glared at her.

She stood up and wiped her hands on her apron. 'He likely had to go off to work, misters. Didn't want to disturb you, I expect.' Then she stood legs apart with her arms folded and her chin sticking out.

'A considerate son,' Dowling smiled.

Between them they had frustrated us. The woman's mouth was reset in the same thin-lipped, sour line we had seen before. There seemed little to be gained by lingering except fleas.

As we made our way back across the courtyard, avoiding as much of the vileness as we could, I wondered aloud what it could be that drove Giles to such distraction.

'Wickedness, condemned by her own witness, is very timorous,' Dowling replied. 'We may not know how Giles puts food on the table, but we can be sure neither gentleman nor soldier he be.'

As we headed out of the slum in which Anne Giles had lived, through the alley, we had to squeeze past two rough-looking fellows pushing forward in haste, one big and stout like a great bear, the other diminutive and thin, like another stoat or ferret. They must be neighbours, I thought at the time, but I was to meet them again shortly. They were not neighbours.

* * *

Later that day Dowling tracked Giles down to Anthony's Pig. Said it was the Mayor's men that did it, at his request. That still didn't sit well with me – the notion that a butcher could order about the Mayor's entourage like he was nobility, but it was a thought that would have to wait for the time being. I knew Anthony's Pig well, for I had been drunk there with William Hill on many an occasion. It was dark and squalid, with a strange mix of clientele: the disreputable and the affluent. It was located close to the Exchange and its forbidding appearance explained its attraction to the more secretive merchants that plied their trade there.

Dowling had accosted me in the street as I wandered towards Cheapside, grabbing me by the jacket, a habit that I had prepared for by donning a brown linen coat, rougher and stronger than was my usual preference. Full of news about John Giles, which he whispered hoarsely into one of my ears whilst propelling me down the street. I smiled wanly at passers-by that regarded us curiously, while trying to pay attention to what he said at the same time. His wet breath in my ear was very unpleasant and did nothing for my concentration. Finally I could stand it no more and detached myself firmly. He declined my invitation to step into The Mermaid, so instead we cut across Paternoster Row into the quieter grounds of Old Paul's. There he shared his news.

'He works at the Exchange. He runs errands mostly, whatever pays. The pages in the City complain that their masters make demands beyond the call of duty. Some bold agents have taken the opportunity to charge for the service.'

He meant buggery. I pulled a face. I had heard of the practice and it sounded painful and messy.

'He hasn't been seen for some weeks. There is a story that

he crossed someone, a fellow he would have been wise to leave well alone. That would explain his manner this morning. His hair grows through his head, and ruin is around the corner. He has taken gold from the goldsmith, and the goldsmith wants it back. I doubt he believed we were who we said we were.'

He was confusing me again. 'What goldsmith?'

Dowling lowered his voice to speak in an exaggerated whisper. 'There is a man called Hewitt, Matthew Hewitt of Basinghall Street. He sent men after Giles. Hewitt is sharp as a blade and merciless as the Devil himself. If Giles played Hewitt, then he was truly a fool, but that's what I heard.' He continued, still unable to stop himself from spraying saliva across my cheek. 'Consider also that Matthew Hewitt lives on his own in a very big house and no one has ever seen him with a woman. That's as much as I will say, but if you follow my logic then contemplate the possibility that Giles might have blackmailed Hewitt, then I begin to see that Hewitt might have decided to frighten Giles out of his wits.'

I frowned. 'Why should he choose to frighten him with the elaborate murder of his wife? Why not beat him and leave him in an alley with no teeth?'

'That is ours to fathom, but mark me! Hewitt has a black soul and a blacker heart and I can well believe that beneath the crags of his ugly frozen face lies a fiery temper that might well contemplate something demonic.'

'What is Hewitt's business? A goldsmith you say?'

Dowling blinked. 'No. He is a merchant.'

I considered our options. Our option. 'We must find out where John Giles fled to.'

'He is at Anthony's Pig behind the Exchange and has been there an hour.'

'How do you know?'

'The Mayor's men tracked him down. I asked them to.'

It was at that point I started questioning Dowling's credentials as a butcher. We hurried to the tavern, anxious to arrive before our quarry fled. It was a strange place for Giles to frequent if he was fleeing Matthew Hewitt, for even if Hewitt himself did not visit that day, others of his acquaintance surely would. So it was with curiosity roused that we entered the tavern early in the afternoon. Lucky for me that I had indeed been here on several occasions before, for strangers were not welcomed. The tavern had a narrow frontage out onto the street, but stretched back the depth of two houses, with private rooms to the rear and cosy booths tucked away in the shadows. In one of those booths we found Giles, on his own, still nervous and agitated. His state did not improve when I sat opposite him. At first he made as if to leave, but stopped once Dowling plugged the gap with his considerable bulk. Eventually he stopped his writhing and sat back, resigned, with his back pressed against the wooden wall of the booth staring out into the tavern.

'Good day, Mr Simpson,' Dowling growled into his ear.

What was he talking about? I stared at him with my heart in my stomach. The only Simpson I knew of was the fellow that had stolen the key to Bride's. Now the butcher didn't think it worthwhile to keep me informed?

'For who did you steal the key of St Bride's?' Dowling wriggled up close. I contemplated kicking him in the shin. He was supposed to be the witless one, not me.

Giles's head jerked round, a grisly taut smile on his thin lips. He blinked repeatedly as if he was about to have a fit. Then he started to laugh; at least I think it was supposed to be a laugh. Then he looked at me with pleading eyes, licking his lips in a state of high anxiety. 'How do you know that?'

I didn't.

'It is not widely known, sir, nor will it be so. The rector gave us a description of this fellow John Simpson which I established must be you through conversations with others of the household.'

When had he done all that?

'Someone deceived you.'

Though I still felt like kicking Dowling in the arse and lecturing him upon the obligations of tradesmen to respect their social betters, the indignation soon passed. This new revelation was more interesting. Why should Giles steal the key to a church then kill his wife inside of it? A foolish way to kill your own wife I would have thought, and in any case, Giles didn't really appear to match the description of the man that Joyce had described. It all seemed most unlikely.

'Ha!' exclaimed John Giles with a loud shrill, but he did not deny it. With his hands to his face he shook his head slowly, muttering to himself in despair, using God's name – though I could not hear how.

'Was it Matthew Hewitt?' Dowling whispered.

'God save us!' Giles exclaimed white-faced, leaning over the table and peering into my eyes. I stopped myself from recoiling as he stared into me as if looking for the bottom of a deep pool of water. 'How do you know these things? Are you a magician? Are you bewitched?'

'No,' I replied nervously, 'we have just been talking to people, trying to establish what happened that night.'

'I did not kill my own wife,' he said very slowly.

I assured him that he had no need to convince us of it, though of course that wasn't true.

Suddenly he looked suspicious. 'Who told you it was Hewitt?' He sat back, more composed, the expression on his face suggesting that he felt he had been tricked.

I sensed that if we did not press home our advantage then we would quickly be stonewalled permanently. 'Is it him that you are waiting for?'

'I will not tell you who I am waiting for, nor will he come until you have left,' Giles answered, deflated but temporarily calm. 'So you may stay here as long as you will. It is nothing to me.'

'Very well.' I sat back and signalled to a wench to deliver me an ale. Dowling could hardly object under the circumstances.

'While we wait, Mr Giles, tell us something of your relations at Epsom. You married into wealth. I don't understand why you live in such poverty.'

'Aye, poverty.' Giles smiled bitterly. 'We live in a stable. We kept a cow there for the first year.'

'How long were you married?'

'Two years.'

'Anne would have been eighteen.' I struggled to recall the legend on the gravestone.

'Aye. Young.'

'Why did you live, then, in such poverty?'

Giles stared into space as if he had the weight of the temple on his shoulders. Then he shrugged. 'Her father would not allow her to marry the son of a farm worker. She went against his will. He gave her no dowry.'

'That must have come as a shock to you both.'

'Aye, a shock. We married anyway, at St Ethelburga, but

that was not the worse of it.' He grasped four fingers of one hand with the other and squeezed hard. 'My father worked on one of Ormonde's estates. Ormonde made him stand for my actions at the borough sessions.'

I grimaced sympathetically. 'Was he pilloried?'

'He was found guilty at the borough sessions, that left the punishment open. The justice was a friend of Ormonde and decided to make an example of him.'

'What do you mean?'

'They hung him by the neck. They said that I had acted in accordance with the Devil and had destroyed any chance Anne had of leading a godly life, so that I condemned her to everlasting torment. If I acted of the Devil, then I was born of the Devil, and all touched by the Devil should perish.'

'An extreme verdict,' I replied, quietly horrified. Now I could understand why Giles had so little desire to stay at Ormonde's side in Epsom. But why had he gone there in the first place? He must hate William Ormonde. He must hate the whole borough.

'Aye. He is a black man with a black soul. He sent men here to fetch me to Epsom for the funeral.'

Neither Dowling nor I said anything for a while, just let time trickle by in silence. Giles sat there calm now, staring away from us out into the tavern with his jaw set rigid.

'You must hate William Ormonde,' I said at last.

Giles closed his eyes and sighed. He looked at me again, this time as if I were a simple fool. 'So you lie. You have decided that I killed my own wife.'

'I didn't say so.' Though the thought had crossed my mind for this man seemed close to insanity. To kill his wife would be to kill Ormonde's daughter and relieve himself of an unexpected financial burden. 'Though I am not yet convinced that you did not steal the key to Bride's of your own initiative.' Looking at him carefully I wished I could see into his soul. 'You were quick to confirm our idea that it may have been Matthew Hewitt.'

'I confirmed nothing. Believe as you will.'

'If it is believed that you killed your wife, then you will hang.' I tapped one finger on the table.

'Richard Joyce will hang for the crime, whatever the truth of it.'

How did Giles know of Joyce, and how was he so sure that the man would hang? What did Giles know?

Dowling's eyes narrowed and he cleared his throat. 'What *is* the truth of it?'

'I don't know who killed my wife, nor why.' I detected a note of resolution in his voice for the first time, and wondered if he was on his own mission to unravel the truth of it.

'You said Matthew Hewitt asked you to steal the key to Bride's. What reason did he give?'

'I did not say Hewitt asked me to steal the key. You did. You also accused me of stealing it of my own initiative. It is clear to me that you know nothing. You are guessing.'

'Of course I am guessing. That is why we are here. Why will you not help us? Tell us what you know, that we might help.'

He shook his head again, expression calm and serious. Biting on his right thumb he refused to make eye contact with me. Once more he ignored my questions, just sat perfectly still. My repeated pleadings, that our aim was only to find out who killed his wife, and my attempts to provoke him, suggesting that his silence indicated either guilt or lack of love for his wife, had no effect.

Our next strategy was to sit in silence with him, to try his patience, counting on his anxiety to talk to whoever he was waiting for, this person who would not come until we left. This did not work either; indeed, I began to suspect that he was relieved that his rendezvous would be delayed.

'If you will not help us, then we must consider speaking to Hewitt ourselves,' I said, inspired. This succeeded in snapping him out of his apparent slumber. He turned to me with a look of pity on his grey, lined face.

'Do not go near Hewitt. He is a dangerous man. You will find out nothing from him, all you will succeed in doing is attracting his attention. You must wish to remain unknown to Matthew Hewitt.'

'What other option do we have, if you will not speak to us?'

Tears appeared at the corners of his eyes and he regarded me with renewed fear and dislike. 'There is nothing I can tell you, but I urge you not to talk to Matthew Hewitt. Leave that to me. He knows me well enough already. I risk nothing by approaching him. You risk more than you understand.' Leaning forward he whispered, 'You were a clerk, you worked at the Tower. You are not Anne's cousin. You know nothing of all this. I cannot understand why anyone would appoint you. You must question the motive of that person, for he is either as innocent as you, or else bears you no love.'

Dumbfounded, I could think of no useful response for a while, for the observation was unarguable. My father was both innocent and loveless. Giles saw my indecision, and sought to persuade me further. 'I did not kill my wife, and I do not believe that Matthew Hewitt did either. He is a trader and merchant, you must know that already. I cannot think of any motive he would have to kill her.'

'We heard that you sought to blackmail him, and that he killed your wife as a warning to you and to others that might contemplate a similar action,' Dowling probed.

Giles dropped his head to the table and his body went limp. When he raised his head he looked wearier than ever. Red eyes and flaky skin, like a fish. 'It is an absurd suggestion. Whoever told you such nonsense knows nothing of the workings of the Exchange. None would be so foolish as to attempt to blackmail Matthew Hewitt. To do so would be to invite death,' The words sounded like his obituary. 'Now please go.'

His request was so heartfelt that it would have been churlish to continue sitting there, knowing that he would tell us no more.

'And please don't tarry in the street, for if you do, you will see none, be assured.'

Nevertheless we did linger a while. And saw none.

'What do you make of that?' I asked Dowling as we walked back towards Newgate.

'Hard to say. He is well informed, though. Hard to look beyond this Hewitt.'

'Aye.'

We spoke no more until we parted company a few minutes later. As I walked home it occurred to me again how unlike any butcher I'd ever met Davy Dowling was. Then I determined to travel to Cocksmouth, though it was the last place in England I wished to go.

* * *

That evening I decided to unburden myself of the whole Anne Giles affair to Jane. She knew of the murder itself – it had been in the newspaper, so she said – though was surprised to hear that Shrewsbury had asked me to investigate it. In fact she said I'd be about as much use as a 'fat, bloaty toad'. Her recommendations were:

One – free Joyce from prison immediately. If I didn't have the brain of an old hog then I would have done it already.

Two – get Dowling to use the Mayor's men to find Mary Bedford. If I didn't have the brain of an old hog then I would have seen to it already.

Three – John Giles was slippery like a horse's cock and I'd get no sense out of him so long as he breathed. If I didn't have the brain of an old hog then I would have realised it already.

Four – Matthew Hewitt was guilty as a quire bird and if I went anywhere near him then I had a head made of mutton. Let Shrewsbury deal with it. The only reason I hadn't worked that out for myself was that I had the brain of an old hog.

All good sound advice, of course. Indeed, as she spoke I wondered why I was not seeing things as clear myself. It occurred to me that it had been a long time since I had really tested my wits. I had concerned myself more with lolling them into a state of gentle stupefaction, with the aid of much ale and wine. This was different. This was important. John Giles, Mary Bedford, and Richard Joyce – all of these people depended on me. It was a sobering thought, or would have been had I been drunk. I decided that night that I had to apply myself to this task with more seriousness than I had so far managed. I considered sharing this new resolution with Jane, but decided against it – I felt sure she would accuse me of being an old hog. But I determined that I did need to sit down and have a serious conversation with the butcher. And Shrewsbury would have to be told about Hewitt.

Chapter Seven

Dwarf Fleabane
In many watery or moist places of the highways.

At the top of Ave Maria Street among the stalls lingered apprentices, scores of them, hanging around in groups of two or three, doing nothing, just standing talking, peering out at the crowds beneath heavy, thick brows, their expressions that curious mixture of aggression and uncertainty that characterises the young and pale. What were they doing here? The apprentices of London were a sorry lot, paid nothing in money, forbidden by their masters to procreate or frequent alehouses or taverns. They vented their frustrations on the rest of the population, doing their best to ensure that none else got to enjoy themselves either. It was unusual to find them gathering in large groups with such brazen disregard. Such congregation usually meant trouble for someone. Last month a band of them had marched out to Moorfields and kicked down the bawdy houses. They cut off one poor woman's breasts to make an example of her to the rest. I detested people that could not just let others be what they would be.

I hurried by, discomforted by narrow-eyed curious stares. Why were they looking at me particularly? Toward the gaol they were crawling like flies on a dead dog, a great teeming mass of them, most still wearing their blue aprons. What were they up to now? Individually the apprentices were nothing to be afraid of – gawky, unhealthy and half grown. Working together as a mob they were to be avoided at all cost, clinging to the devout words and morals of their often insincere masters, seeking a sense of importance and achievement. I kept going, conscious that Joyce was in there.

'Strike!' A big man, older than the rest, stepped forward and pushed me in the chest with a rounded wooden baton. 'What business do you have here?'

'What business do you have asking?' I felt an urge to punch him in the throat.

To my relief Dowling appeared from nowhere to intervene. A second apprentice stepped forward wearing baggy breeches down to his knees, dirty, torn stockings and a faded, patched purple waistcoat. On top of his straggly blond hair he wore a red square hat. Grinning foolishly, blind drunk, his skin was peeling and one of his eyes was badly infected. He looked over his shoulder to where two of his friends stood, also smiling broadly, also stinking of cheap wine.

'You don't go any further without me saying so,' said the big man.

'I have business in the gaol with the head gaoler. There's a man in here what's accused of treason. They say he is to be hung, so I want to confirm it, see what is required in the way of rope.' Dowling pushed his way ahead without waiting for an assessment of his feeble story. I followed, doing my best to look nonchalant, but in truth regretting the fine cut of my clothes. These men made me feel like a fop with their ugly sneers and bad smells.

Inside the evil odour was even worse than last time, some foulness emanating from a small closet that I had not noticed before. Two men stood peering into it, frowns of concentration writ thick upon their swarthy faces. I craned my neck to see what it was they looked at, then withdrew it just as quick. The bodies of two dead men lay there cut into eight pieces, the pieces stacked on top of each other in a higgledy pile, stood in a pool of sticky blackness.

'They was executed three days ago,' said one of the men glumly. 'The family still hasn't got leave to take away the bits and bury 'em. Meanwhile, it's stinking out the place. We was thinking about moving 'em downstairs, but wonderin' which way the air will go, up or down.'

'Where are the heads?' My own head swam and I felt dizzy.

'Upstairs being boiled with cumin seed. Stops the birds peckin' at 'em once they's stuck upon the Nonsuch.' The gaoler closed the door and led the way forward, sneezing violently several times as if to eject the smell of rotting flesh from his nose.

He walked down the dim-lit corridor, not stopping to look either side, seemingly headed for the small door at the end that went to the stone hold. Why was Joyce still down there? We had paid these men good money to have Joyce fetched upstairs.

'Aye, so you did, and so we brought him up. But then we had to take him back down.' The gaoler pulled open the small wooden door and took a torch from the wall.

'Why?' I demanded, standing in front of him, trying to catch his tired unfocused eyes.

He sighed, emitting a cloud of fetid rank-smelling breath. 'You gave us money to bring him up and bring him up we did. Then two officers of the Lord Chief Justice came and told us to take him back down, so we took him back down. After you, if you please. You don't like it, then you tell them yourself.' He rubbed at his eyes waiting for us to pass.

'What do you mean, George?' Dowling asked softly.

George scratched his head, digging his fingers into his oily scalp. 'They came this morning, asked us where he was, we showed them, then they started shouting at us, cursing us. When they finished we took him back downstairs. They's still there.'

With sick stomach I turned to the staircase and the pit beyond it before venturing gingerly downwards. The air was clammy and thick. I coughed and spat, disgusted at the thought that I was actually breathing this stuff, wondering nervously how easy it was to contract the typhus – Newgate was famous for typhus. As we turned the last corner of the spiral stair we saw the silhouettes of two men alone in the tiny vault, talking. A single small torch burnt on the wall. Looking round when they heard our steps, they appeared frightened, staring out of the darkness. Finely dressed, better than me, with long black wigs, feathered hats, petticoat breeches and lots of lace. They wore pattens, wooden clogs with iron bottoms and tie straps, to protect their exquisitely embroidered silk-braided shoes.

'What's the news?' I asked quietly.

Neither man spoke.

'They work for the Lord Chief Justice,' the gaoler said. 'I told you before.'

'Yes,' the man on the left said, 'we work for Lord Keeling.'

'What are you doing here?'

While they looked at each other, uncertain of themselves, Dowling and I stood in patient silence side by side, waiting. There was no way past us.

The gaoler sighed and blinked wearily. 'They said they came here to search the prisoner.'

'Why couldn't you search him upstairs?' I asked, angry. My skin prickled and I could smell my own sweet perfume.

'I searched him myself yesterday,' Dowling said slowly, his voice suspicious, his usual amiability replaced with a quiet wariness. 'I searched him from head to toe.'

The two men fidgeted unhappily. By the flickering light of the torches I could make out their eyes, alive and shifty. 'He must stay down here until such time he is called to trial. That's the order of the Lord Chief Justice. We work for him and take our instruction by him. Now we have to go.'

'What did you find?' Dowling demanded.

'I can't tell you. We can tell only Lord Keeling what we found, if anything. Those are our instructions.'

'They say they found a necklace,' the gaoler piped up indignantly. 'Told *me*, so they did, so don't see why they can't tell you.' A shapeless forefinger slid up his broad nose and scraped around.

Dowling stepped forwards and they stepped backwards. 'Show us what you say you found, or else I'll ask George here to find you cells of your own.'

'You can't do that,' the man snorted, looking at George. George's face was set, expressionless. Whether it was out of support for Dowling or just resigned boredom, impossible to know. I suspected the latter.

'We have our own authority,' the second man said.

'We have the Mayor's authority. Show me yours.' I held out my hand.

'He knows who we are.' The second man pointed at the gaoler.

'Show us what you have,' I insisted.

They turned to each other once more. The one on the left pursed his lips, his face grim, brow set. The one on the right shrugged unhappily. The man on the left dipped his hand into his pocket and took out a small object wrapped in a dirty stained cloth. I took it and unwrapped it. It was a golden necklace cast in the shape of a cross, with surface rough to the touch. Just as John Giles's mother had described it.

'It proves he's guilty. Now you must give it back.' The man put out his hand. He wore leather gloves.

It went in my pocket. 'How do you know it belongs to the girl?'

'We know,' the man replied. 'Now give it!' Dowling pushed him back, nodding apologetically as he did so.

'I will keep it.'

'It doesn't matter.' The second man put a hand on his colleague's shoulder. 'It has been seen.'

'Where was it hidden?' I asked, nodding at Dowling. 'He has already been searched.'

'It was well hidden,' the second man answered. 'Clearly he wasn't searched well enough.'

'You fetched it with you, gentlemen,' Dowling said quietly. 'It wasn't there yesterday.'

'The Lord Chief Justice seeks with undue haste,' I ventured.

'That's *treasonable* talk,' the man on the left said quietly, smiling menacingly as he did so, and even Dowling muttered at me in warning. They waited, sensing my lack of resolve, challenging us to find some excuse to detain them. There was a moment of silence, oppressive and muffled, broken only by the sound of a steady drip. In the absence of any support from Dowling I was wary. I could hardly apprehend agents of the Lord Chief Justice. Shrewsbury would *have* to be involved regardless of his feelings in the matter. Reluctantly I stepped back and gave them room to walk away. They edged past awkwardly and hurried up the stairs out of the stone hold, the clacking of their wooden footsteps echoing loudly as they departed. I cast Dowling a dark stare, unhappy that he had been so useless.

By the light of the gaoler's torch I could make out Joyce's thin shadow in his cell, still and unmoving, hear the quiet wheezing of his steady breathing, see the lice crawling slowly across his close-cropped scalp.

'George,' I turned, 'I will give you another five pounds if you get this man upstairs in front of a fire, unchained and proper food inside of him. If the officers of Lord Keeling return, then by all means fetch him back down, but take him up again when they have left. Can you do that?'

'Not for five pounds.' George screwed up his face and shook his head. 'Ten pounds.'

Ten pounds? Ten pounds was enough to keep Jane going for three months. Ten pounds was a tenth of my entire wealth. And what chance was there that the King would reimburse me – half of London was owed by him. Anyway, I didn't have ten pounds with me. I looked at Dowling. George was *his* friend.

'I'll be wanting that ten pounds today, sir.' The gaoler tapped me on the shoulder. 'Though it's an extravagant way to use your money. He'll be hung and quartered before the week's out.'

'What makes you so sure?'

'They say they found the necklace on him. That's what matters. They said it was the dead girl's necklace.'

'Where *did* they find it?'

'They said they found it on the floor.' He stuck his thumbs in his belt and waddled away. Then stopped. 'That reminds me. I was going to tell you. There's two fellows out there what work for a justice somewhere up north. I forget where exactly, but I recognises them.'

'Out where, George?'

'Outside in the street with them apprentices. You can sees them if you look hard enough – them's the ones with the hair on their faces.'

'Do you know what they're doing there?'

'No idea,' George gestured with his torch. 'Told myself to tell you. Now I told you.'

Dowling grunted, but thumped the gaoler on the shoulder gratefully. We made our way back the way we'd come, pushing past the two men that still stood staring hopelessly into the stinking closet. I felt my stomach cramp again, and pushed my way outside. Ten pounds.

'So you be Lytle.' The man with the baton waited for us. Now he had two, one in each hand. One he lifted to my chin, the other he used to warn off Dowling. 'You here with your bears?'

'Let him be,' Dowling grumbled from the pit of his stomach.

'Your eye's black too, Dowling.' The man held his arm out straight. Others began to crowd in, pushing forward to see what was going on. I recognised the drunkard, with his square red hat drooping over one eye, still grinning foolishly.

'Honey or turd with me, wretch. Stand away.' Dowling's arm whipped out and grabbed the baton, twisting it out of the man's grip. Then he stepped forward and brought it down hard on the arm that reached to my chin, with a cushioned crack. The man doubled over in pain, nursing his broken arm across his chest, and sunk to his knees white-faced.

'Haste now, Lytle. We have one opportunity,' Dowling whispered in my ear, pushing me forward roughly into the crowd. We strode forward, fending off the occasional blow with our arms. Dowling cracked another man over the head with the wooden club, and pushed forward with all his considerable strength against the wall of apprentices, always with an eye for the youngest, the most hesitant, the drunkest. Something hit me on the temple, causing me to stumble in dizzy pain. 'Up!' Dowling roared, grabbing me by the collar of my shirt and dragging me upright. I felt the stitches tear. Struggling to stay on my feet, I was propelled forward by Dowling's shovings, stopped from falling by the wall of people against which I was being pushed. I looked up into the purple face of an older apprentice, pockmarked and gleaming, teeth clenched and eyes blazing. Then Dowling's baton landed on his nose with a heavy crunch and the face disappeared. We were pushed up against the woodwork of a yellow coach that was engulfed by the crowd. I looked aloft, holding up an arm to ward off the blows. Was that the face of Shrewsbury pulling away from the window? Could it be? I clambered up to get a better view, and saw William Hill sat in there too, to my amazement. Neither of them saw me, their efforts focussed on avoiding the eyes of the multitude that swarmed about them. I was pulled roughly backwards by a pair of mighty hands. Dowling again. He pulled me towards an alley mouth, next to the open door of a bawdy house. The noise abated, and the heavy hot air was replaced with a cold, sharp wind and we were running. As we ran, I wondered to myself about the necklace, tucked safely in my pocket. For if it was indeed planted by these men, where did they get it? It must have been taken from Anne Giles's body. What did this imply of Keeling's involvement? And what the boggins was Hill doing with the Earl of Shrewsbury?

John Parsons was waiting for me outside my home. He stood in the street with a sick smirk upon his wretched face, attracting curious glances. People walked round him. When he saw me he leered. I approached reluctantly. What possible good could this satisfaction signify? He didn't wait for me to speak – I had nothing to say to him in any case. He bid me escort him to a low house in Mincing Lane. It wasn't far away and I followed him in silence. When we arrived I could not believe what he showed me there.

The hovel he took us to consisted of rough-hewn planks of wood standing precariously against the sturdier wall of a two-storey house. Parsons stood in front of the open front door with his hands clasped before him. He took off his hat and urged me to enter. The front room was small and damp. Rat droppings peppered the bare boards. A door stood ajar behind. Parsons didn't speak.

'Is she in there?' I asked, pointing at the room behind.

'Of course.' Parsons smiled. Seriously I began to wonder if I had ventured into a world of demons, for he had an air of unworldly evil about him that made me fearful. He said nothing else, just stood there. Suddenly I was sure that this man had done something unspeakable, that he had reneged upon his commitment. There was a thin line of sweat upon his brow and his eyes betrayed a manic intensity that burnt from his soul.

'I assume you kept our pact,' I said levelly, sure that he had not.

'In a manner. I did not test her myself, but it was my judgement that she be tested without delay, else her familiars would have had time to plot her release. I arranged for another to test her, which he did.'

No noise came from behind the door. As I approached it, I could smell the same sweet sticky odour that lingered about Dowling, only whilst on Dowling it was faint, buried beneath the smell of pig grease and other Newgate smells, here it was pure, fresh and overpowering. A loud buzzing of flies.

The first thing I did upon entering the room was to empty the contents of my stomach on the floor. I will not dwell upon what I found, for I don't wish my account to become unpalatable to all but a perverted few. So I will stick to the essentials. I think I half expected to find Mary Bedford dead or mutilated, so this was perhaps not a shock. What appalled me was the state I found her in, and the fact she was not alone. There was another woman in the room; barely recognisable as the woman that Dowling and I had spoken to near Whitefriars, the simple harmless soul that had told us second-hand tales of witchery. They lay side by side stripped of all their clothes. They had not been drowned, nor had they been watched, for their interrogator clearly had not sufficient patience. This, I suppose, must be called searching, but whosoever had done this had searched them with tools the like of which I could not imagine. Every orifice was stretched and torn, leaking pools of blood. Short, sharp cuts and long rounded channels; I will not relate what I saw in greater detail than that. But someone had used implements made of iron or some other metal, to penetrate deep into their bodies; in search of what . . . I still have no idea. They were both dead. Mercifully.

I turned to John Parsons. Did I see pride in those shiny green eyes? He smiled at me *again*. At that moment I felt a greater anger than I had ever felt before in my whole life. My hands started to tremble, so did my whole body, and that smile was the trigger that persuaded me to do what my instinct told me to. I punched him in the throat as hard as I could. He collapsed on the floor, choking, one hand spread in a pool of Mary Bedford's blood. I kicked him on the forehead, kicking high into the air and pulling a muscle at the back of my leg as a result. Then I knelt down, seized him by the ears and rubbed his face in the blood, grinding it into the floor. I wiped one of his cheeks across the floor, then the other, determined that he would never lose the smell of it, the mark of it that showed what an evil coward he was. These parasites were famous for never doing the deed themselves. Picking up his stick, I beat him about the body with it. Then I stamped on his wretched hat and stood there panting, my heart pounding, for the first time questioning whether what I was doing was right. He rolled over slowly, the mask obliterated in the cloying blood, his expression now one of pure contempt.

Once he had slowly got to his feet he stood stooped like an evil little flibbertigibbet. Snarling at me he slowly regarded the surroundings, his clothes, his hat, the dead bodies. He walked slowly over to where his stick lay and picked it up, then stood motionless, staring at me. I stared back. Then he left, without a word, headed back to Hell. I remained there a few moments longer, my wits frozen, then ran after him, determined to seize him and have him incarcerated. My hesitance was my ruin. When I emerged from the house he had gone.

I never did set eyes on him again, which I do not regret. At nights I rest unburdened, certain that his soul rots in Hell. Quite what state my own soul was in upon leaving him there that day, I cannot say. I felt overwhelmed by events and totally out of control of the situation. In truth, I had never felt such black despair. Cocksmouth was too far to travel and the prospect of exchanging conversation with my father too depressing. I would have to talk to Shrewsbury.

Chapter Eight

Water-horehound
*The juice of this herb gives a black dye that clings so
tenaciously that it cannot be washed off or removed.*

I arrived at Westminster to look for Shrewsbury with a
wide, blue silk sash across my tunic, washed, scrubbed and
doused with lavender oil. I reeked like a bawdy house. Not
inappropriate for Westminster Hall. The place was lined
with stalls selling books, clothes, hats and the like, but more
business was done selling the other, if you know what I mean.
National disgrace, I say, though they say that the French are a
lot worse. The French don't have time for running the country;
they're so busy dropping their drawers. I tipped my hat at Mrs
Martin the linen draper. I knew her well, as did many others
in London. She pointed at my sash and placed a hand on her
brow as if about to swoon. I smiled politely and turned away.
Betty Howlett caught my eye, waved and then blushed when
she realised her mother was watching. I made a mental note to
follow that up later. She lived out at White Cock Alley amongst

the dockers and lightermen. I sneezed – too much lavender oil.

I headed towards the Court of the Chancery, for this is where Shrewsbury spent much of his time I knew, but that day was a busy day and sentries barred passage. I managed to make eye contact with one of them, enough that he listened to my request and took the shilling that I gave him to deliver my message to Shrewsbury. Then it was a matter of waiting which I did for more than an hour.

'Lytle.' A quiet voice spake into my ear, little more than a whisper. 'You seek Lord Shrewsbury?'

It was Robert Burton, one of Shrewsbury's chief aides. He stood at my shoulder, a smaller man than me even, with shaven head and large red ears looking at me with his bright little eyes. His glance let you know that he was a lot more intelligent than you could ever hope to be.

'Be at the crypt of St Mary-le-Bow at five. Do not be late and be on your own.' He turned smartly on his heel and was gone before the words had registered.

St Mary-le-Bow was a strange rendezvous. I knew the outside of it very well, for it sat right next door to the Mermaid tavern, on Cheapside. By the time I arrived my tunic was covered in a thin layer of soot and I smelt more like an old shoe than a field of flowers. Never mind.

The bells were ringing loud and bright, but still I felt a clutching reluctance to cross the threshold of the heavy, squat little building. The front door was open, but all was quiet inside with only a few people in view. When I poked my head inside I saw why – there stood Robert Burton, just inside, and next to him a big man with a long sword at his waist. I stopped outside. Perhaps I would forgo this appointment after all. Burton must have seen the fear in me for he bid me enter in a voice that left little opportunity to decline.

The inside of Mary-le-Bow is richly decorated, full of memorials to those who have money to waste, but its polished facade hides a bloody history. Here it was that the friends of Ralph Crepin murdered Lawrence Ducket and hung his body from a window, trying to make it look like suicide. Crepin had been attacked by Ducket in a quarrel over a woman called Alice, yet it was his friends, not he, that took it upon themselves to kill Ducket, for which grim misdemeanour Crepin was hanged. Beaten senseless and then hung for it! Poor old Alice got burnt to death and she knew nothing of any of it.

I followed Burton down the middle of the sunlit centre aisle towards the dark hole that marked the descent towards the crypt. Burton walked at my left shoulder, his eyes watching me like a cat watches a mouse. At the doorway he waved a hand that indicated I was to go first. I had no choice and once I took the first step then I was trapped, for Burton walked behind me blocking the staircase. I walked down those stone steps slowly, feeling a sudden chill at my neck as the air became quickly colder.

This was where the Court of the Arches met. A small place to hold court, I reflected, once we were down. The vault was narrow and the stone arches thick and heavy. The floor was laid with ancient tombstones, shiny and worn. It was dark, lit only by a half-dozen thin candles. Three men sat at the other end of the vault, silent and still. I looked over my shoulder. Burton returned my gaze expressionlessly. He stood in front of the door that led upstairs, blocking my retreat.

The central figure stood up and walked slowly towards me. The other two followed a pace behind at his flanks. As he came closer his black shadow was slowly illuminated and his sharp, bright eyes glistened like paternoster beads. He stopped four yards in front of me and leant forwards, his gloved hands grasping the end of a thick, black lacquered cane. 'Sit down!'

One of his companions strode forward with a chair and placed it firmly where I was to sit. Shrewsbury stayed standing, towering over me like a black demon. His companions both drew their swords and stood one either side of me. Godamercy!

He crashed his cane against the floor of the crypt. Two swords climbed slowly up towards my throat. 'Did I not tell thee that I was not connected with this affair?'

I looked up into his terrible face, remorseless eyes and burning crimson nose. His breath stank of rancid meat. 'Aye, sir, but I have news.'

'What news?'

'I think I know who killed Anne Giles.'

Shrewsbury lowered his head so that I could see the yellow of his rodent eyes. 'Why deliver that news to *me*?' he demanded.

I spoke in a low whisper. 'Sir, you said that the murder falls under the jurisdiction of the Lord Chief Justice Keeling and that if you were to be seen interfering in his jurisdiction, then it would be a great embarrassment to you.'

'Indeed!'

'Yet you said also, sir, that he would not be interested in who killed her. Yet he is a friend of William Ormonde, so it is said, and has made great efforts to apprehend a man called Richard Joyce.'

Shrewsbury's expression did not change. He looked at me as if I had told him it was about to rain.

'Dowling and I found agents of the Lord Chief Justice in the stone hold planting evidence that was taken from Anne Giles's body while she lay at Bride's. He would see Joyce condemned even though it is clear he is *innocent*. I thought that you may after all decide to speak with Lord Keeling since he has shown such keen interest in the murder, and since he is so set upon putting to death the wrong man.'

Shrewsbury suddenly looked weary, like I was the most witless fool on earth. Clearly the notion that an innocent man might suffer an unjust and terrible death did not irk his black, shrivelled soul the way it irked mine. He leant forward over his cane with his eyes fixed on mine so intently that it felt at that moment like we were the only two people in the world. 'Lytle.' He spoke slowly, rolling every word in his mouth before spitting it out. 'I am not connected with this affair. Do you not understand?'

I knew I should say nothing, just nod, yet I did not want to lose his audience without telling him what he had to know. 'We think that a merchant by the name of Matthew Hewitt is the man that killed Anne Giles.'

He snuffled like he was about to choke and his jaw dropped an inch. He stared at me with even more dislike than he had before. Then he seemed to compose himself, straightening his back and dabbing at his mouth with a kerchief before lifting his cane and stroking its tip against my chest. 'Don't waste your time on Richard Joyce. There are hundreds like him in this town and they all end up dead, either on the end of a rope because they have tried in vain to change their lot, or in the river because they haven't. You are not one of God's angels, Lytle.'

'Neither did I venture that I was,' I answered, my mouth dry.

'Find out who killed Anne Giles, Lytle, and do so hastily.

Do you understand?' He crashed his cane to the floor in time with the syllables of the last three words, which he shouted. 'You speak as a weak-minded cowardly fellow, Lytle. Your father would pretend to uphold the honour of your family. You speak like you would have any other man but you perform your filial duties.' He took a sword of one his guards and held it out like a man who is skilled in the art. He pressed the tip against my throat and twisted it so that I had no option but to lift my chin. I felt the blade press into my windpipe and felt my own warm blood trickle down onto my tunic. Ruined. His eyes were flint. 'You say nothing of my involvement to any man. You are investigating the death of your cousin. You do not use my name. Is that understood?'

'Yes, My Lord.'

He lowered the sword at last and stood watching me a minute. Then he was gone, and his dark angels with him.

'Come, Lytle,' Burton beckoned me, a sly smile about his lips.

Darkness fell as I walked back slowly towards home through the emptying streets. I felt a deadening misery wrapped about my throat, hanging heavy across my chest. Why had Shrewsbury offered to help in the first place if he were so determined that his name not be linked to the investigation? It occurred to me that I had been less careful than I might in talking to others of his involvement. Since Hill's warning I was pretty sure that I had mentioned Shrewsbury's name also to William Ormonde and to Jane. William Ormonde had told Mary Ormonde, I knew, since she had mentioned it while I was at Epsom. So it could not be long before someone then mentioned it to Lord

Keeling – and then what did fate hold in store for poor old Harry Lytle? It was my father's fault! He that hid himself away in Cocksmouth and wrote me letters. I had delayed my visit to that place too long. I would go tomorrow.

It was too early to go to bed so I walked down to the riverside, down to the Three Cranes in Vintry. It was a loathsome little dog-hole, but it suited my mood. Taking a mug of poor ale, I settled myself down in a corner. Any that looked at me with curious intent, as if they considered striking up conversation, I glared at. A sorry predicament, indeed.

Woe was me. I downed my third mug dry.

'Lytle.' The sound of Hill's voice in my ear. I looked up in surprise. He crooked a finger and beckoned me out back. I clambered to my feet, cracked my hip against the edge of the thick table and limped after him.

'Sit down.' Hill pulled me into a small room, which was empty save for two mugs of fresh ale and a plate of beef on a small table. 'What have you been doing?' He sat opposite me and leant forward, hands clasped, eyes fixed on mine. This felt like a business negotiation, the way he spoke so clearly and waited for me to speak with matter-of-fact sobriety.

I licked my lips. 'Drinking.'

His puffy eyes were red-rimmed and beady. 'You are making a pest of yourself at Court, Harry. You have been loose-lipped, despite my warnings, and you have antagonised Shrewsbury. He will not see you again, Harry, will not countenance your presence.'

I nodded and picked up the new pot. 'I am of the same mind. I saw him today.'

'I know you did.' How so? 'The Lord Chief Justice is also

aware of you now, though he was not before.' He shook his head sorrowfully. 'Not good for you, Harry.'

'No,' I agreed, 'and you know the worst of it?'

Hill raised his brows enquiringly.

'I am not even related to Anne Giles,' I exclaimed. 'I don't know what put the notion into my father's soft head, but all of this is his doing. Anne Giles is no relation of mine, yet here we all are.' I belched. It was most unjust.

'How do you know you are not related?'

'Everyone tells me so.' I waved a hand. 'Ormonde told me it. John Giles told me it. I didn't need much persuasion, since the only one that says otherwise is my father.'

'Lytle.' Hill bowed his head and laid a hand on the table, chest deflated. He had the air of a man that was about to tell me something very important. But then he said nothing.

'I will go to Cocksmouth tomorrow to find out what this is all about,' I told him. 'Richard Joyce sits in prison, blameless, yet Keeling goes to great lengths to condemn him. Mary Bedford and another old woman lie dead because the rector accuses them of witchery. Yet none of them are guilty.'

'Who is?' Hill asked softly.

'Matthew Hewitt.'

Hill's face turned a curious shade of pink, like a salmon. 'What makes you think it?' he asked, lips pursed like it was an effort to stay calm.

'John Giles is Anne Giles's husband and it is said that he was blackmailing Matthew Hewitt. We have met him and he is clearly terrified of Hewitt.'

'Blackmailing him?'

'Aye, so they say, though we don't know why.' I took a bone of beef and tore a chunk of meat off it with my teeth.

Frowning, Hill looked disappointed. 'Why should a merchant who takes issue with a man decide to kill the man's wife, in so public a fashion?'

The meat tasted old and rotten. Spitting onto the floor I let the bone drop back onto the plate then finished my ale. 'I don't know.'

'You don't know much, Harry.'

I watched him drink. He didn't usually drink so daintily. Usually he drank his ale like a horse slobbers at a pail of water.

'How do you know I saw Shrewsbury today?'

'No matter.'

'I saw you with Shrewsbury,' I remembered. 'You were sitting with him in his coach at Newgate.'

'You are mistaken,' he replied, with a distant calmness that implied he cared not a bushel of peas what I believed. Grimacing he rubbed a finger on the tabletop as if he was thinking hard about what to say. I gave him all the time he required.

He looked up with an open face for the first time that evening. 'Harry, it is no longer important what reason your father had for writing you the letter and soliciting Shrewsbury's help. It's done.'

I started to protest but he held up both hands and glared until I stopped.

'Joyce will hang, Lytle. The day after tomorrow.' He sat back and watched me. I said nothing, for I was too surprised. 'The Lord Chief Justice tried Joyce this afternoon in private.'

'That is impossible!'

'Why is it impossible?' Hill snapped, impatiently.

We both knew that it wasn't impossible, so I sat there like an odd fish, staring at him with my mouth gaping. I croaked out the beginnings of some protest before considering how pointless it would be to protest to Hill.

'Forget Joyce. You won't save him.'

I couldn't forget Joyce. 'Tell me what would you do if you were I.'

'You asked me that before, Harry.' Hill looked up into my eyes and spoke passionately, 'You must go to Epsom. The answer lies there.'

'I did go to Epsom, for the funeral. I found nothing.'

'Then you didn't look hard enough.' He leant forwards again and tapped a forefinger on the table. 'Go to Epsom, Harry.'

I stared back at him, as miserable as ever.

'Go to Epsom.' Hill raised himself and stood over me, his giant girth casting a shadow over the whole table. 'Tomorrow.' He left.

Chapter Nine

Toad-grasse
Because it occurs where toads are found.

Charcoal grey clouds paraded over the smoke and the fog, heavy and threatening. Basinghall Street was quiet. Smoke rose weakly from the chimney of Hewitt's house before being swept away by the strong wind that battered the rooftops. It was said that Hewitt lived here on his own, just him and one servant.

The same wind blew through the coach, a chilly place for me to gather my nerves. Dowling and two of his friends sat silently back on their seats, pressed into the shadows, watching me. Dowling had refused to speak to me for the last hour. He had wanted to involve the Mayor, but the Mayor declined. Since he had no other useful suggestion to make, he was angry, yet still he refused to countenance a direct approach. I reckon he was angrier with himself than he was with me.

I had hurried out of the Three Cranes as soon as Hill left and sent message to Dowling. Hill's opinion counted for nought – I wasn't going to allow Joyce to die for another's sins. Dowling and I were both of one mind – Hewitt was guilty. So we would have to prove it. For my part I had resolved that having lost Mary Bedford I wasn't going to lose Joyce too. Dowling agreed, yet had no remedy other than mine. So he was sulking. He refused to meet my eye as I climbed down out of the coach.

The front door was heavy, carved of an exotic dark wood with strange scenes upon it. Not from the Bible, but from some other religion. I rubbed a finger against the black wood before knocking. My knuckles seemed to make no sound, neither did my fist. In the chill wind I waited, conscious of the three butchers watching me from the coach. The chimney was smoking – there *had* to be someone at home. Sidling around to the left I attempted to peer in through a first-floor window. The room was black, only shadows of furniture were visible. Then a flicker of candlelight betrayed some presence within. I heard shuffling inside and stood back. A window opened, the one into which I had been staring. An old man's head stretched out, the head scabby and grey. The left eye was hooded, but it scanned me just as beadily as its neighbour. A skinny neck, long and scrawny, supported a wizened head that twisted itself to face me with an awkward sneer. The man was very old and his nose was big and hooked, like the beak of a bird of prey.

'I am here to see Matthew Hewitt.' I lifted my chin, hearing myself talk too fast.

'Who are you?'

'Harry Lytle. I am appointed by the Mayor to investigate the death of Anne Giles. I must talk to Matthew Hewitt.'

Head and neck slowly untwisted themselves and then

withdrew. The window was closed and the street was quiet again. It was fully ten minutes before anything more happened. Beginning to think that I had been ignored, I started to simmer in indignant rage, but then I heard the noise of a great bolt being shifted. The door swung slowly open. The head was there, underneath it a body, sinewy and nibbled. His clothes were faded, old and misshapen, but recognisable as those of a servant. The hallway behind was furnished sparsely, but the ornaments that there were, were exotic and rare. Gilt leather panels covered the walls, embossed with gold leaf. Above the panels running around the top of the walls were more strange scenes in plaster, tall, thin characters with their arms as long as their bodies standing in awkward pose wearing elaborate headdresses and skirts and with ornaments on their arms.

I waited for the shrivelled old servant to heave the door closed again and slide back the well-greased bolts, three of them, fashioned out of a heavy metal, twisted and dull. When the servant had finished he gave me a warped stare before leading me deep into the bowels of the house; dark unlit corridors, windows covered with thick screens. Here and there an ornament gleamed and sparkled, gold and silver, cups and candlesticks, shiny shapes reaching out of the gloom like stars. Faces stared down at me from old dusty paintings, men with stern gazes and old fleshy faces, disapproving and contemptuous, lonely and forgotten. I wondered at the value of these items, but was discouraged from exploring their feel or weight by the shuffling old man who wouldn't permit me to linger more than a pace behind. We came to a small flight of wooden stairs to the rear of the house that led straight up to a door. Beneath it was a thin crack of light. The old man didn't climb the stairs but stood at their foot to make sure that

I went up all the way and knocked on the door. I rapped twice and entered.

A small fire and a single candle lit the windowless chamber. The candle stood in a simple silver candlestick on a small circular table in the middle of the room. Two chairs sat next to the fire. In one of these chairs sat a man. His face was in shadow, lit only occasionally by the flicker of the flames. He neither stood up nor made any sound. I walked closer and scrutinised the blank face. His skin was drawn and pockmarked. Long lines ran from his temples down to his chin like knife cuts. Little hairs grew out of his face in small clumps. I took the empty chair, which was pushed well forward so that I would be well lit.

'I am Matthew Hewitt.' His voice was surprisingly soft. 'You would ask me questions about the murder of Anne Giles.'

'Yes.' My voice sounded strange, muffled, no echo.

'Then do so.' Hewitt's eyes were occasionally caught by the light of the fire. They were still and unmoving.

I leant forward and took the poker from by the fireplace. I poked it. There was no new wood. 'Anne Giles was killed at St Bride's, the night of—'

'I know all about her death, Mr Lytle, just as I know that the murderer will soon be hung.'

'Richard Joyce did not kill Anne Giles.'

'I think Lord Keeling would be less than pleased to hear you say so,' Hewitt answered thoughtfully, his tone cold.

I felt a pang of fear in my guts and recalled John Giles's warning. 'I am sure you are right. But the fact remains that Joyce did not kill Anne Giles.'

Hewitt said nothing.

'You know John Giles, don't you?' I asked.

Hewitt was quiet for some time before replying. 'That's my business, Mr Lytle. I have no great desire to discuss my business with you, and no need to either. We both know that you have neither authority nor influence in this affair.'

'John Giles worked for you and stole some money of yours, or something of the sort. Then his wife was murdered.'

Hewitt sat motionless. I sat motionless too, watching his shadowed face. The only sound in the room was the crackle of timber in the grate. The candle burnt down its wick. As the fire slowly died, it rose suddenly, swiftly and briefly, spitting out its last light into the gloom, enough time for me to see the expression on his face. It was rough and grey like the face of a mountain, hairs sprouted from his chest like weeds. The eyes frightened me to my naked nerves. They were round black pebbles, shiny and alight, fixed on mine, questioning and calculating.

'Mr Lytle.' There was a touch of amusement in Hewitt's voice. 'What do you want to know?'

'Who killed Anne Giles?'

'You will have to find that out for yourself, Mr Lytle, for I'm not going to tell you. But to succeed you will have to use rather more brain than I think God blessed you with. Besides which I cannot think of one single reason what you could gain by so finding out.'

'To save an innocent man from the noose.'

'You will not save Joyce. Joyce will be hung and there is nothing that you can do to stop it.'

I frowned, and grunted. 'Is John Giles blackmailing you?'

Hewitt closed his eyes.

'Why did you ask Giles to steal the key to Bride's? He told me that you did.'

'He did not tell you that. You told him that. You also suggested that he stole it of his own initiative.' I was dumbfounded, for he was repeating to me almost exactly the same words that Giles had spoke to us. Had he been spying on us? Had he interrogated Giles after we had met with him? He could not have signalled it thus more clearly. I could think of nothing else to say. I looked around the room, at the leather-bound books that lined the walls. Hewitt still sat with his eyes closed.

I cleared my throat and stood up. I hesitated, uncertain and miserable, before deciding to leave. This had been a mistake. I thought about thanking Hewitt for his time, but didn't. I walked to the door slowly and stretched out my arm to open it.

'Be careful, Lytle.' Hewitt's voice, as I placed my hand upon the handle. 'You are so far out of your league, it should make you shudder.' He smiled gently and tapped his forehead in casual dismissal before closing his eyes again in anticipation of my departure. I stared at his fat, complacent face and was suddenly filled with hatred. I will have you, Matthew Hewitt, and I will see those beady, little eyes wide with fright before I am finished. But not today. I left.

Dowling said nothing when I told him what had happened. To his credit he spared me the avuncular smile and the hand on the shoulder; he just nodded to himself and hummed. Even though he spared me and though it was stormy, I decided to walk home rather than ride. But I managed no more than twenty steps before I sensed his hulking shape lurking beside me.

'I had to try,' I grunted.

'Aye, but I fear our task is even more perilous now.'

'When you stand upon the scaffold with a noose around your neck it is no great concern to learn you have consumption,' I answered. 'I think I have to talk directly to Keeling.' It sounded mad as I said it, particularly given the response I had elicited from Hewitt.

Dowling said nothing.

'What other remedy do we have if it is true that Keeling has personally marked him for the noose?'

'Thy faithfulness reacheth unto the clouds.' Dowling clapped me about the shoulder, grasped my hand, and then let it go. He shook his head slowly in a gesture, the meaning of which I couldn't fathom, then bid me farewell.

Faithfulness? Did he not recognise desperation when he saw it?

Chapter Ten

Narrow-leaved wild Orrache
In stony places.

I went to Whitehall next morn, though I had no appointment, hoping to talk my way through the sentries. I couldn't hope to gain entrance directly into the King's quarters, so I entered through the Court Gate instead. A guard grunted at me and wrinkled his nose in enquiry, but waved me through when I claimed to have an appointment.

I marched through the gallery and out onto the cobbles of the Great Court, overshadowed on one side by the Great Hall with its massive sloping roof, and on the other by the Banqueting House. The Court was busy, lords and dignitaries milling about in small groups. I strode across the Court, in my own finest silks, crossed the covered way and emerged onto Pebble Court. The Great Chamber was to my left. A guard blocked my passage, this one more awake. As I approached he stepped forward. Again, I assured him I had an appointment. He wanted to know with whom.

'With Lord Keeling?' He edged sideways to cover the entrance. 'I reckon your appointment is off, sir. Lord Chief Justice ain't here.'

'I see. Then I would consult with someone in his office.'

'What about?' The guard let the pike in his hand fall forward, in line with my chest.

'I don't care to discuss my business with you.' Trying to assume the arrogant air of an important nobleman, I heard uncertainty in the upward lilt of my voice.

Standing his ground, the guard pointed back the way I had come. 'You is only getting through here if you comes with one of the Lord Chief Justice's clerks from his offices over at Scotland Yard. You turn round, go back the way you come, cross the Great Court and go through into Scotland Yard. Understand? If you get lost, ask for the cider house. The Justice's offices are close by.'

Giving the guard what I hoped was a withering look, I turned and walked back. What was the world coming to? Employing sentries that didn't drink themselves stupid? Scotland Yard was where the offices of the Lord Steward were located, and the Office of Works. Scotland Yard was functional, a mishmash of ordinary buildings, narrow corridors and tiny offices. I knew where the cider house was but it took a while longer to find the offices of the Lord Chief Justice. Eventually I found a narrow building consisting of three floors of small dusty rooms, packed tight with desks and clerks. It reminded me of the Records Office, a memory that encouraged me to pursue my mission with renewed vigour, that I would not need to linger long.

Walking through the offices, I met with no challenge until a deep bright voice sang out confidently from behind me, asking me my business. The man that addressed me had a bald patch in the middle of his head. What hair he had was swept back and tamed with grease. He was older than me, in his forties at least, and had that bright unmoving half smile of a man who likes to know exactly how many hairs there are in a horse's tail. Approaching the desk I introduced myself.

'And my name is Cummins. What do you need?' Each oiled hair lay in a straight line, precisely aligned with its neighbour. His breath smelt of herbs and he was impeccably trimmed.

'Good morning, Mr Cummins, I have heard of you. You are well known about the Palace.' I attempted to flatter him.

'Thanking thee, Mr Lytle, but I doubt it.' He lifted his chin slightly, disapproving. 'I have heard of you, though, I think. You work at the Records Office at the Tower. My colleague, Mr John Wellington, works with you. I hear that you have left the service now?'

I blinked. Who the boggins was John Wellington? Ignoring his sceptical questioning and wrinkled nose, I told myself I was important. 'Aye, indeed. You are well informed, sir. I am charged with finding out whosoever it was that killed Anne Giles at Bride's church a week ago.'

'Aye, sir, a sad event. I have heard much of that killing. It was brutal, I think. I also heard that they caught the scoundrel that did it and tried him. He is to be hung tomorrow, methinks? You are to be praised at finding him so fast, Mr Lytle. I take my hat off to you.' His cheeks gathered into little pouches.

'Thank you, Mr Cummins, but it was not I that caught Richard Joyce, the man of whom you speak. He was caught by the mob. I venture that he holds testament to the killing, but his was not the deed. I must demonstrate the truth of it before

128

tomorrow, else he will be put to death unjustly, which would be a great tragedy and wrongdoing.'

Looking less happy, Cummins addressed me like he was my mother. 'The Lord Chief Justice himself conducted the trial.'

'Aye, Mr Cummins, in all of his wisdom, no doubt, but I sincerely believe that he made an error, and that it is my duty to help him correct it.'

'Well,' Cummins shook his head slowly, 'it sounds like a tangled business, I'm sure. How might *I* be of service to you, Mr Lytle?'

'I must gain an audience with Lord Keeling, Mr Cummins, that I might put my case. It is very important. The sentry at the gate told me that someone here might escort me.'

'I see.' Cummins didn't look surprised. He pondered for a moment before continuing. 'You have come to the right office, but I have to tell you that I cannot help.'

'Why not?'

'It is not in my authority to do so. Were I to try and escort you to the Great Chamber then I can assure you that we would be denied entry.' He shook his head sadly, maddeningly calm, a rueful smile on his lips. I felt my cheeks warm and the old impatient rage well up within me once more. Just as I got ready to say something I knew would do no good, in came a fellow who I recognised, a friend with whom I had been drinking several times. Rolling in cheerfully he greeted me heartily, gripping me about the shoulder and talking into my face. His name was Sandby, and he smiled easily, his brown eyes fixed wide in a permanent surprised stare.

'What news, Harry? I haven't seen you for days! Weeks! What brings you to our cosy little nook?'

'I want to see Lord Keeling.'

He looked to Cummins, who was now writing something. 'Well, you have as much chance of getting to see Keeling as you have of bedding the Lady Castlemayne, Harry, my old friend. You might as well apply for a warrant to exhume the head of Charles's father.'

Cummins raised his head sharply and shot his colleague a stern glance of unmistakable admonishment.

'How so?' I demanded.

'We have been instructed not to assist you under any circumstances whatsoever. So we will not. Not even if you tell us Anne Giles is still alive and trying to get out the box.'

'Mr Sandby!' Cummins snapped, slamming down his quill onto the desk. 'Will you speak with good manners and respect.' The pouched cheeks were bright red now.

'Humbly apologise.' Sandby bowed his head gravely. Shrugging, he looked down at me. 'Still, it's the way of it, Harry.'

'From whom did this instruction come?'

Sandby looked down at Cummins' pink scalp. 'I can't tell you that.'

'From the Lord Chief Justice Keeling, of course,' Cummins answered unexpectedly, to the obvious surprise of the younger man. Others were staring. 'Yes, sir,' Cummins nodded. 'Rumour has it that Keeling is a friend of the family and is sympathetic to their feelings. They want the issue put to rest with all haste and have asked him to intervene.'

'Such hasty determination flies in the face of justice for Richard Joyce.'

Tapping his quill on the desk Cummins regarded me with stern countenance. 'Richard Joyce is condemned.'

'What might a man do?' I looked to Sandby. He just shook his head slowly, saying nothing. The expression on Cummins' face didn't change, nor did he reply. I looked around at the army of scribes all pretending not to be listening. Nothing here.

'Aye, well, gentlemen. Thank you for your candour.' I nodded and turned to leave.

'Good luck, young man,' Cummins called out as I left. I turned to check that he didn't mock me.

'Thank you,' I replied. Sandby waved, again without saying anything, a wry smile on his face. I resolved to hunt him out at the taverns to understand more. The Lord Chief Justice was well organised, I considered, as I left the Palace grounds. So. Direct to his house.

Keeling lived in a fine house north of Whitehall, close to the Great Close Tennis Court. It was a three-storey red-brick house built in a square around its own small courtyard. I pulled on a bell and waited, admiring the scenery, the trees and fields that led to St James's Park. Once I used to go out into the park in search of *Fragaria*, wild strawberries, a custom I had ceased upon being told by Dr Ray that an excess of strawberries may damage the kidneys. The servant that answered the door wore a haughty expression that I found intensely irritating. When I told him I had come to see Keeling, and confirmed that I had no appointment, he looked at me as if I was a common hawker, face frigid and unmoving. Finally he decided to let me in and graciously gestured that I scale the carved wooden staircase. We crossed the hall under the gaze of James I, or rather his portrait, standing with his hand on his hip, wearing full armour. I was shown into a cold, dark room on the first floor. The servant didn't light the fire, only a thin candle that cast unusual shadows on the walls of the large room. Then he left, murmuring that I was to wait. I waited many minutes in the freezing cold, walking in circles to keep warm. Finally, the door opened.

'Mr Lytle. My apologies for keeping you waiting, but I have urgent matters to attend to.' The man who spoke was dressed in expensive clothes, his velvet jacket had a gold trimming, and he wore a fine long wig. I didn't know Keeling well, but had seen him often enough to know that this wasn't him.

'Who are you?' I asked, standing up.

He stepped into the middle of the room with his hands behind his back. 'I am Lord Keeling's chief aide and his representative in this affair. He cannot talk to you and has delegated the task to me.'

'Sir,' I replied, remembering my manners. 'My name is Harry Lytle and I would present to Lord Keeling some evidence that Richard Joyce did not kill Anne Giles.'

'Richard Joyce was charged, tried and found guilty. He will hang tomorrow.'

Stepping forward so that I was within a breath's distance of the man's own face, I could see the blood darken in his cheeks. 'I have testimony that a second man entered the church just before Anne Giles was killed. Richard Joyce did not kill Anne Giles. Yet Lord Keeling held the trial behind closed doors, and I had no opportunity to divulge my knowledge nor to introduce my findings to Lord Keeling. I must have a chance to talk to him.'

'Mr Lytle, Lord Keeling knows more than you think. He knows what you have discovered, and more besides. What for you is the whole story is but a part of the whole to him. He is guided by the divine spirit who protects him from making false accusation.'

Burying my face in my hands I fought to control my temper and voice. 'How can Richard Joyce be found guilty under such circumstances? He ran away from the church after the murder was done – that doesn't make him guilty. The girl's necklace found in his cell – I can tell you who put it there, I saw it done. Lord Keeling knows well, too, for it was his agents. You plot to hang an innocent man, an act that God will frown on. It is my duty in the eyes of the Lord to put my case to Keeling, to be sure that all facts are known before a final decision is made. Otherwise we will see an unlawful killing, which will only serve to compound the evils already done. How can Lord Keeling be content to do nothing while an innocent man is strung up? You tell me!' I jabbed my finger in the air, inadvisedly.

'When you talk to me, Mr Lytle, you are talking to the Lord Chief Justice. I *will* tell him everything you have told me, but I have already told you that Richard Joyce has been tried in God's court and found guilty. The Lord Chief Justice knows Joyce to be guilty because he himself judged it. He is the Lord Chief Justice to King Charles, and King Charles is God's agent on earth. God guides his hand.' He turned on his heel and marched to the door. 'There is nothing more to be said. Thank you for your time and good day to you.'

Growling, I stood my ground. 'Where is Keeling? I want to talk to him myself. He does not know the full circumstances, he cannot.'

'Mr Lytle,' the chief aide barked, straight-backed, patience all but gone. 'Richard Joyce will hang tomorrow. The Lord Chief Justice instructed me to tell you. He also warned me that you are a young man, inexperienced in life and appointed by consequence of political games being conducted by the minor nobility at Court. He will not see you now, nor in the future, and if you do not leave, then you will be escorted out of here all the way to the Tower.'

'When did Keeling tell you all this?' I eyed him suspiciously. 'Today? Did he put all of these words into your mouth? Is he waiting upstairs now to hear the outcome?'

'I told you where he is. He is at the Palace.' There was poison in his voice.

'You must postpone the hanging until I have had the chance to talk to him.'

'The hanging will proceed even if you get down on your knees and confess to the murder of Anne Giles yourself.' Contempt flickered across his face.

That was it! I was fed up of being spoken to like a fool. I was going to check for myself. Striding past the chief aide, I pushed him to one side and headed towards the staircase, but even as I stomped upstairs two of the King's Guards appeared above me to block my path. They descended with intent and picked me up by the elbows so that I could walk only on my toes. I kicked out at one of them and caught him on the top of the thigh, then I wriggled free of the other and turned to the chief aide who had followed me up the stairs and punched him as hard as I could in the side of the face. He went down on his knees and I was buried underneath the two guards who set about me with their fists. Lying there being pummelled, it occurred to me that I could have handled the situation better.

'You will go to the Tower until after tomorrow is finished.' The chief aide stood up with his hand to his cheek, and his wig crooked. 'Thank God, Mr Lytle, that I don't charge you with *common* assault.' The words sounded strangely rehearsed and he disappeared quickly up the stairs and out of sight.

Listening to his steps fade I wondered if he was running straight to Keeling. I lay squashed beneath the two burly guards that beat me. My arms were pinned to my sides, and I took the blows without complaint or struggle, for I could feel no pain, and had lost all hope. My chin was pushed hard against the floor and my arms were pinned behind my back. The blows from the two soldiers became weaker as they tired. I lay still. They pulled me roughly to my feet and bound my wrists. I was hauled down the stairs out through the front door and into the street. There was a small garrison waiting outside the front door, reinforcing the notion that my visit was anticipated, my petulant behaviour predicted. I felt foolish, and avoided the eyes of the guards that had attacked me. They picked me up and threw me across the back of a horse. Looking at the dirt I cursed my stupidity.

The garrison dispersed, only half a dozen accompanying the guards as they led me towards the City. When we reached the end of Whitehall the guards stopped and threw me about so that I was sat upright, a more dignified position. They undid the ropes that bound my wrists behind me and tied them so that my hands were secured around the horse's neck. In this position they led me into the City, through it, and to the end of Tower Street. Our little procession attracted the attention of all, delighted jeers from some who assumed that I was a convicted criminal and hoped for a pillory or a hanging, more subdued jeers for the soldiers from others that assumed the same thing, but suspected the royal motive, and puzzled stares from others that wondered what it was all about. Throughout it all I stared forwards, avoiding the temptation to glance sideways, afraid that this might be what the mob was waiting for, the ones tossing vegetables from one hand to the other. It took us a while to cross the top of Fish Street Hill, but otherwise we made reasonable time, mercifully. We emerged onto the familiar fields of Tower Hill. The guards pulled me off the horse just before they reached the Bulwark Tower. Thank God.

'Mr Lytle, I have been asked to tell you that your job is finished,' the biggest of the two guards spoke with his head bowed so that I couldn't see his eyes.

'Asked by who?' I snorted, looking around at the soldiers and the other guard.

'Your job is finished.' The guard took off his coat and handed it to his colleague. His biceps were thick like a man's legs. He turned round and met my eyes for a moment. He looked sad, upset even. Then he drew back his fist and hit me full in the face.

I woke up lying on a bed. I couldn't see out of my right eye. I tried touching it, very gingerly. My eyelid was much further away from my face than it should have been, and was very tender. Sitting up I pushed aside the curtains. A small, square stone room, dominated by a tall fireplace built into the wall, and a large double-arched window. I stood up slowly with the flat of my hand over my eye and shuffled to the window, which looked out towards the river. A very familiar view.

In the brickwork just under the sill, I found the heart carved into the wall with a big 'E', the handiwork of Giovanni Castiglione, one-time tutor to the young Queen Elizabeth. Next to it were the twelve signs of the zodiac, connected to each other by a criss-cross of lines surrounded by small squares and strange inscriptions, handiwork of Hugh Draper of Bristol, imprisoned there a century ago for sorcery. This was the Salt Tower. The Wakefield Tower where I had worked, day in, day out, these last three years was just fifty paces away, down the Outer Ward.

Few prisoners were ever brought to the Tower. Most people were locked up in Ludgate, Newgate, or elsewhere. I supposed that I should feel privileged. The last to be held here before being executed was, ironically, an ex-lieutenant of the Tower, a signatory to the death warrant of Charles I. Sir John Barkstead's head was still stuck on a stick above St Thomas's Tower. It had been two years now since he had been hung, drawn and quartered. Not much was left hanging from the skull. It had been said that before he died he had hidden the sum of twenty thousand pounds in butter ferkins and buried it all in the basement of the Bell Tower. Men had searched for it for days, weeks and years, so far without success.

It was also said that the intelligence was a ruse, the revenge of Barkstead's mistress who was a bit strange since the death of her beloved. A mad old woman, I had seen her once. Isaac Penington and Robert Tichborne were also ex-lieutenants, and were also both regicides. Penington had died two years ago; Tichborne was still here, somewhere. He had been sentenced to death, but upon pleading youth and inexperience had so far been allowed to live. He would die here eventually, or else on Tyburn.

Looking out over the yard below, I watched the soldiers, sitting in circles playing cards and drinking cheap wine from unstoppered bottles. What a shambles. The King's Lodgings, the Queen's Lodgings and the Royal Wardrobe were all long deserted, now derelict, tapestries removed or rotten, murals faded or chipped and eaten away. Now the Tower was infested by rats and by people, six hundred of them, somehow – clerks, messengers, salesmen, tailors, shopkeepers, innkeepers, bricklayers, labourers, carpenters and painters. Soldiers everywhere, sleeping, drinking, lying around. The White Tower, House of Ordnance and New Armouries were now used to store arms. The Wakefield Tower stored records. The mints stored coins. What had once been a palace was now a giant warehouse.

Night fell. Rats came out to play, running across the floor of the room overhead. I felt wide awake for some strange reason, not a hint of fatigue or weariness. Calm. There was nothing I could do. I had tried my hardest, done my best, and voiced my opinions to all that mattered. What more could I have done to save Joyce? Would it have made any difference if I had spoken diplomatically, if I had managed to control my irritation and impatience? Perhaps I could have caught up with Keeling by some other means, but I doubted it. Just as I doubted that Keeling kept a battalion of guards outside his front doors every night.

I sat there for hours, staring into the darkness. The yeoman peered through the bars of the window at me. I could sense his curiosity, wondering why I was sat there, unmoving. He came by every ten or fifteen minutes, until eventually, with great caution, he opened the door to ask me if I was all right. I wondered if Joyce was enjoying the same human consideration.

I reflected on Jane's advice, advice I hadn't found time to impart to Dowling. Joyce was to be freed from prison tomorrow, though not in the way Jane meant. Mary Bedford had been found, though again not in the way that Jane meant. I had gone to see Hewitt despite her warning. That meant I had the brain of an old hog. The only thing I hadn't done wrong was to spend more time with John Giles. Time to rectify that later.

I felt very lonely that night. For the first time in my life I felt I had no real friends. It was an awful feeling, an unrelenting tug at the pit of my stomach.

A few hours later I contemplated the birth of a new grey winter's day, long and cold.

Chapter Eleuen

Cockle

*The seed of this plant when seen under the microscope
shows a resemblance to a curled up hedgehog.*

They let me out very early. The cobbled walkways and courtyards
were empty as I walked beneath the blanket grey sky. Birds sang
frantically, no doubt trying to keep warm. Through the fog I
saw the outline of a large man the size of a wine barrel waiting
outside the Bulwark Gate. It could only be Dowling. What
words of wisdom would he have prepared for me?

When he saw me he hurried over, took my hand as if to
shake it, but instead gripped it hard and squeezed it, whilst
peering into my swollen eye. In truth I must have looked
terrible. I hadn't slept well, the eye throbbed – as did most
of my ribs and both my thighs, and I felt like my head was
floating two feet above my neck.

'I'm well enough. Tell me what happened while we walk.'
We made our way slowly up Great Tower Street up towards
the City.

'I was allowed to see him in the morning.' He walked with his shoulders scrunched, hands in pockets, looking at the dirt beneath his feet. 'I stayed awhile, waited for them to come and collect him.'

'How was he?'

'Calm. He told me of the trial. They made him stand before the Lord Chief Justice with his back to the court. The Lord Chief Justice said that he would not look into the face of Satan. Various fellows, one after the other, all appeared before the court and told the same story, that they had seen Joyce running from Bride's with blood on his hands, screaming like a devil, with black spirits clambering about his back, attacking him with their talons. He was there two hours listening to the same tales. At the end of it the Lord Chief Justice asked him if he had anything to say. He said, "I think the poorest man in England is not at all bound in a strict sense to that government that he hath not a voice to put himself under."'

'Fine words,' I noted, dubiously.

'They were Rainsborough's words at the Putney Debates.'

'Of course.' The Putney Debates took place twenty years ago, at a time when the army still pretended to rule in place of the King. Rainsborough was a Leveller.

'Aye, but the Lord Chief Justice flew into a frenzy according to Joyce. Jumped to his feet and started shouting and screaming. He had to be becalmed, while Joyce just stood there wondering what he'd said.'

'Odd fish.'

'Aye. Anyhow, Joyce had a better perspective than we did on the certainty of his fate. He was resigned to it.' Dowling laid a meat plate on my shoulder once more. 'He bore you no malice, Harry.'

I didn't need Joyce's perspective to establish the futility of my efforts. 'What next?'

'The old cleric from St Andrew Hubbard came, the fiery fellow with wild white hair. He had been drinking beforetimes to give himself strength methinks. It was he that hung the cross round Joyce's neck. Then they bound him tight. They were all in there, pushing him, prodding him, waiting for him to struggle so they could give him a good beating, but he didn't protest at all. But then, just as they're leading him out, he turned round, and spake out clear as you like, 'Villains!' I thought they would beat him then, but he stared right into their eyes, standing to attention like an old soldier. He looked like a soldier too, even with the cuffs of his jacket halfway up his elbows and his trousers halfway up his knees.'

We walked on past the Custom House, towards the Bridge. At the crossroads with Fish Street Hill we had to stop and wait in a crowd of pedestrians, carriages and sedans. As more traffic arrived from behind we found ourselves jostled and cramped.

'What's going on?' Dowling shouted to a coachman a few yards ahead, up on his seat.

'Turkeys,' the coachman shouted back, shrugging, 'thousands of them.'

Dowling strained his neck above the melee and fidgeted a while, then apparently resigned himself to the delay. 'He stood there like the King himself, looking down on them like they was brutes, which of course they was. You could see they saw it too, didn't know how to respond. Then he looked at one of them and said, "Thou art dull indeed." Thou art dull indeed! As God's my witness, it was the funniest thing I ever saw! The cleric called them to order, told them to stop their growlings and get him to the cart.'

Didn't sound funny to me. There was a clearing in the crowd just ahead of us. Two men ran frantically in circles chasing the birds. 'Did you go with the cart?'

'They allowed me as far as Sepulchras. After that I made my own way to Tyburn. My cousin set his own cart up there. There was a big crowd outside Newgate blocking the gate and stopping the cart from setting off. There were four that went, Joyce and three others, but the crowd was there for Joyce. They threw apples, some old cabbage, but it just bounced off his head. The throwing soon stopped because the guards were having it worse than Joyce. Two of them went into the crowds with their sticks.'

'Who were the other three?'

He pulled me by my jacket, stepping nimbly between a sedan and a woman carrying a pail on her shoulder. I tried to keep up with him so he wouldn't stretch the cloth. 'I don't know, none was interested, it was our Joyce they talked about. But they were all three of them drunk as lords. They started to sing as soon as the cart began to roll. Only Joyce wouldn't take a drink. Like I told you, I went with them as far as Sepulchras. The mob was quiet there, wanting to hear what the clerk had to say, listen to the prayers. He gave each one a small bunch of winter flowers. The drunkards took them and made fun of him, which made the crowd angry. They were angry at Joyce besides, for he just ignored the flowers. The clerk tossed them into his lap in the end, had done with it.'

'He was bound, though, you said?'

'Well aye, he was, that's true, and the only one bound. Reckon they thought they'd keep him tied for his own protection. The other three wasn't. They all three took the ale keenly enough, sat around telling each other stories. Like an alehouse on wheels it was, but with Joyce sitting in the corner like Death.'

The crowds pressed in, squeezing me up against the wheel of a coach. Dowling eased me forwards and off it with one trunk-like forearm. People started to shout, complaining at the squash. Just as I thought my ribs might break, the pressure was relieved and the crowd surged forward. We were carried with it, Dowling as helpless as I, over the crossroads, turkeys running in a panic about our feet, feathers everywhere. At the first opportunity we stepped off the main thoroughfare and into narrow Candlewick Lane. A turkey followed us, gobbling and grumbling.

'I left them there and hurried off to Tyburn. Took me best part of half an hour, the crowds were so thick. No room for a horse or coach. I had to run around the alleys and side roads, but he had a good spot, my cousin, only twenty yards from the gallows. Getting to it was the problem.'

I stopped to take a breath. The crowd had pushed hard onto every tender spot on my body. It felt like I was being beaten up again. I waved away Dowling's fussy concern. 'Go on.'

'The mood was altered by the time they got to Tyburn. Joyce was still in a world of his own, if you ask me. But the other three had lost their nerve. Either they didn't have enough ale or else had too much. Twitching and scratching, wiping their brows and hair, rubbing themselves, licking their lips. They were looking for salvation by that time, but the guards were roused. Having pushed their way through the mob for three miles, been spat on and thrown at, they were of a wicked, foul temper. The crowd had eyes like foxes staring at chickens. Whichever way you looked there was a sea of heads. God's eyes, did they get frightened! They started running about the cart, looking to jump off it into the crowd. Course, the crowd thought that was great fun, just kept picking them up and throwing them back in. Great sport it was, until one of the guards climbed up and started thrashing about with his stick. Then the three of them quietened down, just sat there shivering, terrified almost to death they was, poor souls. Must be a lonely feeling. Hearing the big roar, knowing it's for your own death.'

I felt sick.

'Packed to the galleries, it was. They had two wooden stands set up and they were full. Must have been six or seven thousand. Hanging from windows, perched on the rooftops, leaning from poles and sills. Anyway, as they come up to the gallows, Joyce stood up. The women screamed, all frightened and excited. But Joyce just stood there grinning, grinning I tell you. I never saw anyone look less afraid. People was throwing things at him, but somehow they all missed. Some poor fool hit one of the soldiers with an orange, soon regretted that. The soldier lets out a bellow louder than the bells of Paul's and goes running after him with his pike. Then the crowd sets on him, and it's a right mess. There was almost a riot.'

'And Joyce was alright?'

'Oh aye, he was alright, surveying it all like a badly dressed angel. Things quickened up a bit then; I think the soldiers were keen for it all to end. Four of them lifted him right up into the air for everyone to see. That got the crowd roaring again.' Dowling took a deep breath. 'Then I think his nerve failed him a moment. His knees buckled and he looked up to the sky with his eyes wide open and his mouth gaping. He said something, I don't know what, then fell down and the soldiers had to carry him.'

I felt my eyes fill. 'God have mercy.'

He put an arm around my shoulder. 'Aye, but then he righted himself. He stood up straight again and looked out at the crowd. I could see the right-hand side of his head clearly. Peaceful, I swear.'

'You're pulling my leg.'

'Well, you may say. But I tell you I never saw a wrinkle of remorse. At peace with himself, he was.'

'Aye, well hopefully some others saw that too.'

'People come to a hanging for the show, Harry, they don't come for sober reflection and philosophy.'

'So then they hung him.'

'Aye. The crowd shouted so loud you must of heard it in the Tower. Hangman put the rope round his neck and the crowd went quiet, waiting for him to beg for his life. Holding its breath.'

'Did he beg then?'

'No, just looked up at the sky. The other three were crying and wailing like women, but Joyce actually smiled, grinned over the top of the rope that was wrapped around his throat.'

'You go too far.'

'I'm telling you he smiled. Once the horse was smacked – well *then* he shat himself, his tongue popped out and started going black and all those things, but before that, he smiled.'

I looked away. 'Did they cut him?'

'Aye, they cut him,' Dowling growled and scratched at his cheek. 'One of the soldiers took a blade and cut him from his groin up to his ribs. Three cuts. Did it well.' A look of respect came into his eyes for just a second. 'Then he reached inside his gut, pulled out his innards and set them alight in front of his eyes. Though I think he was dead by then. Then they let him down and cut him into pieces, showed the crowd his head and his heart.'

'I wager the crowd enjoyed that.'

'The mouths of the wicked devoureth iniquity.'

I really had to sit down, and Dowling saw it too. I persuaded him to come with me to a coffee house close by on Eastcheap. We found ourselves a quiet spot where we sat in silence for some minutes, while we waited for coffee to be poured and while I waited for the worst of the pain to subside. Dowling sat with the top of his head forward, looking into my eyes with his mouth set grim. This was not the self-assured Dowling of a few days ago.

'So, Davy,' I managed to speak without my ribs breaking, 'Mary Bedford is dead and now Richard Joyce. Neither our doing, but I don't give much credit to our efforts neither. Do we stop here – tell the story that the affair is ended with the hanging of Joyce? You and I both know it wasn't he that did it.'

'Aye,' Dowling nodded gravely, 'and we have the husband to consider.'

John Giles, of course. The chicken running headless while the fox sits complacently in its lair biding its time. 'What do we do, then, about Hewitt?'

Dowling wriggled on his seat. 'I will talk to the Mayor again, but it will not be easy. He will want to know why we concern ourselves with Hewitt now that Joyce is dead.'

He was right. The Mayor would be a waste of time. 'I will go to Cocksmouth,' I said. 'Perhaps I can establish the source of this mystery there. There is some devilry at the root of this which I do not yet comprehend.'

'Would you have me come with you?' Dowling asked.

It was kind of him, but he didn't know what he was volunteering for. I declined the offer and we went our own ways.

Cocksmouth. Cocksmouth was north and west, beyond Buckingham. It was a long journey and I would be gone from London at least three days. Plenty of time for reflection.

My father was not an educated man, a deficiency that I did not hold against him, God knows. Yet I could not fathom why he made such importance of the need for me to study at Cambridge on the one hand, yet behaved with such stubborn disregard for good logic and sense on the other hand – if ever it came from my mouth. Whatever opinion I expressed, observation I made, could be guaranteed to elicit contradiction. The same determination that I should enjoy greater fortune than he appeared to stir a bitter jealousy against me. His head was like a sealed globe within which wild storms continually raged. Whenever he opened his mouth a violent gale blew. My own policy to deal with such contrariness was to remain silent in his presence. The fewer words I spoke, the kinder the climate. So. Tomorrow to Cocksmouth. Birthplace of my mother's ancestors. A place where pigs foraged before finding themselves strung up with their guts sliced in the front room of my uncle's house. Godamercy.

I walked south, deep in gloomy thought, pushing through the crowds on Cornhill, heading for the bridge. I walked straight, taking no notice of the tradesmen striding down the streets as if they owned it, shouting out their wares so that all could hear within a half-mile radius.

I hated Shrewsbury and Keeling, and all like them. Before I had never cared, they were the distant purveyors of venerable wisdom. Now they were cold calculating politicians, supreme saviours of their own skin – and hunters of mine. It was mid- afternoon and London's walls felt oppressive, the crowds pestilent. I strode out onto the Bridge and marched down the middle of the road, avoiding the clamourings and cajolings of the shopkeepers. By the time I reached the wooden drawbridge to the Southbank I was sweaty and my temper had subsided into a mere simmering brew of resentment. As the mists thinned I became more aware of my surroundings. I passed beneath the arch of Nonsuch House. Its copper-covered cupolas shone like blood. I turned to gaze upon the heads that waved stiffly on the end of tall wooden poles, grinning teeth and dull hair coated with a fine layer of freezing frost. A peeling face stared sadly at me from the top of its pole with dull mouldy eyes as it swung over the edge of the archway. The meat on the head was white and torn. I recognised Colonel James Turner, wealthy goldsmith and embezzler. I looked into his eyes, noted the jagged cuts about his neck, the ragged state of his head where the crows had been feeding. He had been loved and respected once. Not any more.

No politics here on the Southbank. This was where the poor people lived. No politics because there was no money. This was where the leatherworkers and feltmongers lived, free of the powers and sanctions of the livery companies based north of the river. This was where the breweries were based, the brothels, the worst of the alehouses, and most of London's beggars. The City dignitaries would not allow them to cross the Bridge into the City. It was also the place, I suddenly realised, reading the billings plastered here and there, where Harry Hunks was fighting in about twenty minutes' time.

I hurried towards the bear-ring at Paris Gardens. The

crowds milled around, ordinary folk in working clothes, men mostly, debating the prospects of the dogs against blind Harry. I paid my dues and found a seat. The acrid smell of stale sweat filled the air. There were two or three hundred people crammed into the ring, all crowded round the small arena. A single solid pole stood up in the middle of it. Chained to the pole was a big brown bear, his fur matted and dirty, moulded with his own excrement. Peering forth through streaming eyes, small and caked with hard lumps of dried pus, he waved his nose in the air, seeing what he could through smell and sound, his eyes useless. This was blind Harry Hunks, hero of the Southbank.

Two men jumped out into the arena, one struggling to hold a rope attached to the collar of a huge grey wolfhound, big as a man, its mouth and nose strapped in a leather muzzle. The dog strained forward, eyes and nose and every sinew pointed at the prowling bear. Saliva dripped from its muzzle and it growled in violent greedy anticipation. The two men looked much the same. A small fellow with barrel chest strode out into the ring and began introducing the afternoon entertainment, loud and bellowing, striving to rouse the crowd into a state of excitement. At last the time came and the crowd quietened, expectant. The two men crouched and took off the muzzle and the dog sprang forward, launching itself at the bear's neck. But blind Harry could smell the dog, could hear the dog, and had been waiting for this moment just as avidly as the crowd. With perfect timing the bear rose up onto its haunches and casually swiped a great paw with talons extended. The wolfhound caught the blow across its jaw and ended up in the dirt on its head, tumbling over and against the palings. It rose to its feet unsteady and dizzy, shaking its head, surprised and confused. Blind Harry resumed his prowling, facing away, but fully aware of the dog's whereabouts, its uncertainty and reluctance to continue. Blind Harry roared, and the crowd sat back satisfied, their fears that this giant dog might hurt blind Harry allayed. The dog trotted forward, growling again, but more timorous now, hovering out of blind Harry's range, snapping, dashing forward and backward, looking for an opportunity. But blind Harry was ready every time, a seasoned veteran, too clever by half.

'I love old Harry Hunks, don't you, my lover?' A woman leant across me and put a hand on the top of my thigh. She looked at me with bright, lively, brown eyes, round and wide, laughing, enticing. She allowed her hand to drift across my groin, resting momentarily upon my crotch before withdrawing once more to my thigh, then away.

'Aye.' I nodded.

'Let me take you to the Leaguer, lover. We're all clean at the Leaguer, can take away all that anger I see in your face.' She smiled, lips parted, her teeth white and clean. She looked at me with an excitement of her own, the anticipation of a done deal.

'Aye. Why not.' I stood and let her lead me by the hand.

It was a little while later that it again occurred to me that I had been displaying less wit than a Kynchen cove and less fortitude than Agnes Hobson. I had to take to heart the lesson of blind Harry Hunks, and I had to begin by visiting my father.

Chapter Twelue

Hempe
It is very probable the male avoids the female for no other reason than that of nourishment, and the female the male because it is like the hop in being a gross feeder.

'He's gone.' My mother stared into space out of her one good eye. She always stared into space, for she was afraid of people, afraid that they would pick her words to pieces and make her feel foolish.

'What do you mean – gone?' I stood opposite her, ducking and weaving, trying to place my face in her eyeline. Her hand wandered up to her eyepatch – whereupon I stepped back hastily and let her look where she wished. It was a strategy she used that if any got too close, then her hand would go to the eyepatch and lift it. You did not want to see what lay under the eyepatch.

'He went away the day before yesterday.' Her hand stopped in mid-air and slowly sank back to her lap.

'Aye, he did,' her brother Robert called from the table. I

turned to face him, though it was an even more disgusting sight than my mother's ravaged eye. He sat at the table with his stomach hanging naked out of his torn shirt. Grease dripped from his chin and pieces of half-chewed pork flew across the room towards where he spoke. At the moment he was speaking to me.

I sidled around the room to position myself behind a giant pig carcass. The head sat in a dish on the table in front of Robert's right elbow. Its lazy eyes followed me about the room as I walked. 'Where did he go?'

'Don't know,' Robert wiped his sleeve across his mouth, then sneezed. I will not describe one of Robert's sneezes in detail, nor the consequences of it. This place was a disgusting and dirty hovel, populated by imbeciles and Whoballs. It was the country. My mother slowly turned her head towards me, her good eye momentarily making contact with mine before slipping away again to regard the earthy floor. I remembered who had done that to her eye and how. It was a recollection that still froze my thoughts.

'He went with two men.' Robert wiped a palm across his hair so that strands of it stood on end.

My disgust for this place was suddenly forgotten. In the context of events to date, his words made the hairs on my neck prickle. 'What two men?'

Robert picked up a rib and stabbed it at me. He was offering me it to eat. I declined. Shrugging, he started to chew at it himself, making sure he had a mouth full of meat before replying.

'One was the same man what came a week or so ago and helped him write that letter. The second man I have never seen before.' Sticking out his bottom lip and furrowing his brow, he looked to my mother. 'I think they were friends of his from London, wasn't they?'

'I don't know.' My mother shook her head slowly. 'He didn't say nothing to me.'

'What were their names?'

'Din't say.'

I regarded them both with critical eye. My mother sat calm with her hands on her lap, peering at something on the ceiling. Robert drew a pork rib across the edge of his front teeth in an attempt to clean it of every speck of meat that still clung to it. Neither was worried in the least – yet he had left the day before yesterday?

'Tell me what they looked like.'

'They were dressed like city folk, Harry!' Robert screwed up his face and talked to me like I was the idiot. 'They was dressed like you.'

'Where did they go?'

'Don't know. He din't tell us, did he?' Robert belched and noticed his stomach was uncovered. He fiddled with the edges of his shirt then cast an eye in my mother's direction. I hoped she washed it before she attempted to mend it.

'You have no idea where he went?'

'He'll be back,' Robert declared confidently.

'None round here know where he went?'

'You could ask.'

I could stand it no longer. I found that I had stopped breathing, holding my breath that I would not say something that I would later feel ashamed of. I looked to my mother.

'One of the men came here and wrote a letter. Tell me about that.'

Upon seeing that I spoke to my mother Robert stretched

his arms wide, swivelled his beady eyes about his head a few times, then stood up with a mighty grunt. He shuffled out the door in the direction of his shed and was gone.

We were left there, my mother and I, in sad silence. I let the question sit, knowing that she would answer it once she was sure that the words she planned were the best she could think of. I sat myself on the other side of the room with my hands between my knees and looked away.

Finally she spoke. 'They wrote it in here, at the table.'

I looked at the table.

'He told me to leave them alone,' she said quietly, nodding her head in the direction of the back room. 'I went in there.'

I looked towards the back room. My grandmother lay in there with her eyes closed, breathing quietly.

That was it. My mother said no more.

I asked everyone in Cocksmouth if they had seen my father, or could tell me in what direction he had gone with the two men. All that I established was that they had headed south, on the main road to London. I stopped at Byddle and Haremear, the next two villages along the road, but learnt nothing new. Since my face was not known in those parts it was optimistic to expect that I would be told anything – if indeed there was anything to tell.

Fact was – my father was missing.

Chapter Thirteen

Penny-royall
Pulegium when dry is said to flower in midwinter.
Costaeus tells the same story and says there is a similar
example in the case of the Black woodpecker, whose body
hung up by a string has been observed to shed its
old feathers in the Spring and grow new ones.
Both these stories are not worthy of belief.

It took us three hours to get to Epsom – the roads were frozen into hard ridges. I was bounced up and down between roof and seat like a rubber ball. After much experimentation I found a comfortable position with one arm wrapped around the frame of the coach window and one leg held out straight across the seat. Dowling sat opposite me with his baggy, blue cloth cap pulled down over his ears, eyelids drooping, trying hard to stay awake. His guts must have been full of iron shot. My teeth started to rattle.

He was a good man to have on your side, I reflected, even though he was so filthy smelly. When I'd told him what I found at Cocksmouth he had fussed over me like a big, fluffy white hen – assuring me that he would talk to the Mayor, that he would be successful in commandeering enough men to scour the roads between here and Cocksmouth. It was some comfort insofar as I knew it was all that could be done. But they would not find him. Someone had taken him.

We hit a ridge so hard that my legs left the seat and my head hit the roof with such force that I saw lights twinkling before me. I cursed so loudly that Dowling opened one eye and frowned at me disapprovingly. Hill! The knock had juggled my brains and Hill's face appeared before me. I had told Hill that I was going to Cocksmouth before I was locked up in the Tower. Hill, my great friend, who was now snug in Shrewsbury's pocket. I felt an urge to stop and persuade the driver to turn round, go back to London so that I could find Hill, make him talk to me. I sat staring out of the window, not looking at the terrible dreary scenery we passed. No. He had urged me to go to Epsom. It was the only advice he had. If he wanted us to go to Epsom, then we would go. Let's see what he had in store for us. Though I felt like the man that takes an hour to step out onto the ice, only to crash through it and drown.

When we arrived I climbed out of the coach onto Ormonde's driveway with legs of jelly and something trying to drill its way out through my forehead. Dowling stepped out sleepily and took a deep lungful of cold, clean air before smiling happily. The only sound was that of crows complaining in the distant woods. It was an angry, lonely noise that cast a morbid tone upon the frosted fields and the silent, square white house with its big, black empty windows. I noticed a patch of catmint nestled in the grass close to the front door. *If you set it, the cats will eat it; if you sow it, the cats can't know it.*

Another old servant wandered out of the front door to meet

us. The world was full of doddery old servants it seemed. With great enthusiasm Dowling stepped forward to greet him. They had a laugh and a joke about something. It gave me time to empty the contents of my stomach discreetly behind the coach. Our coachman shook his head and regarded me with offended eyes, like it was some comment upon his wretched driving. I spat the last of it and immediately the air tasted fresher and my soul breathed easier.

Dowling appeared at my shoulder. 'He says that William Ormonde is not at home, but that he will ask if we may talk with Mary Ormonde.'

The servant stood waiting for us, blinking anxiously. Once he saw us walking towards him, he turned and trotted back towards the house, hurrying to be first across the threshold. Inside it was much colder and darker than I remembered it. Tapestries hung on the walls I had not noticed the last time, old and frayed, colours faded. Water dripped somewhere, its slow rhythm the only sound to be heard.

Dowling took off his hat and stuck it in his pocket. 'A man might hear a mouse sneeze.'

'We don't receive many visitors. Just Mr Ormonde and his daughter.' The servant coughed breathlessly and bowed again. He led us past a square, wooden staircase with dark polished surface down a dingy corridor. At the end of it was a large room with good light soaking through long windows. Mary Ormonde stood amidst a collection of old embroidered chairs. The room smelt damp and I could almost feel the water clinging to my skin, pervading my clothes. I imagined the chairs to be wet to the touch.

'Please sit,' Mary Ormonde gestured. She still wore mourning clothes, a dark dress that fitted snug about her hips. Her eyes were still bright green, and still stared straight into my soul. Smiling at me gently, she stood calm like an old friend. 'An *unexpected* visit,' she said.

'Aye.' I sat down on one of the chairs. It seemed to be dry.

Her scent drifted up my nose and I immediately started to think about renewing intimate acquaintance. She sat with hands folded neatly on her lovely lap. 'What happened to your head?'

'I was hit on the head in the process of seeking who it was killed your sister.'

She nodded and looked at us both enquiringly, as if to ask why we had come back when all was been and done. 'The man Joyce.'

Dowling spoke with a low sombre tone. 'We think that the Lord Chief Justice has hung an innocent man.'

'An innocent man?' She pursed her lips and sounded very disappointed. Like someone's dog had died. Then she resumed her previous pose and looked at us both with that enquiring gaze again. No sign of remorse. Then she lifted a finger into the air and pursed her beautiful lips again. Those lips transfixed me, luscious and ripe. 'If this man Joyce did not kill my sister, then why was he hung for it?'

'There lies a question, madam.'

'Indeed. Lord Keeling himself tried Joyce, I understand.'

We both nodded.

'My father has known Lord Keeling all his life, you know. They grew up together. Lord Keeling lived in Epsom when he was a little boy.'

There are moments in your life when the same object you have been looking at for months or years suddenly appears different. Breasts are a good example. A baby boy would never suckle on a breast in quite the same way if he had the same perspective on it that he later develops. This is nature and the way that it is intended, of course. It would be no good at all otherwise, else all the little boy babies would never stop drinking milk and would grow up to be very fat. This was one of those moments. William Hill had sent us here for a reason, and Mary Ormonde was going to tell us what that was.

'You know Lord Keeling, then?'

She looked surprised – sort of. 'My father does. They were great friends. He shares many of my father's principles.'

'What principles?'

Leaning forward, she looked at us both conspiratorially. It was a strange pose to adopt with two strangers to talk about your father. I felt a bit awkward, Dowling too, by the look of it. 'My father was a Baptist. Lord Keeling was also a Baptist while he lived at Epsom.'

Dowling gave a little gasp. I had never heard Dowling gasp before, but it was a good time to gasp. Baptists were radicals – dissenters. Though Cromwell tolerated Baptists – barely – now their views were outlawed. That the Lord Chief Justice was once a Baptist was barely credible. Why was Mary Ormonde telling us such things – especially about her own father? Her green eyes watched us carefully, watched us absorb her words.

'It was a long time ago, gentlemen.' She shook her head and watched us some more. Once she was satisfied, she continued. 'Keeling moved to London many years ago. He took his family with him, Jane included. Jane was his daughter. She was good friends with Anne, even though she was ten years older. Anne was upset when they went. They lived in the big house in town. Now a family called Latham lives there. Good people.'

'None of Keeling's family remain?'

'No. Only Mrs Johnson. She's was Janie's nanny, as well

160

as ours. She lives by herself now since her husband died. She was left with a roof over her head, so she will not marry again unless she wishes it.'

'She knew Keeling well?'

'She was *employed* by him when they were here. When they went to London she stayed behind. Jane lodged with her when she came to visit. That was before she died.'

I was confused. 'Who died?'

'Jane Keeling.'

I determined to stay calm. So Anne Giles is murdered and Keeling holds his own trial behind closed doors to see that the man accused of it is condemned. And his own daughter died here a long time ago. This was surely significant.

'What did Jane Keeling die of?'

'A fever – so they said.'

'So they said?'

'Yes.'

'What happened?'

'I would really rather not talk about it, Harry. You might talk to Mrs Johnson who was the nanny.'

I tried to avoid Dowling's eye that was looking at me in puzzlement once she used my name. 'Where might we find her?'

'I'll point you in the right direction once you are ready to leave, Harry.' I wished she would stop doing that. 'What else would you like to know?'

Dowling spoke up. 'Tell us about your sister.'

'Anne.' Mary Ormonde spoke the word affectionately, 'She was three years younger than me. People said that we were very much alike.'

'Did you see her often once she was married?'

'I didn't see her at all. Father forbade me to visit her. She did not come back to Epsom, and I could not go to London without my father's blessing. I have not seen her this past two years, not since a week after her eighteenth birthday. She went with John to his local church to marry without telling any. St Ethelburga near Bishopsgate.' She sat straight, her back rigid as a pole. 'Our family has been at Epsom for many generations. The manner of Anne's leaving of it cast shame onto my father.'

'Worse for John Giles's father, was it not?'

She shook her head regretfully. 'It was of no comfort to my father, I assure you. He is a devout man, but not heartless. The people of the parish assumed that it was his wish that the man be hung, so hung he was. From that time they have behaved with great restraint towards us. I think that they are afraid of us.'

'What was life like for you as children?' Dowling changed the subject.

'Our mother was taken when I was ten. She died in childbirth, as did the infant. There were three besides Anne and I, that all died young. You might have seen their stones at Anne's funeral. Father is a devout man and instructed us in God's word himself. He also encouraged us to read and write, and employed a tutor to teach us the Classics, Hebrew, Latin and Greek. We played together, and with Mrs Johnson, Beth, who cared for us after Mother died.'

'How did your sister meet John Giles?'

'He came from London to visit his father, who worked for a tenant of my father's. One day we ventured into the fields to eat our lunch, Anne, Beth and I. John just appeared. He had the cheek and charm of the Devil himself, and looks to match. He carried bottles of beer in his pack and made us have a sip.

Then he showed us how to dance. Beth would not permit it, so he danced with her instead.'

'Did Beth not tell your father?'

She smiled. 'We begged her not to, it was so exciting, you see. And how could she explain that she danced with him?'

'She was charmed as well, was she?'

'No,' she laughed, 'not Mrs Johnson. I think she thought it was good for us, two young ladies. The days could be very dull you know.'

'An unfortunate judgement, perhaps.'

'What passed between John Giles and Anne was none of Mrs Johnson's doing.' She raised a finger in admonishment. 'The credit for that belongs to my father, God knows, and he has paid dearly for it ever since.'

Dowling leant forward with hands clasped. 'How so?'

'Had he not forbidden Anne from seeing John, then she would never have eloped. John was exciting and charming, but Anne was not simple. Her attentions would have been diverted to another soon enough, some devout young man from the town. But father forbade her to see him, and Anne was stubborn. She got that from him. Then father made up his mind not to give John the dowry. What he should have done was to give John a job, keep him at Epsom, keep Anne safe and sound. But he did neither, so Anne came to be married to John, and lived in a pigsty at Bishopsgate, while he went off at all hours of the day and night doing whatever he could to make a penny.'

'How did they manage to court each other with you and Beth in tow?'

'We didn't realise they were courting. They seemed very fond of each other, and we would leave them sitting and talking sometimes, but we never went far away. Only after they declared their betrothal was I sensible to Anne's feelings.'

Haw, haw, quoth Bagshaw – a likely story.

'I liked him, Mr Lytle, liked him very much and so did Beth. He was a nice man, hardly a man even. He was bold and dashing and full of notions as to what he would make of his life. He wasn't deceiving her; he really did have those ambitions for himself. He was not fain to work on a farm like his father, he was resolute to have his own business in London, acquire some money of his own and grow it, become wealthy.'

Idle, in other words. 'What happened when they announced their plans to marry?'

'When John called at the house, father didn't recognise him, he didn't know his youngest daughter was being courted. He picked up a cane and threatened to beat John with it. Then he summoned two of the servants and commanded them to carry John out of the grounds, where I know that they thrashed him. Father carried on shouting at Anne, you could hear it in all parts of the house. He forbade Anne to see John, said that she was a lady and he was a rogue and a vagabond. But Anne stood up to him. She wouldn't hear his argument. The louder and more frantic father became, the quieter and harder Anne became. By his own actions he ensured that what he feared most came to pass.'

'And then they eloped?'

'Indeed.' She nodded again and sat expectantly, but my poor brain was addled, still trying to appreciate the significance of Jane Keeling's death, and Dowling seemed lost in his own thoughts.

She watched us for a while, a small smile upon her lips. Then she stood and walked out of the room, obliging us to follow. 'You can always come back, gentlemen. Now let me show you how to get to Mrs Johnson's cottage.' I positioned myself behind her so I could watch her swing those fleshy hips.

'A strange woman,' Dowling reflected once we left her behind.

'An odd fish,' I agreed.

'She was very familiar with you,' he noted, clearly troubled.

I shrugged. 'Aye, well, when I was here last time she took me to a quiet room, hitched up her skirts and gave me her strawberry.'

Dowling stopped stock-still in the driveway with his mouth wide open. I fancied there'd be no sympathetic mitt on my shoulder for the rest of the day. He resumed walking, though lagged behind. I heard his steps on the stones.

'It was you that said I should get to know people easily and make myself open to them.'

'Harry! It is no laughing matter!'

'No. But she is an odd fish and no mistake. You said so yourself.'

Dowling recited some phrases from the Good Book as he attempted to soothe his affronted soul. It was quite entertaining. By the time we reached Mrs Johnson's house he had at least stopped twittering and fiddling with the edge of his coat.

Mrs Johnson was a small woman with white hair. Her clothes were old and neat, maintained meticulously with needle and thread. She flashed a happy smile when we explained who had sent us. Her parlour was clean and polished and furnished with bright, shiny furniture and dazzling white linen. Bustling about her table and four chairs, circling, she fretted over which chairs to pull out for us to sit on and then brought out bread and butter for us to eat.

'Tell me about London, Mr Lytle,' she demanded, sitting perched on the end of her chair, knees clasped together and hands folded on her lap. 'Is it busy there?'

'Yes, Mrs Johnson, very busy.'

'Is it dirty?'

'Aye, truth is, it is dirty.' Filthy.

'They have ladies there who take money for carnal vulgarity and lewdness?'

'Aye, they do,' I replied seriously, which was one of its great attractions.

'If you are not careful, men strike you down and take your money. They have places where you can go and see animals tear each other to pieces. There are men there that drink too much every night. They hang people.'

All true of course, but it was not Londoners that put John Giles's father to death. 'Aye, quite often. London is a busy city and all manner of things take place there.'

'Is it a depraved place?' Mrs Johnson beamed with shiny metal eyes.

'There is much that's depraved.'

'Good.' Mrs Johnson stared at me as if she was trying to catch sight of something flitting about behind my eyes. I think that she sought to goad me into argument. It did not concern *me* that funny old women from the country did not share my love of London.

Dowling cleared his throat. 'You've lived here all your life?'

'Yes,' she replied, 'but you didn't come here to talk about me, although it is very sweet of you to ask. Now ask your questions, because I'm sure you have more interesting things to do than sit in a parlour with a little old lady.'

I let Dowling talk. One old woman to another. 'We would like to know more about the children. Anne, Mary and Jane. You looked after Jane when she was a girl?'

'What a question.' She gave me a mock suspicious look. 'Why do you want to know about three little girls? They were like any other little girls. They played little girls' games and talked little girls' talk.'

'What was Jane like?' I asked.

She cocked her head like a sparrow. 'She was very tall and very pale, thin, with hair like a raven. Her eyes were dark brown, almost black. Sometimes you could imagine that she understood every word you said, saw every thought you had, like an angel almost. It was easy to forget she was simple. She died a long time ago.'

'Of a fever?'

She smiled wistfully and held her hands together a little anxiously. 'No,' she shook her head slowly, 'though it is the official record. She died by her own hand. She walked off into the marshes and jumped into a pool. She couldn't swim and so she drowned.'

'Why did she take her own life?'

'She became morose. I don't know why. She was always bright and lively, always laughing. She had a lovely laugh, Mr Lytle, like a little bell. Then she changed.'

'I wonder why?'

'Things happen and nature is unpredictable. They say that a noisy boy grows up to be a noisy man but it's not always true. Nature is less predictable than that. Janie had a little fire that burnt bright in her little heart, but it was as if, as her heart grew bigger, the flame did not. She was a simple soul.' She stared into space and I let her mind wander a while. 'It was ten years ago. She died at twenty. She was foul to everyone when she came back the last time, even to Annie, and she did love little Annie.'

'Madam, how long did Keeling live in Epsom?'

'Until Jane was fifteen, some fourteen or fifteen years ago. Then they moved to London. I wouldn't go, but he let her come and stay with me sometimes. She liked that. But not the last time. Her spirit was sick. Some days she seemed happy, but it was a wild happiness, not real.'

'Were you there when she died?'

'She was staying here, yes. She told me she was going for a walk, and so she did, about four o'clock in the afternoon. She went to the marshes where there is nothing to see and where she knew it was dangerous. She jumped into a pool. They pulled her out next morning.'

'How do you know she jumped?'

'The surgeon that looked at her couldn't find a mark on her, and besides, she left me a note.'

'What did it say?'

'It said "Goodbye".' She tapped her fingers on the table. 'She never left me a note before, she didn't write notes.'

'Who was the surgeon?'

'John Stow. He lives at the other end of town. Turn left up the road and walk on a quarter of a mile or so. If you get lost then just ask anyone where he lives, everyone knows it. But you cannot miss it, he has a plate on the wall with his name on it.'

She began to arrange some flowers that lay on a side table. Humming a little tune, she left us to ourselves. After one last look around the parlour we announced our departure.

Without looking up she made an affectionate, quiet farewell.

We set off to see this man Stow, me reflecting that beneath it all, Mrs Johnson was pleased to see us go.

Stow's house was not far from the town pond, around which was a cluster of small houses and shops. The door was answered by a small woman, dressed plainly, with a billowing white cap holding her hair. We walked out into the garden and found John Stow sitting in a chair. The small garden was full of little apple trees. He was lying back with his nose up in the air and his mouth wide open, snoring majestically. Next to the chair stood an empty jug that smelt of ale, and a plate of cream. A tight, round, little pot belly sat like a ball above his short little legs. His arms hung limp. It was a cold and frosty day.

'He likes his air,' the woman told me, loudly.

'He's taking a big chance sitting out here on a day like this.' A good way to catch a cold fever.

'Oh no,' the woman shouted, 'he says it blows the dampness off his chest. He's always trying to get me to join him, but I can't sleep when he snores like that and my chest is dry.' She leant over and grasped his nose between the fingers of her right hand. He continued to snore muffled snores for a short time before he woke, coughing and spluttering.

'I've told you before not to wake me like that, woman.' He coughed and spluttered some more before hawking phlegm onto the grass, clambering to his feet and grunting in surprise. The woman, his wife I supposed, went back to the house singing. What did she have to be so happy about?

'Who are you, sir?' He stumbled forward, his legs and head still slumbering. I offered my hand, which was taken limply before being dropped. 'Ah,' he squinted at me and eyed me carefully from toe to head, 'and what is wrong with you? I am a surgeon, not a physic.'

'Nothing. We've come to ask you some questions about a matter that happened here ten years ago.'

'Was I in this affair?'

'Indeed. Ten years ago a girl wandered out into the marshes. Her name was Jane Keeling.'

He immediately paled and his fleshy face went lumpen. 'Ah,' he licked his lips, 'I remember.'

'The King depends on it.' This was a big lie, but I reckoned he was a mooning Royalist. Dowling stared at me like I was the Devil himself, but I paid no heed.

'I have already told him that everything he has asked me to accomplish depends upon your willingness to help him,' I said officiously. I imagined that I was Keeling's obnoxious aide. 'Tell me what happened.'

He looked at me with pleading eyes. 'There is little to tell. She took her own life, there was no doubt. She wrote a letter to her nanny with whom she was staying, then she walked out to the marshes and jumped into a bog and drowned. She couldn't swim.'

'How do you know she jumped in? How do you know that she wasn't taken to the marsh and thrown into the bog?'

'She couldn't have. She left a note with the nanny, I told you. She was seen walking on her own, and she didn't have a mark on her. She must have jumped in by herself.' He made a visible effort to keep his hands still, finally sitting on them.

I walked over to the apple tree into whose branches Stow was staring, and leant against it. 'We've spoken to Mrs Johnson, Dr Stow. The note said "Goodbye", it did not say "Goodbye – I am going to jump in a bog". That she was seen walking to the marshes on her own doesn't mean that she didn't meet somebody. If she couldn't swim, then all it would have taken is a little push and she would have fallen in and drowned quickly, without marks. How can I convince the King that your verdict was correct, Mr Stow?'

'We found her there that night with her brown dress blooming upon the surface of the pool like a dead lily. We found her with torches. A crowd of us went, after Beth Johnson told us she was missing. When we fished her out she was white and pale, but her face was peaceful.' He wrung his hands in unhappy memory. 'There was no sign that she died unwillingly.'

'She died on her birthday. A strange day to kill yourself,' I remarked.

'Not if the melancholia has a hold. The days on which others expect you to be happiest can be the hardest. She was very depressed while she was here, Mrs Johnson will have told you. There were no marks on her, no sign of a struggle nor a blow. She most certainly jumped of her own accord. That's the long and the short of it,' he asserted, his mouth set, lower jaw protruded and lips drawn tight.

I was certain that he was holding something back. Why had he gone so pale upon the mention of Jane Keeling's name? 'Mr Stow. If you lie to me, then you lie to the King. That's treason.'

His lip trembled, but he returned my stare with dislike and stubbornness. He said nothing.

'So you would not cooperate with the King.'

'That's not true! I have told you everything you wanted to know!'

'Methinks not, Mr Stow. Once I leave, then your options will be much reduced. For if I discover that you have lied to me, then I will have you arrested for treason.' His eyes goggled and all of his face, except his nose, went white.

'She was with child,' he whispered.

'Who was the father?' I replied, astonished.

'I don't know.' Stow let out a deep breath and sat drooped, looking at the floor. He looked like a man condemned to hang.

An appalling thought struck me suddenly. I turned quickly to Dowling who similarly looked like someone had inserted a large carrot up his rectum. We were so keen to talk to each other that we had to go. Stow watched us leave out the corner of his eye with an expression of unutterable relief.

'An eye for an eye and a tooth for a tooth spells revenge,' I whispered to Dowling as we reached the lane.

'Aye, the same thought occurred to me. Was Anne Giles killed because Jane Keeling was killed?'

We marched quickly. 'Jane Keeling died with child.'

'Yet she was simple.'

'So someone took advantage of her.'

'And Anne Giles was killed as revenge.'

One daughter for another? A devilish thought; yet it had occurred to us both independently. This would imply that William Ormonde had fathered Keeling's child, had used her as his own. I looked at Dowling. He looked shocked, hardly able to meet my eye, just looked to the floor with his mouth grim set, breathing noisily through his nose.

'Are we mad?' I asked him. For this was a mad place. Perhaps it had affected us.

'There is a wicked man that hangeth down his head sadly, but inwardly he is full of deceit.'

That *did* remind me of Ormonde. 'We must confront him.'

'Aye,' Dowling muttered, picking up the pace.

* * *

'Mr Ormonde is not receiving guests, sir.' The old servant came to meet us again. Better than being 'not at home'. 'My master spends his days alone.'

'Aye, then I expect he will relish the opportunity to converse.' I nodded and headed off towards the house. We would have walked through walls had we needed to. The servant blinked and trotted after me. I stopped in the hallway. The servant bustled up behind, rubbing his gloved hands together unhappily. 'My master stays in his study all day.'

'With so little to do outside his study I am not surprised.' I set off briskly down the corridor. Pulling at my jacket he kept urging me to stop and wait, but I paid him no heed, reaching the study door in front of him. I knocked loudly. There was silence. I knocked again. This time the door opened after the sound of key turning in lock. Ormonde stood there in the doorway, face red and ruddy, eyes narrow and shiny, grey hair dishevelled and wild. He leant forward from the waist with his hands on his hips. His legs stood firm, but his trunk trembled.

'Good morning, Mr Ormonde. We are come from London today.' I put a hand against the door and pushed it gently open. A desk stood in the corner of the room, its chair tucked neatly underneath it, its surface free of objects or documents of any kind. I wondered what he did in here, behind locked doors.

'I trust you did not make a special trip for I am not in the mood for talking.' He turned and shuffled back into the room, then sat down in a heavy wooden chair facing away from us so that all we could see was the back of his head. He wore the same coat that he had worn at the funeral, black and old and fraying.

'You know that they have hung a man for the death of your daughter. A man called Joyce.'

Staring out of the window at empty fields leading to thick woods, he sat slouched. 'Who was he?'

'Once a soldier and a landowner. He was struck down on the battlefield. He took an injury so bad that they had to drill holes in his head.'

'Why do they say he killed Anne?' The old man steepled his fingers and looked into space.

'They didn't.'

'Then why did they hang him?' The old man waved a hand impatiently, casting Dowling a quick sideways glance.

'Because the mob saw him running from the church around the time of the killing, and for Keeling that was enough evidence.'

Mumbling something, he gestured feebly with his right hand, a wrinkled claw that protruded from worn cuffs. I sat on the sill of the window through which he was staring.

'Why do you think that Keeling took such a personal interest, sir?'

'He used to be a friend.'

'No more?'

Slumped in the chair, he hid his face. 'We lost contact once he moved to London.'

I looked at Dowling, who stood behind Ormonde. He nodded gently. I sighed before telling him what we had discovered. 'We know that Jane Keeling took her own life ten years ago, on her twentieth birthday, because she was with child. Now another man's daughter has been killed on *her* twentieth birthday, her eyes mutilated and her teeth removed, indications of revenge.' I watched his expressionless dull face. 'Have we intruded upon some private feud?'

As my words sunk in, his eyes widened, his body jerked

in spasm, and a strangled whine escaped his cold blue lips. He stared at me, his tight body twitching, his arm stiff and straight, his hand hovering an inch above his knee. 'Sit down,' he whispered at last.

Neither of us moved.

'Who told you these things?' The old man raised his head slowly, his shoulders still tight and hunched.

'Are they true?'

'You would imply that I fathered the girl's child?' The old man stood and stepped towards me.

'Would you deny it?' I replied, edging sideways.

'Deny it? Naturally, I deny it! You accuse me of the most wicked and foul of all deeds! Who told you that Keeling's daughter was with child? What maul hath unleashed such arrows? All liars shall have their part in the lake, the lake that burneth with fire and brimstone.' He reached me with two long deliberate strides, his hands held out before him like claws.

I stood my ground without raising my hands against him, praying that either he calmed down or that Dowling would step forward to protect me. 'If you speak the truth then you have nothing to fear.'

Ormonde blinked, 'I will ask you one more time, you that speak with black tongue and foul breath. From where did you get these iniquities, this false and vile information?' He let his arms fall to his side. His face was wreathed in hateful disdain.

'I told you that I would not disclose it.'

'Then begone, wretch. But think wisely before you choose to stain my reputation with your vile lies. Put not thine hand with the wicked to be an unrighteous witness. The Lord is the strength of my life; of whom shall I be afraid?' Ormonde laughed, a deep shallow laugh, with no body to it. 'The Lord is *my* helper, and I shall not fear what *man* shall do unto me, for he is mine enemy.'

I took an instant dislike to all and any that shouted Bible quotes at me.

He clasped his hands in front of his waist, sharp smile beneath now hooded eyes. 'Keeling will be full of fury when he hears your accusation. It matters not where the rumour starts, if he hears it then he will now assume that it comes from you. Once it is established that in fact she was not with child, then shall he heap piles of coal on your head. In righteousness, therefore, I am safely established. Good day to thee, Mr Lytle.'

He stepped forward, placed a hand on my shoulder, and with a strength that I had not suspected, tried to propel me towards the door. I was not in the mood to be manhandled by decrepit old Baptists and I stood my ground. Once he realised I had no intention of moving he stood licking his lips, neck crooked, a twisted smile on his bitter face. He stood there frozen for a moment before returning silently to his chair. We watched the back of his scaly head again.

'I was a Baptist,' he said at last. 'So was Keeling. The old King used to send men to arrest people like us. I was imprisoned myself for a short time, about twenty years ago. But his Parliament didn't trust him and after he tried to force money from them to wage war on the Scottish Presbyterians, they killed him. That was the end of it all, I fear, for though those men scoured the Lord's Book and found some words that they said justified their regicide, it was an evil thing that they did. I said nothing then, for I was too passioned by it all, the possibility that man might be free to indulge the indwelling spirit, that he might find his own salvation at last.'

What that had to do with the smell of bacon I had no idea, but I was loath to interrupt. It was an opportunity to learn more about this strange old man.

'Cromwell forsook the dream of Godly reformation in the name of compromise. He spoke to me himself, told me that I lacked prudence, that I might think to avoid the fate of the Fifth Monarchists.'

'What fate?' I asked.

'And in the days of these kings shall the God of heaven set up a kingdom, which shall never be destroyed: and the kingdom shall not be left to other people, but it shall break in pieces and consume all these kingdoms, and it shall stand for ever.'

'Daniel 2: 44. King Nebuchadnezzar's dream,' Dowling said softly.

'Aye, butcher, if butcher is what you be. The Fifth Kingdom. There were many, myself one of them, that believed that the death of the King was a sign from God that the new kingdom was to come. In their eyes Cromwell was God's instrument, he who hath been ordained to make free the path back to Christ. But he betrayed them. He put their leaders into prison. He warned me that my own energies were misdirected, and again I listened. Others did not, I fear, but more than that I fear that they were right, for where now Godly reformation? Where now the new kingdom?'

The old man stood up and walked to the window, from where he looked out onto the dead, frozen countryside. 'It was all for nothing that they killed a King. And now his son is returned, and what do we suppose he thinks of it all?' Ormonde turned to regard me with mocking eyes, looked at my clothes, finer than the old frayed black cloth that he wore. 'He plays games at Court, sets man against man. Why should this King bear any love for us, his people? For there are many of us that were agin him at one time or another, even if we may regret it now. He put to death only those that signed his father's death warrant, the rest of us are free to live, as we will. He could not arrest every man that plotted against him, seize their property, remove them from Court, he does not have that influence. Keeling does not proclaim his past, but it is *no secret.*' He practically shouted the last two words, for no obvious reason. He slumped back into his chair with his hands limp on his lap.

'You are hopeless,' said Dowling.

'Aye. Indeed I would be left in that condition. Now, maybe you would pay me the kindness of leaving me as you find me.'

'Sir, we came on an errand, one which for us does carry hope.'

Ormonde sat silently with eyes closed, ignoring us. What sort of man was this? Old and tired.

'A wicked man hardeneth his face,' Dowling said, breaking his silence.

'As the whirlwind passeth, so is the wicked no more,' Ormonde replied, without looking up. 'Please leave now.'

We stood our ground a while longer, but Ormonde remained motionless, ignoring our presence. There was little more that we could do without more proof.

As soon as we stepped out of the room the door crashed behind us and the key was turned in the lock. Most unwelcoming. I thought to develop our understanding better with Mary Ormonde, but the old servant said that she had left the house and would not be back until the morrow. That was rum too, but no rummer than anything else that had occurred that day.

We talked all the way home. Could it be true – that Ormonde had deflowered his friend's own daughter? Was his violent reaction born out of indignation – or sick fear that his deeds would be publicised? Why had the Lord Chief Justice himself taken such a personal interest in condemning Richard Joyce? There was no love lost between Keeling and Ormonde – that much was now clear – so how could Keeling's involvement be attributed to a desire to help the Ormonde family? Were his efforts instead directed at covering his own misdemeanour? Was it Keeling that killed Anne Giles? Joyce's description of the man he saw at Bride's came to mind – big and bear-like. Hewitt was bear-like – but a very short bear. Keeling was large, yet the idea that the Lord Chief Justice would involve himself in such a wicked affair? And what of Hill in all of this? And Hewitt?

At length, and not without trepidation, Dowling volunteered to talk to some that he knew through the Mayor. He would attempt to probe more into the history between Ormonde and Keeling, that we might develop a better understanding upon which to make our assumptions. When all was said and done, though – we still both believed in our hearts that Hewitt was the beast that murdered Anne Giles, and set ourselves to finding out more about *his* activities.

Chapter Fourteen

Male fern
This plant was hung up in bundles in the Forum Julii on which flies gathered in the evening; they were easily caught when a sack was thrown over each bundle.

At Hill's house the woman that opened the door told me a great lie when she said he wasn't home; I saw his shoes thrown down upon the floor in the hallway. They were the only shoes I'd ever seen him wear these last five years, so if he wasn't at home then he was out and about in his stockings. I did not say as much to the servant for if she spoke a lie then it wasn't hers. I could only assume that Hill was shy of my attentions, so suggested to her that she ask him to meet me at Paul's in one hour, a busy place where we could talk without being noticed. She readily agreed and was happily closing the door upon me when she realised, late, that she could hardly commit to pass on the message to a master who wasn't at home. I cut short her pink-cheeked stutterings, smiled my most charming smile, bowed and took my leave.

I went straight to Paul's. It was my instinct to meet Hill where it was busy. If he had something to do with the disappearance of my father, then I had to regard him as a dangerous enemy, whatever our history.

The cathedral was full. The noise of the printing presses echoed from the eastern vaults, the meat sellers and fruit sellers wandered the nave shouting out the price and quality of their wares. All of London wandered across – east and west – for it was the fastest route between Ludgate and Cheapside. I went out into the churchyard and lingered beneath a great oak tree from where I could see the Cross; the meeting place where Hill would come.

He arrived soon enough, clean, trimmed and fresh. He was looking about him, peering into the grey gloom. He seemed to be alone. There were still folks loitering so I stepped out.

'It's a wet day to be yarning out here, Harry, when we could be tucked up warm in the Crowne.' His breath billowed out into the cold, crisp air like smoke. 'So. What news, Harry? You went to Epsom?' He spoke as a man who knew very well that I went to Epsom.

'Aye.'

'What did you find?'

'It would seem that Keeling's daughter took her own life ten years ago, when secretly carrying a bastard child. She died on her twentieth birthday, the same as Anne Giles.'

'Are you sure?' He looked at me with keen eyes.

I knew what he wanted me to say next. 'Aye. If indeed this affair is about revenge, then the finger points at Keeling. The Lord Chief Justice himself. He is a big man, is he not?'

A change came over William Hill. Whilst before he had stood like he carried the Wisdom of Solomon on his back, now he seemed to float upwards into the grey sky, the arches of his feet curving gracefully upwards. His face changed too, and for a moment I saw the open, carefree expression of the old William Hill, drinker of fine (and not so fine) wines and ales, witty raconteur. Then he blinked and the smile was gone. Yet still he glowed like a fire at the end of a cold winter's night. 'Hold up your head, Harry. Or shall ye have the King's horse?' He punched me on the shoulder, unable to contain himself. His eyes sparkled, laughing with a special delight.

'Why are you so happy to hear of it, William? You are not shocked that I would implicate the Lord Chief Justice?'

He pulled me back towards the dry indoors out of the cold drizzle. 'What did you say when you discovered it, Lytle? It was clear that something strange and evil was at play. Too strange to guess at, but now that the story is told it rings true like these very bells.' He leant close. 'What will you do now?'

'Dowling is going to talk to the Mayor, attempt to establish if there could be any credibility in it.'

His eyes set to twinkling once more; stars sparkled against the black carpet of his oily eyes. 'Excellent.' He patted me on the arm softly and smiled contentedly.

I shook my head. 'Methinks I am still unable to comprehend that the Lord Chief Justice killed a common girl with his own hands. I still believe Hewitt to be the killer.'

Hill grimaced. 'Come, Harry.' He sidled up to me and spoke to me like I was still his younger brother. 'The reason I am so uppity is that your words ring true. I had heard rumours come from Epsom, which is why I insisted that you go. I was afeared that you would not solve this riddle set to you by Shrewsbury, but by heaven I think you have done it! All this business about Hewitt is nonsense. Merchants don't go around murdering people to remedy their woes. If they did then you would not be able to walk the streets without being knocked over by one merchant or another chasing some poor scallywag!'

'You would think so.' I fixed my eyes upon his. 'Yet two men abducted my father three days ago, and he is about as dangerous to any man as a bag of feathers.'

For a moment he looked at me like I held a knife to his balls. Then he recovered and looked at me as if it was all news. He adopted a look of great concern and asked me the story of it but I waved him away. I had seen enough in those big black eyes. 'You know who took him, William. Tell me where I might find him.'

He blinked and lifted his hands to his chest like he was going to sing me a song. 'I have heard nothing of it, Harry, but I will ask.'

I sneered. 'The only reason I can think of that any would have taken him is so that I couldn't speak to him and find out why he wrote me that letter telling me that Anne Giles was my cuz. One of them men that took him was also there the day he wrote the letter. It's all very strange when considered alongside Shrewsbury's strange inclination to put himself out supposedly for the sake of my family.'

Hill's face reddened. I had offended him. 'He is your patron, Harry, and – as I have told you – he is a good patron to have.' He rubbed his nose between thumb and forefinger, a familiar sign of uncertainty. 'If you don't trust me then I suggest you talk to him.'

'I don't think he will talk again with me, Hill. As you know.'

'I think he will be happier once news of what you have found spreads. It will relieve him of some of the concerns he has for his own safety.'

I frowned at him, trying to work out what he assumed. 'I will not be spreading the news, William. It was all too easy. It sits awkwardly with me. Now the story is there in my head it indeed rings true like cathedral bells. The bells ring so loud that I cannot help but feel that they were hung especially for me to hear.'

Hill shook his head. 'I don't understand.'

'Mary Ormonde told us that her father and Keeling were once Baptists.'

Hill interrupted me, putting a finger to his lips bidding me to be quiet.

'So! These are not things to say aloud!' I exclaimed. 'Yet *she* did.'

'She is a country girl, Lytle, innocent in her ways.'

'Not so innocent, Hill,' I assured him, 'for she directed us to her old nanny where next we were told very easily that Jane Keeling took her own life. She then instructed the nanny to direct us to the local surgeon who very easily told us that the girl was with child when she died.' I shook my head.

'Why can you not see that such frankness is born of innocence? These simple country people spake the truth because they did not realise the full consequence of their words.'

'If they are so simple then why should Keeling permit them to live their lives where any might come and discover such a damaging tale? If he is the one that killed Anne Giles and merrily condemned Richard Joyce to an underserved death – then why should he shrink from killing the nanny or the surgeon?' I shook my head again.

Hill now looked guarded, uncertain of himself. He and I both knew that it was he that had insisted I go to Epsom. If there had been any bells hung for my benefit, it was he that did the stringing.

'If I was you, Harry, I would share my doubts with Shrewsbury himself. He is your patron, he will guide you.'

'He did not seem so anxious to guide me last time we spoke. He seemed more concerned that I tell him nothing and be sure his name was not associated with the affair. Would he welcome me mentioning the possibility of the Lord Chief Justice's guilt?'

'Aye, Harry, he would have to. It is not a possibility that he would have you keep from him. Be well advised.' He laid a hand on my shoulder and looked at me seriously. 'Take my word for it.'

I almost laughed, but managed to sneeze instead. 'Aye, well thanks for the kind advice, William. I will see you soon.'

I turned and left him standing there like the mangy dog he was. So Hill *was* working for Shrewsbury in this. The two of them were determined that I dig out this old tale from Epsom. But what was at the root of it? That Shrewsbury should wish Keeling to be implicated was understandable – the two men were rivals – but was this a plot built on rock, or a plot built on sand? And what was the significance of the two old men once having been Baptists together? We would have to work out how to untie that knot once we had further counsel back from Dowling's friends. In the meantime – Matthew Hewitt.

The Royal Exchange is where rich people throw their money away on exotic rubbish. It is also where London's merchants meet to swap news and do deals. At the heart of the Exchange is a massive courtyard, surrounded on all four sides by an arcade behind rows of thin marble columns. Statues of all the kings of England from William to Charles I stand on plinths above the portico peering down onto the throng below. There are nearly two hundred shops trading in the arcades, selling perfumes and scents from the Far East, silk from China, sables, jewels, gold lace and so on. A tall, thin tower with an Arabian roof stands above it all, with a giant grasshopper impaled on its peak. Four more grasshoppers sit on the corners of the roof.

This was the stomping ground of Matthew Hewitt, and I was determined to catch him in some nefarious deed. The courtyard was full today, the merchants gathered in small groups, heads bowed, engaged in quiet negotiation and exchange of information. Straining my ears hopefully to see what I could pick up, I walked slowly. Even the statues seemed to be leaning over, stretching their necks to try and hear what was being said below. I watched the short sharp movements of the merchants' hands, the intensity writ on their faces, the stooped shoulders and low whisperings. The restoration of Charles had done wonders for business. Charles II was following in the footsteps of his father and grandfather, pursuing discreetly the building of relations with Catholic Europe in the name of peace, against the wishes of a vociferous Protestant population who were afraid of the Pope and the insidious tendrils of Rome. The war with the Dutch was the subject of the day; a multitude of guessing games surrounded its outcome.

It took me ten minutes to find Matthew Hewitt, short squat body and stumpy legs. He seemed shrunken outside the dark sanctuary of his little sitting room, some of the menace evaporated in the light of day. His legs were bowed, though not deformed, their curving shape accentuated by the high heels he wore in an attempt to increase his stature. His skin was not just pale, but white like snow, in contrast with the jet black of his hair. Hirsute, but not like Dowling. Dowling's hairs grew in the right places: on his head, arms and chest. The hairs on this man's body were more randomly arranged. There was a patch, for example, of thick black bristles growing in a round patch from a lump on his left cheek. They were trimmed short but impossible to hide. He wore a thick, black little beard trimmed neatly into a blunt point and his eyebrows curved upwards, adding to the intensity of his awful black eyes. Long nails, strong and sturdy, a big pig, yet I admired his clothes – silk and very expensive. His movements were more restrained than those of his colleagues, his manner more calm and confident.

For about ten minutes I watched him before he suddenly looked up. His eyes fixed on mine and his face tightened into a grim mask. I held the stare, though my heart pounded, and then he looked away. Returning to his conversation, he stayed where he was. Three of them talked for about twenty minutes before they were joined by two more. This group carried on talking for another half an hour. During that time another man, obviously not a merchant, came and spoke briefly to Hewitt twice. This man was dressed in rough linen clothes, poorly tailored, the stitch designed to hold, not to impress. He was tall, heavy and ponderous. Had I seen him before?

Then I spotted William Hill standing in easy conversation with two others, apparently unaware of my presence. He must have come direct from Paul's. As Hewitt's bear-like companion trod heavily nearby, Hill acknowledged him and exchanged a few words. One of Hill's companions shook hands with both Hill and the big man, and the two of them departed. What the Devil was Hill's connection to Hewitt? Then suddenly Hewitt took off. He strode purposefully towards the exit, moving fast without stopping to talk on the way. At the last possible moment I saw his wide shoulders disappear. I sprinted out onto the street but he was already gone. I cursed both him and me as I stood looking around, wondering what to do next. In the end I went home, cursing my incompetence.

The day was grey, my mood was black and my feet felt like I was wearing lead shoes. I took off my periwig, before I reached Sopar Lane, to scratch at my itching scalp, ignoring the disapproving stares of a portly man who used to know my father. Calling for Jane as I entered my little house, I was impatient to get my feet into a bowl of hot water. No one answered. I decided to go and sit down with my shoes off to await her return. I pushed open the door to my small sitting room and went to my favourite carved wooden chair with its soft, inviting cushion. Just before my head exploded I heard a noise just behind me, like the soft clearing of a throat.

It was the pain that woke me up, ferocious, burning like a hot iron rod pressed against my temples and driven into the top of my neck, a raging sickening pain that I felt at the pit of my stomach. I was afraid to move lest it encouraged the pain to stab deeper and I couldn't move my eyes without making it worse. Breathing slowly and gently, I could feel the pain throb in rhythm with the beating of my heart. The back of my eyes felt like raw, skinned meat rubbing up against stone. My guts churned, ready to empty. Lying still I became gradually aware that my cheek was lying in a pool of freezing cold water. My body was frozen and stiff.

Darkness. I could just make out a small ladder, wide, with only five or six rungs, leading up to a small archway. To either side of it and above me were thick stone arches forming a vaulted ceiling. There were no windows and the air was cold. I was in a cellar. A weak light flickered from a distant flame, dancing, casting little shadows on the wall ahead. The source of it was behind me. Thinking to turn despite the pain, to try and raise myself, I was dissuaded by a loud sneeze.

'Dusty down here,' said a coarse, strangulated voice, flat and nervous. I visualised the owner as a youngish man, just turning into middle age, fat round the face and waist.

'Aye, but dry,' said another. This voice was younger, but spoke without hesitation. The voice of a brutal man, thin and lithe, not unlike John Giles in appearance, perhaps.

'Must be dark by now.'

'Likely it is, but we don't leave until two of the morning.'

'It's dark enough now,' First Voice insisted.

'We take him out of town at two, like we said,' Second Voice snapped impatiently, on the verge of anger.

'My old lady will be very suspicious – my being out so late without ale on my breath.'

'Aye, well we'll have a pot or two after we've done.'

'I don't see why we can't take him out now. It's pitch-black and no one about. It's just a short way down to the wharf.'

'We said we'd take him out at two, so we'll take him out at two.'

First Voice started to hum, then stopped. 'We got him here safe enough, all the way from Bread Street without being seen, in the middle of the day.'

Second Voice didn't reply.

'Fact I don't see why we has to take him out at all. Why can't we kill him here, be done with it?'

'The man wants him strung up, so we string him up. You

189

fain to argue about it, then you should have argued when you had the chance. Nay quoth Stringer, when his neck was in the halter.'

'At least we could kill him first?'

'We do as we're told. No more to be said.'

'He's probably dead, anyway. You hit him mighty hard.'

'He's not dead. You have made fair speech, now rest.'

First Voice didn't reply. The pain was almost unbearable. I could feel with my fingers, though they were frozen, immersed in the same cold puddle in which my face lay. My stomach still threatened to unload. I could feel a gash on the back of my head, throbbing. I was on my side, curled in a foetal position. Fortunately I wasn't lying on either of my arms. My right arm was lying on a rough and lumpen surface, my hand was dangling limp in the water. I rubbed my arm gently against that surface. It felt like rope.

'Is the rope thick enough?' First Voice spoke, breaking the silence. I froze and held my breath.

'The rope is thick enough.'

'How thick is the pole?'

'Thick enough. I looked at it yesterday. It's been repaired recently, the wood is new and the fitting is sound. It will hold him.'

I was in no fit state to take on these two men. It would take me an age to sit, let alone stand up. My stomach had quietened. I didn't breathe. The blood pounded at the back of my head, the front of my head, the back of my eyes and in my ears.

'Has he paid you yet?' First Voice asked.

'We get paid when we done the job. Why do you challenge me, Mottram? Were you not there?'

'I know, I know,'

'Ye think he won't pay us?'

'No, course he will. Just asking, weren't I?'

There was another long period of silence.

'What should we do if there's people around?'

'We have discussed this many times.' Second Voice sounded like he was talking through clenched teeth.

'Methinks we didn't talk it through well enough. He told a story as if it were simple, but now I am less certain.'

'We'll do the job as we said we would.'

I began to flex my muscles, one by one, slowly and systematically. By flexing my biceps my lower arm began to feel better. I flexed my thighs very slowly in order to avoid attracting attention. I tensed my calf muscles at the same time as my toes. I made no movements with my neck – the slightest movement resulted in searing pain around the wound on my head.

'What time is it now?'

'Half past one.'

'Did he say leave here at two, or leave the wharf at two?'

'He didn't specify.'

'If we get started now, then, we'll likely be ready to leave the wharf at about two, wouldn't you say?'

Second Voice sighed. There was a cracking noise and a shuffling like the sound of a man getting to his feet. 'The candle is nearly dead, anyway. You pick him up and let's be on our way.'

'That's more like it!'

I lay still and listened to Mottram's heavy steps. Big hands grabbed my armpits. Gritting my teeth I stopped myself crying out as he slung me over his shoulder, the back of my head rubbing against his elbow. The pain was twice as bad with my head hanging, the throbbing intensified. His coat was damp. He carried me up a short spiral staircase. As we emerged into a dark room at the top, I looked out of one eye. There was a big table laid out in the middle of the room, thick, with a row of knives hung up on one wall. The room smelt of rotting meat. At the end of the table next to the front door was a barrow. I was swung about and thrown into it, with my legs hanging over one side, and the back of my head landing with a thump on the bottom of it. I thought I was dying. I passed out again.

'It's yonder, just beyond your left shoulder,' Second Voice called out. Those were the words that woke me. A cold wind blew up my trouser legs. There was something on my face that smelt of fish, weighing down on it. I felt rough prickles against my face. More rope.

'Hey!' Mottram said slowly.

'What?' Second Voice snarled.

'I think I just saw him move.' My heart seized.

'How can you see him move when he's bouncing up and down in the bottom of the barrow?' Second Voice sounded fed up. Listen to him!

The wind blew harder and colder and I heard the sound of water lapping against the river wall.

'There she is.' Second Voice was ahead now. Mottram must be pushing the barrow.

'I hope you don't expect me to row us all the way to Westminster by myself,' Mottram grumbled.

'Come and help me get her untied.' There was a thump, the sound of a man stepping down into a boat. The barrow was dropped, again sending fresh waves of pain and nausea from my head to my stomach. It had to be now.

I pushed myself slowly and steadily upwards, my feet slipping to the ground, the rope rolling off my face and falling onto the flagstones.

'Hey!' Mottram's voice shouted. I stood up straight and turned. A big, heavy man was holding a rope in one hand standing at the top of the wharf above the river. Mottram. The man I had seen at the Exchange. The rope led downwards. 'He's got up!'

'Stop him, then!' Second Voice cried out from beyond. There was the sound of feet scrambling on stone steps.

I turned and ran. I saw and recognised the spires of Mary Somerset, Mary Magdalene and Nicholas Cole. Beyond them the big square bulk of Old St Paul's. This was Broken Wharf. Running up the hill as fast as I could I struggled to find strength in my stiff, tired legs.

'You're too damned slow!' Second Voice shouted angrily at Mottram. It was him I was afraid of, not Mottram.

Looking over my shoulder I saw my demons in profile. Mottram was tall and stout and would not catch me, but the other man was shorter, more athletic – and close behind. I tried to run faster. My eyes burnt, my lungs were raw and waves of nausea rippled up from my guts, but I kept going thanks to the grace of . . . Second Voice was catching up, I could hear his steps behind. Fish! Where to go? Where to go? No idea! I darted left into a black alley and sprinted forward, careless of what might lie before me. Slipping twice on the cobbles I slid forward on the sole of one shoe, but righted myself both times. Left, right, left. Not once did I choose a blind alley. I chose the narrowest passages and darkest yards.

I emerged out onto a main street. Knightrider Street! West! St Paul's Bakery! Looking behind, I saw the shadow of Second Voice emerge, turn, spot me and give chase again. But he was farther behind now, forty or fifty yards, and he was alone. I reached the corner of the bakery and headed straight for the wooden row of shops that was there, a hundred yards long. The shops were all alike, with window shutters made of Eastland board. I pulled at the first set of shutters. They were locked tight shut, and the second, and the third, but the lock on the fourth set was looser. I pulled it open with three mighty pulls and leapt through the gap, pushing against the window behind with my body. I landed in a heap on the wooden floor with glass chips all about me. Ignoring the pain of the shards that embedded themselves in my hands, I jumped to my feet. I pulled the shutters closed and held them, leaning backwards with all my weight in case Second Voice tried to pull on them. Breathing hard, my body complaining and threatening to retch I listened hard, but could hear nothing above the noise of the blood pounding in my ears.

Footsteps! Quiet footsteps, quick but cautious, stopping and starting, like a mouse or rat. Footsteps on the street. I held my breath and waited. The steps stopped. No sound. Slowly, very slowly, I leant forward and looked out through the gap in the shutters. Still I could hear nothing. I looked for shadows, listened for the slight crunch of shoe on dirt. Nothing.

'There you are,' said a low voice triumphantly.

Turning round in shock I saw Second Voice walking towards me, through the shops, the passage from one shop to another unbarred. He must have broken in somewhere else. Throwing myself towards him I caught him by surprise. He had expected me to run again. I seized him by the neck with my left hand. He grabbed at me with both of his, leaving me free to punch at his face and ribs with my right, which I did, in panic, with much force. He gasped and fell, losing his balance. I kicked him in the side of the temple, and then kicked him again, before throwing myself back out of the window and onto Godliman Street. Feeling no pain, only the thrill of having escaped and the fear of being chased, I ran east, sprinting, not stopping until I came to the corner of Bread Street. I turned and ran up the middle of the street, not bothering to stay in the shadows, towards home.

My windows were dark and the door was closed. I shook my head and tried to ignore the agonising pain at the back of my skull. Instead I looked to All Hallows, with its broken spire, struck by lightning a century ago. The pain at my temples cut again like a long-bladed knife. I opened my eyes, but couldn't see properly, just a small bright light, which slowly expanded into a curling whorl with blue and green teeth, pulsating and flashing. My stomach contracted and I thought I was going to shit and vomit at the same time. Couldn't see, couldn't walk. Stumbling into the graveyard of All Hallows I prayed that no one was watching me. I made my way slowly to the rear of the graveyard trying to keep my head totally still. There I found a big square gravestone and sat behind it, my back against the stone and my legs out straight in front of me. Closing my eyes, I tipped my head back, waiting grimly for relief from the agony in my head. I stayed in that position for three hours, enduring the pain and the freezing cold, the effort of it exhausting. The pain stayed with me, teasing me, while my joints stiffened, and new pains came. I cannot describe it. At last the cold winter sun rose, casting a red light on the dead morning. My head was still sore, but the sharpest edge of it was dulled. I climbed to my feet gingerly. The streets were still empty, too empty for me to go wandering. Paul's would be busiest soonest. I walked the short distance to the churchyard there; the biggest open space there was in London, silent and comforting at this time of day. Leafless trees stood like twigs in the long grass, their branches quivering in the gentle morning wind. Standing still, I looked up at the great square Norman tower. God's house, indeed. And what the boggins was God trying to do to me?

When Dowling saw me he held one hand to his forehead and just stood there in the doorway of his shop. He danced out like a younger version of Harry Hunks and fussed over me like an old woman. Dirt was ingrained into my skin, hair and shoes. I felt like a dug-up corpse. A dug-up corpse in need of a bath, a drink and a soft bed.

'What happened to you?' He steered me through his shop and out into a room at the back. 'I went to your house yesterday night and that Jane was wailing and gnashing her teeth. She found your wig on the floor, with blood on it, no less. I had every butcher's boy from Newgate searching London for you.'

'I was apprehended.' On the back of the head. My head still throbbed inside and outside and I felt like I was going to be violently sick. The soft morning light speared through my eyes like sharp, shiny skewers. I really wasn't in the mood for talking. 'Can I go to bed now, please?'

There was a woman out the back cleaning up. She was a little old for my tastes, but her calves were lithe and muscular. When she turned to look at me I saw bright blue eyes and a kind, intelligent face. Aye – I could go for that, I reflected. Not now, though. Now bed.

'Meet my wife,' Dowling said proudly. 'Lucy.'

I waved a hand at her, not wanting to bow my head. The room sort of shimmered, with soft, little white lights glistening where there could be no soft, little white lights. Then it suddenly shot off to the left. When I opened my eyes again I could see both Dowling and his wife staring down at me, the ceiling behind their faces. I had never been in so much pain since about an hour before. I spoke very softly so as not to disturb my eyeballs. 'May I lie down on a soft bed in a dark room, please?'

The best part of two days I spent lying in a large lumpy bed in a dark room that actually didn't smell too bad given that it was Dowling's. The back of my head swelled up to the size of a grapefruit and my right eye was now the size of an apple. My ribs pushed down on my chest like the bars of an iron cage and made it hard to breathe. When I did fall asleep I was plagued by visions of Joyce's head swaying on the end of a stick on top of Nonsuch; grey, drawn face, white eyes bulging from red-rimmed sockets. A woman with no eyes, grinning and talking, while blood slowly dripped from two bloody sockets. Though it was winter, I lay bathed in my own cold sweat. The only respite was being able to watch Lucy Dowling's beautifully rounded mature buttocks shift beneath her heavy skirt, imagining my hands stroking them gently.

The third day I woke with a linen bandage wrapped round my head. Dowling sat perched on a tiny three-legged stool next to my head.

'That's a fair old hole you got in the back of your head, Harry,' he said softly. 'Four inches long and half an inch deep.

Reckon I saw the bone. The edges are still blue and puffy, but I think we've got the worst out of it.'

'Thank you.' My mouth was dry. Dowling handed me a cup of ale.

'What happened?'

Though my head still throbbed like a ripe maggot I told him my story. Once I'd finished he sat grim-faced.

'I know Mottram,' he said at last. 'He has the brains of a big cow. His usual trade is thieving or cullying. He works with a partner. He stands up and looks big whilst his partner does the talking. He is a menacer. Never heard of him killing. Methinks you had the Lord's arm about your shoulder, Harry. If it were not Mottram sent to dispatch you, methinks you'd be swinging from that pole as we speak, neck as long as my arm.'

'Do you know where Mottram lives?'

'Aye, Shoreditch, but he won't be there now. He'll be hidden now that he's failed, his mate too. In fear of their own lives, if they be sensible. Whoever it was that paid them to kill you will be determined to make them pay for their failure.'

I closed my eyes.

Dowling cleared his throat and sat back up straight, thick lines across his weather-beaten forehead. 'Harry, you want my wisdom, then I'll tell you that you was saved for a reason. You didn't escape out of your own cleverness. It was God's will. If he saved you then he saved you for a reason. Fear not, saith the Lord, for I have redeemed thee, I have called thee by thy name, and thou art mine.'

'Aye,' I muttered.

'If ye have faith as a grain of mustard seed then ye shall say unto this mountain – remove hence to yonder place – and it shall remove.'

'It is like a church in here. Ye know I don't have that faith.'

'I know that, Harry, one of your many faults. But you need faith now. Think on it. The Lord giveth wisdom.'

I fell asleep – as I always did in church – and dreamt of clerics with big shapely arses, large breasts and, no matter how hard I tried to change it, Dowling's face.

Chapter Fifteen

Columbines
*The leaves of this plant swarm with lice in the month of June,
on account of their exceptional sweetness.*

Commotion. Dowling talking animatedly with someone in the front room. My name. John Giles's name. Sitting upright I forced my stiff limbs to lever me up onto my feet. I staggered out towards the noise, the muscles in my legs tight and bruised. Dowling staring at me with his mouth open, already dressed. The door open. Men waiting outside. They were all about to go somewhere. The look on Dowling's face said that something important was happening. It was dark and freezing cold – still night.

'Wait for me,' I said before returning to my room. All I had to wear was the butcher's clothes. Never mind – it was dark – none would recognise me. I changed quickly. By the time I made it out the door most of the party were already halfway down the street, impatient. Only Dowling waited for me, shaking his head at my folly.

We hurried across the City towards the river, me shivering.

I tried to get Dowling to talk to me, to tell me what was going on, but he wouldn't meet my eye. I perceived that he was not sure of it himself. We reached the Steelyard – already bustling, merchants trading grain, wheat, tea, rope, masts, linen, wax and other goods demanded by the navy and other seafarers. Candlelight shone softly through the fog and smoke, lending a strange air to the surroundings. I didn't venture this way often. The soap boilers and brewers were already up and lively, and though we had to push and shove to get through the alleys, and though my feet sank three inches into the mud with every step, it was well lit and busy, safe to walk through. Ten minutes later we passed across the shadow of St Magnus Martyr, a huge square church with an imposing tower, now black against the orange sky.

A figure stepped out of the mists and came towards us. Young, another butcher, judging by his raw scrubbed hands. He gestured towards the Bridge and led us, hurrying. We ran the first hundred yards of the Bridge, bare as it was of houses to protect us from the icy night winds blowing off the river. After Rock Lock and Gut Lock we reached shelter. The houses here were tall and thin, four storeys high on either side, joined across the Bridge by tie beams. These tie beams held everything together, for the houses were only twelve feet wide, and eight of those twelve feet hung over the rapids that crashed through the starlings that supported the Bridge's stone piers. Every so often, one of these houses crumbled away and dropped off into the river, leaving another gap for the freezing Thames gales to scythe through. There were more than a hundred and fifty shops over the next two hundred yards selling all sorts. The first of them were already open. This was a place to come during the day when the airs were warm; it was not a place for a man to live. The road on the Bridge was just three yards wide and was already congested despite the early hour. The pressure was relieved only at the middle of the Bridge at The Square. The smiths were at work and the first smoke was winding up into the brightening skies.

We emerged onto the south side of the river and traversed the wooden drawbridge passing under the arch of Nonsuch. The man led us to the Bear on the Southwark bank. A sodden dripping bundle lay on the cobbles. It looked like a body, covered with a thin cloth.

'This is what we came for?'

'Aye,' Dowling nodded. He crouched on his haunches and slowly pulled the cloth off the face. John Giles stared up at us.

Huge, white bulging eyes protruded like little bloated guts. The colour in his eyes had dulled, like a new layer of thick white gristle had grown over the top of them. His mouth was pulled tight and wide and his front teeth stuck out – biting into his lower lip. There were deep little stabbing marks all over one cheek. Dowling ran a finger over them.

'He has been cut about the face, cut before he died, else the skin would not have swelled up like that.'

The cuts were clustered around the middle of his right cheek. They seemed to form a deliberate pattern of some kind. A long cylindrical shape with vertical stripes hanging down from it like the branches of a tree, deep reddish-blue gashes sunk into puffy, white, clammy skin. Dowling touched the marks again. 'I think it is supposed to be a grasshopper.'

He was right. The cylinder was the insect's body, and the stripes were its legs. It was a very similar representation to that which sat above the Exchange. The lines were straight and accurate, implying that Giles's face must have been held in a vice-like grip while his face was cut.

'I don't understand.' I turned away.

'The knowledge of wickedness is not wisdom.'

That didn't help. 'He was hanging off the Bridge?'

'Aye, hanging upside down, his head touching the water. Looks like they tied his hands behind his back and tied his feet together. Then they put a rope round both bindings and pulled it tight so he was trussed like a chicken. Then they bound another rope around the knot, a long one, exactly the length of the drop between the Bridge and the river. They tied one end to the top of the Bridge and threw him over.' Dowling gazed up at the Bridge. 'The fall pulled his shoulders and knees right out of their sockets. The pain must have blown every breath from his body. Then he would have drowned I suppose, his head was found hanging just below the surface of the water.'

Dowling rolled the body over so that the face was mercifully hidden and started to wrestle with the thick knots. The rope was wet and the knots had been pulled very tight. He took a short-bladed knife from his belt and cut through the rope around the knots. Giles's limbs fell unnaturally about him like they were not his at all. He lay there like an animal on the slab, ready to be chopped up and parcelled.

'There's a hook above the middle arch. He was hanging off that.' Dowling turned, eyes scanning the surrounds. He pointed at a lone figure sat away from everyone else. 'That man is a boatman. He found the body at dawn.'

He was sat scrunched up on dry frozen mud, knees tucked up against his chest. His shabby wide-brimmed hat was pulled down over his ears, his big red nose stuck out like a lump of raw meat, a drip hanging from its tip over his marbled purple hands. His shoes were sodden and misshapen. We went over.

'Let me alone,' he said gruffly, before either of us got the chance to speak, 'I've had a terrible experience.'

'We work for the Mayor so you have to talk to us,' I replied without sympathy, 'else I will throw you into the stone hold.' It wasn't he who'd been killed. I had no patience for Thames boatmen, no matter how terrible their experiences. They were a foul breed of mongrel scoundrels and I didn't doubt that his apparent reluctance to talk belied his objective to get money from us. 'I'll give you a shilling if you tell me it all, and tell me it quick.'

He stared at me dejectedly then looked out at the river. He cleared his throat and looked a little happier. 'I got up early today, this morning, see? I had a booking first thing at Westminster and I was shooting through the arches, riding the torrent. I almost run into it, but couldn't see what it was, because there was so much fog. I rowed back against the tide so I could see it properly and God's my witness I nearly fell out my boat when I saw it. His face in the water, bouncing on the waves. A rope from his feet climbing up into the fog. His face all white like a mask, grinning.' He pulled a face and looked to the floor. 'Shocking it was. Dropped me oars. Course, I shot off downriver once I'd dropped the oars. Bouncing it was, bouncing on the river.'

I dug out a shilling and dropped it on the cobbles in front of his feet. He picked it up and pocketed it without looking at me. We turned our backs on the wretch and stood in gloomy silence staring out at the Bridge.

'That's five dead now,' I reflected, 'and poor fellows *we* be.'

'Aye, poor fellows, indeed.'

'Have you heard any news of my father?' I asked awkwardly.

'Not yet, Harry.' He laid a hand on my shoulder before wandering off to speak to his colleagues, about cleaning up, I supposed. I stood with my hands in my pockets looking out over the river. Dowling's clothes were warmer than mine. The river was busy now. The boatman had vanished.

'Let me walk you home.' Dowling returned from his directing. 'Make sure it's still there.'

'Jane!' I suddenly thought.

'She went off to stay with her aunt at her house on Little Eastcheap,' Dowling assured me. 'Nice woman, her aunt – don't you think?'

I didn't even know she had an aunt. No desire to meet her neither. Last thing I needed was Jane soliciting reinforcements.

My front door was wide open. When he saw it Dowling bid me wait and went straight inside. No thought for his own safety, I noted approvingly. His turn, I reckoned. While I waited I tipped my hat to the baker who I didn't like much.

Dowling reappeared quickly, even paler than he'd been before. 'Learn to do well. Plead for the widow,' he whispered. What that meant, I had no idea – but something wasn't right. I pushed open the door, stepped in and stood in my own front room with my hands on my hips. There was a funny yet familiar smell. I looked to Dowling who flicked a finger in the direction of my kitchen.

'I could tell you what is in there, indeed it might be better for you. Else you may choose to look for yourself.'

'I choose to look for myself.' I pushed Dowling out the way and threw open the door. I stopped two paces in, just short of a wide, sticky pool of dark-red blood, smelling rich and foul like the waste bins of any abattoir. The blood formed a thick coagulation that covered most of the floor but congealed mainly around one leg of the kitchen table. On that table were two heads. One head was fat and bald with lots of chins and a thin moustache. Its eyes were rolled up and the mouth formed a small 'o'. The lower chins were incomplete, ending in the ragged edge that marked where the head had been hacked from its body. The second head stared forward through narrow black eyes, its lips drawn and teeth bared, as if it blamed me for its predicament. This head was younger, hair thick, straight and brown. The lips were white, but from the corner of the mouth there trickled a still and stagnant line of dark blood. The heads had been cut savagely with some thick saw-edged knife, not very sharp.

'I doubt that you recognise them,' Dowling walked in quietly, 'so I feel bound to introduce you to Mr Mottram and Mr Wilson. That is Mottram.' He pointed to the fat head, 'and that is Wilson.' He pointed to the younger head.

'The men that would have killed me?' I pulled at the shirt about my neck. I felt hot and the room was stuffy.

'Aye, Mottram and Wilson. We were looking for them. We didn't find Mottram, but we found his wife. She gave us the name of the second man. She called him the weasel. That's the weasel there.' Dowling pointed at the second head again. 'Wilson was well known, a thief and a bully. He ventured out with Mottram sometimes. He lived outside the city wall to the east, close to the Tower. We didn't find him neither. Until now, that is.'

The table was thick with blood, soaked. It would never be clean again. What would Jane say? I would just have to get a new one. Dowling put an arm around my shoulder.

'No sign of their bodies? Just the heads?' My stomach

contracted and my skin prickled. I turned and walked weakly out the kitchen.

'Just heads. I think they were killed as punishment for failing to kill you. Their heads I think must be trophies, to scorn our own poor efforts to find them.' He closed the kitchen door quietly.

'Matthew Hewitt, then.' I looked at the walls, and cursed the pervasive malodorous stink that clung to them so tenaciously. 'I *know* it is Hewitt.' Hewitt that invaded my home with the dead, stinking artefacts of life now extinguished. Too many heads today. I shook my own head and walked back out onto the street where the air was clean of the smell of human blood and gore. Clean*er*, anyway.

Dowling sighed. 'I fear that we have come to the end of it. John Giles dead, Joyce dead, now Mottram and Wilson.'

I looked into his big plain face, full of honesty and goodwill. 'No.'

'No?' Dowling's grin returned, faint.

I told him the idea that was taking form in my mind even as I spoke. My next great plan. Dowling's grin disappeared and he started to protest. My soul was set, however. I was not going to let Hewitt go free. But first to Shoreditch to talk to Mottram's wife myself.

Chapter Sixteen

Snakeweed the middle sort
See and consult.

Shoreditch was a little hamlet beyond the city walls to the east. The road that led there was long and winding through tenement after tenement over what had once been lush farmland. The countryside was being ravaged, now covered with house after house after house, a carpet of identical little timber buildings, each with tile roof, each one a small hovel of squalor, damp and pestilence.

I wasn't a very good rider. My arse was sore and the insides of my thighs worn and raw. The rain began to fall, dripping down my back and soaking into my trousers. The rough road, soggy and wet already, churning up. The roads of little Shoreditch were narrow and uncobbled and the mud was inches thick, stirred and layered with refuse and sewage. Suspicious faces peered out at me from behind small, dark windows. Smoke curled upwards out of the roof holes and downwards into the houses. The government had a tax on chimneys; so poor people blocked them up and choked to death instead of starving.

Heading towards the church I called to a man who walked with a basket of what looked like onions, looking for directions to Mottram's house. He looked at me blankly – no surprise there – then shot me a furtive glance and hurried on without saying anything useful in reply. I cursed him impatiently, for the wet weather meant that there were few others around to ask. I rode around a while longer before dismounting clumsily and landing awkwardly on my ankle. I limped towards one of the low houses, one with smoke coming out of its roof, and banged my fist on the top half of the split wooden door.

'What do you want?' shouted a deep, gruff voice from within.

'I'm looking for Mrs Mottram, recently widowed. She lives around here.' I pushed at the door, but it was bolted.

'Aye, well if you knows that, then you should know where she lives.'

'If I knew where she lived I wouldn't be asking, would I?' It was like playing guessing games with a monkey.

There was a silence. I took off my hat and shook it. From every window about me eyes watched. Like flies, they disappeared as I turned towards them, only to resettle once my attention was fixed elsewhere. I could feel them like lice on my body.

'What do you be wanting with Mrs Mottram?' the voice from inside shouted from behind a window across which was stretched a layer of paper soaked in oil. I tapped my finger on the tight paper.

'If you open the door we can talk. Otherwise I'm going to have to cut a hole in your window.'

The top half of the door swung slowly inwards. A long, narrow face poked out, topped with an unruly tangle of rough, wiry, brown-grey hair, bottomed with a thin, unkempt small beard designed to mask a fiercely receding chin. The face stared at me with squinty eyes, both looking inwards, wrinkled nose and raised upper lip. Although it was pouring with rain he looked as if he was struggling with the glare from a tropical sun.

'Who are you?'

'Harry Lytle, and I want to help Mrs Mottram.' I stood back, not wanting to alarm him.

'Be a bit late to try and help her like, Harry Lytle. Her husband's dead and she ain't got no one to look out for her. Unless you intend to provide for her, which I doubt, looking at those fine clothes you got.' I had changed out of the butcher's clothes as quick as I could, so ruining another expensive outfit.

'I want to find out who killed her husband.'

'Not sure how that's going to help her, Harry Lytle. He's dead now and she ain't got no provider. Could help her find his head, though, that'd be helpful. Mighty put out she is, not having his head.'

'How did she find the rest of his body?'

'Weren't hard. It were sitting outside her front door yesterday mornin'. Back up against the wall, legs out straight. Looked very comfortable, by all account.' The man leant forward and wrinkled his nose, smelling the air. 'So what you be wanting with Mrs Mottram, then?'

'Like I told you before, I want to find out who killed her husband.'

'Why you care who killed her husband? He was a fat, ugly

210

old dog. No one liked him, not even Mrs Mottram. Sure he wasn't no friend of yours.'

'Because the same man tried to kill me and is still likely trying to kill me.'

'Ah,' the cross-eyed man leered. 'Self-preservation, isn't it? That I can believe. Keen to find Mrs Mottram, then. Well, I'll tell you. There's no one round here who don't know where she lives, but few will talk to you. So you give me six pennies and I'll tell you now, save you time.' He smiled disconcertingly.

I reached into my pockets without hesitation and gave the man his money. I had had enough of people like this. I waited expectantly, daring him to withhold the information.

'Follow your nose down the road, Harry Lytle. Follow it left down the hill, pass four houses, you want the fifth. May God bless you and watch over you.' The man leered again before closing the door in my face. I turned and looked in the direction that he had given me, into the grey wall of rain, at the pools of thick, stinking mud. Despite the short distance I decided to remount. Each one of the four houses I passed looked sodden and fragile, ready to sink into the soggy quagmire. I dismounted and sunk up to my ankles.

'Mrs Mottram!' I knocked on the door.

'Good morning, sir.' The door opened, and a small, thin shadow of a woman stood there, shoulders drooped, chin dropped and head bowed.

'Good morning, Mrs Mottram.' I took off my hat, baring my head to the heavens. 'I'm sorry to disturb you at this time.'

'Oh, I'm always up at this hour,' she answered in a little voice, eyes glazed.

'No, that's not what I meant.' I looked at her carefully. It had sounded like it might have been a joke. 'I know your

husband was killed. It's what I've come to talk to you about.'
I held my hat in both hands and edged forward into the dry.

'Oh, I see. Come in.' She turned and walked into the house and sat on a chair behind a wooden bucket. The bucket sat under a hole in the roof through which the rain fell straight without touching the sides. There were two other chairs, and I sat on the one closest to her. She sat with her hands clasped on her lap.

'Mrs Mottram, I'm sorry about your husband. You must be upset.'

'Aye, upset is the word alright,' she said very quietly, head still bowed like a little mouse.

'You must miss him.'

'No, I don't miss him. He was a useless lump of lard. He was always getting himself into trouble. Whatever money he made, he spent it. Then he came home and snored like a fat pig. God, I hated that man.' She looked up, pale and expressionless. 'Hated him with passion. Glad to be rid of him, delighted to be rid of him. Sometimes felt like cutting his head off me self.'

I didn't know what to say.

'But he was the one what put food on the table. Now I will have to see how I'm to feed myself.' She smiled faintly.

'Well that's good, I suppose.'

'Oh aye.'

I leant forward, playing with my hat. 'Mrs Mottram, I would find out who killed your husband. Not because I especially care that he's dead, but because the same man tried to kill me, and killed others besides.'

She didn't reply, just sat still with her head cocked, waiting for me to say more.

'Your husband and friend Wilson attacked me in my own

home. They took me to a butcher's shop for the afternoon, and then when night fell they took me onto the river. Lucky for me I woke up and managed to escape.'

'Aye, lucky for you. Not so lucky for old Mottram.'

'No. Listen, Mrs Mottram, I know that your husband wasn't a murderer, he was a cutpurse, a thief.'

'How do you know that, then?' she asked.

'Because a man called Davy Dowling told me. He's the man who came to see you before. You told him about Wilson, the weasel.'

'Another silly, stupid man. Thought he was so clever.'

'Who were they working for, Mrs Mottram? Who told them what to do, paid their wages?' I leant forward a little too eagerly. She noticed, and her eyes narrowed. She licked her lips like a fox outside a henhouse.

'I don't know who they worked for. They didn't tell me their business.'

'He must have talked about the people he worked for, when he was drunk, perhaps. Names . . .'

'Maybe.' She nodded brightly. She looked at the hole in the roof. It was the size of a man's fist.

'Would sixpence help?' I reached into my pocket.

'Five pounds.'

I fell backwards against the seat of the chair and stared at this strange little woman. *Another* five pounds? I was already more than fifteen pounds out of pocket. Had word spread as far as Shoreditch that I was such an easy touch? Anyway, I didn't have five pounds with me. I should refuse her.

'I can write you a promissory note.'

'I'll wait. You go and come back.'

Godamercy. 'Mrs Mottram, I don't have time. The men

who cut off your husband's head are still after me, and I don't have time to be running to and fro from London this morning. I'll give you the note but only if you give me names now.'

She wrinkled her nose and put her finger to her cheek. 'Very well,' she nodded. She put her hand out.

'Names first.' I closed my jacket decisively. I wasn't paying five pounds without knowing what I was paying for.

'Very well, mister. Old Mottram didn't use to work for nobody, you see. He was well known amongst the weasels of this world. They used to ask him to come on their jobs. Just stand there like a big bear. He used to scare the customers. "Customers" is what he called them. He wasn't very bright, old Mottram, not that you could tell him so, but the others didn't pay him full share. They'd give him some money, take him for a drink, get him drunk, and by next day he'd forgotten. He wouldn't be told. He'd just threaten to take his belt to me if I even mentioned it. So I left the stupid brute to the mercy of his friends and sat here while the rain poured in through the roof. You understand?' She pulled her big skirts straight and pulled down her apron tidy.

'Yes, I do understand. That's more or less what Dowling told me,' I replied impatiently.

'Aye. Well, last week he came home all excited. Said the weasel had put them onto more money than we'd ever seen. Must have been taking *you* out onto the river.' Rubbing her eyes, she stretched her arms and yawned. 'Friday night he went off into London, went to meet Wilson. Old Mottram came back before nightfall, sober as a magistrate. Said he had been told to stay sober, not to drink. Never took no notice when I told him not to drink. Stupid sod.'

'Told by who?'

'Told by this gentleman they went to meet Friday afternoon. Met him at Cornhill.'

'Where on Cornhill?'

'I don't know where. I just know it wasn't a tavern or an inn, which is where they usually did their business. The gentleman didn't want to be seen with them in public.'

It made sense given what it was he asked them to do. 'What was the man's name?'

'Pargetter,' Mrs Mottram smiled brightly. 'Least that's what old Mottram called him. Referred to him several times in fact. Called him Pargetter.'

'Any other names, descriptions, address?'

'No, mister. I don't know what he looked like, and old Mottram never said. Took great delight in not telling me any of the details. His big secret, it was; excited, he was. But he called him by name. Pargetter.'

'Thank you, Mrs Mottram.' I could think of nothing else to ask, and I was only too aware of the time slipping away. I stood up, had a final look around at the bare wooden hovel, and the poor furniture that was in it. There was a small table by one wall covered in vegetable peelings. Mrs Mottram watched me from her chair in the middle of the room, her hands still on her knees, as I made a space to write out the promissory note. She took it from my outstretched hand and hid it somewhere inside her clothing. Then she smiled, slightly, and I left.

Now. Who the boggins was Pargetter?

Chapter Seventeen

Dwarfe Mallow
In waste places.

Hill would know who Pargetter was – Hill knew everybody – but he wouldn't tell me. Ne'ertheless, I determined to track him down before putting the great plan into effect. There were elements of the great plan that worried me now and I secretly hoped that Hill might have a better great plan. I sent message for him to meet me at the menagerie.

The menagerie is located close to the Bulwark Gate inside the grounds of the Tower. Hill arrived in the company of a short, squat and very determined beefeater, who was nagging him for money, trying to charge him for escorting him to our meeting place. I cuffed him about the head and bade him leave, ignoring his slurred obscenities. I knew him well – he hung about the Bulwark Gate everyday looking for marks.

'Why did you invite me *here*?' Hill demanded, irritated. He looked tired and uneasy.

I felt safe here, behind the guards that manned the Bulwark. 'It's a quiet place.'

I led him up the short winding staircase to the viewing gallery. It was made of wood and curled off to the left alongside the lions' cages. Light shone from a thin grille set into the wall above, and from the wider grilles of the cages below.

'The smell is foul, it stinks of cat piss,' Hill moaned.

'These are big cats – they piss bucketfuls.'

'Why did you ask me here, Harry?' he asked me again, leaning out over the den of a young lioness. A low growling rumbled forth. Turning, he rested his back against the top of the gallery wall. The lioness suddenly sprang up, roaring, the tips of her unsheathed claws scything past one of Hill's elbows. Hill threw himself forward and fell onto his arse. The lioness stood on her hindquarters for a moment before dropping back to the ground and turning away in a sulk, shoulders stiff and back prickly. It was very funny, I thought, though I didn't smile.

'God's mercy, Lytle!' Hill gasped, climbing to his feet, ashen-faced and shaking. 'That was your doing.' He took off his camelotte coat, shook it hard, then picked at imaginary fragments of lion shit with his thumbnail.

Shouting loudly at the top of his voice the keeper of the menagerie strode in, carrying two buckets full of raw meat dripping blood along the floor. 'Make way! I expect you would like to see them fed, gentlemen. Six lions, two leopards and an eagle. Also there is a dog that lives with one of the lions, but he is famous and you already know that. Now you may look and listen for five minutes while they roar at the smell of the blood. I will be back!' He leered and winked at me before disappearing, leaving the meat standing on the gallery.

Oftentimes I brought ladies here. The lions began to growl and whine. Though the meat was old, it was covered with fat black flies.

'You are a fool.' Hill gave up on his coat and held his fingernails to his nose. He pulled a face and shook his head in disgust. 'I *saw* you at the Exchange.'

I said nothing in reply.

He spoke to me as if I were a snotty urchin. 'It was an idiot thing to do, Harry, stand there watching Hewitt like he was some low criminal. I told you to leave him alone!'

'Was it he who sent Mottram and Wilson to kill me?'

I watched his face closely. Casting a quick glance over his left shoulder like he did when he lied, he shook his head. 'I don't know. God have mercy, Lytle, you are lucky to be alive! Wilson is an evil little man.'

'You know who sent them.'

Hill snorted. 'You wander into the Exchange like a Court fool, you rush round London making loose accusation, and you march into Matthew Hewitt's house and accuse him of murder!' He leant forward and stabbed a finger at my chest, angry now. 'Yes, I know you went to see Hewitt, Harry, and I still cannot believe how you could have been such a witless Whoball!' His face was red, his voice thick and angry.

I didn't answer. He was posturing. I considered whether or not to ask him about Pargetter. Not yet. 'Tell me,' I said, 'who *did* kill Anne Giles?'

His eyes dropped again, shrouded with sly cunning. 'Keeling killed Anne Giles, as you have already discovered for yourself. How else would you hear it?'

Lying, stinking rat. 'I think Hewitt killed Anne Giles, to intimidate John Giles. Then he killed John Giles. He sent

218

Mottram and Wilson to kill me, since I was the only one in London that did not believe Richard Joyce did it.'

Hill shook his head and sighed.

Nodding his head and whistling cheerfully, the menagerie keeper approached. He picked up the first bucket and walked to Old Crowley's cage, a mangy old lion with broken teeth and blackened gums. The keeper threw a slab of the meat at Crowley's splayed feet.

'What *is* your relationship with Shrewsbury?' I demanded, once the menagerie keeper was out of earshot. Hill stood stooped; hands plunged in pockets, looking very miserable.

'I have no relationship with him.'

'You know things, though.'

'Aye, I know things. I know lots of things, but I have no privileged relationship with Shrewsbury. He loves me not and never will. I know him well enough to know that behind that wide, friendly smile is the soul of a wolf. I've told you that before.'

'I don't recall you saying that,' I answered slowly. 'I remember you telling me how lucky I was to have a friend like him. What an excellent patron he was.'

He pulled a face. 'Aye, well he's close to the King, which means he is a good person to know. There's many would say you were very lucky to have a patron of such lofty standing.'

'You said his position at Court was precarious.'

'I never said his position at Court was precarious, Harry. I am not stupid. I know him only by reputation and have some insight as to the comings and goings at Whitehall. This is how our King would have it. He plants seeds, gets others to cultivate them, then finds insects that like to eat these plants, and others who like to eat insects. Keeps everyone on their toes.'

'Tell me what you would do if you were I.'

He looked up into my eyes and spoke passionately. 'Go talk to Shrewsbury. Tell him what you found at Epsom.'

'And Pargetter?'

'Forget him, Harry! He has nothing to do with this! How many times must I tell you!'

'So Pargetter is Hewitt?'

Hill stepped back and regarded me curiously. The veil slid slowly back over his face, eyes wondering what had just happened.

'I have to leave now, Hill. I'll find you later.' I could barely contain my excitement and didn't want him to see it. Pargetter was Hewitt, which left no doubt that it was him that plotted to kill me. Time for the great plan.

Chapter Eighteen

Crocus
*It seems remarkable that the crocus which they say is made
of such feeble and tenuous parts not only stains urine
with its colour but also excrement of the belly.*

I banged my fist on Hewitt's heavy front door. The rains had
started to fall again, big black drops falling down my neck. I
pounded on the thick wood, determined to be heard above the
noise of the wind. The same window opened as before. The
same old, scabby, grey head stretched out, the same hooded
left eye wandered up and down my body. It withdrew. The
great bolt slid and the door opened.

'You should use the bell,' the head sneered at me, the
mouth crooked and turned down at the ends. 'He said you
would come.' He turned to close the door.

'Then he is a genius.' I grabbed him by both ears and
wrapped an arm around his head, covering his mouth. He
coughed and spluttered, eyes wide open. Dowling and two
of his colleagues entered quickly from the street and closed

the big door. I held the old servant while Dowling bound his mouth. Shiny eyes stared at me through Dowling's fingers, black and pupil-less, narrow wells of putrescence.

The corridor was dark, lit only by one candle sat on a small round table twenty yards ahead. We walked as quiet as we could on the polished floorboards, aware of the dark faces watching us from the massive portraits that hung high on the dark wainscoted walls. The candle and table stood at the foot of the small staircase that led up to Hewitt's parlour. I put a hand on the banister and withdrew it quickly. Something sharp. It was the spiky tooth of a grinning serpent, monstrous and twisted, carved into the wooden rail. Composing myself, I turned to the others and signalled silently that they should remain, hidden in cold, black shadows. I climbed the stairs. They creaked. I knocked on the door and entered, closing the door behind me swiftly.

'You are lucky to find me in, I've just returned.' Hewitt stood by the fire looking at me. 'It is raining now, I see.'

I walked towards the heat of the fire. Steam started to rise from my clothes.

'Your manservant told me you were expecting me.'

'I thought you may come again,' Hewitt said slowly, 'one last time.'

'What did you think I'd come for?'

Chuckling, he scratched his head vigorously. Flames from the fire wriggled and danced. He spoke quickly, rubbing his right thumb on his left palm. 'You think I killed John Giles. You think I sent Mottram and Wilson to kill you. You may even think I killed Anne Giles.'

'Did you?'

'Opportunity is whoredom's bawd.'

'What kind of answer is that?'

'The only one you will get from me. I told you last time you came that this is not your affair. I gave you clear warning. Instead you came to the Exchange to observe me, to spy on me.'

'Did you send Mottram and Wilson to kill me?'

'It is as good to be in the dark as without light.'

I snorted. Pompous indulgence. 'Who was John Giles blackmailing if not you?'

'I could write you a list, but I will not.' Hewitt spoke with quiet amusement in his voice. He poured himself a glass of wine without offering one to me. He sat, sighing as he fell back into the soft leather upholstery.

'You are a devil.'

'Speak to me like that again and I will have your throat cut,' Hewitt answered lazily. I couldn't think of a suitable riposte. He sipped unhurriedly at his wine. 'I take no pleasure in Anne Giles's death, much less that it was you appointed to investigate it, but I'm no different to any of the others that work the Exchange. Look at me, Lytle.'

I looked.

'What do you see?'

'Your face.' Like the skin of a dead animal hung out to dry.

'*Every* face at the Exchange is the same as this face, Lytle. Do you understand?' He let me look upon him a moment longer before sitting back.

I realised, startled, that he was surely talking about William Hill. Why? I shook my head, confused. 'How does that excuse you from telling me what I would know?'

'I don't need an excuse.'

'Was it you that sent Mottram and Wilson to kill me?'

'If it had been me, would I tell you?' He was playing with me.

'You're hung one way or the other.'

'Enough!' He snarled, jerking forward, his white face scowling, black eyes fixed on mine.

I walked towards the door.

'Goodbye.' Hewitt sat back again, fingers arched, contemplative. 'Don't come back.'

I opened the door to Dowling and his colleagues, who bounded up the stairs, boots crashing thunder on the wooden boards. Hewitt leapt to his feet, crouched, legs spread. His head jerked to look at me, outraged and incredulous. I tried to avoid his gaze.

'I think you killed Anne Giles and John Giles, and tried to kill me. So I am going to take you somewhere where you may be persuaded to make your confession.'

'You would do *what*?' Hewitt almost laughed. 'By whose authority?'

'By my authority.'

'Lytle. You . . . are . . . mad.' He paused to scrutinise my nervous expression. 'Quite mad.'

I signalled to Dowling. He and the others bound Hewitt with rope. Hewitt made a couple of token movements to resist but was still overcome with astonishment. Only when Dowling wrapped a cloth around his mouth did his eyes flash. He tried to kick out, but it was too late. He stopped quickly, unwilling to make a fool of himself. The three of them carried Hewitt down the narrow stairs and I followed close behind. All of us were uneasy now, unsure of ourselves, and the cold, murderous, furious sparks flying from the cold flints of Hewitt's eyes did nothing to comfort us. We left the house quickly, as fast as we could, and hauled Hewitt into the back of a coach we had left parked by the front door.

I think I said somewhere earlier in this narrative that I had never been into Alsatia and never would. That was my view at the time, which I had shared with Dowling. He responded by telling me that it wasn't so bad, that he knew a couple of fellows that lived inside its boundaries. This remark had surfaced in my mind the night I had formulated the great plan. So now we would take Hewitt there and keep him at a place known by one of Dowling's fellows.

Alsatia was a swarming, stinking nest of rats. Every house was split into twenty or more tenements, each tenement housing up to ten men each. There lived debtors, cheats, liars, forgers, thieves and murderers, living in cellars, in kitchens, first-floor rooms and garrets. There lived rufflers, who made their living pretending to be old, maimed soldiers, begging from royalist commanders who they claimed to have served. Strowling morts pretending to be widows. Fraters who collected money for hospitals, keeping the money for themselves. Polliards and clapperdogeons, who used children to extort money from wealthy passers-by. Tom O'Bedlams, thieves that feigned madness. Anglers that earned their name fishing through open windows with a rod and hook. It was a dangerous place policed by gangs of ten or more, burly thugs armed with poles and knives that stood for the only law that applied there. Worse than The Exchange. Just.

We stopped on Fleet Street at the mouth to Shoe Lane. I watched nervously the characters that wandered in and out the tops of the narrow alleys that led down into Alsatia, dirty rogues, walking slowly and without haste, masters of their territory. The streets were narrow, doors were public thoroughfares, and the noise from within tumbled out loud and crude. The area swarmed. Houses so overfilled and overpopulated that the sewage formed a thick river that covered the width of the street. This was the dirtiest and unhealthiest district in the whole of London.

Dowling strode over, having been stuck in conversation with the driver of the coach. The coach rumbled forward gently and came to a stop at the top of Salisbury Alley.

'We all four go together, Harry, it's safer that way.' Dowling took my jacket in his hand and shook his head sorrowfully, gazing at my oldest and least fashionable clothes. Still they might as well have been the King's robes. Snatching my jacket out of his hand I pushed him forward, I had no appetite for discussing it. We paused at the top of the alley and looked down. Walls closed in on either side of the running sewer. Faces stared out from doorways and windows.

'Right, let's take him.' Dowling and one of the others hauled Hewitt out onto the street and pushed him forward. Someone had put an old linen bag over his head. We walked with purpose following Dowling into the maze. I didn't try and avoid the eyes of the dirty flea-bitten wretches that stared at me with greedy malice, but I didn't hold their gaze long either. I tried to look unworried and disinterested, as if I was on my way home after a day at work. Dowling led us onwards, marching forward, keen not to linger. My boots sank into the filth with every step I took and I felt the shit seep through the leather and into my stockings and soak up my hose. Every face in every window, every body on every street corner, turned to watch us walk by. Conversations died, laughter stopped, arguments were postponed. Suspicious faces, frowning countenances, beetled brows, low murmurings.

People here had all day to do nothing very much.

A trio of particularly ugly and vicious-looking young men kicked their heels as we walked by, then slowly followed. One of them carried a long truncheon, two feet long and made of hard, dark wood. This was the upright man, the leader of the pack. There was no stepping off these dank and humid lanes, for the doorways led straight into people's living spaces, and the alleys were blocked with piles of rotting rubbish. Eyes watched us out of every door and window. The old and young hung out of every upper-floor window. There was nowhere to stop or rest, no coaches to hail, no wharf or boats. The lanes wound on, lined with eyes, watching and waiting. I thought we were about to die.

'Have at thee, Dowling. What have you there?' The upright man drew alongside Dowling and poked Hewitt with his stick. My chest relaxed and fell, my breathing resumed. I felt like dancing. Then he grinned at me, an unpleasant display of thin, sharp, brown teeth. His brow was greasy, his eyes dull and cruel. He lifted his truncheon and held it out to one side, its end resting gently on the floor.

'Nothing that would interest you, my friend.' Dowling smiled lazily. Friend? The upright man laughed and slapped Dowling on the back. A loud buzz rumbled forth from all around, tumbling down towards the river, a thick cloud of disappointment. The mob had wanted a fight. Heads dropped, faces sneered, and the rabble went back to their chattering and bickering. The upright man didn't care. He was the pack leader, free to please or displease.

'This way.' Dowling headed towards what looked like no more than a crack in the wall, but it was a tall, narrow alley, dark and wet. The upright man stopped and watched us squeeze down it. He turned, leered, and was gone. What next?

The alley was quiet. Now the only noise was the abrupt sound of little running feet, rats emerging into the cover of darkness, interrupted by the occasional scream and groan or drunken laugh escaping from behind walls and unseen closed doors. We slid slowly down the slope, until Dowling stopped. Pushing open a door to his left, he led us into a gloomy room with crumbling walls. The floor was covered with wet straw mixed with the excrement of the two chickens and the pig that scrambled out of our way. The chickens were scrawny, all skin and bones, but the pig was plump and well fed. Stolen. Holes peppered the walls and the air was foul. An old woman sat on a chair with her head bowed. She looked up as we entered, licking her lips and rubbing her hands. Struggling to her feet, back bent and twisted, she gasped as she steadied herself. Shuffling forward with tiny crabby steps, feet not leaving the floor, she put out her hand.

'Davy. What you bring us today?'

'Thomas said that I might use your basement for a while. I have something I need to keep in there.' Dowling took a coin from his pocket, that I had given him, and pressed it into the old woman's hand. 'I have paid him some already, and will pay him more by the day, so long as my goods stay unharmed and untouched.' He had 'paid him some already' with my money, too.

'That your goods, is it?' The old woman answered eagerly, stepping quickly over to look closely at Hewitt. She pulled at the silk of his jacket and ran her fingers up the cloth of his trousers. 'Precious, are they?'

'Aye, precious and dangerous, Mary. This is one that you'd best leave be. I don't want to find him gone, nor untied, nor stripped of his clothes. He would kill you without fear nor hesitation.' Dowling gently pushed her hand away.

The old woman laughed in a hoarse whisper. 'Have some sack. Best sack in Alsatia.' She turned and hurried back into the shadows. 'Only a penny a bottle.' I would have paid a guinea if I thought it would help, but Dowling swore and spat on the floor, and told her a halfpenny or nothing. The old woman laughed quietly to herself and came back with a basket full of dirty-looking bottles that she lined up on a table. Opening four of them, she poured their contents into filthy cups. I wiped at the rim of the cup with my thumb and forefinger, determined not to examine too closely what might be floating in it. The sack was strong and acidic, twice as strong as it ought to be. My stomach and throat burnt.

'So what you be in Alsatia for, my little flower?' The old woman held out the bottle to refill my cup. Dowling's friends laughed along at her joke.

I held my cup in front of my nose and tried to ease myself gently away. 'This is fine sack.'

She followed me as I stepped backwards, clinging like a leech. 'You didn't answer my question.'

Dowling took the bottle off the old woman. 'He's got the same interest as me, Mary. I'll pay thee well if you keep this bundle safe. But you think to market it yourself for whatever you can get, then mark my words all you'll get is your throat cut.'

'All's rug here, Davy.' The woman stood up close to me, studying my face. I nearly choked on the smell of rotting meat that blew out of her diseased mouth, struggling to keep the look of disgust off my face. Dowling tapped her on the shoulder and waved a hand, urging her to fill up the others' cups. She looked sadly at the table, covered in empty bottles, whereupon Dowling pressed upon her some more pennies. Sighing happily, she pulled out another two bottles from the basket, then returned to me.

'I be an unholy wretch, my pretty gentleman,' she grinned, eyes bright, 'which be my role in the world, but I don't profit by it. If I am to look after your goods then I do you a service, for which ye shall pay me well. And if you pay me well, then you may leave your goods here, and be sure they will still be here upon your return.'

'Aye, woman.' The sack was thick and heavy. It soaked into my blood quickly and hit my head hard, catching me unawares. The room began to swim.

'My name is Mary.' She turned to Dowling and pointed towards the far corner of the dark room. 'Bring it over this way.' Picking up a broom as she walked forwards, she set about sweeping the straw off a wooden door, laid flat in the floor. She pointed at a great rusty ring. 'You pull it open. It is too heavy for me.'

Dowling found a short metal rod with a hook at the end of it. Placing the hook in the ring, he pulled. The door swung slowly open, though Dowling had to exert himself mightily to achieve it. Once open we stood in a ring staring down into the blackness. Wooden steps led down. The old woman grumbled and muttered and shuffled away to fetch a torch.

'Harry and I will go down. You two stay here.' Dowling cast the old woman a quick glance, before gently steering Hewitt towards the black hole. I followed, carrying the flaming stick that the old woman had given me.

'I don't reckon it's been opened for a while.' Dowling looked back over his shoulder. The staircase was short, and led down into a small cellar four yards square. It smelt damp and stale, but I could see no pools of water, nothing growing on the walls.

'Clean and dry,' Dowling announced. He pushed Hewitt down against a wall, arms still tied behind his back, and pulled the bag off his head. Still I couldn't see Hewitt's eyes. Dowling pulled a piece of rope from his pocket and tied Hewitt's legs together tight at the ankle and at the knee. I pulled the gag from Hewitt's mouth. Crouching on my haunches I watched him closely. He opened and closed his mouth a few times, before settling motionless to stare back. We sat like that a little while, Hewitt expressionless, his black eyes promising horrible vengeance, me staring back, my drunken brain wandering painlessly. This was the Devil, and he was in the dungeon where he should be. I felt brave.

'We will leave you here awhile, Hewitt. A day or so. I fear that you'll not have light, for there is nowhere for me to put the torch.' I smiled humourlessly. 'You'll not have food for a while, either. That's by choice. I will leave you here for a day or so and then I'll be back. When I come back, I'll ask you again who killed Anne Giles, who killed John Giles, who sent Mottram and Wilson, who killed Mottram and Wilson. I pray that you will give me good answers, Hewitt. If not, then we will leave you here to rot. Lock the door and not come back. Do you understand, Hewitt?'

'I understand,' spake the Devil at last. 'You're trying to scare me.'

'Aye,' I nodded, for he was right. 'All true. Also true that I will leave you here for good if you don't tell me what I need to know. Consider it, Hewitt. How may I let you go? You tried to kill me once, methinks. What would I do tomorrow?

Release you? Then you would try and kill me again. This is my dilemma. I hope that you have an answer for me tomorrow. Leaving you here to starve doesn't appear to be so stupid, for none would ever find you.' I stood slowly, my knees cracking. I had made up the words as they entered my brain, but it was a profound analysis, I decided.

'I can't tell you, Lytle,' he shook his head slowly, 'even if I wanted to.'

'I will see you tomorrow, God willing.' I turned and headed back to the staircase. 'I will leave the gag out, Hewitt, but if you call out then they will throw water over you until you stop.' I climbed the stairs, and heaved the trapdoor closed again. It fell with a crash. Dowling secured it with a chain, locked it, and handed the key to me with a solemn face. Unhappy.

'I like this less than you do,' I told them all, 'but remind yourselves what Hewitt is, and of the blackness of his heart. Remember Anne Giles.'

'Aye, right enough, Harry,' Dowling muttered. 'If there be found among you any man who hath wrought wickedness in the sight of the Lord, thou shalt bring him forth and stone him with stones until he dies.'

'I have to go,' I wiped my brow. I sensed that I was very close to unravelling this great mystery and was feverish to see it broken. I just needed a quart of sack to lubricate my thinking. 'Walk me back to Fleet Street.'

Chapter Nineteen

Crow-garlick
Weeping ulcers in diseased limbs when lanced or cauterised smell of onions three to four hours after it has been eaten.

Stinking Lane was a narrow passage of small cramped houses that ran north of Newgate Market, east to Christ Church. It was a loud and lively neighbourhood where children ran about your feet and grabbed at your pocket. And it did stink. An open sewer ran almost the width of the lane. Marching fast, we attracted stares and curious looks. A very old and rotten apple missed the back of Dowling's head by about two inches. A child shrieked with laughter. A man leant against his doorway unshaven and unclean, only half attired, despite the cold, wintry air.

'Who is this witness?' I pulled my coat about my neck. I had been settled down for the evening in front of a new fire when Dowling had arrived suddenly. Said he had a witness to the John Giles murder.

'A slaughterer. Lives close by.'

It was indeed close by, a small cramped house. We were ushered in by a nervous old woman, who laughed constantly with her mouth, if not with her eyes. Trying to both lead and shepherd us to a table where the slaughterer sat, she giggled as she breathed, the giggles interrupted only by a twitch and occasional wild gasping laugh.

An aura surrounded him. His skin was white and clear as if he had been hosed down, but there were patches that had been missed – under his nails, at the roots of his hair. A bit like Dowling – only worse. My knees buckled when the woman pushed a chair at me from behind. The slaughterer sat slumped, exhausted by his day's efforts. He didn't look like a slaughterer; he was old, thin and wiry.

'You saw the killing on the Bridge.' Dowling's low pronouncement was more of a statement than a question. The woman collapsed in a bout of particularly violent cackling, but her face gave lie to the apparent mirth. She looked terrified, fit to burst into tears. The slaughterer shot her a veiled look and she almost exploded out of the room into the back.

'Aye, I saw it.'

'You were up at that hour of the morning?' If he was up at that hour of the morning then he could only have been drunk.

'Aye.'

'What was it you saw?'

'Aye, well,' the old slaughterer sighed deeply. 'I was walking slowly across the Bridge from the Bear. I was in no hurry, so perhaps my feet were quiet. I saw the man who was killed. He was standing at the palings. I couldn't see him very well. Then I saw the other man and I stopped, to make sure that there was no villainy.'

'Villainy?'

'He looked like he had a knife, so I stood in the shadow like any man would. He was big, built like the tower of St Paul's. He had broad shoulders and was taller than any man I've seen for a long time. I can't give you a better description because he was clothed from head to toe, I couldn't see no part of him. He wore a scarf around the bottom of his face, round his mouth, and he had a hat pulled down over his eyes. He had a rope. Not on his person, but at the floor by his feet. One end was tied to a big hook, a hook in the wall of the building. I don't know why there was a hook there.'

He stopped speaking and looked like he had fallen asleep. I leant over and prodded him, to make him start talking again.

'Maybe it had been put there special. He had another rope he used to truss him like he was a chicken. He just walked over, took him in one hand and placed him on the floor face down. Then he put one knee on his back and bound him up. It's no easy thing to bind an animal on your own. Bind him he did, though, fast. He tied his hands first and then his legs. The little man kicked and screamed, but he was too small. The big man put a knee on his neck. That stopped the screaming.' The slaughterer's eyes were distant as if he was seeing it all again. Sweat beads formed at his temples, his cheeks were drawn. 'You might ask me why I did nothing.' He sighed and shook his head. 'It wasn't that I was afeared, though I was. I just couldn't think what to do. So I stood there watching until it was too late. It's difficult to fathom.'

'Aye,' Dowling said softly.

'He picked up the body with two hands. The little man stared up at the big man in terror. He wriggled. His face was white and every muscle of it was drawn tight. The big man said something to him before he threw him off, but I couldn't

235

hear what it was. Then there was a snapping noise. It was only then I saw what he'd done, tied one end of the rope to the hook.'

It made me feel ill just to think of it again, the sound of a joint being ripped from its socket. I wouldn't be eating chicken legs for a while.

The slaughterer turned to look us in the eyes. 'I tell you, the man who did that murder is a devil and will ne'er be forgiven. It was planned to cause most pain and most spectacle. By God you should have seen that little man's face. He knew what was going to happen before it happened. I would rather be hung, drawn and quartered.'

It was quiet in the room. Neither of us could think of anything to ask or to say, and the slaughterer sat in bitter silence.

'Thank you, sir. I think we'll leave you for now.' Dowling picked up his hat. The slaughterer muttered something that neither of us heard. We found our way out quietly, the slaughterer's wife having hidden herself away somewhere, as far away from her husband and his experience as she could get. We walked slowly back towards Newgate Street.

'You know, I am not so sure now that Hewitt is our man,' Dowling whispered into my ear. 'Before, I was certain.'

'Aye, unless we can show that he is acquainted with a giant that wears a scarf and hat.'

This was not all that troubled me. Baptists. I wanted to talk to someone who could help me understand better the significance of the religious connection. Despite every best effort, I could think of none better than Prynne for that.

* * *

I went to the Tower straightaway, though it was late, for I wanted to talk to Prynne alone. The porter at the Bulwark Gate looked at me strangely but was not disposed to engage me in conversation. Miserable low dog of a fellow. Speaking of loathsome creatures, I bumped into Wade on his way home for the day.

'Harry Lytle! Truly as I live!' he exclaimed, wrinkling his nose and grinning. 'What's news in the world? Your custom is out, so we hear? Labouring for the King himself, so we are told? This is something like!'

'Aye, something like. Would you do me a favour, Wade?'

'What favour?'

'Ask Prynne that I would see him over at John's Chapel.'

'Tell him yourself, I'm going home,' Wade retorted, looking most offended. 'Why would you meet him in John's Chapel anyway? It's a right old mess, no one's yet been fain to touch it. No one goes near it.'

'I need to speak to him alone, Wade. Give him the message else I promise you he will be vexed.'

Wade scowled at me, keen to be away, but his fear of Prynne prevented him from declining my request. Swearing and stamping his feet, he turned on his heel and headed back whence he had come. I hurried past the low portcullis of the Bloody Tower before climbing the slope beneath the cold shadow of the forbidding White Tower. I touched my forelock to a yeoman, a man I recognised. Stinking of wine, his eyes rolling, he was wearing only the top half of his uniform and walked unsteadily. I gave him wide berth. A group of five soldiers stood at the bottom of the wooden steps that led up to the Tower entrance, chatting, bored. I walked past without stopping. The White Tower stood the height of twenty men; its

237

walls were thirteen feet thick. Commissioned in the eleventh century by William the Conqueror, it was built to serve both as palace and fortress. Nowadays it was used to store rifles, ammunition, and lots and lots of gunpowder.

At the top of the staircase I turned right, and climbed the spiral staircase to the first floor. The chapel was located at the top of the staircase before the entrance to the rest of the floor. The frozen winter sky shone chilling white through the arched windows over the nave, framing a simple wooden cross in silhouette. I walked across the stone flagstones, cleared of seating. To either side, in aisles behind sturdy stone arcades, were newly fitted wooden shelves, all of them packed tight with scrolls. Most were property rights for parishes towards the northern city walls. Dust hung in the air like fine white gauze. I waited there in one of the aisles, out of sight of any that might pass idly by.

Prynne was famous for having lost his ears – bit by bit. The flappy top bits were cropped thirty years ago before I was even born, after he published *Histriomastix*, a long, boring tirade against every form of entertainment that man had invented. In it he called women actors 'notorious whores', an insult said to be directed at the Queen. The King fined him, pilloried him at Westminster and cut the tops off his ears. Don't know why he bothered. No one would have read the book if he'd just let it be. He was a frightening, furious man whose acquaintance I had avoided whenever possible when he had been my better and superior. Now I was free of him, yet here I was again.

'Lytle?' A familiar voice snapped, not much later.

'Mr Prynne.' I emerged out of my hiding place.

'Thee would speak to me, Mr Lytle, before Keeling's soldiers come to take you to Tyburn.' His long face stared at me mournfully through the gloom. Walking towards me he ran a long crooked forefinger over the wooden shelves, eyeing the scrolls with steely resolve. I couldn't help but stare at the long curls that covered his temples on their way down to his chin. Three years after *Histriomastix* he got into trouble again, this time for publishing 'News from Ipswich'. I haven't read that either – caring little what happens in Ipswich – but it is said to be another long, weary collection of your usual Puritan rantings, not stuff I'd think twice about if I was King. Charles, though, cut off the hard gristly bits of his ears and branded him on the face with a burning iron 'S L' – seditious libeller. Not what I would call setting a good example when it comes to toleration and goodwill unto others. But then what would I know? Prynne twitched his nose.

'Sir, I need your counsel.'

Prynne snorted, though I could tell that he was flattered. 'What counsel would thee seek of me, Lytle?'

Prynne had been in Parliament many years ago. He was kicked out for opposing the army, both their intention to execute Charles I, and their advocacy of religious toleration. A Puritan, he had been utterly opposed to Charles I's policies, but he was no regicide. Now he was no royal confidant, nor was he a politician or schemer about Court – just an eccentric, old outcast. I felt I could trust him, yet I was wary. In him I saw something of John Parsons.

'I think that the Lord Chief Justice may be involved.'

'Of course he is involved. He is Lord Chief Justice, and put Joyce to death.'

'Yes, which is strange in itself, methinks, that he should take such an active interest when the evidence against Joyce was so questionable. Since then I have found out that his

239

daughter may have taken her own life ten years ago when she was with child. Perhaps it was William Ormonde's child.'

'William Ormonde's child?' Prynne's old face turned a deep crimson. Standing silent, his thin body shook with wrath, eyes fixed on mine. 'Who says so?'

'The surgeon that found Jane Keeling's body says that she was with child when she took her own life. When you consider the nature of Anne Giles's death – an eye for an eye and a tooth for a tooth – and Keeling's own behaviour in this matter – then it is easy to come to that conclusion. I think Shrewsbury heard the rumours too, though I am not supposed to mention his name, and I think he has laboured to have me discover it.'

Prynne stared at me, his lips twisted into a gnarled scar. His eyes were a watery light blue, pinhole black pupils aimed at me. Clenching his fists, he breathed noisily through his nostrils. 'Then now you know it all.'

I picked up a scroll and blew the dust off it. So many secrets. 'I am not so sure. The trail was laid so carefully. There is one thing that troubles me.'

'Speak!'

'While at Epsom, both Mary Ormonde and William Ormonde himself let it be known that Ormonde and Keeling were once great friends.'

'It's well known. That is no great mystery.'

I looked into Prynne's poisonous face. 'Aye, but they were both Baptists.'

Prynne's body stilled. 'They told you this?'

I nodded. 'Mary Ormonde did so with great deliberation, William Ormonde seemed to speak it more casually. But why should either of them tell us, strangers, that the two of them were once dissenters? Even if it is known widely, and I know not whether it is the case, why make particular mention of it to the strangers?'

'Why indeed?' Prynne put a hand to his chin, his brow lowered as he paced the floor in puzzled thought. 'Why indeed?' He found an old stool buried beneath a pile of parchment and sat on it, sending the records flying through the air. 'Give me time to think.' With his head in his hands and his elbows on his knees, all I could see was the back of his old head.

It was silent in the chapel. The bright white light that shone through the long narrow windows turned to grey, and shadows crept out from the ends of the aisles. I sat down on the floor, my back against a shelf and waited. I would wait all night if necessary.

Prynne sat straight then pointed at me. 'Ye said that Ormonde was *not* father of the girl's child?'

'No,' he could point at me all he liked. 'I said that I was not sure that he *was*.'

'Then why did Keeling kill Anne Ormonde, if it were not so?'

'Perhaps he didn't.'

'Oh no. He killed the girl, that much is clear.'

'How do you know?'

'Because Shrewsbury believes it to be so. Shrewsbury is the Devil himself, the serpent that winds itself about the tree in the garden of England. He that is deceitful and self-serving.'

'Oh.' That was my beloved patron he was talking about.

'Both Ormonde and the girl tell thee they were Baptists. Keeling kills the daughter. There must be something that Ormonde did in the past, or something that Ormonde knows that Keeling would not have him divulge – aye, that's it!' Prynne stood suddenly. The stool slowly toppled over and rolled away. 'That must be it.' He descended upon me with his arms held wide – a fearsome sight. 'They were Baptists together. They were involved in some plot, some malicious scheming. Ormonde has threatened to divulge it so Keeling has killed his daughter.'

'Would that not make him more determined to tell what he knows?'

'No!' snapped Prynne, tight-lipped. 'For he has two daughters!'

Keeling murdered Anne Giles as a grisly threat that Mary Ormonde might suffer a similar fate? It explained William Ormonde's agonised writhings, his determination to do and say nothing though his daughter lay butchered.

'I am suspicious,' Prynne prowled the floor again, his tail up like an arthritic goose.

'Suspicious of who?'

'Some misguided wretches were convinced that the execution of Charles I was a sign from God that the resurrection was at hand, the coming of the Fifth Kingdom. They were the Fifth Monarchists. Some of those were Baptists.'

'Lord Keeling was a Fifth Monarchist? How could he keep such a thing secret?'

'There are many secrets at Court, Mr Lytle. Sorting out truth from mischievous gossip is nigh impossible. That's why the King encourages it to the extent that he does. He builds a haystack in which he may hide his own needles. Also, there were many that chose to conform upon the Restoration, and Charles was tolerant and forgiving. So!' Prynne held up his arms aloft. 'Were Keeling and Ormonde among those that plotted the new King's downfall? For until the King was once more dispatched, then there could be no Fifth Kingdom.'

'Plotted the King's downfall?'

Prynne's bright blue eyes fixed on mine, his expression lively and bright, all primness now dissipated. 'The revolt of Thomas Venner. The King made merry of it and used it to advance his own agenda. In the end it was hardly a revolt.'

The revolt of Thomas Venner? A rabble that tried to storm Parliament. It lasted a few hours and Venner was hung. 'Sir, forgive me, but this seems fanciful.'

'So!' Prynne waved his arms in the air, unable to restrain himself. 'Now I will tell you of William Ormonde.' He clasped his hands and took stage in the middle of the room. 'Ormonde and Keeling both started off as Baptists. Ormonde espoused radical views for a while, until the Protector persuaded him that the radical agenda was a distraction to the commonwealth and endangered Godly reformation. Ormonde was still a close friend to Keeling, who continued to regard him as a like-minded fellow.' Prynne wagged a finger. 'But it wasn't so. They remained friends until after the Restoration. What changed things was the death of Thomas Harrison.'

'Major-General Harrison?' Harrison was one of those that signed Charles I's death warrant. He had been hung, drawn and quartered by Charles II shortly after the Restoration.

'Verily. The leader of the Fifth Monarchists. It was about that time that Ormonde changed his views. I doubt if Keeling did, for he is a fanatic. I doubt that Ormonde supported the Venner affair, though it may have been his great misfortune to be privy to it.'

'But how can you be sure that this concerns the Venner's Revolt? It was such a pitiful affair.'

'Keeling and Ormonde are at loggers. Remember that Keeling killed Ormonde's daughter in bestial fashion. We know that they were both Baptists and I know that something happened between them shortly after the Restoration.'

I was far from convinced. 'If this is the case and Shrewsbury knows of it, then why would he not expose it, rather than go to the trouble of having the world believe another motive?'

'He has no evidence of it. Were he to make such an accusation without being sure that it would stick, then Keeling would kill him. Sooner or later, by whatever means, Keeling would have his head. For the same reason he cannot bring forward witnesses. None would provide testimony against Keeling.'

It was bemusing and fantastic, yet I knew Prynne well enough to know that he would not be dissuaded. His chin gently rose, his lips thinned and his blue eyes glazed over with their customary stern disdain. That icy, patronising smirk returned. Slipping his fingers under his locks, he lifted them up so that the grisly stumps that served for ears were fully exposed. I didn't want to look, yet he would not stop staring at me with his hair held up. 'Do I look like a humorous fellow – or a fool?'

'Neither, sir.'

'Mr Lytle. Last time we met I told thee that thou art effeminate and whorish, a bawd Godless ruffian, that thee haunt plays and indulge in lust-exciting dancing, all of which is to Christ's dishonour and sin's advantage and that thee art abominable. Now I am hopeful for thee. Thine efforts have been noble and for that I commend thee. May God have mercy on thy soul.' He held out his wooden cane by the tip. On the end of it was a silver handle, cast in the shape of a sheep. 'Yea, though I walk through the valley of the shadow of death, I will fear no evil: for thou art with me; thy rod and thy staff they comfort me.' He pressed the cane into my hand. 'If I am right, then consider; Keeling will want you silenced, and Shrewsbury besides if you pull Keeling's tail too hard. It is in Keeling's interests that this whole affair is put to bed. Shrewsbury would have the world believe that Keeling killed Ormonde in revenge.'

Then he turned on his heel and left me, all alone. I had never been more confused in all my life.

Yet at the crux of all of this was this girl that died ten years ago. Jane Keeling – was she pregnant when she died or was she not? Which tale was true?

Chapter Twenty

Ribwort
*Two species of this plant are defined by botanists: we think
that each of the two species is found with us, but we
have not yet distinguished them accurately.*

By the time the sun rose weakly to cast its white light on
the grey winter countryside, I was almost at Epsom. Hiring
a horse to ride myself I was oblivious to the possibilities of
tobymen. I had nothing much left to steal. I felt more miserable
and frightened than I had ever felt in my whole life, but also
determined not to be humbled by the likes of Shrewsbury,
Keeling and Hill. Dowling had refused to come with me,
though he had, finally, at least ceded that I was sincere in my
convictions. I had decided to dig up Jane Keeling's corpse.

If I discovered that she was with child when she died, then
I would accept the story as true. If not – then I would know
that the story was false, arranged by Shrewsbury. Dowling's
idea was to press the surgeon John Stow, but that was no
remedy. Stow was a weak and miserable fellow and would say

whatever needed to be said to save his skin. I had to be certain. Still – it was not a happy prospect that I had committed myself to.

Bleakness enveloped me like a damp blanket until, with just five miles to go, I came round a rolling curve in the road and saw a turnpike, a heavy gate with metal spikes on top of it, just a hundred yards in front. This was new. It had not been here before. There were three horses tied to it. Pulling up my horse I leant forward against its ears, peering into the faint light, listening. Three horses and no riders. No one would leave horses unguarded. Birds scrabbled in the hedgerows, an owl hooted, late back to its nest. Sitting a while I watched and listened. It was meant for me, this new construction. I was certain that men were out looking for me now that we had taken Hewitt. But why would they hunt for me on the road to Epsom? Had Hill betrayed me? Even if I cleared the turnpike, just being spotted would mean at least three men on my tail, each with a fresh horse. How many more were lurking further on? I considered kicking on anyway, in the hope that this was nothing to do with me at all, but I didn't. That would be a final mistake.

Pulling the horse round I rode back the way I had come, looking for a different road. I felt panicked, for I had counted on arriving before dawn, that I might work in the graveyard undisturbed. I did not want to arrive late, I could not! Half a mile back I found a narrow lane to my left. It was chewed up and rutted but solid underfoot, still frozen by the freezing night airs. Hesitating for just one moment, I kicked at the horse's flanks with my heels, forcing it into a trot, but before we had got a mile the lane had got narrower, the trees were shorter and the overhanging branches reached lower. Soon I had to bend double over the neck of the horse to avoid being dislodged from the saddle. Then I cursed, screamed out loud in frustration as the lane petered out altogether. Forced to dismount I pulled the damned horse through clinging brambles and prickled bushes. Walking, I followed what I thought was a straight line for half an hour. My guts were churning and my temper was brittle, almost broken. As I watched, the pale sun rose sickly through the web of dead branches that spread their long, spindly fingers above my head. Veering left I prayed that the road lay in that direction, beyond the turnpike. But I was still walking another half-hour later, my soul dead, pushing on forwards, oblivious to the thorns and spikes that tore at my clothes and skin. Then the trees began to thin out, and the brambles gave way to low ferns. Remounting, I rode at a steady pace, but still all I could see was a wall of trees, the silent forest floor laid out before me like an endless twisting carpet of twigs winding a crazy path through the banks of still ferns. I was hopelessly lost.

I smelt the smoke before I saw it. It wafted gently through the woods, hanging in the windless air. Climbing down cautiously I looked for movements, listened for unnatural sounds. All I could hear was the sound of the horse's hooves and my own feet. I walked to what looked like the source of the smoke and soon emerged into a small clearing. There was a hut. The smoke came from a makeshift chimney. Should I skirt round it? But what then? I had to rediscover the trail to Epsom. The soldiers would not have come this way, surely? I tied the horse and walked forward as quietly as I could, anxious not to scare whoever it was that lived in the ramshackle wooden hut with its pitched roof and crooked walls. The door was crudely hewn of thick wood.

'Hello there!' I called, with more confidence than I felt.

'Hello.' A pair of curious pebbly eyes emerged from inside and stared out at me from beneath a furrowed brow, above pursed, questioning lips. The man had wild, unkempt, straggly white hair and pouched cheeks. Nose wrinkled and twitching. 'What do you want?'

'Can you tell me how to get back onto the road? I'm headed for Epsom.'

'Oh aye? What you doing here?'

'I got lost back there in the forest.' Beyond the small clearing there were woods in all directions. 'Is this where you live?'

'Aye. Where I live and where I work. What were you doing riding your horse in the forest? What do you want here? You ain't from around here.'

No one was from 'around here' – there *was* no one around here. 'I got lost.' In the hut I saw four rabbits and a pheasant strung up hanging from the ceiling. A poacher. Scum.

His upper lip curled up, revealing thin yellow pegs growing out of shrivelled grey gums. Contemptuous eyes skinned me. 'No you din't get lost. You din't get lost. You came ridin' down the road, saw the turnpike, thought you'd try and ride round it. I saw yer. I was there, weren't I? You was trying to avoid the soldiers. There's a reward on you, I reckon.'

'There's a reward on you too, I reckon,' I snorted.

Eyeing me up and down, he blinked slowly. Then he grunted and withdrew into his cabin for a moment, returning with a large skinning knife, very sharp and with a wicked serrated edge. His legs were very short – *really* stumpy. Carrying the knife in the palm of his hand he looked me in the eye. There was neither malice nor anger in his expression, just the same matter-of-fact puzzled sneer. He was going to kill me with that knife.

'I wasn't threatening you,' I said quietly.

Staring at me for what seemed like an age, the little man stood his ground. He was in control, this poacher, not me. 'Don't matter if you was,' he said at last, plunging the knife into his belt then beckoning me to follow him into his hut. I didn't want to go with him, but wanted to ride around the woods in circles all day even less. There was a small stove in the centre with a pot on it. The little man spooned out two bowls and handed one to me. The broth was thick and grey with bundles of herbs sticking out of it. I took a sip. It tasted of unlawful rabbit.

'Now then. Who are yer? Dressed nice. Why are the soldiers after yer?' The poacher sipped at his bowl gracelessly, spilling the thick soup down his shirt.

'I'm trying to get to Epsom. I have to get there quickly and don't want to be bothered by soldiers at turnpikes.' I ate. I was ravenous.

Drinking noisily then smacking his lips, the poacher stared at a point about halfway up the wall in front of him. 'Well that's very interr-restin'. Also it's a load of old cobblers. Wandering off into these woods rather than have a chat with a load of sleepy soldiers. What sort of story is that? Unless you be the one they's lookin', for of course. You don't want to be tellin' me your business, then that's fine by me, mister, and I won't be tellin' you mine. Part of my business is knowin' how to get from here to Epsom without using the main road.'

'They are looking for me because I took a man prisoner, a man who killed a woman. He has friends in high places it seems, determined to set him free.'

'What's he ever done to you, this prisoner of yours?'

'He sent two men to try and kill me.'

'Why'd he send two men to try and kill yer?'

'Because he saw me following him, I reckon, watching him at his place of work.'

'Why'd he be bothered by the likes of you watching him at his place of work? You don't look much of a danger to me.'

'Because I was hired by the Mayor himself to find out who killed this woman. I was watching him to see what he might be doing.'

'Why'd the Mayor hire you? You got soft hands and the wit of an old chicken, if you ask me. A fellow what goes riding into the woods to avoid three soldiers what all be fast asleep anyway, then gets himself lost, is not a sharp fellow. I took three shillings and a pair of new boots off those fine soldiers without them knowing it, while you go running off into a forest you don't know and get lost. Reckon the Mayor should hire me, I'd find out who killed this woman quick enough.'

I was not in the mood for hearing how stupid I was. That I knew already. 'You asked me my story, now you have it.'

'Some of it. One thing I'll let you knows for nothin' is I ain't no poacher, though I sees it in your eyes you be thinkin' I am. I live off these woods legitimate. Rabbits are powerful breeders. What I take off the land gets put back just as quick. I work when there's work, I eat when there isn't. Why you going to Epsom?'

I looked into his cunning eyes. He held my gaze without discomfort. I felt like he was listening to me think, counting the seconds, waiting for the lie.

'I have to dig up a corpse.'

He coughed. Just once. Then resumed his chewing. The lines on his forehead were thicker and deeper. I smiled to myself, though he was onto it like a snare.

251

'What you got to smile about?' he demanded. 'Best not laugh at me, mister.'

Staring at the bottom of the bowl, I didn't care whether he believed me or not. Nor did I much fear him bringing soldiers to capture me in return for a reward. I could lose myself in these woods in a second – that much I had proved already. 'I'm not laughing at you. I have been told a tale that a girl that died ten years ago died with child. I am not inclined to believe it, but I know not which way to turn if I cannot be sure of it.'

'You going to Epsom to dig up a grave.' He laughed and stood staring at the floor with a hand on top of his head. Then he looked up at me sharply to make sure I wasn't lying. 'Where's your shovel?'

Good question. 'I will get one at Epsom.'

Sitting opposite me he regarded me with pity. 'Aye. So you will ask for a shovel there, and worry not that your face will be the first they think of once they find a grave has been disturbed. And you planning to dig in the daylight?'

'I had hoped to be at Epsom before dawn. I did not count upon the turnpike being there.'

'Don't think you counted on much.' He continued to stare at me like I was a strange animal. 'Din't count on the turnpike, din't count on finding a shovel, din't count on the fact it takes half a day to dig a grave. You know where in the graveyard is the grave?'

'The plot of Lord Keeling.'

'You know where it is?'

'No.'

Sitting back, he lit a pipe then turned away from me and gazed into the oven. We sat in silence a while, just the sound of birds singing. Then he moved, with purpose. Turning his pipe upside down, he emptied the bowl onto the floor of the hut.

'You can stay here until nightfall. I'll get you a shovel, not from Epsom. I'll get you clothes too, clothes you can dig in, and I'll go with you tonight to watch out for you, make sure you isn't disturbed. And I'll find out where in the graveyard this body is buried. You has to pay for that though, pay a lot, 'cos I don't like yer.'

I had pissed a quarter of my entire wealth into the gutter in just the last few days. A small fortune had gone on coaches and horses and gratuities and none was likely to be repaid. I watched the little man lick his bowl clean. 'I haven't any money with me.'

'Twenty pounds,' he said. 'A promise is fine.'

I looked at the bottom of my bowl and reckoned I ought lick it clean too. This was becoming absurd. 'A promissory note, you mean?'

'No, I mean a promise. You promise to give me twenty pounds and I'll save your neck from the noose.'

'That's very trusting of you.'

'No it's not. You make me that promise and don't show up inside a day with my money then I'll come and find you and take you for fifty, leave you a little souvenir for nothin' too.'

'Very well.'

'Very well, indeed. Then I must be gone. Stay here. We leave an hour after nightfall.' He marched off into the forest and out of sight without looking back.

Left by myself, I reflected. It was possible that he had gone to do what he said he would do. Far more likely he had gone to fetch soldiers and collect the prize that was no doubt on offer for my head. But there was something about this little man with his big knife that I trusted. Were he to betray me and stare at me with his cold eyes, tell me I was simple, then I would not have been surprised. Yet I didn't think that would happen and I resolved to trust my instinct. So I waited.

Simon with the big knife was true to his word. That is what he called himself – Simon with the big knife of Little Millpond. Little Millpond was a very small village between his hut and Epsom, which we passed through on our way to the town as the sun went down. A vain and self-important little fellow, he was never shy of relating a story that cast him in a heroic light. He was a poor fellow that took pride in being without riches, would rather have been cast into the pits of Hell than live the life of a wealthy nobleman. The tales he told were tedious and vainglorious, yet I was careful not to betray my disrespect, for he was also very strong and clearly both brave and efficient. I needed him.

Though I had done little that day other than sit in a forest, still I was tired and bleary-headed by the evening. I had never dug up a grave before, nor had I fully imagined the task that I had committed to. The hole would have to be dug deep and the earth would be hard, set solid after so many years. Far worse, though, was the thought of what I would do once I got to the bottom of that hole. Would the wood be solid still, or would it be rotten and broken? How would I open the box? Would I seek to lift it – no, for it would take several men to achieve that, so I would have to break it open with my shovel. And what would I find inside the box? In what state would I find the corpse? I had imagined a pile of bones, neatly set, either with or without a miniature set within. But what if the body was still fleshy and clothed? How would I establish that that I sought to establish? These were the thoughts that haunted me all that day.

It was a relief when the poacher returned early, for it gave me someone to share my doubts with, or so I thought, but he quickly dispelled that notion. Holding up his palm he bid me save my problems for myself. His task was clear, and that was all he cared to consider. No sooner had he arrived than he announced that he was going to rest. Entering his hut he closed the door firmly behind him, leaving at the door a pile. Sorting through it I found an old shovel (robust), old clothes (clean and voluminous), a pickaxe and an oil lamp.

Setting off at last, shortly after the sun's rays had deserted the little clearing, we both rode on my horse, since he seemed to have none. I rode and he sat squat behind me with his thick, stubby arms wrapped about my waist, his head pushed hard against my back, his grip uncomfortable. He had not ridden much before – that was clear. We navigated by grunts, he grunting at me when he wanted me to turn left or right, instructions upon which I was dependent, for the evening was darkly gloomy and I had no sense at all of where we were headed.

I don't know if it was a long journey or not, for I have never returned to the hut of Simon with the big knife, but it seemed to take no time at all. Soon we were sat together on the horse, peering into the darkness over the wall of the church into the graveyard.

'No time for pretty thoughts nor womanly misgivings. It would take me half the night to dig that grave – I fancy it will take you half a week.'

The dwarf poacher slid off the horse sideways, freed the shovel, pick and oil lamp from their bindings, then stood waiting for me to tie the horse. I led it off the main thoroughfare and tied it to a tree that was enveloped in black shadow. The poacher marched off into the graveyard assuming that I would trail him. We walked deep amongst the stones, the night sky cloudless and blue, and a light wind the only noise. I recognised nothing from my previous visit.

'This one,' my partner whispered, pointing with a crooked finger after he threw the shovel and pick to the ground. 'I will make sure you that none disturb you, but you had better dig quickly, for your arms are thick as twigs. The day will come sooner than you think. I will get this lit.'

He disappeared into the night with the lamp, leaving me alone. Soon all I could hear was the gentle dancing of the wind, the sound of leaves rustling. It was mild and calm, not a night to be digging up corpses. I ran my fingers through the grooves of the stone letters of the gravestone. The luxury of a minute or two of tranquillity. When the poacher returned with the oil lamp lit, he stood with a hand on one hip with a look of disgust evident, though I could see only one side of his face in the lamplight. Taking off my coat I laid it on the stone, picked up the shovel and started to cut the turf into large squares for peeling off the soil beneath. He made no move to help, just stood watching for a few minutes before grunting in apparent satisfaction and disappearing once more into the night.

The soil was soft, the autumn having been wet and mild. This gave me enormous encouragement and I dug with great gusto, forgetting for a while what I would do when I struck wood. That was until again I was struck by self-doubt. What if the poacher still planned to betray me, had decided that to deliver me in the act of gravedigging would be more rewarding? What would happen to me if I was caught here, now? They would hang me by the neck – Keeling would see to it. I dug even faster, out of fear now, reflecting on the stupidity and foolhardiness of my even being there. I contemplated throwing the shovel to one side and running as fast as I could. I stopped digging for a moment, listened to the silence, waited for my body to recover, the pounding in my ears to slow. Was the poacher still out there? Picking up the oil lamp I stepped out tentatively into the darkness.

'Where you goin'?' a low voice growled into my left ear. A small scream escaped my lips and my bowels came to within a sneeze of emptying themselves into my drawers. Gritting my teeth I growled, hating the poacher for frightening me so badly.

'I wanted to be sure you were still about. I couldn't hear you, nor see you.'

'Nor will you.' The poacher wandered towards my hole. 'That's half a hole, best dig the rest.' He turned his back on me again and disappeared.

It was still night when my shovel hit the lid of the coffin. The contact was solid, the wood still strong. Clearing the lid right the way across the bottom of the hole, I discovered in the process that my hole was too narrow on all sides. Tired and sweating, my muscles ached and my fingers were raw and swollen. Then the lid was clear enough. I reached out of the hole for the pickaxe, readied myself, then said a little prayer before swinging it.

The corpse was dry and shrunken, skin drawn tight like tree bark, brown, ridged and hard. Yellow teeth stood bared, exposed by the withering of the lips. The eyes were gone, dried and shrunken like two small peas. An awful sight, but no worse than I had imagined. The smell was as a dead fox or dog, no worse than that. The face had no expression on it, it was just a dried-out shell.

Reaching for the oil lamp I stood it as far away from the

hole in the wood as I could. The body was still clothed, but the cloth was thin and easy to tear. It resembled nothing more nothing less than a giant seedpod. I could not take the pick to her, the thought made me ill. Nor the shovel. I stood straight and took lungfuls of clean air. My hands were shaking and my stomach cramped. Jumping out of the hole, on impulse, I was suddenly fearful. Where was the poacher? Simon with the big knife? Calling out his name softly, I waited. Turning slowly, listening for a sign of his approach, I called again.

'You finished?' He emerged from the gloom.

'I need your knife.'

I will not relate the detail of what followed. It was disgusting and unpleasant. Sufficient to tell that the corpse opened like a dried fruit and was hollow inside with no sign that a smaller corpse had ever lain there.

Once I had filled the hole, replaced the turf and taken my leave of Simon with the knife, I headed directly to the house of John Stow. My goal was achieved before the sun showed its face and I would be away from Epsom before dawn, but I wasn't leaving without hearing what Stow had to say. My trousers were seeped in mud from ankle to thigh, my skin was raw and cut, I could feel the sweat and mud encasing my face like a thin mask. No matter. If I scared him to death, then he would deserve it. I tied my horse to the same great oak tree. The cottage was silent, the windows dark, and the chimney lifeless. I walked up the little path and tried the door. It was locked, so I knocked, hard, and kept knocking until I heard movement within. The same small woman as before opened the door to me, slowly. Her face paled and her eyes rolled and there was a loud thud as she landed on the floor. Pushing the door firmly open, I stepped over her body still sat upright, and headed straight for the staircase, following the weak flickerings of candlelight. Stood over his bed I looked down on the small, round, bald patch in the middle of his thin brown hair. He was still fast asleep, faced away from me.

'Mr Stow,' I announced myself loudly. Mrs Stow appeared again, peering round the door, wide-eyed and shivering. A brave woman, I considered, and I held out an outstretched palm in an attempt to reassure her. 'Wake up, Mr Stow!' I poked him in the ribs with a stiff forefinger. Rolling round to face me, slowly with eyes still closed, scrunched and squinting, he made a disgusting grunting snuffling noise – like a little pig.

'Methinks you were not expecting me to visit you, else I would not have found you here.'

Stow's breathing stopped entirely and his eyes opened slowly.

'Methinks that someone told you I would inform *them* of what you had told me, and that I would not bother you again.' I crouched down that I might see Stow better in the moonlight. The hairs in his nose were still and unmoving. 'Methinks they gave you money.'

Stow pulled himself up in the bed, his eyes wide and unblinking, scanning my filthy face and soiled clothes.

'What say ye?'

Nothing.

'I told Ormonde this story, that Keeling's daughter was with child when she died.' I stared into Stow's face, watching to see if he told truth or lie. His little mouth fell open, his brows climbed so that they touched the fringe of his mousy hair.

He licked his lips. 'That was a secret that I told you.'

'I fancy it wasn't a secret, Mr Stow, I fancy that it was a

lie. No matter for the moment, because I did not tell Ormonde that it was you that told me. I have not told that to anyone yet. I was keen to do so, yesterday, but now methinks I will not allow it to be told further afield until I have checked the truth of it with Lord Keeling himself. In that case I will be bound to share with him the source of the intelligence,' I smiled, 'unless you confess to me yourself that it was a lie, in which case it will be forgotten.'

'Aye,' Stow whispered, looking round for his wife, 'it was a lie.'

'And you were paid money.'

Peering up, aghast, he stared in horror at my stiff face. 'Aye, I was paid money. I was told that other men would come to check the rumour, and that so long as I denied it then, that nothing more would come to pass. I would deny that I had told it thee.'

'Who paid you money?'

He looked at me, horrified. 'I will never say.'

It was no matter, I reckoned I knew the answer anyway. 'Why did Jane Keeling throw herself into a pond?'

Stow shook his head. 'I don't know. Methinks it was an accident, though Beth Johnson insists she writ a note. None other saw it. Anyhow, there were no marks on her, no sign of a struggle nor a blow. That's the long and the short of it.'

'You are a fine actor, Mr Stow. You should be at the playhouse.'

'Thank you,' Stow mumbled, not looking up.

'Farewell.'

Chapter Twenty-One

Adders-tongue
In Grantcester meadow abundantly.

Alsatia was quiet. Those that had business abroad scurried out of their hovels like cockroaches in search of morsels to eat, infesting the City like vermin. Those that had nothing to do would wait until the freezing dawn gave way to something warmer before surfacing. We reached the narrow alley without being bothered and slipped into its black shadows. I was dressed in Dowling's butcher clothes I had worn before. Suitable attire for interrogating Hewitt, the mood I was in.

'Methinks they may be home at this hour,' Dowling whispered. Thomas and Mary, I supposed he meant.

Inside was empty. The pigs and chickens were gone too.

'The way of the slothful man is as a hedge of thorns; but the way of the righteous is made plain.' Dowling suggested happily. Thomas was out working, in other words.

I snorted, 'What does this man Thomas do to earn his bread?'

'He labours honestly, but knows not how to store his daily bread once earned.'

'I suppose he sells stolen pork and chicken meat as part of his righteous way.' I kicked at the straw and wandered over to the corner, the great trapdoor. There was something on it, moving and rustling. I squinted in the darkness then – Godamercy! Disgusting! – It was a giant rat crouched nibbling at something, unafraid of my approach. I took a broken plank from the debris and threw it at the rat. It ambled off, though only to the nearest black shadow.

The door was closed, but not locked. The lock lay to one side and the chain was broken. There was something on it, whatever it was that the rat had been chewing. It was a piece of meat, a small steak, or an ox's tongue. It was nailed there with a big iron nail. I poked at it. The rat squeaked. I stepped back suddenly, heart in my head, for it was a man's tongue, cut off neatly at the root. I took several steps back and stood breathing deep, slow breaths, eyes closed, trying to control the nausea.

Dowling knelt next to it. 'A man's tongue.'

We pulled the door open together and descended the steps slowly. Hewitt sat where he'd sat last time I'd seen him, his hands and legs bound, his back against the wall. But now his head hung to one side and his jaw was dropped, mouth agape. Blood stained his chin and neck and soaked the front of his shirt. Half-open eyes, unfocussed, disgusted expression on his face.

'Hewitt's tongue.' Dowling spat on the floor once we had escaped the scene. The rat crept back to the trapdoor.

'Harry Lytle?' A rough-hewn voice, with a deep crack in it. Turning, we saw a swarthy-faced man, six foot tall, broad shoulders, with a mop of filthy matted black hair on top of his grizzled greasy head.

'Who are you?'

'It's him.' What did that mean? Who was he talking to? Three more men pushed into the room from outside. All of them were big, black-haired and unwashed, like great bears, ponderous but dangerous. They were dressed like working men or tradesmen: rough shirts with sleeves rolled up and bare chests.

'Are you the ones who cut out Hewitt's tongue?'

'Not us, mate. You and he did that, not us.' They all laughed, loud raucous laughter, hard-edged and mocking, cruel and gloating. 'Make haste, now.' His smile faded.

Reaching for our faces, two went for me and two for Dowling. One of them pulled my arms hard behind my back, wrenched them with a mighty force and tied them with a rope that bit into my flesh. A cloth was thrust into my mouth and I had to open wide, else he would have broken my teeth. He pushed it so far it made me gag and I had to bite down onto it despite its foul taste. Then a bag was pulled down on my head. It happened so fast and yet these men were so strong that there was no way to avoid it.

Someone seized my upper arm and pulled me forwards. Stumbling, I tried tripping gracefully forward with small delicate strides so I wouldn't fall, but I fell anyway as I was pulled forwards faster than I could walk. Tripping over what must have been the threshold of the door, someone grabbed at my sleeve just as I went over. The winter wind cut through my trousers – we were outside. As we walked up the hill we were still pushed hard from one side to the other, for the sport of it I supposed. My head crashed against something sharp, right on the fresh wound. Warm blood trickled down the back of my neck. Then we stopped and I felt a great hand grab me by the collar. We must be at the top of the narrow alley, I thought, preparing to advance out into Salisbury Alley. The alley was too narrow for horses, so they must be thinking of walking us up the alley in full view. I was pushed forward again, one man holding my left bicep, another holding my right bicep. Footsteps on either side, and then I was lifted upwards. We stopped again, my shirt almost severing my throat.

'Who are ye? What's your business?' It sounded like the voice of the upright man, though I couldn't be sure. The bag on my head rendered all sounds muffled.

'Our business is none of thy business. Stand aside or suffer the consequences.'

The grip on my right arm tightened like a vice.

'Unless I be much mistaken those is Davy Dowling's legs I see running beneath that sack. If those be Davy Dowling's legs, then your business *is* my business, for he be a friend of mine.'

'They ain't Davy Dowling's legs.'

'Well, they be Davy Dowling's old trousers, and Davy Dowling's old shoes. And those short stumpy legs, well they look like the legs of Davy Dowling's friend.'

Short and stumpy? My legs were not stumpy. I heard a clatter, what sounded like a wooden truncheon tapping on the floor.

'Out of my way,' a voice growled just in front of me.

'And what makes this all the more interestin' is that Mary Hutch, what lives just round the corner, says that a group of soldiers, dressed most unlike soldiers, have just taken Davy Dowling and his friend out of her house, 'gainst their will.' The upright man shouted now, a rallying call to the local neighbourhood.

A low murmuring became a buzzing and a roar. It sounded like we were in the middle of a riot. The air felt hot, and then I was being jostled and pushed. The hands that held my arms disappeared, and all I could hear was shouting and cussing, and the sound of men grunting. I tried pushing forward, but I was pushing against a wall of wriggling, shoving elbows and knees. So I tried to walk sideways, in search of a wall to lean against, determined not to fall onto the floor where I feared I would be crushed. I found my wall and dug my heels into the floor pushing myself against it. Bending my knees I rested most of my weight onto my right foot, which is where most of the buffeting was coming from. Then suddenly – light! The bag on my head was whisked off. I looked into Dowling's solemn face as he pulled the foul gag from my mouth. Friendly hands untied my wrists. The alley was full of men, sweating and panting, clapping each other on the back and congratulating themselves. Women and children leant out of first-floor windows enjoying the entertainment. The earth floor was dug up and rutted as if a herd of cows had been chased down the alley. Hats and shoes lay discarded and torn.

The upright man appeared next to Dowling, his sharp teeth glistening, his brown eyes alive and darting. He had a long cut down one cheek, but didn't seem to know it. Picking up his truncheon he laid it across his shoulders with arms resting on it, like he was tied to a cross. I wiped the dust off my face and looked up the alley to see what was happening. A pile of men sat on three of our assailants, pinning them to the floor. They were covered in dirt, and stared out from beneath the human pyramid with scared faces.

'What'll they do to them?' I demanded, ridding my hands and wrists of the last of the rope.

'Same as we'll do to him.' The upright man pointed back the other way. Four men were holding the last soldier, while two more tied his chest and stomach to a massive cartwheel. Wriggling and squirming, he kicked and screamed out at the top of his voice, but none would hear outside of Alsatia, for the excited celebrations of the crowd drowned out his frantic protests.

'And what's that?' I asked, afraid of what the answer might be.

'We'll cut off his arms and then we'll cut off his legs, then we'll wheel him down the hill into the river.' The upright man leered.

And this was civilisation.

'I'll thank you for saving our lives,' Dowling said quietly to the upright man, fingering his jaw.

'It be a pleasure, Davy Dowling, I know that ye'll return the favour one day.' The upright man swung his truncheon through the air and turned to supervise the execution of the first soldier. A man appeared with a short, squat little axe. Its blade was chipped and blunt.

The faces of those that still lay squashed stared out in terror. Yet there was no possibility that the crowd would be deprived of its entertainment. 'Can we go?' I pulled on Dowling's sleeve.

'Aye. There's nothing to be done here.' Dowling replied in a hoarse whisper. He pulled me back into the alley. 'God will not cast away a perfect man; neither will he help evildoers.'

I suppose.

'I promised Mary and Thomas ten shillings,' he looked to my pocket.

'Make it a guinea,' I replied wearily.

We made our way quickly back up to the top of Salisbury

Alley, moving fast, without talking to one another, keen to put as much distance as possible between us and the horrors that were taking place behind us. Hewitt's murder was all the more confusing. If he was the murderer, then who had motive to kill *him*? Someone that could command soldiers – but to what end? If he was not the murderer then why kill him? As a convenience? But Joyce was already hung – why go to the trouble of killing Hewitt besides? Before we parted company I suggested that Dowling take advantage of his connections with the Mayor to go search Hewitt's house now that he was dead. Perhaps there would be a letter there, or a diary, or best of all a confession signed by all involved. I would find Hill and attempt to get some sense from him as to what this latest development signified.

Hill was not at home and nor were his shoes. I was tired and could think of little else to do, so went to the Crowne leaving message that I would wait for Hill there. Perhaps not the safest place to be, given that we had quite possibly precipitated the death of a powerful merchant, but it served good ale.

As I sat and supped and watched ordinary people going about their ordinary lives, it all seemed absurd. Hewitt now a victim, apparently not the man that killed Anne Giles, nor the man that butchered her husband. Why then had he behaved so strangely? Why had he sent men to kill me? It made no sense. With Hewitt dead and Hill's Epsom story exposed as the fraud it so clearly was, this left us then with only one other account – Prynne's bizarre theory of Fifth Monarchists, treason and plot – for which there was no evidence whatsoever. In the meantime someone else would have us dead, someone who could command soldiers to do his deeds. And my father was still missing. All very odd and no mistake.

I watched a large fellow scratch at his balls and pass comment to a friend that I could not hear. It was clearly funny, since both of them laughed with great gusto. Strange to think that we all lived in the same world, yet they felt safe and happy and I was alone and in great danger. All I needed was a change of face, so that none would recognise me.

'Mr Lytle?' Hill's maidservant appeared next to me, flustered and ill at ease, eyeing warily the men that cast her sly glances. She handed me a note and was gone. The note was from Hill, of course, though I didn't recognise the writing.

Meet me at Bride's at ten. News of your father.

It was fifteen minutes before. I left the mug unfinished and hurried out.

Chapter Twenty-Two

The Wallnut-tree
An antipathy seems to exist between this tree and the oak with the result that one does not tolerate the other.

The strange church stood as it always had, quiet and still. I dismounted and wandered through the churchyard past a patch of white-bottle. The door was open – someone was at home other than God. I crossed the threshold slowly, peering into the darkness. No light. No candles. Then a thick arm wrapped itself round my neck, a knife pricked hard at my throat and a low, deep voice whispered into my ear. 'Harry Lytle.' The knife dug in just below my Adam's apple, 'Shrewsbury's hound.'

I struggled to breathe. A cloth was clamped down hard over my mouth and nose. I couldn't move my Adam's apple without forcing it down onto the razor-sharp blade.

'Walk.'

I couldn't walk. The knife was hard against my throat and he was pulling my neck back so hard I couldn't stand on my own, let alone walk. A trickle of blood dripped down to my chest. The knife moved swiftly to my ribs, and he grabbed my hair. I fingered my throat. The wound stung, but it wasn't deep, just a scratch. Steered by the hand that held my hair, I walked forward into the cool interior of the silent church, towards the lectern by the far wall. He marched me towards the front pew, the door to which stood open, and forced me to sit, pulling my hair down with one hand and digging the knife into my waist with the other. I dropped my cane, which clattered to the floor. Then the knife was withdrawn and his face appeared in front of me. Hiding his knife inside his coat he grabbed my wrist. His hands moved like lightning, and before I could think what to do he had bound it to the wooden lattice that decorated the front of the simple pew. Then he grabbed for my other wrist. I whipped it back behind my shoulder until the knife appeared again. His wrists were as thick as most men's legs. Now I understood how John Giles had been trussed and bound so easily.

At least I could see him now, but the church was poorly lit, and all I could really make out was that he was dressed from head to toe in black. A thick cloak flowed from his chin down to the tops of his big muddy boots. An ordinary hat hid his brow and a scarf covered his mouth. I was in real pain; my wrists were bound so tight that my fingertips were numb, but he just pulled the rope tighter, puffing with satisfied exertion. He sat down next to me on my right. I was forced to lean forwards, held there by the ropes.

'God bringeth out those that are bound by chains.' Leaning back, he wrapped his left arm across the back of the pew, while the right hand held the knife. It had a long, thin blade. His eyes burnt, a bright incandescent blue.

Fighting to stay calm I could not stop my arms and legs

from shaking. 'You killed Anne Giles here. Joyce saw you do it, didn't he?'

'Whosoever believeth in him shall have eternal life.'

I pulled gently at the ropes, but my wrists might as well have been set in stone. 'Am I to die as she did?'

'No. Thy death will be swift. Then will I take thy body to the river and throw it there. It is time for all of this to end, now that all knoweth that I will be their plagues.'

'You will be judged after this life if not in it.' My voice trembled like a woman.

The black-robed figure shook his head. 'Mark the perfect man, and behold the upright: for the end of that man is peace. Anne Giles was innocent, and she shall have her reward in the Kingdom of our Lord. The rest were evil sinners, and I have done God's work in dispatching them to the eternal flames of Hell.'

'Richard Joyce was not an evil sinner.'

The blue eyes fixed upon me. 'That man was dead already. It was God's mercy that led him here that night. Blessed are they which are persecuted for righteousness' sake; for theirs is the Kingdom of Heaven.'

I pulled harder, without success. 'It is not your place to walk the streets of London like the Lord God himself, making judgements as to the worth of men.'

Laughing out loud with real mirth he exclaimed, 'Ah, but I am the Lord Chief Justice. Indeed it is by my judgement that men live or die in this City. It is my job to dispatch you poor wretches. If I say you are guilty then it is in God's name that you are pronounced guilty. And the fault is yours.'

'What was Anne Giles guilty of?'

'She died for another's sin. I told her how I got her own

husband to steal the key to this church. She wept. Not for herself, but for him, though he did not deserve her tears.'

'You knew her since she was a baby.' His blue eyes narrowed. 'I know who you are, and why you killed Anne Giles.'

'I just told you who I am.' The cold blade wormed its way up my right nostril. 'But it would please me greatly to hear thy account. Speak well, friend, or else I will slit thy nose.' His voice was black velvet.

'I will say nothing with your blade up my nose.'

The knife wormed its way higher up my nostril, towards my brain. I felt a lump in my throat and had to cough and splutter, drawing back my head. The knife stayed where it was a while, but then it was slowly withdrawn. I sneezed and wiped my nose hard against my upper arm, desperate to be rid of the foul tickle.

'Entertain me with thy words of wisdom and insight,' he mocked me.

I cleared my throat and rubbed my nose again. 'You are Keeling.' I looked again into the blue eyes. 'You killed Anne Giles in fear that William Ormonde would disclose your part in a plot to kill the King. You are a Fifth Monarchist. You knew that Ormonde is too much of a coward to do anything about it, for fear of his own reputation, and for fear of you, I suppose. And he is a wretch. He allowed Joyce to hang for his cowardice, and your sins.'

'My sins?' The blue eyes stared at me with such unrelenting intensity that I felt dry-mouthed terror.

'You killed a sweet, innocent girl for no other reason than to quieten William Ormonde. Why kill her? Why not simply make your intentions clear, it would have been enough?

Methinks that you kill for the pleasure it gives you. Why else did you kill Mottram and Wilson, and then go to the trouble of cutting off their heads?'

I held my breath.

Keeling breathed quietly, saying nothing. 'Your meddling hath served no purpose other than to please your master. And believe me, Lytle, he doth not deserve it.'

'It was my duty to try and save Richard Joyce from your justice. He died as a murderer.'

'Not in God's eyes.'

'You had no right to kill him, nor her.'

'Now the Lord of peace himself gives her peace always, by all means.'

'God didn't say that. It was a man that said that.'

'Art thou ungodly, Lytle? What amazement is this? Or indeed, shouldst we be amazed at all? 'Tis true that thou art a drunkard, a dancing fairy that doth frequent whorehouses, and alehouses. All these unlawful pursuits you indulge in on the Lord's Day, betimes. The Lord saveth such as be of contrite spirit, Lytle, but if you will not turn from all your sins, then ye shall die, ye shall not live.' He picked up the knife again.

I looked to the pulpit that Anne Giles had been tied to. 'Torturing a young woman, poking out her eyes from their sockets. How did that feel, Keeling?' I asked with sick wonder. 'So great is your mercy. I don't believe Richard Joyce's death troubles you one degree.'

'Quiet!' He stuck the knife into my ribs.

'Ah,' I snorted, 'you're a savage brute.'

He growled. 'I was born a common man, Lytle, like your father. I laboured hard.' The knife lashed out suddenly. I jerked my head back, yet he still caught my cheek. I took a deep, short breath in shock. If I hadn't seen the blade coming then I would have been cut to the bone. The sweat prickled on my brow and on my back. His eyes were wide and his mouth was open slightly, panting like a terrified cat. He held the knife out, up and wide to his right, hanging majestically in the air. I waited breathlessly, the blood streaming down my cheek and neck.

Smiling a tight, twisted smile, he lowered his knife and tucked it between his legs. 'One thing more I will tell thee, before thou art dead. I have watched thee keenly, through my eyes and those of others, to see what sort of man you are, what sort of man it was that Shrewsbury sent against me. I still know not why he picked you. It is my place to ensure that justice is done within my jurisdiction, and that is what I do. I administer justice, not the law, for the law and justice are as far apart as my left ear and my right ear. It is justice that decreed Anne Giles must die, to atone for the sins of her father, and it is not ungodly, for I remind you that the innocent often die for the guilty, so that the guilty might be saved. It is a blessing for her that she died as she did and God will reward her for it. And it is justice that Ormonde now bears the grief and the guilt of his daughter's death, the knowledge that he killed his own daughter, not me, but him. For he would have betrayed me, and in doing so, betrayed the Lord Jesus Christ. Now justice will see him suffer for it, here, and beyond if he does not repent. You must understand the difference between law and justice. John Giles broke many laws, as did the beasts that Hewitt sent after you. They all had learnt how to dance round the law, but they could not dance away from justice. I am Justice.'

'What is just about my death?' I asked with warm tears in

my eyes, the cold misery of helpless fear lying heavy on my heart.

'I am thy salvation, scoundrel! Ye will die because Shrewsbury, who is a devil, hath laid the path for you. But I will save thee. I will sprinkle clean water upon you, and ye shall be clean. I will take away the stony heart out of your flesh, and I will give thee a heart of flesh. For then thou shalt lift up thy face without spot. Repent, Lytle.'

Smiling faintly he seemed to regain his composure. He tested the point of his knife on his thumb, seemingly lost for a moment inside his own reflections. I peered around the inside of the church. This was the view that Anne Giles had seen not so very long ago. And so, I thought, ends the short life of Harry Lytle. I tried to quell the fear that came unwelcome, tried to make peace with the God above that I had supposedly forsaken. My father was a Puritan, John Ray had been a Puritan too, but both of them preached too hard. I needed time to consider for myself. It was too soon to be asked to repent. The church offered no comment. But as I stared at the screen through misty eyes my heart jumped. Movement! Was it Hill, here to fulfil our appointment?

'Who appoints you justice?' I asked, seeking time to think and watch.

'God.' He held the blade before him.

'The King, not God! God appoints the King, the King appoints you. Ye must do the King's bidding!'

'Thus hath the Lord God shewed unto me. I am a herdsman, a gatherer of sycamore fruit.' His eyes were bright again and alert. Suddenly he slashed again, this time at the rope that tied me to the pew. 'The time is fulfilled, and the Kingdom of God is at hand: repent ye, and believe the gospel. It will be hastier and easier if thee sit back and push out thy ribs as far as they will go. I will slip the blade between thy ribs and into thy heart. Thee will be dead quickly. If thee sit in a ball with thy shoulders tight then I will have to stab you in the gut and you will bleed slowly.'

I looked into those blue eyes and foresaw my death. I pulled a face and did not sit back and push out my ribs. This was his act, not mine. He shook his head sadly. 'The spirit of truth dwelleth in you, and shall be with you.'

As I looked steadily into his eyes my moment of weakness passed. Leaning back I pulled on the cords that he had chopped. They stretched and strained, the threads on the edge of the ropes breaking away, leaving only two or three inner strands binding me to the pew. Keeling cut at them contemptuously. Sitting back I puffed out my chest. He smiled gently, with cruel eyes, then tossed his long-bladed dagger from hand to hand so it flashed in the dark gloom. I watched his hands without moving my head. He stopped, feinted, then lunged forward, the blade aimed straight at my heart, but I had been waiting for the blow, sitting with my weight on my left thigh. As his arm snaked forward I pushed to my right and twisted inwards. Drawing back my arms, hands still tangled together, I pushed myself forward and punched Keeling hard in the mouth with both fists so that he fell over the back of the pew. He stood up quickly, blood pouring from his lower lip, then stared at me in incredulous fury. Reaching for his knife, he dropped to the floor. Snapping my wrists apart I fell to my right and pushed myself scrabbling towards the right end of the pew. My blood was hot and saucy and I bounced off posts and benches without feeling the impact. I ran to the back of the church, towards the font, rushed to the door and pulled on the handle, but it was locked. Turning, my field of vision was filled with the figure of Keeling charging at me with knife drawn back ready to strike. I leant back against the door and kicked out hard and high, catching him in the stomach so he doubled up wheezing. This time he didn't drop the knife. I charged into him sideways, knocked him out of the way and pushed past, then ran down the aisle towards the pulpit, the pulpit that stood over the spot where Anne Giles had died.

'They being ignorant of God's righteousness have not submitted themselves unto the righteousness of God!' Keeling roared furiously from the back of the church, his voice ringing out clearly like a bell, filling every corner of the old building, bouncing from its walls and ringing in my ears.

Kneeling down I slipped off my shoes. I slid them behind the pulpit then ran silently off to the left, heading for the shadows of the speaking pew. Keeling's long, heavy stride echoed down the central aisle from font to pulpit. I ran on my toes towards the back of the church again, stooping down, hoping that he wouldn't see me in the murky grey light.

'Be not curious how the ungodly shall be punished, but ask how the righteous shall be saved, whose world it is, and for whom the world is created,' Keeling shouted again from the pulpit. I watched him from above the side of a pew, a few feet inside the western wall of the church standing motionless, legs a few inches apart with his back to the pulpit. His head moved very slowly from left to right as he scanned the interior of the silent church. A soft virgin light floated down from the heights of the tall windows set into the eastern wall, reaching down to about chest height before choking in the black darkness that engulfed the floor. I found myself staring not at Keeling, but beyond. Behind him, ten or twelve paces behind him, was another door, the door to the vestry – where all this started. Thinking for a minute, I then dropped to my hands and knees. There was a door out into the street from the vestry. Crawling quickly back towards the font, my hand landed on something hard and rod-shaped. My cane. I stood up straight in the font's shadow and projected my voice with all the confidence I could muster.

'The souls of the righteous are in the hand of God, and no torment shall touch them.' Immediately I dropped back down to my hands and knees and scurried back the way I'd come, with the cane tucked into my shirt.

'Dearly beloved, avenge not yourselves, but rather give place unto wrath: for it was written, Vengeance is mine; I will repay, saith the Lord,' he roared again, his giant steps cracking the air as he strode back again to the main door.

Crawling and slithering as fast as I could down the side of the church across the stone floor, I kept my head down, determined to make as much time as possible to try the vestry door and get away again in case it was locked.

'Lytle.' Keeling's voice was lower this time, smooth as silk, polished like a precious stone. 'I have changed my mind, Lytle. I must inflict great pain on thee before I kill thee. I must make thee wriggle and squirm like a fish on a stick, like a cock with its eyes pecked out. So that thee may repent! Thou hath forsaken justice, neglected the opportunity of a noble trial. Now justice must show thee the error of thy ways. Ye must repent!'

I reached the vestry door, grasped the handle and slowly turned it. I pushed. To my delight the door opened, silently. Easing it open eighteen inches, I slowly got to my feet then squeezed through the gap, at the same time peering back into the darkness. Keeling was quiet now; there were no steps, no breathing, no shadow. I slipped into the vestry. The door that led out was bigger with a heavy lock. Running across the room I seized the handle with both hands. Locked! I cursed, a silent scream of anguish and rage. Closing my eyes, I let the anger wash over me like a wave before turning slowly back to the vestry. The same wooden crucifix on the wall, table and chairs. I turned to the door that led back into the church, suddenly sure that Keeling was behind it. I stepped backwards behind the table. The vestry door slowly opened. Taking the cane out of my shirt I held it before me with both hands.

'Judge me, O Lord, according to my righteousness, and according to mine integrity that is in me,' Keeling said quietly as he entered. His eyes were narrowed, the sparkle of the luminous blue now subdued beneath a layer of thick sea-green ice. Drawing his hands up in front of him he steepled his fingers. 'Thus saith the Lord God: Behold, I judge between cattle and cattle, between the rams and the goats. I, even I, will judge between the fat cattle and between the lean cattle.' Reaching into the deep folds of his voluminous black coat he pulled the knife out again, then kicked at the table with a heavy black boot.

Standing up straight I swung the cane about my head, catching Keeling a heavy blow to the side of the head as he walked forward. He staggered, his left hand clutching for support. He caught the back of a chair and fell forward onto it. The chair gave way and he fell onto both knees and I swung the stick again and hit him square across the back of his head, so hard that the stick broke. I stood panting, holding the top half of the stick in my right hand. Crouching, I heaved his body round. His eyes were half closed and his breathing was irregular. I pulled the folds of his coat apart, and started rifling through the pockets for a key. Both inner breast pockets were empty. Both side pockets were empty. I ran my hands up and down his body looking for more pockets, but couldn't find any. Cursing, I turned to the main door. Just in time I turned back as Keeling lunged. Screaming in shock, I scrabbled backwards, kicking myself away from him. He stood, pushing himself up with his left hand, holding the knife steady with his right. The left side of his face was purple and swollen and he bared his teeth.

I stood up to face him. 'No more preaching?'

He roared and threw himself forward, knife to my throat. We fell against each other, clutching and grappling. We writhed and wrestled on the floor, each struggling for the better position until he gasped, throwing back his head, eyes tight shut and teeth bared, white-lipped. His back arched and he peeled away from me, rolling gently across the floor.

I stood up and looked down. One half of my cane stuck out neatly from between two of his ribs, the tip poking into the ventricle of his heart, the silver lamb sitting aloft, untouched by the bright-red blood that pumped out around the bottom of the stick.

I pulled his body around a second time, and as I did so a glint of metal shone about his neck. It was a chain and the key to Bride's was on the end of it. I walked out of the vestry door and painfully up the centre aisle. As I walked I saw movement again, out the corner of my eye, over to the east side beneath the tall, narrow windows.

'Who's there?' I called, spotting a shadowy figure lurking in the gloomy south-east corner. No one answered.

'Come out now,' I shouted, walking across the pews towards it, beside myself with rage, relief and fear. But none replied. I walked slowly out of the church and into the wintry air I thought never to breathe again.

A familiar figure stood at the church gate, a large man with a hard potbelly and broad shoulders.

'Hill?'

'Aye, Harry.'

'What are you doing out here for God's sake?'

I saw the beads of sweat on his upper lip, the lines around his eyes. 'I heard that you were to meet Keeling here. Has he come?'

This made no sense. 'Heard what? I was here to meet you!'

Standing with his arms crossed and legs astride, he was barring my exit. 'It is no matter.'

Walking up close I returned his unfriendly gaze. 'You sent me a note.' I pulled it from my pocket and gave it to him. 'Where were you?'

Crumpling it into a ball, he thrust it deep into one of his pockets. 'This is not from me.'

Lying cock. 'You've been here the whole while. You would have watched me die.'

'No,' he shook his head slowly. 'You don't understand.'

'You are Shrewsbury's agent. Why would you betray me?' A lump formed in my throat, unexpected and unwanted. 'No, I don't understand. Less it be for money. Ready whore, ready money. It is what you value above all things, is it not?'

'Let me alone. Had it not been me then it would have been

another, and I would have found myself floating in Thames river.'

'My life for yours, then.'

'I was around to watch over you, Lytle. I have met with Shrewsbury every day since this started, telling him what you have been doing, to whom you have been talking. I've hightailed it after you from here to Epsom, here to Shoreditch, here to Epsom again, and all about the slums and filthy pits of London. God's mercy, it hath been most taxing.'

'What assistance have ye lent me? Even now, you would have stood back and watched me killed.' I shook my head sorrowfully. 'You are no friend of mine, you shitty piece of scum.'

'Aye, well.' He bowed his head. 'Soon we will all be dead, and I'll receive judgement and so will you, and I am sure we will both be saying that we made mistakes and should have done better.'

'You set me up to die.'

'For God's sake, Lytle! That is enough! I am fed up with your whining and complaining. I have been tending you like a wet nurse these last days, watching over you, making sure nothing happens to you. You don't know what it has been like.' He stepped forwards and tapped me hard on the forehead with his finger. I had to stop myself from snapping it off. Instead I punched him as hard as I could in the mouth. When he didn't fall I hit him again, harder. He stumbled back with a hand up to his jaw. I had caught him hard and cut his lip and his gum. His lip was starting to swell already. I smiled.

'Thanks be to thee,' he mumbled.

I went to pass him. 'Keep your thanks to feed your chickens, you piece of filthy scum. I'll see you later.'

Three men I'd not seen before appeared from nowhere and blocked my passage.

'What's this, Hill?'

'You are under arrest, Lytle. For the killing of Lord Keeling.' Busying himself with his bleeding mouth, he would not look me in the eye.

Chapter Twenty-Three

Dogges-rose
*Sometimes a smooth hairy lump grows on the stalks of
this plant. If you cut open this gall, you will find it
packed with small white maggots.*

That they put me in the same cell as Joyce may have been
coincidence, I suppose. They took me to Newgate in a coach,
wrists and ankles manacled. These men were sober, serious
and very determined. They didn't beat me or foul-mouth me,
or indeed take any notice of me whatever, just made me go
where they wanted me to go without any fuss or effort. In the
coach one sat either side of me and one opposite. All three of
them looked out of the window, eyes alert, practically silent.
They spoke only when they had to, in short crisp sentences,
very quietly.

We were at Newgate inside twenty minutes. They themselves
escorted me through the prison, along the corridor and down
the slimy steps into the stone hold, never once uttering a
word to any. My protests were ignored, my feelings were of

284

no importance. Once the door was open, they propelled me firmly across the threshold and clapped manacles about my wrists and ankles before closing it behind me. When the sound of their steps had petered out it was silent and utterly dark.

The floor beneath my feet was slimy and thick. It stank of piss and shit as it had done before. Through my shoes I could feel a thickish layer of mud and straw. God knows what lived in it. I leant against the wall as best I could, but the stonework was uneven and scattered with sharp edges. All was silent, save for the occasional rustle and squeak from the rats. Something bit at my ankle. I kicked out, though without much force. The manacles prevented it. No light, no noise, just me, all alone. I felt a sudden panic – what if none came to feed me? What if no one told any that knew me where I was? I stood there for an age, trying to quell the fear. But it was so black and so noiseless, and the rats kept nibbling at my feet. No hope. No life.

Why was I here? Shrewsbury had what he wanted, didn't he? He wanted to have it over Keeling. Well Keeling was dead – I had killed him. So why was I here? Hadn't I given him what he wanted? My legs began to ache, first at the knees, then the ankles, and then my thighs. My muscles got stiffer and stiffer as if I had been walking for miles. No way of knowing how quickly time passed, I tried to think of something else. My stomach rumbled, despite the foul air. My tongue was dry. Things kept biting at my ankles if I didn't move my legs constantly. The manacles started to rub raw against my wrists and feet. My head started to throb and the backs of my eyes began to burn. If there was a Hell, it would be like this. Where the worm dieth not, and the fire is not quenched. Well, my fire would not be quenched either. Sometime soon someone would open that door. In the meantime there was nothing to do but wait.

It was not soon, but someone did eventually come. One of the gaolers strode in holding a torch above his head and gave me a ladle of foul water to sip. He threw a piece of green bread at my feet and then was gone.

At some point there came a time when I could no longer stand. I searched for the driest quarter of the small cell floor and gathered there the driest straw. Then I sat down and waited for the water to soak into the seat of my trousers.

There are lessons to be learnt in the art of being imprisoned. These include:

1) Eat all the food they give you, no matter how foul it is. Else the rats will come and eat it.

2) Choose one corner in which to sit. Take care that it is not the lowest part of the floor. Use the farthest corner to piss in and shit.

3) Regard your body and your mind as two different entities. If you cannot dissociate your brain from the rats and the roaches and all the bugs that walk about your body, then you will go mad.

A man came to see me. He looked like a clerk, like I did a week or so ago. His face betrayed disgust, like I was an animal or a madman. He looked at me like I probably looked at Joyce just a fortnight ago.

'You have been indicted,' he told me, as if he expected some reaction. He pulled out a piece of paper from his jacket and read it aloud. I don't recall exactly what he said, but it was basically an indictment for the murder of Lord Keeling. Sitting in my pool of crap and piss I watched him speak. It was a good thing, I reflected, for it meant that I would be going to trial – and soon. Out of this hole.

It had occurred to me before this fellow arrived that I had two choices, should I be indicted. I could talk about what we had discovered at Epsom, with no mention of my doubts concerning the truth of it, nor of course the disinterment – the tale that Shrewsbury clearly wished spoken in other words. Or I could tell the whole truth. This was my dilemma. The more time dragged on, with my wrists and ankles burning like they were doused in lime, the less well disposed I was towards Shrewsbury, and the more I felt inclined to speak plainly. Now that I had been arrested, by Hill of all people, and indicted, now I could not trust Shrewsbury to safeguard my well-being – this was obvious.

I had thought through all of my witnesses. First I would call Dowling, who could testify all that I had seen. The slaughterer that had seen Keeling kill John Giles. As my star witness I would call William Ormonde, who could surely now speak openly, and I would consider calling Mrs Johnson and John Stow. The combined testimony of all these witnesses would surely be enough to acquit me.

'What is your plea?' the clerk asked me.

Ah now! This was important. I struggled to pull myself up to my feet. He stepped back uncertainly so that his face sunk back a little into the shadows of the torch held by the gaoler.

'Might we speak upstairs?' I enquired politely, bowing

slightly, trying my best to put the fellow at ease.

The clerk opened his mouth then shut it again, looking at the gaoler as if for guidance before realising the absurdity of it and becoming flustered. I avoided his eye. 'Yes.' He wrinkled his nose. 'That is a very good idea.'

Never has a shithouse smelt so fresh as Newgate once we climbed out of the stone hold. When he saw me in the light I fancy he was able to see that I was unlikely to pounce upon him in some manic frenzy. Optimistic that this fellow would listen to me, I began to feel quite rejuvenated, hopeful that I would be able to put forward my point of view. When he dug into his pocket and purchased a meat pie and a jug of ale for me, then I almost danced for him.

'Well,' he said, sat on a little stool opposite me, 'what is your plea?'

My mouth was full of gravy and thick, dry crumbs.

'You may wish for the judgement of God, or you may go to trial. I assume you wish to go to trial?' I nodded vigorously. If you wished for the judgement of God, then there was no disgrace upon your family, nor would you be executed in public. However, you were laid upon your back on the floor over a large boulder. A board was placed upon your stomach upon which were loaded heavy stones. One by one. Over the course of several days.

'Then you may plead innocence, self-defence or provocation.' He regarded me earnestly with anxious brown eyes. I considered. The fact was that I had stuck Prynne's stick into Keeling's ribs. That was an accident, self-defence or provocation? If I was successful in pleading an accident then I would be acquitted. If I was found guilty of self-defence then I would be pardoned, but would be fined a sum of money equivalent to the value of all my goods. Which by now was half what it had been anyway. If found guilty of killing Keeling under provocation, then I'd lose my property and be branded on one hand. The jury would never believe it was an accident; he came at me with a knife and I stabbed him.

'Self-defence,' I replied.

'Very well.' He opened a volume that lay upon his knee and wrote in it. He then closed it and stood up.

I was by no means ready to go back into the stone hold. 'When will the trial be?'

Sitting down again he replied. 'I think the day after tomorrow, or perhaps even tomorrow. They are keen to try you quickly.'

'Who will be my counsel? Will it be you?'

'No-o, Mr Lytle. In cases such as these you are not permitted counsel. You will represent yourself.'

I had thought so. 'To whom then do I submit my list of witnesses?'

The young fellow looked at me wonderingly from out of his fresh innocent face. Like mine had been. 'You are not entitled to submit a list of witnesses.'

'But I have witnesses who I believe will be willing to testify.'

'No matter. There will be only one witness, I believe.'

I was frightened. I knew that you could not force a man to testify against his will, but I felt sure that at least William Ormonde would want to set the record straight, and I was sure that Dowling would speak up for me. 'Who is the witness?'

The young clerk opened his book again and turned its pages. With one finger he slowly traced a line down one page and then another, until he found what he was looking for. 'Ah-ha.' He looked up and regarded me enquiringly. 'A friend of yours, I think?'

Dowling?

'William Hill of Basinghall Street?'

'Hill?' Hill as sole witness? What did that signify?

'I think the only other thing I can tell you is that the judge will be the Right Honourable James, Earl of Mansfield and the prosecutor is the Attorney General himself.' I knew neither. 'And you can of course challenge up to thirty-five jurymen, though I would consider challenging none.'

'Why so?'

Pulling a face he whispered, 'The Earl of Mansfield will not like it. He has a foul temper and little patience, and may hold it against you.'

'I see.' No counsel, no witnesses and a judge keen to finish quickly. It did not bode well.

'I will leave you some clean clothes to change into.'

'That is good of you.'

'No, sir,' he grimaced. 'It is not for you, it is for the judge – he would not let you in his courtroom smelling as you do.'

'Of course.'

'Good luck.' He stood and regarded me awkwardly. 'May God be with you.'

'Thank you.' I sat and looked at the flagstoned floor. He hadn't been so far.

Back in the hold I racked my poor brains. What could it mean, calling Hill as the only witness? True – he seemed to be working for Shrewsbury, but what motive could Shrewsbury have for seeing me condemned? I had spoken to Hill three times during this affair. Every time he had urged me to Epsom. So I had gone to Epsom, discovered what he wanted me to find, and got rid of Keeling for him besides. Hill was my *friend*. We had spent countless nights together drinking ale, smoking pipes and sharing our lives. Surely he would not turn the tale so that I was found guilty? Surely?

Chapter Twenty-Four

Thistle with a bending head
*All the plants that grow freely with us have a nodding head,
which feature easily distinguishes it from others and
it has no need of further description.*

They allowed me to wash, gave me new clothes and removed my manacles for the trial. The clothes did not fit well, were made of rough linen and indeed were not all that clean, but they were a great improvement on those that had begun to stick to my skin down in the putrid environs of the stone hold. I felt like the King of England himself as I walked into the courtroom, my newly shaven head free of lice, my feet and arse mercifully dry.

As we walked down the bright wooden corridor, alive with people going out about their business with energy and commitment, I felt my own soul awaken. It was contagious, and I found myself imagining all kinds of optimistic outcomes. After all, was not my fate in the hands of my closest friend?

My mood changed completely when we entered the

courtroom. There was not a face I recognised. To my left was a crowd of men, gentlemen they looked like, gathered in small groups of two or three talking seriously. When I entered, flanked on either side by my guards, all eyes turned to me and the din transformed itself instantaneously into a low buzz. I saw horrified fascination and disgust, timorous excitement, anger and fear. None of these men were my friends. I was escorted to a seat at the front of the court where again I sat with guards on either side, and waited.

The Attorney General and the judge entered together, which did not seem proper to me. They spoke to each other in rapid serious staccato, talking as fast as they walked. Obviously they knew each other well, but were in serious mood. They looked at me together, at the same time, short, sharp glances, then strode on. The Attorney General settled himself to my right where he was immediately engulfed in a small army of assistants that had been following at a distance. The judge climbed a short staircase, sat down and started a conversation with one of the clerks at court. They talked for many minutes, never once looking in my direction. I wondered if any would notice were I to discreetly depart. I doubted whether I was to be a real player in this drama at all.

At last the court was called to order. Now the judge looked at me, peering at me down his long nose with cold, stern eyes as the indictment was read out for all to hear. An old man with a long, narrow face, his lips seemed to be curled inwards in a sign of universal disapproval. I returned his stare for a while, which he didn't seem to like, for his cheeks went red, so then I looked the other way, towards the prosecutor, upon reflecting that it would not be a good idea to anger the man unnecessarily. The prosecutor was also staring at me, but with a broad, contented smile. A stout fellow, but much younger than the judge. Underneath the edges of his periwig I could see strands of straight black hair, ungreyed and oiled. His brows were thick and black, his eyes a very dark brown, deep and impenetrable. He sat back carelessly with his well-rounded stomach sitting up for all the world to gaze on – if they so cared. After watching me for a while his eyes returned to scanning a paper he held in one hand, just in front of his double chin, caring not if I continued to stare at him, nor who looked away first. Indeed he reminded me of a wealthy merchant sitting in the corner of a coffee house reading the daily news-sheet, happily anticipating a large breakfast.

A clerk began to read a long list of names; Henry Busby of Greatwood Street, George Wheatley of Coleman Street, Richard Gildhart of Friday Street and so on. These were the jurors, sitting on their own bench to our left all in a long row. Another thirty or more stood in a crowd to the left of the bench. All were dressed in their finest silks; dark blues and greens mostly, with brilliant white cuffs and scarves. A fine bunch, indeed. Lords for the day. Those that looked at me now tried to do so in a manner that was both stern and munificent. Today was their finest hour, and it was I that could spoil it for them. The others stood impatiently and anxious, keen that they might be called to serve if others were ejected. Today could be their finest hour too, if I were to make it so.

'Mr Attorney General.' The judge addressed my learned colleague in a voice that reminded me of dry toast. 'Do thee challenge any that hath been selected as juror?'

'My Lord, I do not,' my learned colleague replied loudly, smiling at the jury as he did so.

'Doth the accused challenge any that hath been selected as

juror?' the judge asked without even bothering to look at me. Feeling so small and insignificant as I did, it would have been an effort simply to say 'nay' in a very quiet voice, but I stopped myself from it. The judge was such a dreadfully pompous bag of goose bones that I did not feel inclined to make his day easy. I felt sure that his idea of this easy day was a quick guilty verdict; so the sooner I woke him up the better. The judge looked up with weary impatience, sure, no doubt, either that I was too dull to know that it was my place to speak, or that I was too timorous. Turning my attention to the jurors I ignored him.

Of the twelve, five were looking at me. I could not pretend that they were friendly, but at least they were looking at me. The other seven were sitting with their finely sculpted chins held high in the air or were seeking to establish sympathetic eye contact with the judge, or both.

I stood up. 'Aye, I challenge seven.' The guards stood up too, flustered, and the judge looked at me with real hatred.

'Tyburn calls,' whispered one of the guards into my ear. It was the first thing I had heard him speak.

'I challenge seven, My Lord.'

All of the jurors were looking at me now, suddenly concerned, afraid that this great day was to be taken from them. It suddenly occurred to me that those I left behind would feel compelled to show that they felt no gratitude to me. No matter, I had chosen my path, so now was the time to walk it.

'Which?' the judge snapped.

'Well, I forget their names, but I can point them out to you.'

'Do so!'

The guards showed no sign of allowing me to pass, so I extended my arm and pointed carefully at each of the seven.

The first blinked and looked at me disbelievingly. He seemed surprised to learn that I was even in the room. No matter. The seven of them walked off, shoulders slumped. Back to work you leery rascals. Seven more took their place. After watching them for a while, three returned my stare and four of them stood self-consciously straight backed, gazing forwards. Those four went. Those four were replaced. Of those four all went. Of the next four I kept two, and so on. Finally we were left with a new jury all of whom now stared at me.

By now the judge looked ready to chew on his desk. 'Mr Attorney General,' he snarled. 'Do thee challenge any that hath been selected as juror?'

'I do not, My Lord.' The Attorney General looked across at me with laughing eyes like I had made his day more interesting.

'Thanks be!' exclaimed the judge, turning to me again. 'Thy plea is self-defence. Be that still the case, or do thee seek to change that besides?'

'No, My Lord. My plea remains that of self-defence.'

'Very well, then call the first witness,' the judge said more calmly, flicking the instruction at his chief clerk as he spoke.

'Mr William Marmaduke Hill!' the clerk summoned solemnly.

Marmaduke? It was with some discomfort that I heard the unfamiliar name. If we were such friends then how was it that I didn't know he had the name of Marmaduke? Looking over my shoulder I saw the benches were full now, of clerks and other anonymous-looking fellows, sitting in groups, some of them with notebooks and quills, others with nothing at all, yet still poised to do something, go somewhere, take a message, run an errand. Then the doors opened and Hill appeared, escorted by one of the court clerks. Though it was I who was on trial, it was he that walked as if fettered in chains. Shoulders slumped and head rigid, like he was afraid to look about him for fear of being beaten with a stick. He took short, slow strides towards the witness box as if it were his own scaffold. The old brown shoes had been replaced with new, shiny black shoes with a large brass buckle. He coughed a lot and was sweating about his brow even though it was cold. A very fat man, I reflected, who did not look odd in the corner of a dark tavern at night, but in the cold, bright light of the courtroom he looked out of place and uncomfortable. Only once as he stood in the dock alone did his eyes wander curiously about the courtroom. When he saw me sat there opposite, his eyes dropped and so did his head. I fancied he had been hoping I would be absent.

'What is your name?' The clerk stood with his back to Hill speaking very loudly and looking at the ceiling.

'William Hill of Basinghall Street.' It wasn't loud enough for the judge who made him repeat himself. The clerk sat down and the Attorney General stood up.

'Mr Hill.' The Attorney General stuck his chest out so far that his belly sat almost unnoticed just above his belt.

'Yes?' Hill looked up at his inquisitor, and none other.

'Describe to me your profession, if you will?'

'I am a merchant.'

'A merchant of what?'

'A merchant of goods.' I recognised his reluctance to divulge any one thing.

The Attorney General licked his lips and smiled with all his teeth. 'What goods, Mr Hill?'

'Various goods,' Hill glowered at him. 'I inherited my

father's business and I import goods from outside England, and sell them inside England.'

'A merchant, then?' The Attorney General spoke as if it was a new revelation. The jury were looking at him as if he were either a little mad or very intelligent. He had their attention in any case.

Hill didn't bother replying, just looked at the Attorney General resignedly in anticipation of further bothersome questions.

'In the case that we are here to speak of today, Mr Hill, I believe that you had a *particular* role, did you not?' The Attorney General leant forward with his hands on his desk. 'A role unrelated to that of merchant?'

'Aye. I was paid by Lord Shrewsbury to investigate the death of Anne Giles.' That could not be right. I stared at him, keen to catch his eye.

'Lord Shrewsbury, acting Lord Chief Justice?' The Attorney General rolled the last three words round his mouth like a large plum. Shrewsbury had already supplanted Keeling? That was quick work! In which case Shrewsbury had appointed this judge and Shrewsbury it was that had arranged this trial so that I could not call my own witnesses, nor seek help to make my case. Godamercy – it was worse than it could be!

'Aye, the same.'

'The defendant, Mr Harry Lytle, has also made claim that he was employed by Lord Shrewsbury to investigate the death of Anne Giles. Is that correct?'

'Yes,' I replied loudly. The Attorney General froze, dramatically, and turned to face me very, very slowly, with an appalled expression upon his face. Everyone else in the court took his lead, except Hill. The judge breathed noisily through his nose as if he couldn't force his mouth to open.

'The defendant will not speak again unless I ask him a question directly. If he speaks again then he will be taken away from this place and the proceedings shall continue without him.' He looked at me severely. 'Does the court understand?'

The court murmured its assent. I tried to look suitably chastened.

'Mr Hill.' The Attorney General returned to his witness with great fortitude, still struggling to recover from the shock. 'Mr Lytle has also made claim that he was employed by Lord Shrewsbury to investigate the death of Anne Giles. Is that correct?'

'No.' Hill shuffled uncomfortably. 'Mr Lytle was asked to investigate the death of Anne Giles by his father, who was mistakenly of the belief that Anne Giles was a relation of the family.'

'A relation of the family?' The Attorney General looked suitably perplexed. 'Can it really be so?'

'Aye, sir I have a letter to that effect.'

'May I see the letter?' the Attorney General asked, one of his clerks hurrying forward to the witness box. Hill fished out a letter from within the folds of his jacket and handed it to the clerk. Well, I didn't see how this could fly. How could that be my letter?

'Allow me to read the letter, My Lord.' The Attorney General bowed to the judge, who nodded his head.

'Son.' The Attorney General declared solemnly, pausing for comic effect. Members of the jury sniggered dutifully. I began to despise this preening cockerel.

'Still here. In this lairy place.' Cue widespread laughter.

'Your mother seems happy, tho. Must be the pigs that they

breed here *coz she likes pigs*.' The clerks were laughing now with mouths wide open and hands to their stomachs, seeing who could make the most noise. The jury were not much more restrained. Even the judge smiled. Looking thoroughly ashamed of himself, looking at the toes of his feet, only Hill was not amused. So it should be. It was clear which way he had chosen to walk.

'Nothing to gladden a man's heart in Cocksmouth. Nothing for me to do save help her brother in the shed. Can't make shoes here. You caring for the shop? *Some hope*.' Disapproving groans from the Attorney General's willing audience. It was almost artistic the way he orchestrated their reactions. I had to acknowledge his expertise.

'I note you haven't been to visit. Your mother notes it too.' More of the same.

'You have a cuz, name of Anne. Married to a man called John Giles. Don't think you knew your cuz Anne. Not likely to now coz she dead. Someone killed her. I took the liberty of telling Mr Prynne esq. that you have to leave his employ.' There were some low groans and mutterings at the mention of Prynne's name.

'We'll be back when your grandmother has died. *About time, I say*.' The paid help behind me gasped their horror at such callous words and the jury turned to look at me, eyes burning with affronted loathing. Me? I just sat there fuming. Some villain had taken this letter from my house – which implied prior knowledge of its existence. And where the boggins was my father?

'Mr Hill,' cried the Attorney General in a strident tone designed to bring the court to order. 'Did you succeed in establishing who murdered Anne Giles?'

'Aye, sir. A man named Richard Joyce killed Anne Giles and was hung for it.' I looked at Hill. This was a lesson. The face of a man telling a very big lie. This was the same man that had casually dismissed the possibility that Joyce was the killer and had urged me hasten to Epsom.

The Attorney General feigned puzzlement. 'The accused protested against Joyce's indictment and said that in fact he did not kill Anne Giles and that there was none that saw him do it. That he was merely seen running from the church of St Bride's . . .' he paused for theatrical effect '. . . in fear.'

Hill said nothing.

'Who was this man Joyce?'

Hill cleared his throat and wiped his brow. 'Joyce was an old soldier, a Roundhead. He was injured on the field of battle, an injury that left him unbalanced, indeed mad. He had been trepanned.' The jurors all wrinkled their noses in revolted synchronicity. 'He was a man that often showed signs of furious rage. The killing itself was not witnessed, true, but he was seen running the streets of London with blood all over his hands, on his clothes and on his face. Later the girl's necklace was found about his person. All this was shown at his trial.'

'A trial conducted by Lord Keeling,' the Attorney General finished, looking to Hill for confirmation. Hill nodded.

'How did the accused respond to the conviction of Richard Joyce?'

'He was unhappy and came to talk to me.'

The Attorney General sat down. 'Why did he come to talk to you? Did he know that you were conducting the enquiry on behalf of Lord Shrewsbury?'

Hill at last turned to look in my direction. His eyes were

rheumy, red-rimmed and bloodshot. He looked very tired. 'No, he did not. Harry Lytle is an old friend of mine. We went to Cambridge together.' More gasps from the audience. I sat back, vexed. Not only was the sole witness testifying to my own misguided depravity, but he was doing so from the perspective of 'old friend'. Old friend, indeed. I narrowed my eyes, bared my teeth and glowered at Hill, who quickly looked away.

'So he came to you as an old friend.' The Attorney General waved a hand in my direction. 'What did you advise him as an old friend?'

'I advised him to go to Epsom to make peace with the Ormonde family.' Not entirely untrue, I supposed.

'What did he do instead?' The Attorney General stood up again suddenly with arms outstretched, succeeding in focussing the jury's attention on Hill.

'He was certain that Anne Giles had been killed by Matthew Hewitt of Basinghall Street. He believed that John Giles had been blackmailing Matthew Hewitt and that Hewitt murdered his wife as a warning to him.'

'Could that have been the case?'

'No, sir. It is inconceivable that a man as esteemed as Matthew Hewitt would kill Anne Giles, especially if you consider the manner in which she was killed. It is clear that Anne Giles was killed in a mad frenzy by Richard Joyce.'

'But Hewitt was a bit of a scoundrel?' The Attorney General winked. Oh aye, a bit of a ruffian and a scallywag. Again I had to congratulate the Attorney General for the way he was leading his jury. Meantime they sat there all self-important.

'He may have been,' Hill nodded, 'but no more than that. The Exchange is a place where hard words are often spoken and agreements sealed by a handshake. I think that Harry Lytle mistook what he saw there. I have a better understanding, since it is my trade.'

'Mistook what he saw there, you say.' The Attorney General grasped his chin between forefinger and thumb. 'How did this ignorance manifest itself, I wonder?'

'He came down to the Exchange and followed Matthew Hewitt about the place. It was inconvenient for Hewitt since it prohibited him going about his business as he would.'

'How do you know that the accused went to the Exchange and followed him about the place?'

'I was there and saw it.'

There was one of the jurors that I was beginning to loathe with a passion. He kept looking over at me, shaking his head and tutting audibly.

'I see.' The Attorney General shuffled some papers in silence. The jurors' heads slowly stretched outwards in his direction, necks craned, as if to try and read those papers. 'John Giles died soon after, did he not?'

'Aye, he did.' Hill's eyes started to dart and flicker and he started shuffling again.

'How did he die?'

'He hung himself by the neck,' Hill replied.

'Godamercy,' I muttered to myself. I turned to the guard on my left and whispered into his ear. 'That is the biggest lie he has spoken today!'

The court quietened and I found myself being stared at once more. The guard inched himself away from me, looking embarrassed. I could feel the judge's stern gaze upon me though I chose not to meet his stare. The prosecutor shook his head slowly and smiled sympathetically at me. I waited for the judge to speak, but it was the prosecutor that broke the silence.

'The accused would have us believe, I understand, that John Giles was thrown off London Bridge with a rope tied about his arms and legs by a villain?' He turned to Hill.

'Not possible,' Hill shook his head, 'and besides, I saw the rope marks around his neck.'

'Why did he take his own life?'

'Hard to say, sir, though there were rumours that he was at odds with Matthew Hewitt. Also the accused spent time with John Giles speaking of Matthew Hewitt, and may have put the fear of God into him.'

So! I was no longer even Harry Lytle. Even Hill was now referring to me as 'the accused'. Would I were able to put the fear of God into a man like I saw it in John Giles – then I would put it into William Hill! May his soul rot in Hell and be devoured by maggots.

'Did the accused come to speak with you again?' The Attorney General raised his eyebrows enquiringly. 'Perchance?'

'Aye, he came to see me. We met at the menagerie since he said he did not feel safe elsewhere.'

'Did not feel safe?' the Attorney General frowned. 'Why not?'

'I don't know,' Hill replied, 'though I fear the strain of it all was greatly bothering him. Besides, he told me that John Giles was murdered and renewed his vow to bring Hewitt to justice.' This was not right either, not that it would make any difference. I was sure that I had made no mention of John Giles's death to Hill.

The Attorney General stood with his legs together, one leg crooked, his arms folded and one finger pointed upwards. A man in contemplative repose. The jury leant forward eagerly. 'So, Mr Hill. You quickly discharged your duties in establishing who killed Anne Giles, but you also discovered that your best friend was engaged in the same pursuit at the bidding of a – shall we say – *eccentric* patriarch.' He paused and looked to the judge as if for Godly inspiration. 'Your friend, who is a clerk and is of a – shall we say – *lowly* background, comes to a different conclusion, based on – shall we say – *scatterbrained* suppositions, and begins to lose his sense of reason. Is that a fair summation?'

I glared at Hill. I didn't mind the 'eccentric patriarch' nor the 'lowly background' – it would be hard to refute either assertion, despite the conceit and pomposity in which the words were dressed, but 'scatterbrained suppositions'? His black eyes glistened, then he sighed, and looked like a man who wished he could go back a year and live his time again. 'Aye, fair.'

'Matthew Hewitt was murdered too, was he not?' The Attorney General suddenly looked very serious, and why not? The death of a couple of commoners is hardly worth writing home about, but Hewitt was almost a gentleman.

'He was.'

'What knowledge do you have of that killing?'

'I saw it happen,' Hill replied very quietly. The Attorney General shook his head sharply, as if he had a flea in his ear, and feigned amazement. Could the jury not see that this performance had clearly been rehearsed many times? This was the best play in town. The juror whose posturings were fraying at my nerves looked at me as if I were the Devil himself. I shrugged and stared him out until he looked away. Inside, though, I was looking forward to Hill's reply as much as any in court. Was it possible that he *had* been there in Alsatia? Was he implicated in Hewitt's death himself?

'Tell us,' the Attorney General said quietly before sitting again and leaving the stage to Hill.

'Hewitt was at the time imprisoned in a cellar in Alsatia,' Hill explained.

'A cellar in Alsatia?' The Attorney General struggled to his feet again. 'Imprisoned by whom?'

'By the accused,' Hill answered.

'The accused imprisoned Matthew Hewitt in a cellar in Alsatia?' The Attorney General left his position and wandered across the front of the bench until he stood opposite me. He stood with his legs astride and his hands on his hips and glared. 'Is this true?' he demanded.

He seemed to be speaking to me. 'I thought that I was not permitted to speak?' I replied, trying to see the judge.

'The accused has been asked a question by the Attorney General. He must answer the question directly,' I heard the judge snarl.

'Hewitt was—' I started.

'Did you imprison Matthew Hewitt in a cellar in Alsatia? State "aye" or "nay",' the Attorney General interrupted me, speaking with such passion that he left spittle on his chin.

'Aye.'

The Attorney General relaxed. He clasped his hands in front of his plums and bowed his head like he was the Lord Jesus Christ, before raising his chin and regarding me like I was one of the two robbers. 'Pray continue!' He returned to his station.

'Well,' Hill stuttered. 'By this time I was concerned. The accused was a friend of mine and I heard word that he had abducted Hewitt in order to extract confession from him.'

'Confession to what crime?'

'Confession that he had killed both Anne Ormonde and John Giles.'

'Ah yes!' the Attorney General proclaimed, ensuring that the jury did not become confused, 'because he was at odds with John Giles over some affair at the Exchange.'

'Indeed,' Hill continued, 'and so I followed him into Alsatia that I might find where he had Hewitt kept, and seek to persuade him to liberate him.'

'Very noble of you,' the Attorney General remarked reverentially. The first time in my life I had heard anyone refer to Hill as noble. Him too, I supposed, judging by the pink patches that appeared on his cheeks. Godamercy – he was blushing! With shame, I hoped.

'Aye well, not so noble I suppose.'

'What happened?'

'I followed him deep into the tenements there. He went to a house that was derelict.'

Now what was happening? I suddenly realised that he had made no reference to Davy Dowling in any of this. And he was deliberately omitting Thomas and Mary besides, two acquaintances of Dowling's. I didn't *mind* him leaving Dowling out of this tale, indeed it was a blessing, but I wondered what was his motive? By leaving Dowling out of his account he effectively isolated me in the telling of it, but I was not permitted to call witnesses. By leaving Dowling out of it he lost a chance to condemn the butcher alongside me, leaving him free to tell what tales he may. Why would he do that? Why would Shrewsbury wish it so? Unless Dowling had betrayed me too? That was difficult to credit. Yet I felt momentarily shocked and my already downtrodden soul lost another drop of spirit.

'Derelict, you say?'

'Aye, not habitable. There were some animals there that I suppose were kept by folks that lived close by. Also there was a cellar, and it was there that the accused had imprisoned Hewitt.'

'You saw it?'

'I saw the accused go into this ruin. He had a key with him that he used to unlock a chain that lay on the floor. He then pulled the cellar door up open, which was when I realised what it was. He descended down some steps and then came up with Hewitt who was bound in ropes and in a very sorry state.'

'A very sorry state?'

'Aye, I reckon he had been down there for at least two days.' Aye – and so he had. Hill described the scene too well.

'Then what happened?'

'Well, the accused asked him questions about the murders. He was seeking for Matthew Hewitt to confess to the crimes. When Hewitt did not, then the accused became enraged. He kicked Hewitt while he was on the floor, still bound with the ropes. Eventually he kicked him so hard that he started to bleed from the mouth.'

'Did the accused then administer aid?'

'No, sir. I fancy that he lost his senses at that point and kicked Hewitt all the harder.'

'What a brute,' whispered the Attorney General. Now I had all the jurors staring at me again and the judge besides. What nonsense. I sat dejected waiting for Hill to resume his silly tale.

'Aye, well once he had seemingly killed Hewitt he took a

knife from his pocket and cut the man's tongue out.' I gasped myself at this atrocity – the atrocity that Hill should lay the ownership of that barbaric act at my door. The rest of the court started shouting curses at me because they believed it. It took the clerks some minutes to restore order while I sat there embarrassed and fuming. Hill looked at me again, this time openly and boldly. So – he had finally sold his soul and cared not who knew it.

Puffing up his chest and straightening his jacket he declared in loud voice, 'Then he nailed it onto the trapdoor and walked out in a tremendous fury!'

I wondered from where I had got hammer and nail in this derelict hovel, but did not of course have the opportunity to ask. It was several minutes before the clerks could persuade the assembled throng to at least stop shouting and wailing. The judge sat impassive throughout, eyes fixed on my miserable self. When he cleared his throat all were quiet. 'Doth the accused understand the testimony that hath been spake thus far?' He leant forward and eyed me like his lunch.

'I *understand* it,' I replied, attempting to establish that did not mean that I agreed it was true without incurring the judge's wrath.

'Very well. Proceed!'

'Mr Hill,' the Attorney General said in a whisper, so that all had to hush in order to hear him speak, 'what did the accused do next? Was this not enough?'

'No, sir. For he then went to Epsom.'

'Why did he do that?'

A better question would have been – *when* did he do that? Hill had the timings all wrong.

'I think it was because I advised him, if you will recall.'

'Ah yes! You had suggested to him earlier that he go to Epsom to make peace with the family of Anne Ormonde.'

'Aye, sir, well now he did go. I don't know why he decided to go at this particular time, but I think it may have been to deliver his account of the death of Anne Ormonde and the motives behind it.'

'I see. That is logical.'

Very logical now that the order of events had been so neatly amended.

'Aye, well, whatever the reason he went, he was not permitted audience. Neither William Ormonde nor any of his family was willing to speak to him. He was not of their family, of course, and they were in mourning.'

'Understandable. So he came home again.'

'No, sir.'

'No?'

'No. He went to see a woman called Elizabeth Johnson.'

'Who is Elizabeth Johnson?'

'She is an old woman who used to be nanny to Anne Ormonde, and Jane Keeling besides.'

'Jane Keeling is the daughter of Lord Keeling?'

'Aye sir, she was. She died of a fever ten years ago.'

'I see. And why did the accused go to see Elizabeth Johnson?'

'I don't know what led him to her house, but once he made acquaintance then I fear that he allowed himself to be led astray once more.' Hill paused, confident now. The Attorney General saw it, and let him have his moment. 'She is a very old woman and is known at Epsom for being weak in the head. The accused would not know this, since he does not come from Epsom.'

'Naturally.'

'Aye, naturally. Well, she told the accused a tall tale that Jane Keeling took her own life because she was with child, and that the child was fathered by William Ormonde.'

'How so?' The Attorney General cut short the hysteria that threatened to engulf the court once more, his whole body proclaiming the absurdity of the idea.

'Aye, sir – an absurd notion, but the woman is very old and, it is said, is prone to fabricating such stories. Those that know her humour her in this, because she is old and has given many years of service to some great families at Epsom.'

'Indeed.' The Attorney General bowed his head. At least they weren't going to accuse her of being a witch.

'Aye, well at this the accused became convinced that he had been misled. He became sure that it was Keeling himself that had killed Anne Ormonde, and John Giles besides, as revenge upon William Ormonde.'

'Ludicrous.' The Attorney General shook his head doubtfully. 'That an old woman might peddle strange tales is one thing, that the accused should credit such tales is another. Are you sure it was so?'

'Yes, sir. I am sure.'

'How so?'

'Well, what he did next was proof of it.' Hill looked at me again. Black bottomless pits. Here we go. The coup de grâce. Keeling had asked me to puff out my chest that the sword would glide easily through my ribs. I had escaped then, but I saw no way out now. Hill kept his eyes on mine as he told the tale of how I had disinterred the body of Jane Keeling. The court exploded in a frenzy of collective rage. There were only two souls that stayed calm while the storm raged above our heads – the only two that knew the truth of it – myself and Hill. Hill, my old friend and confidant, stood six paces from me, weaving with his tongue the web that would entrap me, watching me with steady black eyes while he did it. Seemed to me that moment lasted many minutes. It was a reckoning of sorts. Slowly the din subsided and the court was silent again, the audience awaiting the final act.

'What then, Mr Hill?'

'He left Epsom and returned to London in haste to find Keeling and confront him.'

'How so, Mr Hill? If he disinterred the body of Jane Keeling then surely he must have been dissuaded from the foul notion he had heard from the lips of Elizabeth Johnson?'

Hill shrugged. 'The body was ten years old. There is no telling what he thought he had found.' Very neat.

'So he flew to London?'

'Aye, I think that someone at Keeling's residence was unwise enough to inform him that Keeling was at the church of St Bride's, praying for the soul of Anne Ormonde.'

'God have mercy.' The Attorney General put an arm across his chest and looked to the floor with his eyes closed.

'The Lord preserveth the faithful,' replied Hill, adopting the same pose. God have mercy indeed. On Hill's worm-ridden, crumbly black soul.

'What happened at the church?'

'I arrived late,' Hill shook his head mournfully. 'I found them in the vestry. Just as I entered I witnessed the accused thrust a knife into Keeling's heart. He died in my arms.'

'In my house have I found their wickedness, saith the Lord,' the Attorney General whispered.

And so fell the curtain on a wondrous performance. Of

course the audience did not stand and applaud rapturously, they didn't shout for more and refuse to cease until the players lined up before them to take a bow. But the effect was the same. The jurors began talking to each other, telling each other what wickedness lurked within the hearts of men, asking themselves if they could truly believe that one man could be capable of such sins, assuring each other that they had a God-given duty to make sure that these sins were punished in public, that the people should see what happens when man gives way to the demons that betimes may cling to his back. When Hill descended from the dock, helped by two clerks, the Attorney General stepped forward and put an arm around his shoulders and uttered sympathetic words. Me? I just sat there, a man condemned.

'The jury will now retire to consider their verdict,' announced the judge, in slow sombre tone. 'They will consider that there are three possible verdicts.'

The jury ceased their pratings and listened to their instructions.

'Acquittal is not a possible verdict, for the accused hath pleaded self-defence.' The jurors nodded wisely.

'To deliver a verdict of self-defence the jury must be of the opinion that Lord Keeling set about the accused with murderous intent. In this case it hath been established that the accused sought out Lord Keeling whilst of unsound mind and with the blood of Matthew Hewitt already on his hands. A verdict of self defence would not be a wise verdict under such circumstance.' The jurors all faithfully shook their heads.

'A verdict of provocation doth imply that the accused was motivated to kill Lord Keeling because of the sins of Lord Keeling against his person. In this case there is no evidence that the Lord Chief Justice was guilty of any such actions.' The jurors smiled as if the notion was absurd.

'We are left with a verdict of guilty. The indictment was for the wicked murder of Lord Keeling.' The judge looked up at the jury. 'In this case, though it is not usual, I am willing that you consider the other crimes that this man may have committed, namely the murder of Matthew Hewitt and the desecration of the grave of Jane Keeling. You will retire until you are all of one mind, without food nor water.'

They trailed out in a line, following one another across the bench to a door at the back of the court. Some of them looked at me as they passed, others would not. What I saw in their faces left me without hope.

'Up you get.' One of my guards lifted me gently by the elbow. I was led back across the court in the opposite direction, out towards the holding cells.

To my pleasant surprise they didn't put the manacles back on my wrists and ankles. No doubt they didn't think it worth the effort given that mine would be a short wait. One of the guards stopped on his way out, turned swiftly, and put in my hand a piece of paper, surreptitiously. Then he was gone and the door was locked.

Everyone stood.

'Harry Lytle. Thou art condemned for the murder of Thomas, Lord Keeling. Thou art condemned for the murder of Matthew Solomon Hewitt. Thou art condemned for the wrongful desecration of the grave of Jane Bridget Keeling.'

Not surprising.

'Ye will be taken from Newgate prison, tomorrow, to Tyburn. At that place thee will be hung by the neck then cut down before thee have expired. Thine entrails will be drawn from your body and burnt before thee. Thy body will be cut into four pieces and thy head will be posted for all to see so that thy death shall be a warning unto others. May God have—'

'Excuse me,' I said very clearly, that all would hear. Then I read out the words on the piece of paper given to me by the guard. 'I appeal to the King for a pardon.'

The judge looked at me as if I was mad and the Attorney General looked at me as if I was hiding some intelligent plan. Then the judge pulled a face as if to say, do as you will, and finished – 'May God have mercy on thy soul.'

Chapter Twenty-Five

The male Fools-stones
*The colour of the flower is generally purple,
less often a reddish colour.*

The manacles went back on as soon as we stepped out of
the courtroom and back we went to Newgate. In the coach
I wondered who it was had written the note, and why? I
knew that any man might ask the King for a pardon, but I
had not thought to do so since there seemed so little remedy.
It was clear to me now that whilst I had been an instrument
of Shrewsbury's, part of the grand scheme of things to clear
Keeling from his path, that I was always to have been sacrificed
at the end of it. I suppose that is why someone had persuaded
my father to write a letter. I suppose that is why Hill had been
appointed as my guardian – a face that I would trust – to act as
a conduit that Shrewsbury might easily wipe his hands clean.
I was another Richard Joyce, a little fellow that none would
miss. I say this without any self-pity – for I have no desire to be
a big fellow that all would miss. My partaking of this journey

had reinforced my view that there was little good in the world, and that which did exist was pale, unformed and wriggling next to the doughty forces of the two selfs – self-preservation and self-advancement. So goodbye to Harry Lytle, I supposed. Yet the question remained – who had written me that note, and why?

At Newgate they led me not to the stone hold, but to a single cell on the ground floor. There was a barred window high up the wall casting a soft light onto a dry straw-covered floor. It was bare and almost clean. There was a table and on it was a plate of meat and a flagon of ale. This was something! Who had paid for that, besides?

Sitting at the table I ate and drank as best I could. It was not so difficult for I was getting used to the restrictions, and the sores on my wrists and ankles had begun to rub rough. So this was to be where I spent my last night? Unless my appeal was granted and I was to receive the King's pardon. Would he not at least cast an eye over an affair that included the killing of his Chief Justice? But what if he did – the evidence had been so artfully caressed that to any man's eye it would appear that I was guilty, surely? Unless Shrewsbury's deviations were not yet fully unwound. Perhaps it was in his interest that I be condemned, yet then pardoned; that I might not be killed, yet still be restricted in the tales that I could tell. For had not the trial confirmed the official view of events and provided neat endings for all loose ends? If Shrewsbury had one ounce of a heart beating behind those bony ribs perhaps this was a way of expressing it. Perhaps it was a promise extracted by Hill in exchange for his damned testimony. I began to calculate the minutes and hours that it would take a man to ride to the King's Palace and then back again to Newgate. It wasn't a long journey. What did they do if the King was indisposed or not at the Palace? I didn't know, though I harboured a fear that in such cases the execution was never stayed. These were the thoughts that trooped in circles about my mind as I lay there in lonely contemplation as the light of the day waned and reddened.

Until just before dusk.

'You has a visitor.' The gaoler opened the door and stood there unsteadily.

I don't know who I was expecting, but it wasn't the Attorney General. He walked in briskly, eyeing my cell as if it were too grand for the likes of me.

'Good evening, Mr Lytle,' he declared, pulling the door closed behind him. 'Please stay seated, I will stand.' Dark curls tickled his forehead and his head was bare, no periwig now, concerned, no doubt, that it did not become lice infested.

I stood anyway. 'Have you brought the result of my appeal?'

'Hah!' he snapped. 'The road to Whitehall is long and winding. If you harbour hopes that a man may ride that way and back before your execution, then you are a fool. Is it not already plain to you that you are to die tomorrow?'

It was like a stab to the heart. He looked at me with curling lip, and the hint of a sneer, the face of a man that believes he has done a job well and will brook no argument with any man that would argue otherwise.

'Why, then, have you come?'

He smiled at me with his shining teeth and fixed me with a stare that willed me to see the world through the same eyes. 'To tell you that your appeal will not succeed. I would not have you wasting your time indulging in idle fantasy that you will live more than another twelve hours. I am sure that you have many reparations to make with the Lord your God.'

'That is very good of you. You must be very busy.'

He showed no signs of moving. 'Indeed I am. It would make my journey worthwhile were you to show me the paper that you read from.'

So that was it. He wanted to know who had prompted me to appeal in the first place. He must be worried to come all the way here just to ask me it. Poor fellow. I fetched the paper from my pocket where it sat screwed up. Unfolding it, I read it once more, and held it out to this awful man. One arm snaked out, whereupon I placed the paper in my mouth and swallowed it whole.

His face froze, then relaxed. 'No matter, Lytle. I will retrieve it from your guts tomorrow morning. Farewell.' Turning on his heel, he was gone.

I really didn't see why he had to be so mean-spirited. But that was his affair. I had my own affair to worry about.

Next morning it was raining and windy. I knew this to be so because it was a drop of rain that woke me, landing on my nose. It could not have made its way through the high barred window without some help from the wind. I was quite pleased, all things considered. A rainy day meant smaller crowds and that all concerned would want to hurry things along so that they may spend as little time possible outside getting wet.

It didn't feel like my last day on earth.

I decided to be calm and reasonable, in the hope that everyone else would be calm and reasonable too. I didn't want to spend the day wrapped up in tight knots. In truth, I was very tired, having lain awake all the night, contemplating the silence. As the sun rose so did the fear subside a little.

It was still several hours before the key turned in the lock.

'Good morning!' I didn't stand, for fear they would assume that I was lunging at them, just sat with my legs and arms out straight, manacles to the fore.

It was the old cleric from St Andrew Hubbard that entered, a short, old man with white hair that stood up straight in untidy clumps. The same fellow that had attended to Joyce. He breathed into my face and I nearly died there and then – how much had this fellow had to drink?

'Stand up,' a dour-faced fellow ordered me. He wore a strange brown skullcap and a long, brown leather apron. Odd fish. His hand was as big as Dowling's and he held me by the shirt with it while he looked into my eyes, as though he was searching for something. I looked at his eyebrows so he wouldn't think that I was staring at him. Then he let me go, roughly, and marched out.

'He is the executioner,' the cleric slurred while fumbling with a large wooden cross tied to a piece of thick cord. 'He is very good at his job. You are fortunate.' He held out the cord around my neck and let the cross bounce gently upon my chest. So, I had been measured up. A day of reckoning, indeed.

There were four other strangers in the cell stood officiously, but I didn't look at them. They were big and very ugly, ill-disposed towards me, I felt sure. The cleric drew out a Bible from his inside pocket and began to read out snatches from it. Either he had poor eyesight, else he had drunk enough to render him unable, for few of the words were intelligible. His two eyes worked as they would, rarely arriving in the same place at the same time. We all waited patiently for him to complete his task.

Then the time came to leave. They attached a chain to the manacles that bound my wrists and led me forward like a dog. We walked down the main corridor out towards the entrance. Men stood at the bars to the public cells staring out. Some watched seriously, perhaps contemplating their own demise. Others leered and shouted, a couple even spat at me, though thankfully they succeeded only in hitting the sleeves of my shirt. Someone else could wash that later.

It was a relief on climbing into the cart to find that I would not be making the journey alone that morning. Rain still fell, though not hard, and there sat on a rough cloth sack was my travelling companion. Younger than me, and very thin, he sat with his knees bent outwards and ankles together, leaning forward with his wrists against the cart floor in front of his feet. He looked up at me with dull eyes beneath oily, black hair.

'Good morning!' I greeted him, determined that we not sit morose. I calculated that we needed each other's good cheer if we were to support ourselves through the abuse we would surely experience on the way to Tyburn.

'Hardly that!' he mumbled. 'Why are you so happy this day?'

'I think I might be released. Though they found me guilty, I asked for the King's pardon.'

'Many ask for the King's pardon, friend. Not many receive it. None have received it that I know of while on the cart.'

'Methinks it is necessary to look on the bright side.' Which was true. Though it was but a silly notion, the longer I managed to stay calm then the shorter the time I would suffer.

'Methinks it is the sign of a simpleton, the kind of nonsense spake by those that have not yet understood what fate beholds them. When you see the scaffold and the crowds that surround it, then ye will start moaning and crying.' He shrugged, 'I have seen it.'

'Are you complete with what fate awaits you?'

'I will not know that for sure until I find myself standing there with the rope round my neck. If I ask the Lord God for forgiveness before I drop, then I will know that I am complete. If I shit my trousers and start panting like a dog, then I will know otherwise.' He looked at me. 'You will shit your trousers and pant like a dog.'

'I wager I will not,' I assured him.

'I accept,' he grinned.

I liked this fellow. I wondered what he'd done. 'First to Sepulchras. To partake of wine, I believe?'

'Indeed, though it is not a great vintage.'

The crowd was thin outside Newgate and at Sepulchras. We drank as much wine as they would give us, while the clerk read the prayers. A pale-looking fellow, weedy and yellow, he looked ill to me. He had a habit of snorting phlegm up his throat upon pausing for breath between verses. An unpleasant custom that rather spoilt the effect of his words. The small crowd didn't appear to be disappointed, for their attentions were fixed upon us, regarding us with a hungry leer, keenly anticipating that one or other of us would lose control and give way to a bout of frantic pleading. The soldiers that accompanied us would be wishing for a quiet day. The one that walked closest to me frowned unhappily; nose and mouth bunched up like someone had tied up his snout with twine. He kept flicking sideways glances at me as if concerned that I would laugh at him. A strange idea under the circumstances.

We took our winter flowers and pinned them to our shirts,

like gentlemen. The cart made good time up the road towards Tyburn, with the rain giving way to a steady drizzle. The crowds that there were shouted and cursed, but the guard that walked with us almost outnumbered them. It was a quiet journey compared to some I'd witnessed, and by the time we arrived we had barely enough cabbages to open a shop. I'd seen men have to be carried to the scaffold barely conscious from the batterings they'd taken on the cart. We should have counted ourselves fortunate, I suppose, yet I felt a sudden wistful grief that somehow London was full of people that had woken up that morning, looked out of the window and said to themselves 'Ah – Harry Lytle is to be executed this day. Ne'er mind – it's raining – let's to the Crowne instead.' What would I have given to be in the Crowne that morning?

We talked all the way, a good way to take your mind off what was to come. His name was Roger North and he was condemned for robbing men on the road to Epsom. He was a tobyman, in other words, and I had never met a tobyman before. It wasn't such a glamorous life he described, even without the unhappy ending. He had been betrayed by a colleague of his that had objected to his flowery tales of brave words and valiant deeds. They had contested a lady's hand in a tavern one night, and North had won. Next morning he'd awoken with empty arms and a sword at his eye.

As we got closer to Tyburn, so the crowds began to swell and thicken. By the time we reached the foot of the hill they were five or six deep on either side of us. Now the guards had to earn their money, pushing and prodding with their long pikes to keep the road free. I found myself scanning the throng, seeking familiar faces, people that I knew. Not a fruitful way to pass the time, I knew; yet I could not help it. Quite suddenly the prospect of death felt real. It was at this time that Joyce's companions had lost their composure, so I recalled Dowling relating. The drink was all drunk, and it was time for repose. Roger North watched me carefully for sign of panic, I knew. He himself remained composed, though the veins on his face now looked very green against his marble-white skin.

At the scaffold the crowds were thick, swarming and buzzing. Galleries had been erected on either side and not a seat was to be had. I looked around for just one familiar face but saw none. Ugly faces, drunk and lairy. I ducked to avoid an orange. North was hit on the back of the head by a hard, young apple. He gritted his teeth and looked angry. All the faces I looked into were bleary and hard, impatient for the show to begin. No respect for death, I felt, and it was *my* death – surely it deserved *some* respect? I felt more like a player on the stage than a man about to reconcile himself with the Lord, unhappily aware of an expectation to perform – or be damned.

We stopped. I stood up and never had I felt so tall. The crowd were all looking at me. I scanned the galleries. Men sat forward with their elbows on their knees staring intently. Women sat too, heads stretched back over their shoulders to talk to their neighbours. They were out there and I was here, with Roger North, exposed and afraid. Stepping down off the cart was a relief. The soldier that helped me step down cast me a quick glance, assessing my state of mind with expert eye, no doubt. It was so damn noisy! No longer could we see above the heads of the vast gathering. It was like a tunnel opened up before us walled with people. We were pulled forwards by our chains, desperate to stay on our feet and not slide over in the slippery brown mud. No man wanted to die with wet brown filth on the seat of his pants. The scaffold waited for us ahead.

It looked so small from here. The horses danced next to it, skittish and nervous, ready to hold us beneath the gallows. A wall of people barred any attempt to flee.

The tall man in the brown leather apron stood above us, waiting. The heat, the smell of sweat, vomit and ale, the obscenities and blasphemies that I could hear, despite trying not to listen, pressed down on me. North was ahead of me, yet the spell of our companionship was broken. I could see the fear in his eyes, the tears on his cheeks. I felt my own bladder weaken, felt the crap in my bowels begin to churn. It was too noisy to exchange words of comfort. We were in the pit of Hell, burning in the flames of man's hatred. Words were no use here.

'Hold fast!' a voice shouted from somewhere up in front, from somewhere past the horses.

'Hold fast!' it shouted again, this time louder. It sounded like someone was in trouble. I waited for a scream. The guards slowed, mumbling and impatient, pikes held aloft.

'Hold fast!' A body appeared in front between the scaffold and us. 'I have a document signed by King Charles himself! Harry Lytle is to be trialled anew!'

Trialled anew? Trialled anew? Trialled anew! God have mercy on my soul! I felt like singing, yet would the guards oblige? I felt a sudden fear that they would dismiss this man with his document signed by King Charles and insist on carrying out their task. Could they read? I stood with my feet dug firmly into the mud, determined not to take a single further step towards the gallows while the chief of the guards took the paper and read it, then ran his fingers across the seal. He read slowly, I watched his eyes move from side to side, letter by letter, word by word. He mouthed the words as he read them, his face a picture of anxious puzzlement. Then he turned to his colleagues and shrugged. My chest was squeezed so tight it felt like I was being crushed beneath a great stone.

'Back to Newgate for this one.' The guard pointed at me. 'Onward-ho for the other.'

Back to Newgate! My very own Garden of Eden! I looked for Roger North up ahead. I caught a quick glimpse of his face, mouth wide open and tongue lolling, his eyes frantically scanning the sky for some angel of salvation. He walked with his shoulders slumped forwards and his trousers were soiled. He had shat his trousers and was panting like a dog.

I never saw Roger North alive again. Though his head sat above Nonsuch for about six months.

Chapter Twenty-Six

The common Cotten-thistle
The first leaves produced by the roots are very nutritious and restore strength if taken either as a distilled juice or roasted in the oven in the manner of artichokes in meat pies.

I was back in the same courtroom the very next day. This time none came to see me at all before the day started, so I resigned myself to another session of ritual public humiliation. I wondered what witnesses would be called today? They might as well collect the heads of Giles, Hewitt and Keeling, attach them to the end of sticks and have Shrewsbury perform a puppet show. Yet I was not entirely pessimistic. There must be some reason for initiating the rigmarole one more time.

I resolved beforetimes not to mess about with the jury unless there sat a genuine lunatic. On second thoughts perhaps I would be better off with a jury selected from Bedlam. That was a thought indeed!

I asked one of the guards who were to be the judge and prosecutor as we travelled. The judge, I was told, was one

Nicholas Earl of Newcastle, a scholarly sort of fellow by reputation. The prosecutor on the other hand, was none other than the Attorney General, the same that had told me that I should be dead by now. He should be glad to see me then.

We resumed our old familiar seats. I couldn't tell this set of the jurors from the last, so ignored them. They would do as they were told, no doubt, so there was little point in concerning myself. I was more interested in observing the Attorney General. He came in on his own in advance of the judge and settled himself quickly. I received a brief glance, but no more. Gone were the flummery and flammery, the posturing and theatre. Sitting with his arms folded, he looked like a man denied his favourite pudding.

The judge entered by himself, a slight man. He walked quickly with short little strides, head lowered, muttering to himself. After he jumped the steps up to his little wooden throne he peered about him short-sightedly until he spotted me. He glanced me up and down, blinked and was satisfied.

The same clerk as before read out the names of the jurors.

'Mr Attorney General,' the judge spoke very fast, 'do you wish to challenge any of the jurors?'

'My Lord, I do not.'

'And you?' he looked at me.

'My Lord, I do not.'

'Very well. Last time you pleaded self-defence. Does that remain your plea?'

'Yes, My Lord.'

'Good. Then let's begin. First witness.' He paused to read a parchment on his desk. 'And only witness. David Dowling.'

Dowling? I turned to see him escorted towards the witness box. He regarded me calmly and gave me a big wink. The Attorney General saw it and glared.

'What is your name?' The clerk adopted the same ceremonial position and manner as he had before.

'His name is Dowling, as I have already made clear. Please be seated.' The judge waved a hand irritably, sending the poor man scurrying for cover away from the eyes of his junior colleagues. 'Mr Dowling, I will be asking you some questions. From time to time I will permit the Attorney General to ask you some questions of his own. Is that clear?'

'Yes, My Lord.' Dowling was looking quite splendid today I thought, having forsaken his usual sorry attire in favour of a fine suit. It wasn't expensive or particularly finely tailored, but was well cut and very stylish. It really quite became him.

'Dowling, your profession?'

'These days I am a butcher.' Dowling turned to face the judge and gave a deferential little bow.

'Butcher? You don't look much like a butcher.' The judge squinted. Wait until someone told him that he could read and write and bore the saddle off a donkey with Bible talk.

'It is not my usual occupation, My Lord.'

'Well, what's your usual occupation? Come on now, Mr Dowling, we don't have time for games.' The judge cast an eye in the Attorney General's direction as he spoke.

'My usual occupation is agent for King Charles II. I am employed by His Majesty to look after his interests about London.' He turned and smiled broadly at me.

Well, as I am a sinner, which I certainly am, Dowling was the Bishop's sister's son! This was something! And I thought he was only fit for ruffians! This could only be a poke in the eye with a burnt stick. The Attorney General sat slouched in his chair, sullen but not surprised. You are on a different field today, my friend!

'What is your role in this sorry affair?' the judge asked.

'I was asked by His Majesty to assist Mr Lytle in his quest to discover who killed Anne Giles. His Majesty was interested in the affair and knew that the Earl of Shrewsbury had chosen to support Mr Lytle in his efforts. He was intrigued to understand better the Earl of Shrewsbury's motivations. So he ensured that I was nominated to assist Mr Lytle, whose appointment he did not entirely fathom.'

'Lytle was appointed by whom?' The judge tapped a finger on his desk.

'Mr Lytle was not officially appointed by any. He was informed by his father that Anne Ormonde was related and his father asked the Earl of Shrewsbury for his assistance which he agreed to bestow. That is the official story.'

'I see,' the judge mused, 'this is at odds with the testimony given by Mr William Hill, who testified that he was the only agent employed by Shrewsbury.'

'That may be true, My Lord. The Earl of Shrewsbury did not employ Mr Lytle. That is, he did not pay him any money for his labours. He merely agreed to support Mr Lytle in his efforts. Though I have to make it known to Your Honour that Mr Lytle's father was only under the impression that they were related because he was told so by one Robert Burton.'

Burton?

'Who is Robert Burton?'

'He is another employee of the Earl of Shrewsbury. He has made written testament of it and delivered it to His Majesty.'

That made sense, at last. The silly old fool had his tail twisted by Shrewsbury. Well – he wasn't the only one.

'I see. Mr Attorney General – did you know of this?'

'No, My Lord, I did not,' replied my learned colleague

quietly. He didn't look very surprised, though.

'Very well, let us proceed. The death of Anne Giles.' He looked around the court again as if to make sure that everyone was listening. 'Anne Giles was killed by Richard Joyce. Richard Joyce was tried for it and condemned. This is a matter of public record, is it not?'

'My Lord, it is a matter of public record,' Dowling bowed his big, grey head. The judge seemed to like his soft Scots accent. It was certainly a soothing noise he made when he spoke. The jury looked like they might go to sleep. 'However, I think we might reconsider the findings of the court in the light of subsequent events.'

'Why should we do that?'

'To explain that fully, My Lord, I must give you my account of those subsequent events. For now I would note only that Joyce himself spoke to us lucidly and categorically denied that he murdered Anne Giles. Furthermore he described the man that did kill Anne Giles as being a big man wearing a thick black cloak, a hat and a scarf.'

'That is not much of a description,' snorted the judge.

'No, My Lord. It is not much of a description, but it is the exact same description that we were given by a slaughterer that saw John Giles thrown off London Bridge.'

'The court was told that John Giles killed himself by throwing himself from London Bridge. William Hill testified that he saw the marks about the man's neck.'

Dowling shook his head. 'No, My Lord. They were my men that recovered John Giles's body from the river and I can assure the court that there were no marks about his neck. His arms and legs were bound and he was thrown from the Bridge so that he died a most painful death. I have the boatman that found him and several of my own men that will testify it.'

'I see. Mr Attorney General – what say you of this?' The judge looked at the Attorney General with a sceptical eye.

The Attorney General stood up. 'This testimony is at odds with the testimony of Mr William Hill.' He sat down again. This was going well!

'Aye, well I know who I believe.' The judge looked at Dowling with respect. 'So who did kill Anne Giles and John Giles, Mr Dowling?'

'Lord Keeling,' Dowling replied brightly. The judge pulled a face as if to express severe disappointment with a favoured son. 'Sir, that is too much to credit.' The court seemed to agree, for everyone started to talk in low, quiet tones and shake their heads. The Attorney General joined in theatrically, tutting loudly and laughing contemptuously. The judge silenced them all with one sweep of his arm.

'My Lord, this is not a simple affair. I beg your indulgence.' Dowling bowed, completely unworried, it seemed.

'Proceed,' the judge declared, with apparent reservations.

'It was clear to us that Richard Joyce did not kill Anne Giles and it was clear that he did not kill John Giles – since Joyce was executed before John Giles died. Our attentions turned at that time to Matthew Hewitt.'

'Why Matthew Hewitt? This is the fellow that Lytle says was being blackmailed by John Giles?'

'Aye, though it wasn't any detailed account of what the disagreement was between them that alerted us to it. We spoke to John Giles and he was deeply afraid of Matthew Hewitt and what he might do to him.'

'William Hill would have us believe that such rumours

were nonsense.' The judge still looked sceptical. The Attorney General muttered and snorted.

'Aye, but there is a piece of evidence which we did not have at the time, which explains the nature of the disagreement. It was not an ordinary disagreement.' Dowling looked at me and winked again. I didn't wink back. I hoped he knew what he was doing.

'Enlighten us.' The judge put his chin in his hand, looking curious.

'After Hewitt was killed I went to his house with some of my men, on Mr Lytle's instruction.'

'On what authority?' the Attorney General stood up and barked.

'Mr Attorney General, kindly be quiet unless I ask you to speak,' the judge shouted, furious. The Attorney General sat down angrily and buried his head in his shoulders. 'Now, Mr Dowling. Upon whose authority?'

'My apologies, My Lord. I spoke in error. It was Mr Lytle's *suggestion*. We entered the house on the authority of His Majesty.'

'There.' The judge waved a hand at the Attorney General. 'Are you satisfied?'

The Attorney General slumped back in his seat.

'We were looking for some evidence that explained why Matthew Hewitt should have been so distressed by our attentions that he sent two men to kill Mr Lytle.'

The court responded with a series of 'oohs' and 'aahs'. This was the first revelation that did not result in everyone looking at me as if I were Satan's bag carrier.

'And why, pray, did Matthew Hewitt send two men to kill Mr Lytle?'

'We found letters at Hewitt's house, various documents. Of

no great importance of themselves. However, they indicated that Matthew Hewitt had changed his name a few years previously.'

'Changed his name from what?' The judge demanded, incredulous. The Attorney General stopped picking at his fingernails and raised his head in interest too.

'Venner,' replied Dowling.

Venner! So Matthew Hewitt was Matthew Venner? A relation. Dowling was implying that Hewitt was associated with the Thomas Venner revolt! Then Hewitt was a Fifth Monarchist too, and therein lay his relationship with Keeling. This explained how it was that Keeling had told me that Hewitt had unleashed his dogs upon me. The two of them were connected!

'You have lost me, Mr Dowling.' The judge shook his head in confusion. 'You are looking at me as if you have presented me with a barrel of cream, and I have no idea why.'

'Lord Keeling was a Baptist, as was William Ormonde. Lord Keeling remained fanatical even after the Restoration whilst Ormonde did not. Keeling backed Venner's Revolt and Ormonde threatened to expose him. Keeling killed Ormonde's daughter so that he would remain quiet – for Ormonde has two daughters. However, John Giles had learnt of Hewitt's involvement, probably through his wife, and was blackmailing him. Keeling killed John Giles to protect Hewitt. Hewitt sent two men to kill Mr Lytle, because he threatened to expose the whole affair anyway.'

The court fell silent. Everyone looked at the judge, who looked confused. We sat like this for at least a minute. The judge cast an eye about the court, anxious not to be seen to make a fool of himself. 'You mean Venner sent two men to kill Mr Lytle?'

334

'Aye, sir,' Dowling nodded. 'His manservant has 'fessed all.'

'And I suppose William Ormonde will testify accordingly?'

'Yes, My Lord. Now that Keeling is dead William Ormonde is able to speak without fear.'

The judge still looked bemused. He turned to the Attorney General as if he genuinely sought his views. 'Mr Attorney General, do you know *anything* about this at all?'

The Attorney General stood up with a weary expression on his face, wondering perhaps if he still had a career. 'My Lord, all I can say is that this testimony is at odds with the testimony of Mr William Hill. I have no knowledge of all that Mr Dowling sets before us and, indeed, were he not in the employ of His Majesty then I would find his testimony incredible.' He sat down and flicked his quill to one side.

'I agree, sir. Mr Dowling, I will need to see all of this testimony you refer to.'

'Of course, My Lord. I have it with me today.'

'Very well, pray continue.'

'The men that Hewitt sent to kill Mr Lytle failed. Unfortunate for Hewitt I think, for once Mr Lytle had taken him prisoner, Keeling must have feared that he would talk.'

'Mr William Hill testifies that he witnessed the accused kill Matthew Hewitt then sever his tongue with a knife and nail it to a . . .' he rifled through some papers '. . . trapdoor.'

Dowling arched his eyebrows and sighed deeply. 'Mr Hill lies, My Lord. Soldiers killed Matthew Hewitt, soldiers sent by Keeling. These same soldiers attempted to abduct us both besides, until we were rescued by men I know that live in Alsatia.'

'Whose testimony do you have to substantiate that?'

'Just mine and Mr Lytle's I fear,' Dowling grimaced, 'for

none from that part of London would ever come here to testify.'

The judge muttered unhappily.

'Though I fancy we may be able to find the bones of the soldiers that killed Hewitt if I be permitted to search for them.'

'I see.' The judge still looked most bemused. 'And then I suppose that Lord Keeling pursued Mr Lytle to Bride's to kill him, and the accused was forced to defend himself. Hence the plea.'

'Yes, My Lord.'

'Mr Dowling, what evidence do you have of that? Mr Hill says he saw the accused plunge a knife into Keeling's ribs.'

'Sir, I have testimony from several of the soldiers that escorted Mr Hill to St Bride's and from those that prepared the body for burial. The only knife discovered at the scene remained clenched in Lord Keeling's fist. They had to drop a stone on his fingers to free it. Between his ribs he had half a walking cane.'

The judge eyed the Attorney General with open contempt, yet refrained from asking him his opinion another time. The Attorney General appeared to be beyond caring.

'How do you explain that the accused desecrated the grave of Jane Keeling?' the judge asked at last. 'I may safely assume that whatever fantastic story you are about to tell me is well documented?'

'Certainly, My Lord.' Dowling scratched his head, rubbed his cheeks with his palms and stretched. 'First I must tell you that he informed me in advance that he was going to desecrate the grave. I did not approve, but neither did I stop him.'

'True,' I said aloud, without meaning to. 'That he advised me not to do it.'

'Then why did you?' the judge asked me directly.

I blinked, and then slowly stood. None pulled me back down. Dowling smiled back encouragingly. The Attorney General looked at me out of the corner of his eye, but looked away again just as quickly.

'Sir, we were convinced that Matthew Hewitt had killed both Anne and John Giles. Yet Hill kept insisting that I go to Epsom. When I did go to Epsom, then I was directed by Mary Ormonde to visit Beth Johnson.'

'The same Elizabeth Johnson?' the judge asked.

'I suppose,' I affirmed, 'and she did not tell me that Jane Keeling was with child, as Hill claimed, but she did say that she took her own life and she had a letter affirming it.'

'Did you see this letter?'

'No, sir. But she directed me to the house of Dr John Stow, who told me that she had been with child. From that I presumed Keeling had killed Anne Giles out of revenge, and when I related my idea to William Hill then he assured me that I was correct and that he had heard rumours to that effect besides.'

'So why did you desecrate a grave, Mr Lytle?' the judge demanded, incredulous.

'Because I did not believe the story. It was so easy to discover, and Hill had insisted so absolutely that I go to Epsom, that I doubted the veracity of it. Yet what if it were true?'

The judge shook his head and waggled his finger at me as if I were a naughty boy caught stealing apples. 'Mr Lytle, it will not do. I appreciate that you were in a predicament, but desecrating a grave is ungodly and wicked.'

I contemplated asking him what he would have done in my place, but decided against it.

Dowling cleared his throat, seeking permission to intervene. 'My Lord, it's true. I went to Epsom not two days ago and spoke to this John Stow. He tells me that he was paid by one Robert Burton to tell his tale to Mr Lytle. He was assured that he would be visited only once, and then should deny all knowledge of the story.'

'This would be the same Robert Burton that you suggest was employed by the Earl of Shrewsbury?' The judge read back over notes that he had been scribing.

'Aye, My Lord.'

'And so you found that she was without child, Mr Lytle?'

'Aye, sir.'

The judge sat back and pursed his lips. With his face so set he read back through his papers for ten or fifteen minutes. As he did so he made little noises with his mouth, as if all were becoming clear to him. Then he shuffled the papers into a pile, rested forwards onto his arms and regarded the Attorney General. 'Sir, you are the prosecutor. What do you make of it?'

The Attorney General looked surprised. 'My Lord, I think I would need to see this testimony referred to before venturing an opinion.'

'Very wise,' the judge nodded. 'Let us go and review it together. The papers please.' He gestured to Dowling with his head then stood, descended the steps and left the courtroom with the Attorney General trailing him disconsolately.

The rest of us were to wait. The jurors all looked vaguely worried, yet excited at the same time, not sure what had been going on, yet confident it was important. A few of them craned their necks in the direction that the judge had disappeared, wondering perhaps why they too hadn't been invited to see this vital evidence. Dowling sat down in the witness box, so that all the rest of us could see was the top of his head. There was to be no talking, a rule that a couple of the clerks enforced by stalking the courtroom like carnivorous herons, hissing loudly at any that dared whisper.

I was feeling much more optimistic. Dowling had answered the judge's questions so well that the case looked as white now as it had done black just the day before yesterday. Yet I was not so simple as to think that the truth would be the only factor that decided my fate. Foremost in my mind was seeking to understand why the judge had taken the Attorney General away. Certainly the Attorney General did not seem to be a happy man, yet could the private meeting have been called in the way of working out how to surmount the obstacle that Dowling's testimony presented? Why should this judge be any different to the previous in terms of his objectives? Such were the thoughts going through my brain during the one hour or more that we sat in silence, waiting. Dowling's head slowly disappeared and we were treated to the sound of a Scotsman snoring.

When they came back in I looked straight for the expression on the face of the Attorney General. If he bounced in full of new-found energy then I was in trouble. But he did not. Returning to his seat and sitting down he looked as he had before, only wearier. The judge didn't bother climbing back up his perch but instead crooked fingers at me and at Dowling. I stood and was escorted by my two guards to the bench.

The judge looked different close up. Though his whiskers were very neatly trimmed you could see that they were white. The lines on his face were sort of velvety, suggesting to me that he was extremely advanced in years. Yet I imagined that there was nothing soft about his mind, for his eyes were calm and piercing. He gave the impression that he asked questions merely to confirm what he could already read on your face. Waving a hand in the direction of my shackles, he indicated with a frown to one of the guards that they should be removed. 'Mr Lytle and Mr Dowling, will you come with me, please?'

'Sit down,' he commanded once we had reached his room. It was a small, oak-panelled room with a wooden bench across one wall and several large upholstered chairs scattered about the place. They were fine old chairs, but worn, with the leather fraying and holes beginning to develop like an old man's liver spots.

The judge crossed his legs and placed his hands in a neat pile upon his lap. 'Mr Dowling, please tell me what is going on.'

'My Lord, I think you now have all the facts at your disposal.'

'Mr Dowling, if I am to believe what I have heard today, then I can only conclude that the Earl of Shrewsbury engaged Mr Lytle here to establish a ludicrous plot that he himself had seeded.'

'Indeed.'

'In order to discredit Lord Keeling.'

'Indeed.'

'Why then, Mr Dowling, should the Earl of Shrewsbury have invented such a ludicrous story when all he had to do was to expose the fact that Lord Keeling was a Fifth Monarchist and had conspired to kill the King?'

'He had no evidence, My Lord. Nor could he hope to persuade William Ormonde or Matthew Hewitt to testify.' I repeated Prynne's argument as it was spelt out to me.

'Logical,' Dowling nodded. 'Shrewsbury was in no

position to make accusations. Had he sent agents to seek out the evidence, then he may quickly have alerted Keeling to his activities and, God knows, no man would want to incur Keeling's wrath. Keeling would have had him killed.'

'So he made up this bizarre story.'

'My Lord, it was very clever. Not only did he appoint Harry, but also he arranged for Harry to have an assistant from the Mayor's office. This ensured that when Harry uncovered the story it would quickly be recounted to the Mayor without the Earl having to become involved. Indeed, I did take our findings to the Mayor to consult. Sooner or later rumours would have spread. Then Keeling would have been faced with the prospect of having to explain his poor relations with Ormonde, without reference to the real cause. It would have put Lord Keeling in a difficult position, almost certainly all that would have been required to tilt the scales against him.'

'I don't know if it was very clever or very foolish.' The judge shook his head doubtfully. 'You are sure of this?'

'Aye, My Lord, and it was cleverer than you think. Shrewsbury knew Keeling well. If such a rumour had spread, then you can be sure that Keeling would have pursued Harry to the ends of the earth to have his vengeance. His part in the affair would thus be lost for ever.'

'Which is nearly what happened, I am led to believe.' The judge nodded at me, even looked me in the eye. He still looked unsure. He removed his periwig, revealing very short-cropped white bristles, and scratched himself. 'How well do you know this man?' He waved a hand in my direction while looking at Dowling.

'We had not met before this affair, and so have not known each other long,' Dowling turned to grin broadly, 'but I feel

I know him well enough now. He has plenty of blood in his body and not a little phlegm. He is rarely choleric and quick to rouse himself from melancholy.'

'Indeed?' The judge considered me. 'And is he honest?'

'Aye, My Lord, more honest than he knows. I can see why Shrewsbury picked him for the task. Shrewsbury's only error, I think, was to discredit his intelligence.'

'Aye,' the judge nodded grimly, 'one of the man's worst faults. He is so busy scheming and plotting that he oft forgets that others are not wholly incapable themselves.' He pulled his wig back on his head. 'Ah well, time for a verdict.'

'Sir!' I leapt up.

The judge turned to me sombrely.

'Davy!' I clenched my fists and struggled to unfreeze my brain. 'You said that part of Shrewsbury's plan was that all record of my involvement in the case was to be lost with my demise.'

Now they both stood looking at me, the judge curiously, Davy like I had just realised something he had known for some time. He nodded.

'So what has Shrewsbury done with my father? He could tell of the letter!'

Dowling put an arm about my shoulder and squeezed me gently. 'We still haven't found him, Harry, but we're still looking.'

Chapter Twenty-Seven

Sea Starwort
It is tall or short according to the nature of the soil.

They found my father a week later lying on his back in a watery hollow deep in Byddle Wood. He had been knifed in the guts and struck on the back of the head so hard that pieces of his skull were missing. They found the men that did it too, one of them Robert Burton. Both were tried and hung inside two days. I didn't go to watch it, but went to Newgate to see the cruel face of my tormentor. When I saw him he was pale and lost, still not come to terms with his fate. He wouldn't talk to me nor meet my eye, just sat in the corner of his cell with his wrists and ankles manacled, contemplating his poor fortune. Not so intelligent, after all. Shrewsbury was nowhere to be found, naturally – on his way to Holland no doubt.

Soon after it was all over I found myself pushing open the little wooden gate that marked the entry into the graveyard of All Hallows. Negotiating a route through the stones, I headed off the path into the long, wet grass towards the shade of a strangely shaped oak tree, its roots thick and twisted, its lowest branches reaching down to the ground where a child might climb upon it. Its canopy spread far and wide, offering shade to the fifty or more dead souls that lay there. To the far side, north and east, a small plot had been cleared anew and two short, square stones stood there, glistening in the morning sun. On one was carved the name of my father, on the other the name of Richard Joyce. An unlikely pair.

Death comes to all, I know. My father was very put out when they executed Charles I and gave short thrift to those that sought permission for regicide in the Holy Book. Me myself, I don't really see what the Holy Book has to do with anything. The King's head was so big they couldn't get him out of the stables – that was his problem. Death comes to us all in one form or another, sooner or later.

When I was small we came here often as a family. This had been my tree. We stopped coming as my father's preferences had become more and more extreme. It was like he had stopped thinking for himself and let others define a strict doctrine by which he would live his life. I laid a hand upon the top of my father's stone. Just a chunk of granite underneath which lay a pile of bones. Yet it gave me some consolation.

I could not help but wonder whether I might have done things differently. I had spent so much time wishing that the whole affair would be finished early and cursing my father for involving me in it. And I had put off going to Cocksmouth until it was too late. And Joyce. I reckon he was probably a good man, a man that deserved better. God knows he wasn't the only man in London that had met with a poor fate, but he had surely not deserved to end up with his head stuck on a pole for all to mock at, with the birds feeding on his eyes and sharpening their claws on his scalp. It was me that asked that they take down his head and restore it to the rest of his body. What remained of it. They had done it inside a day. That he died bravely and now lay with some dignity – that gave me some consolation too.

'Good afternoon, Harry Lytle,' a voice piped clearly in my ear, making me jump so violently that I could not help but fart. I looked up into a familiar, old face.

'You remember me, then?' I stood up and straightened my clothes. I felt like an overdressed child.

'Of course.' He looked down at the stone then back at me. 'Why did you ask that they bury them here, and under this tree?'

I turned away from him and towards the stones. 'This is the only church I know and I knew you would sanction it.' Which was the truth; I did not spend much time considering it. 'The tree is the best place to be in this graveyard, the rest of it is lonely and forsaken.'

'Not by me,' the rector protested, appearing to be offended, though I knew he was not.

'Aye, true, but you are too old to visit every grave often.'

The rector laughed. What was I doing here talking to a man of God, I asked myself. When was the last time I gained solace from one of these strange creatures? I regarded closely his lined forehead, his closely cropped white hair. He was just a man.

'This was not your father's church recently,' he gently pointed out.

'Aye, but it was his church for longest, and I had no appetite to bury him elsewhere.'

The rector grunted. 'Everyone has been talking about you, Harry. You behaved with great courage and fortitude. You performed great deeds in the eyes of the Lord.'

'You think so?'

'You do not?'

I shrugged. It seemed to me it had little enough to do with the Lord. An affair of men.

'I invite you to come to this church more often, Harry,' the rector said softly. 'In accordance with the King's law, thou knowst.' He grinned.

'Would you have me fined?'

He waved a hand. 'I would have you come of your own free will, Harry. You might come when ye visit your father and Richard Joyce.'

'They are both dead,' I reminded him.

The rector grimaced and clicked his tongue. He regarded me out the corner of his eye like I was sent to test him. 'You have a clean soul, Harry, though perhaps you do not believe it yourself.'

It wasn't a conversation I wanted to have. I sighed and bid him walk with me back to the street. I had learnt how evil some men could be. It wasn't 'News from Ipswich' but it was news to me. Hypocrisy and conceit I had lived with all my life, cold-hearted murderous intent was new. I had known of its existence, but not made its acquaintance.

The rector stopped at the gate. 'This is a place you might come to share those thoughts, Harry.'

'Aye.' I stopped too and shook his hand. Perhaps. Perhaps not.

Chapter Twenty-Eight

Star-thistle
It never has real thorns except on the flower heads; the tiny thorns on the apices of the leaves are almost innocuous.

The air was particularly bad in the kitchen. I had thrown open all the windows before I left, but it hadn't made much difference. I had thought to scrub and mop things, but I didn't really know how, so I just sat there a while and relaxed, enjoying the feeling of the day washing past me. The door flew open and crashed against the wall.

'What do you think you're doing?' Jane stormed into the kitchen with her coat on and carrying a small bag, breathing in the air and pulling a face.

'I'm sitting here minding my own business. What are you doing?' I did my best to ignore her.

'You're sitting there on your fat arse feeling pleased with yourself is what you're doing. What the devil is that God-awful stink? The whole house smells like the butcher's armpit, but this room smells like his crotch.' She rushed to her cupboard full of cleaning materials, mops, beazoms and polish.

'There's a reason for that.' I leant back and watched her.

'Aye, no doubt. And what might that be?' Her muffled voice echoed from inside the closet.

I mulled it over a while, wondered whether I was cruel enough to tell her about the heads. Aye, I decided, I was.

She screamed at me, made me cower with those wild green eyes, made me feel it had been my fault, regarding me as she might a great black roach. 'Well you will have to find the money for a new table, won't you – *sir*?'

I could but agree.

'I will arrange for this table to be chopped up and taken away. Today. You have money?'

'Half as much as I had before,' I admitted, 'but I have a new job working for the King as a King's agent. Dowling recommended me.'

'You, a King's agent? God have mercy on us all. Bring on the next republic.' She took off her coat and hung it on a hook. 'And I thought Mr Dowling was an able man.'

'I might remind you that you said Hewitt was as guilty as a quire bird.'

'So he was, wasn't he?' she snapped, then disappeared out of the kitchen with her bag. The house shook as she stomped up the stairs.

I reminded myself that it was *my* house, screwed my courage to the sticking plate and lit up a pipe. I sucked in the smoke and let it run slowly out of my nose. Harry Lytle – King's agent. A fine young man worth fifty pounds. All in all, a very pleasing conclusion.

The judge had issued an indictment for the arrest of William Hill, much to my satisfaction. He wasn't able to do much about Shrewsbury – that noble Lord would find it easy enough to dissociate himself from Hill and Burton, but Dowling assured me that he was finished. Be in Holland by morning. Yes, I had done very well – well done, Harry!

'Harry?' Jane entered quietly. Unlike her.

'Yes?' I tilted back on my chair with my feet on the table and puffed at my pipe.

'There is a man at the door called Simon. He has a big knife. He says that since you didn't pay him what you owed him he is come for retribution.'

Boggins!

I fell off my chair and knocked myself unconscious on the hearth.

Acknowledgements

With sincere thanks to Tara Wynne for retrieving *Sweet Smell* from her slush pile, and to Annabel Blay at Curtis Brown.

To Susie Dunlop, Sophie Robinson and the rest of the crew at Allison & Busby - thanks for brushing Harry down and helping him back to his feet.

With gratitude to my parents and brother Mark. And with all the love in the world to Ruth, Charlotte, Callum, Cameron and Ashleigh.

Finally I must acknowledge John Ray for his wonderfully rich descriptions of the flora of Cambridge that head every chapter of this book.